EMPRESS THERESA

Norman Boutin

Copyright 2010 Norman Boutin

Cover image by Norman Boutin

This book is a work of fiction. Any resemblance to actual persons or events is a coincidence.

September 2020 version

"I'm very simple. I follow my conscience. I am what I do. If you think that's easy, try it for one day!"
----- Theresa Elizabeth Sullivan Hartley, the World Empress

"Staying alive for me is like surviving a train wreck."
----- Theresa

"You can teach millions something more important. When the world falls apart around us, we look within ourselves and find ourselves. Show us what's within you."
----- British Prime Minister to Theresa Hartley

EMPRESS THERESA

Chapter 1

I'm Theresa, the younger daughter of Edward and Elizabeth Sullivan, and I hope it's not bragging to say I was cute as heck at age ten. Everybody in the family said so. I was the princess in the Sullivan clan of Framingham, Massachusetts because besides being cute I was a whiz in school and had a good disposition. All the relatives expected great things from me.

Nobody could have dreamed of what I would do a few years later, and nobody would have believed it if they'd been told. Prime Minister Blair said I'd still be remembered in a million years.

Did you catch that?

Churchill, Hitler, and Lincoln will be footnotes in dusty history books a thousand years from now, and nobody remembers Charles Martel who saved Christianity in Europe by winning the Battle of Tours thirteen hundred years ago to set up the world as we know it today, but Prime Minister Blair said I'd be remembered for a million years. Mr. Blair is not inclined to exaggerating. I was the last person you would expect to earn that accolade. I was a nobody from nowhere. When this story began I was a little girl who didn't have much of a clue about anything. My job as a kid was to figure out what the heck was going on and what to do about it. It's not easy when you're young and everything is brand new.

My father once served a tour in the Navy. He said I had to be the captain of my ship but sometimes the seas would be rough. I had to learn all I could about the world. I wondered why should I be worrying about it in the fourth grade? I'd soon find out.

We're lost in this confusing world unless we follow the directions of its Maker. I did. It's the only thing that got me through.

Everybody has pressures. There are two kinds. One is threats to your life and health. I had more than my share of that with a thousand assassins wanting to get me. The other kind is bearing responsibility for other people's lives and welfare. That's really tough if you care about them. I set new world records in that department. People were sure I'd crack under the pressure, but I didn't. It will take smarter heads than mine to figure out why.

You can't do anything without the courage to do it. I had plenty of courage and I did plenty.

I'll be telling my own story which is a good thing because nobody knows it as well as me. The drawback is that there are some things I can't know because I wasn't there. For example, Prime Minister Blair and President Stinson mentioned they talked to each other on the phone. They must have talked with many other heads of state and it would be interesting to know what was said. It's a sure bet they discussed how to eliminate me if I got out of control, but I can't know any of that. It can be frustrating not knowing these things. But remember, you'll learn things in the same sequence I did. Somebody else telling my story could only say what I did in the world. They couldn't get in my head like you will. You'll see what a horrible, worldwide mess I had to deal with.

My story began quietly with no hint of what was coming.

I was home with my 17 year old sister Catherine who was old enough to be my babysitter. She made it possible for mom to go back to her part time job without leaving me alone. Catherine hadn't been a whiz in school like me, and she was thinking of going to one of the many trade schools around Boston after high school. Mom and dad said I should go to college.

Oops! Before going on I have to mention an odd incident that happened six months before I was born. Mom was raking leaves in the backyard when she noticed a fox sitting on its haunches ten feet away. It was staring at her. A metal rake is a good weapon against a creature as small as a fox and mom held her ground. After five minutes the fox walked away. This strange event seemed unimportant. My parents forgot about it for eighteen years.

OK. Now I can begin my story.

Our house was next to a pond close to the river, where all the neighborhood's kids spent many happy hours looking for turtles and frogs. I was lounging on the deck reading a book on the school summer list. Catherine was inside reading a magazine.

Taking a momentary break from the book, I noticed a red fox walking along the pond's edge. It disappeared behind the little patch of woods which dad let grow wild like most of the neighbors. This was very rare. Red foxes were never seen in broad daylight during the summer months. It didn't happen.

Then something really amazing happened. It came out of the woods and walked towards me!

I kept still and waited to see how close it came before noticing me. It was sixty feet away, forty, twenty. By now it was clear it was looking at me. I considered running into the house, but curiosity won out.

The fox reached the four steps of the deck. It came up the steps, stopped, and sat on its haunches staring at me. It did not seem vicious so I waited.

In an instant, faster than you could blink an eye, a softball sized white ball emerged from the fox and went straight into my stomach.

I screamed and ran into the house. The fox ran away. I slid the glass deck door closed and locked it just in time to see the fox disappear in the woods.

"What did you scream for?" asked Catherine who had walked into the kitchen.

"There was a fox out there."

"He won't hurt you," she said, and went back to the living room.

I stood at the glass door for five minutes watching for anything else that might happen. At last I thought it was all over.

I went into the living room to sit down and think. What was that white thing? I couldn't come up with any theory. It was nothing I had ever seen on those television nature programs.

Perhaps it was a daydream from not eating enough. Mom had warned me about that. At age ten I was already conscious of my weight and tried to stay skinny. I should eat something.

I went into the kitchen to prepare an early lunch of fried eggs, a strip of bacon, toast, and milk. I gobbled all this down in a couple of minutes and soon felt better. It was too little eating after all. Nothing had really happened.

Satisfied, I walked back into the living room to find something else to do. I turned on the television and watched the late morning talk shows for a while.

I heard fire trucks in the distance blaring their deep toned sirens. These trucks could be heard from a mile away. They were coming closer. And closer. Soon the sound made it obvious they were in the vicinity of our street. My intuition told me this had something to do with the white thing that jumped at me.

I went out the front door and waited on the lawn. The sirens were very close, and, yes, there they were turning into the street, a tanker truck and a small ladder truck. The two vehicles went halfway down the street and stopped. Already people were coming out of houses to watch the excitement.

The yellow fire engines had loudspeakers that sent out vocal messages loud enough to rattle windows. A conversation was going on between the firemen and the station.

"What do you have?"

"A hundred and fifteen degrees here" a fireman shouted.

"It's seventy here."

"Yup. We have something."

A crowd of neighbors was gathering near the confused firemen. I walked over to join the onlookers. "What's going on?" I asked one of my girlfriends.

"They're looking for a fire."

The girl's father said, "The temperature jumped up in a few minutes. Somebody called the fire department."

It was hot. It was nice a little while ago. I thought it over. A fox appears in daylight which never happens, it comes up practically to my feet, the white thing jumps into me, and the firemen look for a fire that doesn't exist. All this happened within an hour. There had to be a connection.

Before long the fire chief arrived in his yellow sedan. He asked the lead fireman if anything had been found. Then they walked over somebody's property to look at the pond. Nothing there.

"Could it be a ground fire?" the fireman asked the chief.

"Not likely with water over there unless there's a rock ledge underneath. We have to check it out."

Thermistor probes were brought from the station, and firemen spent the rest of the morning pushing the probes a few inches into the ground to check the temperature. They did this on everyone's lawn, the area inside the turnaround at the end of the street, and finally went into people's back yards. They found nothing.

Around one o'clock the temperature in our neighborhood had dropped back down to eighty degrees. The firemen gave up and left.

I was young and inexperienced, but I wasn't a dumbbell. If people found out what happened today they'd pester me about it forever. My Cousin Mary was diagnosed a schizophrenic and the whole Sullivan clan was biting their nails waiting for the gene to show up in some other family member. It wasn't going to be me! I resolved to never tell anybody. Not even my parents would know. They'd think I was ill like Cousin Mary. I didn't need it.

Two days later I woke up early and walked into the living room. Mom was looking intently out the window. "What's going on?" I asked.

"There's some men parked down next to the turnaround. They've been there all night."

I looked and sure enough a van and a four door sedan were parked in the turnaround where they could see every house on the street.

"Mrs. Gagnon said a police car stopped to talk to them at two a.m." said mom. "They showed IDs and a little later the police left."

Dad woke up and heard the same story. As mom and dad got ready for work, another police car came around the street, but left without stopping.

Other people left for work. The morning wore on. The mail truck came by at ten. I walked out to get the mail while Catherine was in her room. Two minutes after I got back in the house the car and van drove away. They had spotted me.

How did they know about me?

I sat on the sofa thinking for a while. I felt I was being watched. Or was somebody listening?

I spotted the phone. Was somebody listening on the phone?

I dialed 0 for the operator.

"Operator. How may I help you?"

"Can I have the number for Alice Pizza in Framingham?"

"One moment, please."

Ten seconds later another woman said, "Alice Pizza, 555-8402."

"Thanks." I hung up. So they weren't listening.

The weekend arrived. Mom and I went to Boston to shop in the Washington Street shopping district. We drove down to the Boston Commons underground parking garage. I thought I saw some car come in right behind us and park close to our car.

We got up to the surface and a man followed us. We went to the Barnes and Noble bookstore first, because if we bought something, it would be small and easy to carry the rest of the day. I looked through the books on sale and thought I saw a different man watching me. Barnes and Noble had two floors. "I'm going upstairs, mom" I said.

There was an escalator to the second floor. I went along the wall, stopping now and then pretending to look at books, and that same man from downstairs always seemed to be close to me. He was spying on me.

Later, we went to McDonald's and I spotted another man who walked behind us into the restaurant. He was there as long as we were, and after we left, I looked back and he was coming out too. But he stopped at a corner. Another man standing on the corner started walking in our direction.

We got back home and mom took things into the bedroom. I dialed the operator again.

"Operator. How may I help you?"

"Can you give me the number for Alice Pizza in Framingham?"

"One moment, please."

I waited. And waited. And waited. A full minute passed by and she hadn't come up with the number yet.

I hung up the phone. Now they knew I knew.

While I was young I had some feeble ideas of what this all meant. My life wasn't going to be like that of other kids. I had to think like somebody important, somebody with responsibilities. I was something special. Maybe I was dangerous, or that was what the government was thinking. Someday they would come around and talk to me. I wasn't stupid enough to think they would just watch me for the rest of my life.

Two days later mom took me to a nearby strip mall. There was a DVD movie rental store. I looked around for the classic movie *2001: A Space Odyssey*. They'd shown it on television two months earlier.

I played and replayed the parts of the movie where the astronauts talked to HAL. The most chilling scene was when astronaut Dave Bowman left the spaceship in a pod to retrieve the body of his dead astronaut partner drifting through space. When he flew back to the spaceship, he said one of Hollywood's most famous lines:

"Open the pod bay doors, HAL."

But the spaceship's computer, HAL, wouldn't open the door. It was a creepy scene.

The summer days rolled by. I saw the watchers following me everywhere. Mom did most of her grocery shopping on Saturday and I usually went with her because Catherine wandered off with her friends. While mom was talking to the meat counter clerk I went down the breakfast cereal aisle to choose something.

"Hi, Theresa."

Some woman I didn't know was standing next to me. She looked to be in her early twenties and had a friendly smile.

"Hi," I said with a young kid's taciturnity.

"Do you have a cellphone?"

"Yeah."

"Call me when you're alone." She handed me a piece of paper with a phone number.

The woman knew that I knew about my watchers. I had often stared at them. So this woman also knew I had to think she was one of them and I had to be curious enough to talk to her.

When we got back home I went to my room and called the number. My curiosity about the watchers overcame my wish to keep HAL secret. I wanted to know how they knew about me. The woman answered. Her spies must have told her I was home.

"Hi" said the cheerful woman. "I'm Jan Struthers from the United States Government. Are you alone?"

"Yeah. Are you?"

"You know I'm not. There are twenty people with me in this room. Can we talk?"

My childhood was over. All I wanted was an ordinary life like everybody else. It looked like I wouldn't get it.

"About what?"

"About your little secret. We know it."

I thought about that. Everybody had secrets. Talking to this woman wouldn't be admitting mine.

"Something happened to you to make those fire trucks come to your neighborhood. You were giving off a lot of heat. We know you were because we saw it all around you. What happened before the fire trucks came?"

"I don't have to tell you anything, do I?"

Jan Struthers maintained her friendly attitude.

"No, you don't. But it will make things a lot easier if you tell us something. We're not going away. We will be spying on you from now on. We have to. Whatever happened is very important."

"You don't know anything that happened?"

"We know a lot. Something from outer space came to Earth seven years ago. We've been looking for it ever since. That heat you were giving off has to have something to do with that thing from outer space."

I considered that. Jan Struthers gave me a moment and then brought out a point.

"There is nothing natural to Earth that could have caused that heat. The thing from space did it. We watched you rent that movie *2001: A Space Odyssey*. You are aware of that thing. What happened before the fire trucks came?"

There was no use denying something happened. They already knew.

"I saw a fox walking near the water. It came up close to me and a white thing jumped out of it. That's all."

"Where did the white thing go?"

"In me."

"How big was this white thing?"

"Like a softball."

"Did it come from the fox?"

"Yup. Came right out."

"What part of the fox?"

"The stomach."

"How did it jump out at you?"

"It moved in my stomach."

I wasn't very enthusiastic about telling the story. Jan Struthers had to force it out of me one tiny piece at a time.

"How long did that take?"

"Like that." I snapped my fingers at the phone.

"Did you feel anything?"

"Nope."

"Did this white ball look solid like a steel ball?"

"Nope. Fuzzy like cotton."

"What happened then?"

"I ran into the house and waited. Then I ate breakfast. I thought I was going crazy."

"How long after the white ball jumped at you did the fire trucks come?"

"Half an hour."

"Did the white thing change you in any way?"

"No."

"Does it make sounds or talk to you?"

"No."

"Have you seen it again?"

"No. It's like it went away."

"How have you been eating lately?"

"Like I always do."

Jan took a break to think what else she should ask. This was the most important interview since Moses came down the mountain.

"Would you be willing to come in to talk to some smart people and figure out what this thing is?"

"I didn't do anything."

"All right." She dropped that line immediately! "You rented *2001:A Space Odyssey*. What did it show you?"

"It showed me don't talk to this thing. It's like

talking to the devil."

"Do you have a name for it?"

"HAL."

"Like the computer. The monolith was the alien, not the computer."

"The monolith didn't talk."

"Does HAL talk?"

"No."

"It's a good idea not to try to talk to it. Don't stir it up."

"What is HAL?"

"We don't know. We saw it seven years ago but haven't seen or heard about it since. You're the only one who's seen it."

"Does it come from space?"

"Probably, but that may not be bad. This thing may never do anything.

"I think that covers everything. I have to emphasize how important it is to tell nobody about this. Don't give a hint to anybody. If you talk to somebody, they will too, and you will never be able to live the life you want. No college. No job. No marriage. No friends. You'll have to stay at home all the time. This is the last thing we want. A lot of people are trying to keep this secret."

"What if one of my watchers talks?"

"Most of our people don't know why they're watching you. Only the people at the top know. I'm one of the few people who knows you give off heat. Without knowing that, nobody can prove you have anything to do with HAL. That's the biggest secret. Without knowing about the heat, they can't spot you or suspect anything."

"Don't those twenty people know about me?"

"Very good, Theresa! I'm impressed! These people are top ranking officials from the Defense Intelligence Agency. Your watchers are people hired from outside. They know nothing."

"Can I tell my parents?"

"That's up to you. But remember, if you can't keep it a secret, why should your parents? Your mother will want to share it with Aunt Jessica. Then Aunt Jessica will want to share it with Uncle John. Before you know it, ten thousand reporters will be parked in front of your house for the rest of your life."

"Not if HAL never does anything."

"All the more so. It's anticipating something that hasn't happened yet that interests people."

A break in the conversation let me absorb this new idea. This was heavy stuff for a ten year old to think about.

Something else had made me wonder. "Why is the operator one of you guys?"

"You might ask the operator to connect you to somebody, maybe somebody outside the country. We need to know who it is. It's for your protection."

"How can I give off heat without burning up?"

"Hold on."

There was a moment of silence. I had stumped her!

"Theresa, we think HAL is doing a lot of things around you but not inside you. It's like you're in a party. A lot of people are dancing around you but they're not making you dance."

That sounded reasonable. "Okay."

"Well, I'll leave you alone now. Thanks for talking

with me. Call anytime you have questions."

She hung up. I'll bet the twenty people cheered her for doing a good job.

There it was. They tapped the phone and watched me all the time. And they knew I knew I was being watched. But I said nothing to mom and dad. What must the spies be thinking about that?

In a moment I realized Jan Struthers hadn't asked me if I'd told anybody besides my parents the secret. They knew I hadn't. How did they know that?

One day I woke up at 6:30 a.m., tumbled out of bed, and changed to jeans and sweatshirt before my groggy eyes cleared and I noticed an orange spot in the middle of my field of view. It was right there in the exact middle no matter where I looked. I hadn't noticed immediately because it was small. It was like an orange golf ball at forty feet.

I put on shoes and walked to the living room. The orange spot was always there. I went out to the backyard. Likewise, the little orange ball was always there even when I looked up at the sky. HAL must have had something to do with it.

"What is that for?" I whispered.

A few days later I was working in the tiny garden I kept in the backyard. I liked to grow pumpkins, which were fairly easy to grow, and would grow eight plants a year in the small plot. The plants now had vines three feet long with little one inch pumpkins. They would expand rapidly in the next month until they reached eight or ten inches in diameter in September.

I was pulling up the annoying weeds that kept

sprouting up all the time. The worst was that prickly weed whose name I didn't know that would grow three feet tall if you let it. I used a hand spade to dig one of the prickly weeds up by the roots and felt a rock. I brought up the three inch wide flat rock and threw it at a gallon water sprinkler can ten feet away. The rock hit the can dead center. I hadn't even tried to do that. I found another rock and threw it at the can. It too hit the can.

I got the rocks and walked fifteen away from the can. I threw the rocks while keeping the orange dot in my eye field on the can. The rocks hit the can again.

I got the rocks once more and walked fifty feet away. Nobody could hit the can from this distance. I threw. The rocks hit the can. So that's what the orange dot was for. It was an aiming device. It got the rocks to whatever I was looking at. Interesting, but I couldn't see any use for it.

Two days later I saw ten year old Tommy Kearns walking back from the nearby convenience store. I sometimes saw him throwing a baseball with another boy.

"Going to Tommy's house, mom."

"OK, dear."

Tommy's house was four homes down the street. I knocked on the Kearns door. The mother answered.

"Hi. Is Tommy here?"

The mother found Tommy and told him Theresa was visiting. Tommy came to the door.

"Hi, Theresa."

"Hi. You want to pass the ball?"

"Sure. I'll get it."

He retrieved a baseball and two baseball gloves

and we went to the street. We stood roughly fifteen feet apart and passed the ball back and forth. I backed up to twenty feet and we continued passing. I was getting the ball straight to Tommy's chest. He was not doing as well. I had to take a step or two to the side to catch the ball. Tommy stood in place.

"Hey! You're good!" Tommy exclaimed. "How do you do that?"

"I'm a natural" I said.

I backed up to thirty feet. It went the same way. I hit Tommy dead on while Tommy's aim was typical for a ten year old. Bad.

Tommy's father came out and walked to Tommy.

"Can I take over, son?"

Tommy was glad to be relieved.

The father smiled and asked, "Ready?"

"Yeah" I said.

We tossed back and forth. Tommy's father had an accurate aim. I didn't have to step side to side to catch the ball.

After a few throws Tommy's father backed up to around forty feet. No ten year old could throw accurately at this distance, he must have thought. We tossed the ball. I invariably got the ball straight to Tommy's father. This went on for another ten minutes. Other people had been coming out to watch.

At last, the father noticed that I was getting tired. This was August and it was very hot.

"Let's call it quits, Theresa" the father said. "It's getting hot."

"OK."

I went aside to talk to Tommy. Several adults came up to Tommy's father. One of them asked him,

"How good is she?"

"She's incredible. Someday she might pitch for the Red Sox."

August rolled on. It was a week before I was to begin the fifth grade and I could think of little else. Most kids said they hated school. I loved it. It was there that I met all my friends who were scattered all over town in the summer, there that the girls invited each other to each other's homes.

It was a working day for my parents and Catherine had eaten something. I began throwing together lunch for myself. Mom had bought steaks. There was a new bottle of steak sauce. I tried to open it but it was tight. The trouble with these steak bottles was that the cap was so narrow. There was no leverage to twist it. I tried harder. No wonder little old ladies starved to death. A little more effort and the bottle broke. Steak sauce spilled on the counter. A steak sauce bottle had particularly thick glass and should be unbreakable.

I cleaned up the mess and put away the rest of the food. I wanted to think. How had I broken the thick glass bottle which not even a strong man could have done? Did I have a lot of strength?

I looked around for something to lift. The living room sofa was the heaviest piece of furniture in the house. I lifted one end of it easily. But so did dad. How could I tell how strong I was?

I went to the basement and looked around. Like many people we Sullivans kept lots of junk we never used. I rummaged around and found two complete sets of old lawn horseshoes, grabbed a horseshoe with both hands and tried to twist it. At first it didn't change, but as I applied more force HAL seemed to get the idea. The horseshoe bent easily.

The next morning I approached mom.

"I want to see Father Richard."

She spun her head around in surprise.

"What about?"

"I can't tell you."

"Honey, you can tell me anything. Maybe I can help."

"I can't tell you."

Mom was worried. Something serious must be going on, but even at age ten I had certain rights to privacy.

"All right, dear. I'll drive you."

On the way through the living room I picked up a burlap shopping bag used by environmentally conscious people who didn't want paper or plastic.

"What's in there?" mom asked.

"Horseshoes."

"Why are you taking those?"

"It's a secret."

Mom was really worried. She made a quick call to the rectory to make sure Father Richard Donoughty would be there. We drove the one and a half miles to the rectory and were met at the door by the smiling twenty-nine year old priest. I knew I could trust him to keep my secret. Priests were supposed to be beyond salvation if they revealed a secret, or something like that. That's what I thought then.

"Ah. Theresa wants to be a nun?" he joked.

"She won't tell me what it's about."

"Oh." He got more serious. "Do we all talk

together?"

"No" I said. "Me alone."

"Very well. Mrs. Sullivan…" He indicated the living room which served as a waiting room. "This way," he smiled showing me to his office.

Father Donoughty sat at his desk and I sat in a chair in front of him.

"Now, Theresa. What's on your mind?"

"I have to show you something."

I took three horseshoes out of the bag and stacked them together. The ends had small bends and I had to arrange the horseshoes with one advanced over the one below so that the rest of the structures would lie flat on top of each other. Then I grabbed all three shoes at once by the ends and started trying to twist them. I applied more and more pressure over some fifteen or so seconds until I did succeed in bending the horseshoes about fifty degrees. I put them down on his desk.

The priest thought it had to be a trick. He picked up a horseshoe and tried to bend it with all his strength. It didn't budge. He tried the other two with the same result. It was no trick. I had bent all three at once.

He tried to remain calm as I waited patiently for his comment. The thought of diabolic possession had to be the first thought that came to him. Possession was often manifested by super strength.

He managed to say, "How did you do that?"

"I have something from space. The government knows about it. They watch me all the time. They followed me. I saw them."

"When?"

"When we came here. Mom doesn't know."

"They followed you here?"

"Yeah. They're in the green car." I pointed in the direction of the parking lot.

He got up to look out the window at the small parking lot. There was a green car out there, a four door sedan. Instead of driving into the parking space as everybody did, they had backed up so that the two men inside could watch the rectory. There was a blue car next to it similarly backed in to watch the rectory. This car had a male driver and female passenger.

"Can you wait here a minute, Theresa?"

"Yeah."

He went outside. The window was open in the heat, so I walked over to listen to whatever I might hear. When Jan Struthers saw him she instantly got out of the blue car and quickly walked over to him.

"These men don't know everything. Only I do. What did Theresa say?"

"I'm not at liberty to say."

"It's not the usual stuff?"

"It isn't."

"It's critical you tell no one. Theresa will be the first to suffer. People will come after her. They'll kidnap her, kill her, or worse."

"Who are you?"

"I work for the American government."

"How many of you are there?"

"Hundreds."

"That's a lot of people."

"Do you understand how important this is?"

"I'm beginning to."

Father Donoughty thought things over for a

moment.

"I'll need to tell the Cardinal."

"Why?"

"Theresa needs one person she can trust. I need the Cardinal's help to stay close to her wherever she is."

"All right, but it goes no further. Don't call him on the phone. Talk to him in person."

Jan Struthers walked back to her car and he returned to his office.

"I'd like the Cardinal to come here and talk with you some time. Is that all right?"

"Sure" I said.

A meeting was arranged with the Cardinal. It was concluded that there was no diabolical possession. I was a perfectly normal good girl. My story, confirmed by the brief visit of Jan Struthers, had to be true no matter how amazing it was.

I did so well in the fifth grade it was decided I'd skip the sixth and go straight into seventh. I would graduate from high school at seventeen. Part of the decision to let me skip a year was my hair. It started growing very thick after HAL came around. I mean, you could grab a handful of my hair and feel the weight like it was wet. Mom was sure this was a sign of my "change of life" and I needed to be with girls my own emotional age.

Yeah, well, I was growing up fast, but it wasn't because of hormones. I was worrying about HAL, and so were a lot of others. Jan Struthers walked by me sometimes in a store or someplace when mom and dad were out of sight. She asked how things were going and asked was there any news about HAL. I never told her about the orange spot in my eye field or the strength HAL gave me. They'd haul me off to some laboratory. One time I asked her how many people were watching me. "Four hundred," she said! It takes that many people to watch somebody twenty-four hours a day without being noticed. It would be easier if I lived in an Iowa farmhouse. They could keep an eye on me from a distance. But when mom and I went into Boston, a hundred and fifty watchers had to spread out to keep an eye on me. It would be just as bad when I went to high school and moved around a lot.

Jan said, "I suggested we just give you ten million dollars if you promised to stay home. They turned it down."

They were right. I wouldn't stay home.

Chapter 2

The high school years go by quickly when you're having a good time, and I did. The strength and throwing accuracy HAL gave me got me on the boys' baseball team where I was a star pitcher. I threw the ball up to eighty-five miles an hour, rarely seen in a high school kid and never in a girl. Actually, I could have thrown the ball well over a hundred m.p.h., but I had to hold myself back or people would realize there was something special going on. My speed was explained as being the advantage of being small, like a lightweight boxer being much faster than a heavyweight but not as strong a hitter.

In middle school I'd played unofficial baseball with a group of boys who recognized my talents. When the playing field wasn't being used we went out there and practiced. I was still twelve when people started hanging around the field watching us. They were amazed at what I could do with the ball. The high school baseball coaches came around one day and the boys made sure I was on the mound all the time. They wanted me on the boys' team. The coaches seemed interested, but were they impressed enough to let me on the team?

There had been a few girl quarterbacks around the country. This usually happened at a small school where they had a hard time recruiting enough boys to make up a football team. So being a pitcher on a boys' baseball team wouldn't be such a big deal, you'd think. And it wasn't. I made the boys' team in my freshman year.

I was on television all the time. Now I learned something about the world. People said bad things about me on the internet.

I wouldn't have thought it was possible. Complete strangers on the internet's social media said all kinds of terrible things about me. Even worse were the websites that a few people started about me. They questioned my sexual orientation or said I must have gone to bed with the coach to get on the team. They said I was making out with everybody on the team. There was nothing I could do about these people. I didn't know their names or addresses. They were internet trolls, jealous cowards who attack from the safety of anonymity and distance. I was told my only strategy was to ignore them.

Being young, I felt the pain of rejection strongly. Kids couldn't deal with this. I complained to the school principal and a teacher took it upon herself to counsel me.

Mrs. Steinfeld, one of my teachers, approached one day and explained these trolls.

"These kids are being defiant. You are beautiful, intelligent, and you're often on television. You're a sports star. You have straight A's and high morals. All these things represent what people want in kids. You're the daughter every parent wants. You're the student every teacher wants, the young person society wants. You fulfill all the authorities' expectations. So these kids attack you. Don't let them bother you. There's one last question a person should ask before she dies: 'Do I feel good about who I was?'"

"OK, but what do I do now?"

"There isn't anything you can do. Just try to think of the future. When you go to college, nobody will ask how your high school was, and you will care least of all.

"There was a TV commercial years ago I never forgot. A young woman had three horses and bought a fourth, a miniature horse only two feet high. She put the little horse in the corral with the three normal sized horses. They sniffed the little horse and ran away from him. The little horse had very short legs and couldn't run. He walked towards the big horses who kept running away. He followed them everywhere but couldn't get within fifty feet of them. Finally, the little horse gave up and stared at the big horses and towards the house where the young woman watched out of her window. It was very sad. The little horse didn't understand why he was being rejected.

"Then the woman ordered something online. That was what the commercial was about. She ordered a dog door for the front door of her house. Now the little horse could come into the house and be with the woman anytime he wanted. She talked to him and patted him on the head while she read a book or watched television. Intelligent animals like horses and dogs love close contact with humans. We must seem like gods to them. The little horse ended up better off than the other horses.

"Keep plugging away, Theresa. You will be better off than these trolls. They can't follow where you will go."

I saw why the trolls were angry. They knew they

couldn't go where I was going. I'd have a good life. They wouldn't. What they said made no sense. They were really mixed up big time! I blamed the parents for not raising them right.

My parents did a good job teaching me the important things. What I learned came to mean something when I was ten. I didn't know what HAL would mean to me at first, but gradually I came to understand that someday I would have great responsibilities. By the time I was fifteen I was almost grown up.

My mom, who came from another town, went to a Catholic high school. A teacher told her something the ancient Greeks said: An unexamined life is not worth living. Know thyself. Mom said too many people never question who they are and how they're doing. This is a fast track to disaster. They're not equipped to get through troubles and be successful. The television news showed examples every day.

My parents gave a good example of the kind of people to be. I'd have to write a book about them to explain. It's enough to say I wanted to be a woman like mom and I wanted a husband like dad. That says it all, don't you think?

So I thought a lot about who I was and who I wanted to become. This assured I would get there.

Nothing else bad happened to me in high school besides the social media bozos' hatred.

The kids I hung around with weren't like the phony kids in Hollywood movies. They couldn't be because nobody likes obnoxious elitists who form cliques and wear fancy clothes, drive expensive cars, and lord it over the less beautiful and talented. Eventually people like that have nobody's respect. In the movies the cheerleaders are cliquish snobs who make all the other girls feel inferior. In my school the cheerleaders were my friends. They were among the best athletes in school and admired a girl pitcher on the boys' team. They suggested I try out for their cheerleader team, but I decided I had my share of celebrity. Let some other girl cheer. Anyways, my schoolmates were good kids and they probably were at your school too.

In the beginning of my Senior year, still only sixteen after skipping the sixth grade, I began to think about college. I had one more thing to worry about that other kids didn't. What about HAL? Did the government know anything about him that might guide me in what to study?

It was time to meet Jan Struthers for an update. She agreed to a meeting in a nearby Burger King where the noise gave privacy as good the Sahara Desert to update each other's thoughts and info about HAL.

When I was ten years old I hadn't worried much about how the government had found HAL before he merged with me. Now I was curious and asked Jan about it.

"When you were three years old an amateur astronomer in Arizona was looking for comets. He had a telescope in his backyard. He noticed a curved streak of light in the sky. A comet will move in a straight line, not a curve. He sent a message to all his comet hunting friends and the government heard about it. The military sent up planes to watch this thing coming down to Earth. It was a hundred foot wide white ball. It headed down to Framingham and helicopters watched it reach the ground. They thought it might bounce or explode when it hit the ground. It didn't. It just went into the ground without rustling the leaves on the trees it passed through. The helicopter crews couldn't believe their eyes.

"President Sheffield authorized a secret office in the Pentagon, the Office of Orbital Phenomena Surveillance. OOPS for short. It was supposed to keep track of all the space junk we put into orbit. Its real purpose was to watch for anything going on anywhere in the world that would be something HAL was doing. Seven years later, HAL merged with you and gave off enough heat for a few hours to bring in the fire trucks. This was the kind of thing OOPS was looking for. They came to your street and aimed sensitive infrared cameras at everything. They saw the heat coming from you. President Gardner had an intelligence agency set up your watchers."

"How did you get involved?"

"When you rented that *2001* movie they knew you were aware of HAL. The President wanted somebody to go talk to you and find out what you knew. But you were only ten years old. I was chosen because they thought you would trust a young woman."

Jan and I updated each other on our thoughts.

I hadn't heard a peep out of HAL in the six years since he merged with me. It was a safe bet he didn't travel a million light years just to watch me take showers and neither could he be interested only in me. His interest must be the world but for some mysterious reason he'd chosen me as his base of operations. Perhaps he had no real interest in me at all but only used my senses to see and hear the world I lived in.

Perhaps he'd leave me sometime and merge with somebody else. As for why so much time was spent watching me, Jan revealed that no other HAL had been detected anywhere in the world. I was an exclusive club of one.

"How do you know there's no other HAL? Did you ask around?"

"No. If we did that, somebody would talk, and even if we didn't give your name, your watchers would know that's why they watch you. They would give you away.

"Years ago we noticed a column of disturbed air above you that goes right up to space. We see it with Doppler radar. It's too faint to be seen by those weather station Doppler radars because they scan horizontally, but we can see it with a radar beam aimed down. We sent up a spy satellite looking for these columns and yours was the only one we found."

"How much does a satellite cost?"

"Over a hundred million. Mostly it's the rocket."

"Tell you what. Give me the money and I'll give you HAL."

The talk moved on. What HAL was made of and how he worked was still a mystery. More important was his purpose. What could that be?

It could be anything. Jan was reminded of those lines in the movie *Contact*. A female astronomer is about to go on a trip to meet an alien race. Technicians give her a cyanide pill saying they could think of a thousand things that could go wrong, but what worried them the most was what they couldn't think of. "It's the same here. There's no guessing why HAL is here."

Jan told me I must get as broad an education as possible to be ready to deal with any unimaginable challenge HAL gave me. It was possible I would have to be the ambassador between the world and the aliens. The odds were they'd be benevolent, but if not, I had to be prepared to deal with great difficulties. What these might be was completely unpredictable. I had to be ready for anything. Other people thought about their home, their neighborhood, their town. I had to think globally.

This was a new concept for me. In every book, movie and TV show I'd ever seen, the issue was about something local. Never did the whole world become part of the story. It was nearly overwhelming.

"How much do you expect from me?" I asked.

"Don't lose sleep over it. You have the United States government ready to help you. But if HAL starts talking and asking questions, he may demand instant answers. You may have to act quickly. You might need the knowledge of Thomas Jefferson, and the wisdom of Abraham Lincoln."

"Oh, is that all?"

"Nothing might happen for forty years. Don't worry about it now."

"If I have that much time I'll major in alien relations."

I got home from school before my parents got back from work and brought in the mail. In late March of my Senior year I got a letter with no postage stamp and no address except my name, Theresa Sullivan. It read like this:

Where is Jan Struthers?

Meet me in the Framingham Library
Saturday 1:00 p.m.
Jeremy Benton

Who the heck was Jeremy Benton? And what was he saying about Jan?

Jan had given me an email address I used to contact her to set up meetings such as the update meeting last Fall. It was janswatchers at snoop.gov. I could find no such government website. Obviously it was something created just for her. I sent an email. A few minutes later I got a response:

Failure Notice   No MX or A records for snoop.gov

For the first time since HAL merged with me I was afraid.

What happened to Jan? Who was Jeremy Benton and what did he want with me?

Who could I talk to? Not to mom and dad! I was too afraid to go meet this guy. I had decided not to meet him when I had a good idea. Father Donoughty knew everything. If I brought him along what could happen at a public library?

Father Donoughty and I entered the library and looked around. A neatly dressed man in his forties waved to us from a corner table. This had to be Jeremy. We walked over and he introduced himself.

"Hello. I'm Jeremy Benton, personal aide to Prime Minister of England Peter Blair. Please sit down."

We sat. But instead of talking Jeremy stared at me.

"What's the matter?" I asked.

"Seeing you close like this took my breath away. Do you realize the effect you have on people?"

He meant the effect I had on people who were

aware that I was the world's telephone connection to the aliens.

"I'm beginning to."

"Can we talk about HAL?"

"Sure" I said. "Father Donoughty knows about him."

"Your friend Jan Struthers mailed a package of four volumes to Canadian Prime Minister Jean Turgeon. He sent it to Prime Minister Blair. It's clearly a call for help."

"What happened to Jan?"

"We don't know. All traces of her end when President Martin was sworn in."

"How do you know that?"

"We have people looking for her. She had credit cards and bank accounts. They were closed. She seems to have disappeared from the Earth. Somebody thought she knew too much. Jan Struthers documented everything. The volumes contain thousands of pictures of you from age ten, your activities day by day, your school records and papers, information about your parents and the people who live on your street. I assure you no biography I've read has so much information about a human being. Jan Struthers asked that if anything happened to you the Canadian Prime Minister make a big fuss about it to the press. Apparently something happened to Jan Struthers herself, but the package she sent was actually mailed by her father, Charles Struthers. We think they had some kind of pre-arrangement. We have spied on her father. He appears happy enough. His daughter must be safe somewhere."

I thought about all this while my companions

waited. If they thought I had ideas about what the heck was going on they were wrong.

"What do you think happened?" I asked.

"Your President William Martin was sworn in two months ago. May we assume he didn't know about you and HAL before then?"

"Yeah. Jan said somebody elected President is briefed on all burning issues before taking office so he could take off running. But I don't think HAL was an emergency. He didn't find out until he was sworn in."

"Then we can presume he didn't like the table setting and changed it."

"Yeah. Didn't Prime Minister Blair ask him?"

"Good Lord no! This might make things very difficult for your friend."

"Oh. Yeah."

Great! We had a perfectly harmless thing going on and President Martin didn't like it. What was he thinking?

"What do you think President Martin is doing?"

"That is impossible to guess. Prime Minister Blair assured me he would do nothing."

"But we don't know what kind of guy the President is."

"Quite right. You've had a President Gardner who knew about you . He changed nothing about your arrangement with Miss Struthers?"

"No. Do you think President Martin may cause trouble for me?"

"Jan Struthers believed so. We assume she talked with him but didn't like what he said."

"What do you suggest I do?"

"You could talk to President Martin yourself or

come to England with your parents. We'll give you new identities."

Father Donoughty spoke. "The Holy Father is interested in your case. He'll protect you in Rome."

I had options. None of them were very good.

"No, I'll wait a while and see what happens."

"Miss Struthers suggested we bring your situation to the public and get you the public's support. Perhaps you can do that yourself. Is there any way you can prove HAL's presence?"

Father Donoughty touched my foot with his to warn me. Jeremy might be from the President and trying to get new information about HAL. I didn't have to tell him anything new.

"I give off heat. That's how the government found me. If you have the right equipment you can see the heat around me."

"Ah! We can do that and show the press."

"Then what kind of life do I have? They'll never leave me alone."

"I see your point. It is a difficult problem."

The discussion was over. Father Donoughty said he'd keep an eye on me and call the Canadian Prime Minister if anything went wrong. There was nothing else to do for now.

Who said youth is the happiest time? That's when we're most vulnerable! I couldn't even share this with my parents. One mistake on their part and my future was ruined before I had it.

All this started with damn HAL. What was HAL? Would I ever know?

And as for President Martin! I'd learned that somebody with eloquence may not have seen his powers of understanding receive any aid from education. Ignorance and deficiency of mental improvement could still remain. There's some quirk in their personality that keeps them from becoming wise. The President gave great orations, but he was a babe in the woods when it came to dealing with me. Instead of shutting Jan up, why didn't he send her to talk to me? If she told me the President was worried I'd agree to meet with him somewhere. What was there in my history that made him think I couldn't be trusted? It was like some of my fellow Seniors. Twelve years of education hadn't taught them a thing about human nature. They labeled people. They were suspicious. They bullied or were obnoxious in some way. They were not worth much to themselves or anybody else.

From age ten when HAL merged with me, I had tried to make myself the best person I could. If HAL wanted me to do something good I was ready, if something bad, I wouldn't do it. President Martin should have left things alone.

Chapter 3

Boston College isn't a small college and it's not in Boston. It's a large university in Newton, Massachusetts six miles from Boston. The location is as good as it gets. Newton is an upscale neighborhood, downtown Boston is accessible on the T which has a terminus right next to campus, and the campus itself is small enough to make walking to any part of it quick.

BC has nine thousand undergraduates and a nationally known football team, but that's not why I went there. I got a full scholarship plus room and board. It had to be the work of Father Donoughty and the Cardinal. With these people fighting for me I would be stretching my luck going my own way. Besides, I had some responsibilities to my parents who were comfortably well off but not rich enough for astronomical tuition costs.

Father Donoughty remained in Framingham, again probably the work of the Cardinal. Priests are usually moved around more often. He was not too many miles from me and I might move back to Framingham.

Every Freshman wants to make a good first impression. The first night on campus the girls wandered from room to room socializing with their dormitory mates as if the first day determined their social life for the next four years. I soon found how sheltered I'd been in Framingham compared to the sophisticated kids from New York and other big cities. That night I realized I was not going to be the sparkplug of the college scene, but that was okay. Just as Framingham High hadn't been the final definition of my life, neither would BC.

Monday brought the chaos of finding my way around campus, finding the classrooms of my courses which had been set up before I arrived, and standing in line at the bookstore. The assignments I got in my classes seemed endless. Could anybody do all that work in a semester?

After my last Monday class I relaxed in my room to unwind. Then a group of girls invited me to join them at supper and we walked to the cafeteria.

We got our food and sat down. From long habit I looked around the room. There was a group of kids at a nearby table looking at me. A girl learns to read expressions. One boy was intently looking at me. I called him Mr. Intense. He was very handsome, with short hair as black as my own, and he was around six feet which was a good match for my five feet four inches. I liked taller guys and apparently he liked smaller girls. He wasn't gawking at a pretty girl, or lusting for her body. He looked interested. And that's ok. A girl gets used to being looked at.

But it wasn't Mr. Intense who made the first move. A boy next to him, Mr. Fastmove, brought his food tray over to my table.

"Hi," said Mr. Fastmove. "Can I sit here?"

"Sure," I said with a smile. I had been advised to be friendly from day one or be labeled a tease for the rest of our four years.

"I'm Jack Koster," said Mr. Fastmove. "Aren't

you Theresa Sullivan, the baseball player?"

I had been on television a lot.

"I am," I said, and we were off and running. I noticed that Mr. Intense looked disappointed. It made me think of someone whose neighbor won the lottery.

That night I looked up both Jack Koster and Mr. Intense on the computer. BC provided free disk space and all the students were urged to set up a webpage about themselves before they got to school. The kids' dormitories were listed which made it easy to find people if you didn't know their names. It turned out that not only did Jack and Mr. Intense both live in my dormitory, they were two doors away from each other. So, if Jack and I were an item, Mr. Intense was unlikely to interfere.

I read the computer screen. Jack was a boy from close to New York City but not in it. His father was owner of a specialty food store. Jack was going to be a history major, a guarantee of a job in his father's store.

Mr. Intense was Steve Hartley. His father was a physicist for Intel and Steve was majoring in physics too. That was interesting. He mentioned he was Catholic. Also interesting. Students' personalities showed in their personal pages. Steve's page showed the kid of a research physicist, precise, succinct, and somewhat lacking in spontaneity. Something like myself, actually. It wasn't a bad thing, except in reality TV shows where they have to keep the gab going all the time.

Jack was a genuinely nice guy, a good talker, and the stereotypical boy from New York City who had plenty of stories to tell. He seemed to be a gentleman.

Jack knew I was not the kind of girl who had to put up with foul language or crude jokes, and he carefully avoided them. He was one smooth operator.

We were soon seen eating in the cafeteria together whenever our schedules allowed and around campus generally. One Sunday Steve saw me at Mass. He looked embarrassed, like somebody who had missed his chance, not somebody who did something bad. Well, four years is a long time and the campus had a lot of women.

Steve seemed nice in person. He always gave me a little smile like he was glad to see me. He and Jack were casual friends and apparently didn't talk about me. But I'd seen the looks. Steve was genuinely interested.

I didn't know what I felt about him; we never had a conversation alone. There was nothing wrong with dating Jack for a while. It was already clear that we were not compatible enough for a lifetime of commitment. He was a little careless about schoolwork and had no passion for his major. I was fanatical about mine. But Jack was fun to be around for the time being.

I was walking out of biology lecture on the way back to the dorm to wait for lunch when I heard an authoritative male voice: "Theresa Sullivan?"

It was a campus cop. "Yes?"

"We have a problem. Can you come to our office?"

"I don't know where it is. I'll follow you."

A campus wasn't so big that you couldn't reach any central place in five minutes. I followed a hundred feet behind the cop so people wouldn't notice.

We arrived at the campus police office. I was led to a conference room, nothing but a room with a long table and chairs and a grease board. There were nine police there, two twenty-something guys who looked like upperclassmen, and a priest in his sixties. The senior cop painted the picture.

"This is BC President Father Walter Haynes" he said. "We saw these two men following you around the campus. Do you know them?"

I looked at the two men. They were either my watchers or nutcases. If they were watchers they must not have said anything yet. They'd be ordered not to. But there they were and the school had to be told something.

I thought about all this a moment. Father Haynes interrupted my thoughts.

"You seem to be a very interesting young lady, Miss Sullivan. The Holy Father himself paid for your scholarship."

"Did he say why?"

"No. It's a big secret."

I spoke to the two young guys assuming they were watchers. "I've been here a week. It's not so easy following somebody on a campus, hunh?"

"It isn't" said one of them looking for guidance. They were watchers.

I said, "It's gone too far. They'll go to the FBI and the newspaper. Call your boss."

He pulled out a cell phone and whispered to somebody. After a few moments he said, "He's calling the Director."

Eyebrows went up around the room. The tension

built as we waited for something to happen on the other end of the phone call. Then the watcher told me, "The Director is calling the President of the United States."

Did I have everybody's attention now? You bet!

A few more moments and the watcher handed the phone to the senior cop. "He wants to talk to you."

The cop took the phone and was read the riot act. "Yes, sir...." "Yes, sir...." "No, sir...." "I understand, sir...." "I wouldn't want that either, sir...."

After a minute the senior cop handed the phone back to my watcher. He told everybody the facts of life.

"We will say nothing about this to anybody, not to each other, not to our wives, not to our dogs. This situation does not exist, nor will it ever exist. That's all."

I could have walked out in an instant but hung around a moment for effect. I looked at each person with an air of confidence. I looked like I had the situation well under control and they'd better listen to the Prez. Then I walked out.

Come October it was Homecoming week, always a big weekend on any college campus. There were many special activities going on and we had to choose a list.

Friday nights, the kids would 'hang' around, meaning drift up and down the dormitory hall talking and joking with anybody there. Jack had suggested we go to a movie at eight. I went down to the second floor to hang around until movie time.

Jack's door was open and I walked in. There were six boys visiting Jack including Steve Hartley, and one girl. As soon as I entered everybody went silent. I knew something was very wrong. I waited as everyone looked embarrassed. The girl stood next to Jack. She looked possessive.

"Hi, Theresa," said Jack with not a lot of enthusiasm. "This is Ginny."

"Hi," I said. There was not much else to say until I found out something.

"Ginny dropped in by surprise," Jack said.

Yeah! I could see that! I couldn't remember seeing her around campus, or at least not in our complex. She might be somebody from outside.

The embarrassing silence continued. Ginny looked very uncomfortable. She had known no more about me than the other way around. Ginny's position near Jack made it clear she considered herself his girlfriend.

"Do you have anything to say, Jack?" I asked.

"I'll be up in a few minutes."

I went back upstairs. This was the most humiliating experience I ever had. All those boys were watching.

So! Two timing Jack was coming up for a last look, was he? I'd give him something to look at!

I went to the closet and pulled out my 'little black nothing'. It was a backless dress made of flimsy, clingy material. It was something appropriate for a party, but in my room, with no other girls to look at, Jack would find it hard to forget. He deserved the VIP treatment.

Six inches above the knee wasn't a big deal these days, but to make it more interesting I folded back the hemline three more inches inside the skirt and taped it. Now that was a dress!

I put it on and looked in the full length mirror on the door. Yup. This would kill Jack. He'd promise to throw Ginny out the window if I took him back. Sorry, Jack. Too late for that.

I waited a few minutes. There was no knock on the door. I sat on the bed and turned on the television. They were showing the early part of "The Caine Mutiny". I'd seen it before. Captain Queeg was a paranoid personality who couldn't take adversity. It made him a dictator on the ship. He made his men miserable with his inflexible demands. Later, there would be an ultimate crisis, a monstrous typhoon that threatened to sink the ship. That's when the Captain lost it and his chief mate Maryk took over the ship on the grounds that the Captain was nuts. As a reward for his courageous saving of the ship, Maryk was put on trial for mutiny.

My dad who'd been in the Navy read the book and said half of it was about a love story between Ensign Keith and a girl who wanted to be a singer. Eventually her career took off and she left the Ensign. Dad guessed that this boring love story meant something to the author, but it dragged down the book. The movie producers wisely dropped the singer's story and concentrated on the mutiny. It worked because the chief mate's willingness to sacrifice his career to save the crew was a very effective love story of sorts.

I noticed something similar in a book called "The Robe" which my grandmother gave me. It was written by a Methodist minister who filled it with quotes from the Bible. It was a spectacular bestselling book in

World War II when the world looked like it was falling apart, but it would probably bomb today. In the Hollywood movie starring Richard Burton, all the Bible quotes were dropped, and they concentrated on the conflict between Burton and Caligula. But Burton and his girl marched off to martyrdom from a more dramatic Emperor's throne room scene than was in the book. Sometimes subtle messages work better than speeches.

That's how I operate. I could have criticized Jack in front of his friends for dating me without telling about Ginny, but I said nothing. I let people think it out for themselves.

The movie ended with the Caine sailing back out to sea. Ensign Keith was the only officer of the original crew left after the devastating trial. The next movie was one of those horrible made-for-TV - walking-dead movies. I couldn't stand them and turned off the TV. The problem with that trash is it didn't address an individual's decisions in life. It was insulting to avoid challenging the viewer's ideas as if his ideas didn't matter. At least in 'The Caine Mutiny' you were challenged to think whether you would have the courage to take over the ship like Maryk. If you were a real thinker, you'd consider why the Navy didn't look into the circumstances of the monsoon scene before rushing into putting Maryk on trial. Apparently nothing had been said before the trial.

I stared at my roommate's wall. There was nothing to do and I was milking my loneliness. People who never went to college believed it was one continuous party. In fact, parties were rare. Some colleges had nearby drinking spots just outside the campus where kids crowded in until the fire codes were broken twice over, but BC wasn't like that. It was all residential zone and no commercial. College life was mostly studying and killing time with inane activities. It was a test. If you could stand this life for four years you could stand anything. A lot of kids went nuts and dropped out.

After half an hour moping on my bed I moved to my desk and resumed moping. Paging through old magazines was my pretense of doing something. The truth was I was desperately lonely. I thought of going downstairs to see what was going on, but after the scene in Jack's room my loneliness would be too obvious. I still had a little pride. It was amazing how quiet it could be on the girl's floor. That was another thing people got wrong.

It was now nearly nine o'clock and I was near tears. There was nobody around here who cared for me. There wasn't one person I could walk up to and call 'friend' to their face.

There was a knock on the door. "Come in,-" I said.

Steve Hartley walked in.

He walked up close to my desk and said, "Ginny is Jack's hometown girlfriend. They've been seeing each other for years. She was supposed to show up next week but she came early."

So. It was going to be all over anyway.

"Did you know about her?"

"No. None of us did."

"Have a seat." I indicated the bed. He sat down on the edge of it. We looked at each other. I must have looked pretty sad after a miserable evening. I sensed that he was aware of how lonely I'd been, but somehow I didn't mind his knowing.

"Anything going on in the dorm?" I suggested.

"There's an all night card game."

I heard about the boys playing cards all night. You would think something exciting was going on, but all they did was throw cards around. There was no intelligent conversation possible when all you did was look at your cards. Why did they do it?

He glanced at my legs. My hemline was practically up to my hips when I sat down. Nothing excited boys more than a shirt skirt. Bikinis didn't do as much.

"You're quiet, Steve. Something on your mind?"

'Yeah. You want me to leave?"

"If you leave now I'll have to kill myself."

It took a few seconds before Steve got the joke and laughed. The ice was broken and we each had that little smile of people comfortable in their situation. Next came planning the night's campaign.

"Will you stay with me a while, Steve?"

"I want to."

I smiled. "I think we can find something interesting to talk about."

I stood up and reached for a deck of DVDs high on my bookcase. The DVDs were of the famous BBC production series 'Victoria'."

"You ever watch this, Steve?"

"No."

"You'll like it" I said while walking over to put the first disk in the player. "An eighteen year old girl becomes Queen of England and Empress of the British Empire. Everybody wants something from her. She survives eight assassination attempts. You wonder how a teenage girl got through it. You wonder if you'd have the nerve to take on what she did."

I indicated that he move over a couple of feet and sit back against the pile of cushions. I sat next to him with my left arm in reach of my desk. "This is more interesting that playing cards, don't you think?"

"Yeah" he said with a smile.

"You'll get used to me soon, Steve. We have to get over this awkward moment."

The feelings of an eighteen year old boy in this close encounter weren't hard to guess. I felt safe. There was no way he was going to try to take advantage of me like some boy who would keep trying to get something that wasn't his right. Anyway, I could throw him out the window.

'Victoria' was made for the English who already knew the story. It was very complicated with rapid changes from one subplot to another. I had to explain the characters and their motivations. Steve seemed interested. There was much to talk about. We both marveled at the responsibility the girl took on. She could have withdrawn in her castle and ignored everything going on in the world. She went out to be seen by the people despite assassination attempts, and made heavy decisions like sending a band of traitors to Australia instead of letting them being drawn and quartered. Her uncle was next in line if she abdicated. He did maneuvers to bring this about. The girl queen told him, "I have made mistakes and perhaps I will make more, but I'm a better monarch than you could ever be." I wondered if I could do as well at her age.

We took two breaks during the night to go

downstairs and get little snacks out of the food machine. Some people saw us at two a.m. which was sure to start rumors. By daylight we were giggling from fatigue.

We went to breakfast. I was still wearing my little black nothing dress which stood out at breakfast. It was obvious from our demeanors that we'd been up all night. Girls gave us the eye. I didn't care. Let them think what they wanted. We hadn't done anything we couldn't tell our parents. Nosy girls filled our table and asked what we did all night.

"Nothing," I said.

"Surrrrrrrrrrrrrrrre, Theresa!"

Steve joked, "The video is on YouTube".

We suddenly had lots of friends. An attractive couple was invited to everything.

Steve and I were perfect for each other. We could spend hours together without talking, or we could chatter like eight year olds when the mood struck us. I fell for him like a fifteen year old girl in her first love because, really, Steve was my first love. He was too smart to take advantage of me. He also felt he'd found the right mate and didn't want to mess things up.

We had differences in interests and opinions but nothing critical. Taking a hint from comments of our parents and grandparents, we promised not to try to change each other. That's what kills a lot of marriages. Nobody could change a spouse, and if you even wanted to, hadn't the marriage already failed? We promised that Theresa would always be Theresa, Steve would always be Steve, and that's the way it would be forever.

It was like the situation with Alexander Hamilton and Thomas Jefferson we studied in American History class. The two men were both in Washington's Cabinet and argued about everything. Washington had a hard time keeping them from killing each other. Jefferson had been a wealthy kid and had an easy time of it. Hamilton spent his youth on a horrible Caribbean island that made Devil's Island look good. It was the last refuge of criminals trying to escape the law. Slaves had a five year life expectancy. Human life had no value. So, Jefferson trusted human nature and wanted a nation of gentlemen farmers with little government. Hamilton thought men were scum and wanted a strong central government in control. Between Jefferson's Declaration of Independence and Louisiana Purchase, and Hamilton's central bank and other government institutions, these two men built the America we know. So why did they fight each other in the Cabinet? They were founding a nation. They should have been friends.

Like those two founding fathers, Steve and I had different childhoods. I had HAL to worry about since age ten. I had to consider that someday I would have to take part in world affairs. What would happen if the world found out about HAL? It would be chaos! That's why the government was watching me day and night. My father said I'd be captain of my ship and had to learn all I could about the world. Yeah, well, I might be captain of a lot more than my ship! I took an interest in politics, sociology and history, though not enough to want a career in any of them. Steve had two sisters and a brother, happily married parents, and a good family income. If he had a theme song, it would be "Everything Is Beautiful, In Its Own Way". He wanted to be a physicist like his father and had no interest in politics. He was Jefferson who thought people would turn out all right, and I was Hamilton worried about the worst.

But we never argued. We got along beautifully. Steve was years ahead of boys his age. He understood that a girl wants romance, not sex just to fulfill some urge. He did nothing ungentlemanly the first time he entered my dorm room despite my compromising situation. He wanted a lifetime commitment as I did. Despite almost universal skepticism, there really are gentlemen like Steve in the world, and every girl wants to be a lady who catches one. The current Miss Massachusetts was at BC. She went out with a guy with glasses and an extroverted jolly personality that reminded me of Jeff Winslow, my high school steady. This was not what people would call a man's man, but eat your hearts out, guys, he was dating Miss Massachusetts. I found out that the previous year he had been the steady escort of that year's Miss Massachusetts too! He'd found the secret of dating outstanding women; he treated them like ladies.

So it was with Steve. I noticed girls looked at us with envy. They could see we had that eternal love of a Disney full length animated movie. "Someday my prince will come," sang Snow White. Yeah, well, I had my prince.

In a month we knew we'd get married and we wanted it soon. Well really, now! Could we go four years without doing it?

Mom and dad raised the parental eyebrows when they learned of our plans following a whirlwind courtship. Fortunately Father Donoughty got to know Steve well in our meetings to plan the wedding. Father convinced my parents that Steve was as fine a boy as I was ever likely to meet, and while we were young, he'd found that some young couples were still together sixty years later. There was nothing to indicate our marriage wouldn't work. On the other hand, discouraging it might cause harm. It was a dilemma for my parents. Eventually they approved.

It all came down to one question. Did Steve and I know what we were doing? Father Donoughty had seen many young marriages fail and knew the reasons. He believed Steve and I would succeed.

The large Sullivan clan had waited for years to see *this* girl's wedding and they weren't disappointed. I was gorgeous as a recently turned eighteen year old. For the church service I wore a two piece wedding gown. A floor length wide skirt with spaghetti shoulder straps was made from matte duchess satin. Over this I had a jacket made of peekaboo cotton Venice lace that more or less covered my shoulders and the top half of my upper arms so as not to scandalize the congregation. At the reception the jacket and train came off and my shoulders and cleavage charmed the crowd.

And now we set off to find out what life was all about. Henry David Thoreau was a 19th century philosopher who lived not far from Boston. He spent a year in a one room shack in the woods next to Walden Pond to find himself. He said other men could journey to Africa to shoot giraffes if they wanted, but he preferred to stay home and shoot himself. What he meant was you should explore your inner self. You'll find you own a territory greater than the Russian Czar's. Men try to prove their courage by going to unexplored jungles, hunting lions with spears, or climbing the tallest mountain, but they don't have the courage to examine themselves. Thoreau said that, not me. Blame him.

Anyway, Steve and I would explore ourselves and each other. We hoped to like what we found.

We moved into a small apartment for privacy during the summer break. It belonged to a retired couple who spent all the warm months touring the United States in an RV, something a lot of retirees did, we learned. Steve's father gave us a new Chevrolet as a wedding present. I was driving the car alone one Saturday to go grocery shopping, thinking of the wonderful future waiting for me.

Chapter 4

I preferred to go to a supermarket in a direction away from Framingham because the extra three miles it took to drive along this isolated road more than made up for the waiting in Framingham traffic. It was on this road that three cars ahead of me suddenly drew abreast of each other and stopped. I was forced to stop too. Six men with handguns drawn got out of these cars and surrounded me.

"Get out of the car!" one man ordered.

I got out just as a van pulled up from behind. It was a large van with three bench seats. "Get in!" someone yelled as the door to the middle seat opened. I got in, sat down, and found myself surrounded by men pointing guns at me, three behind me and two more in the front seat.

"Isn't this overdoing it?" I asked.

"We have our orders."

The van started moving and I looked around at what might be my last look at familiar surroundings. I'd known for a year that the President was stewing over me and a struggle seemed pointless.

We drove a couple miles to a field where two military helicopters were waiting. "Follow us" said one of the goons. I got out of the van and followed them to the nearest helicopter. It was some kind of VIP transportation helicopter with seats looking forward like in airplanes. It was probably used to haul generals' butts around to important military spots like Las Vegas and Disney World. I sat in the seat they indicated and was strapped in. Both helicopters took off and headed south. We passed within sight of my car still on the road a quarter mile below. It was surrounded by dozens of cars and trucks. People were standing around talking about what happened.

Even in the helicopter they kept several guns on me. They must have suspected I had powers I didn't admit. Well, I did.

We headed south over water at a slight angle to the east. I could see the Massachusetts and Rhode Island coastlines in the distance.

"Where are you taking me?"

"To an aircraft carrier" answered one of the men holding guns on me.

"Am I coming back?"

"No."

There it was. The death sentence. This was the last I'd see of Massachusetts.

My face softened and tears gathered in my eyes. How many thousands of stories had I seen on the news about young people like myself being killed by murderers or in accidents and I didn't think about it long. Now it was my turn to face death. Death! Death at eighteen! My mind could scarcely believe it. The unfairness of it made my body shake with revulsion. Dead at the peak of my beauty and youth when I was just beginning to taste the best life offered! I was a little angry for a moment but returned to sorrow.

But I didn't cry. I wasn't a phony movie actress using hysterics to milk all the drama she could out of every moment. I was a real person and I didn't give a damn what these kidnappers thought. I'd had years to consider something like this might happen someday.

Besides, I had a solid upbringing. I'd been taught that this life was just the beginning. Death wasn't the end. It was the start of a wonderful eternity. Still it was natural to mourn the loss of this world.

These guys probably had never told a girl she was going to be killed and must have expected a soap opera scene. I gave them Navy SEAL. They said a few words to each other once in a while. I noticed their voices softened. I sensed I'd won their admiration.

Time passed. I waxed poetic. This trip was analogous to a journey through life. I could see the thousands of buildings below with their tens of thousands of people, and this was like a journey to see the world. All those people down there going through their daily routines didn't give a thought to the meaning of it all. But I did now, maybe a little too late.

The helicopters headed south approximately parallel to the East coast. Beaches and cities could be seen on the right. I could no longer recognize them.

"How are you going to do it?"

"You'll be put in a plane with an atom bomb."

My eyebrows went up a little. Wouldn't a bullet save taxpayers a hundred million dollars? But then I realized they wanted to destroy HAL, not me, and everybody said nothing could survive an A-bomb.

"When is this going to happen?"

"Tomorrow afternoon. It's far away."

They were becoming more talkative. Apparently they were relieved that I hadn't put on the hysterical scene they expected. I had a day to think of something, if anything could be done.

"What did they tell you about me?"

"You're a danger to the security of the United States."

"How?"

"They didn't say. No need to know."

They didn't know about HAL. Should I tell them and demonstrate the strength HAL gave me? No. That would definitely convince them I was dangerous and the President knew what he was doing. My chances were better leaving them in the dark. They might chicken out at the last minute and let me go.

I remained quiet after learning of my death sentence while the helicopters continued down the coast. I couldn't recognize the landscapes. The helicopters landed for refueling at some military airbase next to some nondescript building that might be used for anything. I was allowed to use the restroom with a warning that armed guards had the building surrounded and I couldn't escape.

The fully fueled helicopters took off again. I let my mind wander aimlessly over the incidents of my short stay on Earth. In retrospect I'd had a charmed life. Nothing had happened to me. No attacks by sex-crazed boys. No illnesses. No traffic accidents. No run ins with the police. Nothing. If I were to write my autobiography now I'd write three lines: "I was born. I had a good time. I was vaporized by a bomb". The negative incidents I remembered, mostly childhood experiences, were so trivial in nature they wouldn't be worth telling in a letter. An ill-tempered dog barked and lunged at me but did not touch me. From this I had no love for dogs. When I was twelve and in my mother's car I saw a traffic accident a short distance in front of us. Everybody drives by hundreds of accidents after they happen, but rare was the person who actually saw one happen. It was a grisly scene, a head-on collision with one driver instantly killed and two other people severely injured. Mom had to be a witness in court. This experience shook me up for a while.

Other than that my life had been an amalgam of routines. And this is what made up a life, not the spectacular events that make the news. I'd been satisfied with my quiet life.

After three helicopter flights we finally ended the day's traveling at some kind of airbase far south. Maybe we were in Florida or somewhere around there. It had been dark for a while and I couldn't recognize cities from lights alone. The East coast was nearly continuous densely packed residential areas with lights everywhere. Not one person down there knew what was happening to me.

I figured out why we were in helicopters. A chopper could land anywhere such as this quiet part of the airbase while planes had to land at the airstrip with lots of people watching.

They marched me to another one of those nondescript military buildings that only had numbers on them. Building number 39 turned out to be a cafeteria. It was late and no crew was on duty. The government men told me they'd arranged for food to be left out and I could help myself. I grabbed a tray while looking down the line. There was a beverage dispensing cabinet at the end. Hopefully it had plastic bottles. I walked along and picked up two tuna sandwiches, a piece of chocolate cake, an 8 oz carton of milk, and a cup of coffee. Finally, I arrived at the beverage dispenser. It was the size of a refrigerator and had a glass door you could open and grab a drink from a shelf. There were 20 oz bottles of Coke in there. I grabbed twelve bottles and put them on my tray. The men guarding me dismissed this as the irrational behavior of someone who knew she'd die in hours. One could not expect much better.

A few feet beyond the end of the cafeteria line was a garbage can. Leaving my tray on the end of the slide shelf for a moment, I walked to the garbage can to retrieve the garbage bag. It was after hours and the crew had cleaned up and put in a new bag before leaving. I pulled up the plastic bag and returned to my tray to put eleven of the twelve Coke bottles in the bag. Then I sat at the nearest table to eat.

The men watching me, three of them aiming guns at all times, were impressed by my calm. A thousand miles from home and anybody I wanted to see, surrounded by executioners, I ate methodically keeping my eyes down as if I were alone in the room. I glanced at them once in a while. Hardened as they were by a cruel world, their eyes softened at the sight of me. Perhaps they had daughters. How could they justify this?

Building 39 had a cot in a back office. They took me to it.

"Try to get some sleep" I was told. "We leave at four a. m."

They left me alone. No doubt they had every escape route guarded. I could have easily killed all of them by throwing hard objects at them, but where could I go? An army would be sent out looking for me.

I laid down on the cot and slipped the garbage bag of Coke bottles under the blanket so that it couldn't be removed without disturbing me.

What was I to think about for the next six hours? My first thoughts were of Steve. I smiled as I recalled how awkward he looked when he walked into my dormitory room for the first time. I wore that flimsy little black dress outfit and wondered if he'd attack me or run for his life. He handled it well. Before long people saw how hard we'd fallen for each other. Girls asked if we'd been to bed. That was none of their business, but in fact we did wait for marriage. We knew we had something special and didn't want to spoil it with regrets.

"Wake up. It's four o'clock."

God! I'd fallen asleep! The whole night was wasted.

I was put in a car and driven to a landing strip while it was still dark. We got into a twin turboprop used for short commutes between minor airports. It had fourteen seats in single rows separated by an aisle. It was too small for an enclosed cockpit; in fact I could see over the pilot and co-pilot's shoulders through the windshield for a spectacular view.

As we headed out to sea the government men finally put away their guns. They weren't needed. From this point on there was no escape.

I spoke for the first time since they put me in the first helicopter.

"I have to know. Exactly when does the bomb go off?"

"When you reach sixty thousand feet."

"They go that high?"

"They can reach a hundred thousand for a few seconds. Reminds me." He held up an airman's jumpsuit, a one piece covering something like the thermal underwear used by Northern outdoor workers in the winter. "You'll have this if you want it. It gets cold like you won't believe up there."

"Thanks. I will."

It fit in perfectly with my plan. I looked away so they wouldn't see my interest. This was the last time I spoke to them.

Perhaps it was moving away from land, but for the moment Steve and my parents seemed in another world I had already left. There was nothing they could do for me. I turned to thoughts of my eternity.

When pushed to the brink someone can panic, or despair, or hope. I had always believed. Some people said they had doubts about God. I pitied them. How could they have doubts? Simple reasoning told me the universe could not be in the form it was without design. It might be a chaos, but the beautiful way it was ordered against a trillion to one odds of elements just happening to have exactly the properties needed to sustain life could only be somebody's design. Besides that, people's intellects could not be material alone and could not be hardwired to understand any concept presented to it. The human mind held universal ideas beyond the reach of matter and evolution. The intellect could not be made of matter. Nor could the human soul operate on its own. It needed an omniscient and omnipotent intelligence to move its thoughts. But most of all, the unselfish self-sacrificing goodness of my mother, father, and Steve was not something that could exist in animals.

When Socrates was in prison waiting to be executed, his friend Crito urged him to escape and go to another country. Socrates said he enjoyed living in Athens all his life and owed everything to Athens. If he ran away he would be betraying the decision of the Athens people even if it was wrong in his case. If we want the life God gives us we must accept the bad along with the good. That is a life well-spent.

I recited a prayer in my mind as best I could remember it. It was not a standard Church prayer but was fitting for the end.

The Lord is my shepherd; I shall not want. He maketh me to lie in green pastures; he leadeth me to still waters. Though I walk through the valley of death I will fear no evil for thou art with me. Goodness and mercy shall follow me all the days of my life and I will dwell in the house of the Lord forever.

The flight lasted for hours. I'd grown tired of thinking hard and let my mind wander through simple memories. My time had run out. The important issues were settled. My name was written in the book. There was nothing left to do.

I saw an aircraft carrier and its half dozen support ships many miles in the distance. So this was the end. But strangely I was not afraid. I was past that.

"This is a refueling stop" said the nearest government man. "Our destination is further on."

He got up and moved closer to me.

"When we land the plane stops with a jolt. It can break your neck. We have to get you ready."

He and his partner got to work. They buckled the

seat belt across my hips. They stuffed large pillows in front of my legs until they were packed in so tightly they couldn't slip a hand in.

"Raise your arms" I was told. I did and they unrolled a long belt, wrapped it around the seat and my armpits, and secured it high on my chest.

"Put your hands on your forehead." I did. "When we approach the deck close your eyes and push back on your forehead hard or you could break your neck. Can you remember that?"

I nodded.

We descended and slowed down. It was somewhat dramatic to watch the approach to the carrier deck. Few people had experienced this.

"Sixty seconds" said the pilot over the intercom. Groups of sailors could be seen on the edge of the deck furthest from the landing strip. "Thirty seconds." The sailors disappeared over the deck's edge although they could keep their heads up to watch the landing. "Fifteen seconds." I put my hands to my forehead. "Five seconds." I closed my eyes.

The wheels hit the deck and squealed. The tail hook snared a cable and the plane decelerated from 110 m.p.h. to zero in a second. The G-forces were incredible. It felt like a giant was trying to rip my arms out of their sockets. My head floated around a bit because I was dizzy.

"You did well" said one of them.

He came over to remove my chest harness and the pillows packed in front of my legs.

A vehicle that looked like a small tanker truck rolled out and the plane was refueled. Then the plane taxied up to the catapult cable. The catapult was a large piston and cylinder hidden under the deck that was powered by steam. When it was actuated steam pushed the piston down the long cylinder and the piston pulled a cable attached to a hook at the front of the plane.

The cable was attached. The engines were revved up to the max and we took off from zero to 120 m.p.h. in three and a half seconds. I was crushed back in my seat. No wonder the pilots liked the thrill of their job.

"That was nothing" said the man to my left. "Wait 'til the jet takeoff."

I rolled my eyes to Heaven. These guys had to be crazy. Did they think I was enjoying this adventure? I was getting tired of it. It seemed like a week since they forced me out of the car. I just wanted to get this business done.

I checked my watch. Three o'clock. It was another long, boring flight which left my tired mind nearly blank. I'd almost forgotten what the trip was for. Through blurry eyes I saw the second carrier in the distance.

The procedure was the same. Pillows were tightly packed in front of my legs. The chest harness was secured. I was reminded about closing my eyes and pushing back on my head. We landed with the same instant stop. This was the end of the line.

They removed the pillows and belts and handed me the jumpsuit. I stepped in the aisle to put it on. I picked up the garbage bag of Coke bottles and followed the goons out the door.

The carrier had thousands of sailors but they were all below except for a few men needed to handle the planes. There was a group of a dozen officers some distance away. The goons and I walked to them.

The officers seemed shocked to see me. I guessed they had not been told the person being executed was an eighteen year old girl. It was lucky everybody else was below deck. I could have caused a mutiny.

We arrived at the group of officers and waited while the jet plane was prepared. The oldest looking officer said, "They didn't tell me you were a girl." I was right. They hadn't known. Would it have made a difference? Probably not.

There were three female officers in this group. The Captain probably thought the condemned man deserved a last look at females.

One of the women asked my goons, "What did she do?"

"We don't know, ma'am."

"How long were you with her?"

"Since yesterday morning. She hasn't said fifty words. She's a tough little lady."

This triggered something in the young woman's brain. She thought I should have the opportunity to say something in my defense. Nobody had been given a protocol, so this young woman pulled a cellphone from her pants pocket, and boldly walked around the government men until she was almost in front of me. She held up the cellphone and activated the video mode.

"Do you have anything to say?" she asked.

I was nervous, but at this point I was more disgusted than nervous.

"This is the most stupid thing ever done. I'm glad I won't be here to see what happens."

She sounded disappointed. "Is that all you have to say?"

My face softened. Yes, that was the wrong way to leave my family hanging.

I once read a famous quote by the Shawnee Indian Chief Tecumseh about singing a death song and going out like a hero. I had rewritten it for more universal use, never dreaming that I'd use it myself so soon.

"If people grieve your passing, rejoice in the good you did, and die like a hero going home. I feel good about who I was."

She was more than satisfied with that. She was thrilled. Surely nothing better could be said.

One of the goons said, "Time to go". Everybody advanced to the jet.

I climbed a ladder and awkwardly got into the cockpit still carrying the garbage bag of Coke bottles. A seaman on another ladder on the other side of the plane reached into the cockpit to get an oxygen mask attached to a long plastic tube. He put it on to make sure it was working. "This is oxygen. You'll need it up there" he explained and put the mask over my nose and mouth. An elastic strap around my head secured it in place. He waited a moment. "Are you getting oxygen?" I nodded.

An X shaped seat belt was attached to my seat near my shoulders and by my hips. This was two belts stitched together over my chest. Given my small size and this device's tight fit, besides its impracticality for escaping the plane quickly, I guessed they'd designed it just for me.

The canopy was mounted on a heavy frame. The crewman lowered it like a closing clamshell and moved it forward. Something slid into place to lock the canopy.

While all this was being done, the catapult cable was put on the bow hook. Everything was ready. The crewman climbed down and the ladders were removed.

The officers disappeared into the conning tower to watch the show. A couple minutes later the jet engine of my plane started up. In thirty seconds engine thrust reached a stable speed. They had to be checking it for problems by remote control sensors. The plane was freed and the catapult engaged. I was accelerated from zero to 165 mph in two seconds. The pressure on my back was unbelievable. It was unimaginable. The man had not exaggerated.

The plane climbed steadily. There was no time to lose. I went to work immediately.

First, the seat belt harness had to go. I felt around the belt attachments next to my hips for release buttons. I couldn't find any. The belts seemed to disappear into metal slots. It was the same at my shoulders. There was no time to waste looking for the release mechanism. I reached my right hand down to grasp the belt at my left hip. I pulled and pulled with ever increasing force. The belt stretched and grew thinner until it snapped with a dull pop. I repeated the procedure on the belt next to my right hip with my left hand. I did the same with the belt attachments at my shoulders, pulling forward with both hands, my back pressing against the seat to provide a counterforce. The harness was free. It was much simpler to pull the stitched X in the middle apart. This gave me two belts. I tied two ends together to give me one. Finally, I wrapped it around my waist and tied the other two ends together. This would keep the Coke bottles from moving below my waist. I wanted them to stay up around my chest. The jumpsuit had a zipper from the collar to the crotch. I unzipped it down to the makeshift belt.

I checked the instrument panel. The important mechanical altimeter was easy to find. 11,320 feet. Two miles. All right. I was doing well. I had time to do some of the bottles.

I grabbed the garbage bag of Coke bottles and put it in my lap. I uncapped a bottle, poured its contents on the floor, tore off a small piece of garbage bag, wrapped it over the opening of the empty bottle, and screwed the cap over the plastic covered neck. That would make a water tight seal. The bottle went inside the jumpsuit under my left armpit. I did the same procedure with a second bottle which went under my right armpit. And a third bottle went on my left side. A fourth bottle went on the right.

The altimeter read 22,190 feet. I was doing great.

More bottles were emptied, sealed with plastic and capped, and jammed into my jumpsuit. Eleven bottles would provide enough buoyancy to keep my head well above water.

The altimeter read 47,520 feet. I watched it carefully. It was nearly over.

I thought once more of Steve, of the good times, of the funny moments, of the private hours. I now understood his purpose. He helped me walk over the unsteady ground to home. In him, I had a foretaste of the Father.

The altimeter read 54,140 feet. It was time to go home. As a believer I was sure I was immortal and that gave me courage. I pulled off the oxygen mask and said a silent prayer in my mind.

Father, forgive me for all my sins. Take me into your house forever.

I stood up on the seat and turned around to face the rear of the plane. The canopy was a few inches above my head. I pushed my hands up against it hard. It didn't budge. I increased the pressure and kept increasing it. Still it didn't move. How much pressure could I exert? I didn't know. There was never a reason to find out but it had to be enormous.

The canopy was moving! Something somewhere was distorting. Metal or something was being stretched, torn, destroyed.........

The canopy suddenly flew off. I instantly covered my face with my arms as my body was sucked out of the plane. I rapidly somersaulted head over heels.

I was very afraid because leaving the plane guaranteed my death. But I was nowhere near panicking. I knew there was a better world after this one.

The first thing I noticed was the complete silence. The scream of the jet had lasted only a few seconds. As the plane moved away it quickly went silent. Except for my breathing which sent throat sounds through bone to my ear there was absolutely no sound. On the ground there was always some background sound even if a person wasn't aware of it. Up here there was nothing.

The second thing I noticed was the extreme cold. My fingers went numb in seconds. Without the jumpsuit I might already be dead.

The bomb went off miles away. The light was so

intense I could see it through the flesh of my arms.

As I fell the air temperature climbed rapidly. A minute after leaving the plane, it was no longer cold enough to suck the heat right through my jumpsuit. I was keeping some of the heat.

I still somersaulted wildly. I took my arms off my face but kept my eyes shut. Films of skydivers showed them stretching their arms and legs out with knees slightly bent and arms back past the plane of the torso. This had the effect of a badminton shuttlecock to keep the body falling true. I stretched out my arms and legs. Momentum from the somersaulting kept my body turning over in all kinds of angles, but the turning was slowing down. Finally, I stopped turning over. My body was in a stable face down position.

The air temperature had passed into tolerable territory. I opened my eyes slightly, just enough to see something. The clouds were still far below. I closed my eyes for a while.

I opened my eyes again and saw the cotton ball clouds just below. It appeared I was going to pass between two of them somewhat close to one. I reached the top of the cloud layer, fell between the half mile thick clouds, and finally I was below them.

I'd been falling for minutes. Choppy waves in the thousands were visible on the ocean's surface. The strong wind that buffeted my hair on the carrier deck stirred the water. I was glad to see the waves. They'd make it possible to know exactly when I'd hit the water.

The waves appeared larger every second. Their approach seemed to speed up and I knew there were only seconds left. Once again I covered my face with my arms. My body made a hard belly flop. I was knocked out.

The waves brushing my face were stimulating. I regained consciousness. It was the South Atlantic, far below the equator, and for the Southern Hemisphere, June was like December in the North. The water was ice cold. My feet and ankles hurt but there was no escaping it. I started whimpering. The cold sank deeper into my bones. I yelled and thrashed the water. It got worse and worse. Now I was close to panic and screamed. Dying was bad enough. How painful would this get?

In a couple of minutes my lower legs went numb. The skin all over my body was losing nervous sensation. My screaming stopped to be replaced by intermittent whimpering and groans.

It was nearly over now. I quieted down.

It was time. All accounts were settled. All debts were paid. I had no more use for this world.

I passed out.

Chapter 5

I woke up and remembered my horrible experience in the water. I cried and violently thrashed around. Memory can be as bad as the experience itself, and this experience was terrible. In a minute I calmed down.

I was in a hospital room. Some electrodes were attached to my head. There were doctors and nurses around me and I recognized Peter Blair, the popular Prime Minister of England whom I'd often seen on the news. I slammed my hand on the mattress in frustration. For eight years I had kept HAL a secret. My life was ruined. All I wanted was a quiet life. I didn't get it. What was I supposed to do next?

"I'll bet my secret is out."

"It is."

"Terrific. Some maniac will kill me in a week. How did you get to me in time?"

"We didn't. You've been dead for two weeks."

"What? That can't happen."

"It did. A most remarkable story."

"So I went through all that for nothing?"

I was referring to my kidnapping and fall from the plane.

"I'm afraid so."

Could my anonymity still be preserved? "I'll bet there's a lot of news stories about me."

"About a million if you include all languages around the world. You are discussed continuously."

No anonymity! "Anybody say anything bad about me?"

"No. I have seen nothing negative."

"I knew I might become famous and kept myself squeaky clean."

"People with problems can be interesting too."

"Yeah, well, people with problems don't change the world."

His eyes opened up. What I said surprised him. It was as if the concept was a new one to him. I saw the nurses were also staring at me. I'd said something important. What did I say?

The Prime Minister turned his back and moved away a few feet. He seemed to be pondering something. What the heck was going on in the world?

He turned around again and smiled.

"It hadn't occurred to me. Perhaps only the kind of person you want to be can do what's needed."

"What's needed?"

"Later. I'll leave you with the nurses."

He left with the doctors. Nurses took off the electroencephalograph electrodes from my head. I heard a large crowd of people cheering.

The nurses took other things off me, including a thermometer out of my you-know-what and brushed my hair. I was still wearing the clothes I had on when I fell in the ocean.

I noticed my clothes were stained with some reddish-brown stuff. "What's this?" I asked.

"Blood."

Peter Blair came back to the room. By now I was sitting in a chair chatting with the nurses.

"How are you?" asked Blair.

"I'm good."

"Any nausea?"

"No." Why did he ask that? "Where am I?"

"In London. This hospital is on the periphery of the city. We couldn't bring you into the heart of London. The traffic obstruction would have been horrendous."

Why was I so important? Never mind. I could find out later.

"Can I go to a hotel or something?"

"We hold a floor of a new hotel tower for visiting dignitaries. It's yours."

"Do they have shops?"

"They do."

"I need fresh clothes but I don't have money."

"The British nation will gladly pay. We've already spent millions on you."

Everybody laughed at that. Something else that made no sense! I could find out about it later.

"I need something to eat. They didn't feed me my last day."

"The nurses will get you something."

He left again and the nurses got me some 'fish and chips'. Blair came back.

"How is your stomach taking the food?"

"Fine. That's the second time you asked that."

"The doctors warned me you might revive briefly but soon sicken and die. It would be like radiation sickness. First, nausea within the hour, then rapid deterioration. It can't be stopped. I'm glad it didn't happen."

What? More mysteries to find out about later.

"Can I go to the hotel now?"

"Of course, but first would you mind coming upstairs to the sunroom and let television cameras see you? Your family will see you."

"Sure."

Having Steve and my parents see that I was alive was too good to resist. The PM and I left the room. The PM's people followed as we walked towards the center of the building with greatly excited hospital staff and visitors cheering. There was a staircase near the front entrance. We went up to the second floor and walked to a patient lounge which had observation windows on three sides. This hospital was on the outskirts of London with plenty of open space in front.

Peter Blair guided me to the center window. A crowd of people large enough to fill a dozen NFL stadiums waited. In a moment they spotted me and cheered. Half a million people were cheering me! I felt a thrill going up and down my spine.

I was not used to this kind of attention and had no set responses like a seasoned celebrity would. I stared out at them amazed that they would find me so interesting. I was in my usual youthful situation of wondering what was going on.

"Why are they here?" I asked the PM.

"It took fourteen hours to revive you. People like that. The suspense, you know."

Television camera crews had claimed the spaces closest to the hospital and aimed their cameras at me. The world saw me standing in my blood soaked clothes. People held up hand painted signs. "HELLO", "WELCOME", and "COME TO IRELAND" were typical comments. One woman held a sign that read, "SAVE US".

"Save us? What's that about?"

"The wind is stopping everywhere."

"Where's everywhere?"

"All over the world."

I looked and saw those spherical cotton ball clouds that form when there's no wind. They weren't moving at all. They just hung there. It was like looking at a postcard.

"What does it mean?" I asked.

"No wind means no rain and no food."

"How bad will it get?"

"We may see the whole world starve to death."

The television cameras must have taken close ups of my face. The crowd became silent as they waited to see if I lost it.

"How will it happen?"

"Only the coastlines will have enough rain to grow a few crops. The inland areas will turn to desert. Europe and the United States can survive for two years by marshaling all their resources. Every square inch of the coasts will be cultivated. Unfortunately the rest of the world can't do this. We'll lose a billion people in the first year. Beyond two years our economies totally collapse. Everybody abandons their jobs. All social structures break down. It's every man for himself. All animals are slaughtered for food. With birds extinct the insects will multiply a thousand times spreading uncontrollable epidemics. In five years there will be few of us left. The world is dying."

Horrible! Inconceivable! And I was supposed to do something about this mess? I didn't even know how it happened!

The crowd was absolutely still. They knew I'd just learned the facts of life and my reaction showed I didn't know what to do. This unimaginable horror was likely to be their future. No wonder they came here to see me.

I walked inside and stopped at a nurse's station. Blair followed and stood next to me. He was the world's lifeline to me now—if that meant anything. He had to suspect by now that I didn't know what to do with the wind situation. Somehow he would have to pull a miracle out of me.

"I feel like running away," I said. "You couldn't stop me."

"I know we couldn't."

"All I wanted to do was be a high school math teacher."

"You can teach millions something more important. When the world falls apart around us, we look within ourselves and find ourselves. Show us what's within you."

I had no response to that. How did I know what was within me? Nothing could have prepared me for this kind of challenge!

"The world waits to hear you. Would you agree to speak with me on television? The topic is HAL."

"The government hasn't figured out HAL after eight years. You want me to do it in one day?"

"Not one day. We must begin."

"I need to see everything that happened in the last two weeks."

"Agreed. I'll speak to the BBC. They'll put together a montage for you."

"I need to see it in the exact sequence it happened to guess what HAL was thinking."

"Agreed. We'll see his thinking."

"This is what I was afraid of. I knew if my secret

came out people would never let me alone. I never wanted to be famous. I dont want television cameras in my face. I just want to live privately. Is there anything wrong with that?"

"There isn't. We'll shelter you as much as possible. Shall we go to the hotel?"

"Sure. It won't take me long to pack."

He laughed. I had nothing but the clothes on my back.

London's skyscraper district had a new sixty story hotel with two thousand rooms and every amenity. We arrived unexpected. A crowd gathered immediately as we walked to the desk.

"Mrs. Hartley needs a diplomatic room on the government floor," the PM announced.

The desk clerk signaled a young female hotel worker to follow. We went up to the 58th floor. My "room" was a suite with two bedrooms, a separate sitting room, and a kitchenette. It was far better than any hotel I stayed in before. The desk clerk who also went up with us said, "Nancy will attend you this evening".

Nancy was the hotel worker. "At your service, mum," she said to me, very excited about her assignment.

The men left us two girls alone. Blair said it would take some time for the BBC to put together the montage. There was a lot of film to edit.

I turned on the television and of course most channels were talking about me. I stumbled upon a channel that was showing the wedding of Prince William and Kate Middleton.

"That happened a long time ago" I said to Nancy.

"Why are they showing it now?"

"People need cheering up. It's been a horrible week. Royal weddings are rare and glorious. They have been showing it all week."

Well, yeah, America had no royal weddings, just the trash weddings of tabloid celebrities, if anybody cared. I watched the highlights of the wedding. The commentators gave much related information. I especially noticed how nervous Kate was.

After seeing everything I turned to a priority.

"I need some clothes. These are two weeks old. I must smell like hell."

While the world's people waited to hear whether their death sentence was commuted, Nancy and I went shopping. A swarm of security people hastily summoned by Blair kept the curious away. I selected four skirt and jacket outfits, lots of casual clothes, accessories, underwear, and every kind of personal item. I broke a world speed record in doing all this in 110 minutes.

The PM was alerted when I returned to my suite. He came over right away, but I had jumped into the shower when Nancy let him into the room. He waited patiently for half an hour. I came out in a flattering Irish green dress.

"A tribute to my ancestors" I said with a smile.

My hair was still damp and a mess but already expanding out to that mane that had startled many.

"Very lovely," the PM said. "I presented the final section of the montage being prepared for you. It will begin playing in a few minutes. After it's done, could we appear on the air twenty minutes later?"

"Sure."

"Excellent. I'll arrange it. Very lovely," he repeated and left. He looked encouraged by my cooperation.

The phone rang. With a million people wanting to talk to me there could only be one person who got through.

"That has to be my husband" I said to Nancy. "Tell him we can't talk on the phone. People are listening. Tell him no matter what I say tonight I can change my mind tomorrow."

The first person to speak on the BBC montage was an anchorman who had recorded his comments in a documentary on an earlier date.

"United States Navy Admiral Ruck was ordered to the White House to meet the President. President Martin told him sometimes a person was a clear and present danger to the United States but could not be neutralized by ordinary rules of law. What did the Admiral think was done with such people? The Admiral said he had no idea. The President said such a person was eliminated. One person could not be allowed to endanger three hundred million Americans.

"The Admiral was told such a person was a problem now. A plane was being prepared with an atom bomb. Would the Admiral cooperate in launching the plane from his ship, the U.S. carrier Ronald Reagan?

"The Admiral asked why the person was being executed and in this extreme manner? He was told the President would explain it on television immediately after the bomb was detonated. Other countries would detect it. The President had to explain it. Would the Admiral cooperate?

"He said he would, but he didn't like it. The President responded nobody was enjoying the operation, but if the Admiral was ordered to launch a nuclear missile to kill a million people, he would do it.

"The Admiral agreed to bring the Ronald Reagan around South America to the Atlantic for the operation. An F-22 Raptor was prepared with a bomb and remote control and loaded on the Admiral's ship. Then it was a matter of waiting for an opportunity to abduct Mrs. Hartley."

The next person to speak in the BBC montage was another announcer.

"Theresa Hartley was seized from her car on Saturday, June 12 and put in a helicopter. The witnesses who had seen Theresa Hartley's car forced to stop and the government men forcing her into the van at gunpoint called 911 to report a kidnapping. The police arrived in five minutes and were astonished at the witnesses' story. Usually a kidnapping was committed by one or two men. This time six kidnappers were seen and there' had to be at least one more in the van. The police wasted no time in calling the FBI. Kidnapping was a federal offense in America. Investigation of kidnappings must include all the States.

"Two FBI agents, each with an assistant, came over from Boston. They listened to the strange story and in turn questioned the witnesses. This could not be the act of criminals. A quick check showed Theresa's family had no ransom money to speak of. The kidnappers sounded like federal agents. Who were they? Who were those people in the numerous cars rushing past the scene minutes later? Why was

Theresa Hartley so important? Mystery upon mystery upon mystery! One agent said, 'If this was federal and we uncover it, it will make Watergate look like a tea party.'

"Steve Hartley was called in to the police station to meet the FBI men and was questioned about his wife's friends and routines. He could give no reason why Theresa would be kidnapped.

"After a few questions about her activity which revealed nothing, Mr. Hartley was asked if she had disk space on the Boston College computer system. Yes she did, he told them.

"Thereupon the FBI and Steve Hartley went to Boston College. A computer center technician there had the password to Mrs. Hartley's files. They found one called MISSION IMPOSSIBLE. It was two hundred and sixty pages of mathematical jargon, completely incomprehensible to anyone but a mathematician. Four math professors were called in to exam the file. They could not understand what it was for. Mrs. Hartley used many abbreviations and terms without definitions. If she were intending to hide her work's purpose, she did very well.

"The computer tech suggested the file be shared with everybody on the Boston College campus. Somebody might know what this was for. It brought no response. Theresa Hartley had been working alone."

The BBC montage did not have information about my Odyssey on the helicopter and twin engine prop plane to the carriers. But I knew all about that. Maybe they left it out for that reason.

The next part was a video of President Martin on

television.

"My fellow Americans. A short time ago the United States exploded a small atomic bomb in the atmosphere over the South Atlantic. It was scheduled. It was a one time event and will not be repeated.

"In an attempt to calm world fears I will immediately and fully disclose the reasons for this operation.

"Fifteen years ago an alien entity entered Earth. It disappeared and could not be found for seven years. Eight years ago it associated itself with an American named Theresa Sullivan.

"We observed her. The alien interacted with her influencing, her physical activity. She could not or would not explain what the alien was. We were patient, but this situation could not be tolerated indefinitely. We could not wait while this alien was as likely to be involved in hostile activities as friendly. It made no announcement to us in fifteen years, which we considered an unfriendly relationship. Therefore, we destroyed it with an atomic bomb.

"Sadly, this young woman had to be sacrificed. The alien remained with her at all times. We could not destroy the alien without destroying her too. We put her on a plane with the bomb.

"My fellow Americans. We took this action after careful deliberation. When we are at war, we send thousands of soldiers to their deaths. This was the loss of one person to eliminate a potential threat greater than any war.

"She was told what would be done. She went to her death bravely with no resistance. Her courage was magnificent. She gave credit to the human spirit.

"There is no medal designed for courageous conduct in this kind of situation, but let me console her family by saying her dignified and brave sacrifice did more good for the world than any Medal of Honor winner. We offer thanks from a grateful nation."

I imagined Steve and my parents were crushed by this news. How horrible it must have been to learn I'd been vaporized out of existence, nothing left behind, no body to bury, not a trace to mourn over, no known place at which to drop a flower wreath on the water. It was as if I never existed. Terrible!

Then came another shock for the world.

There were six thousand sailors on the Ronald Reagan. They could not be kept silent and no effort was made to make them shut up. They had cell phones connected to a satellite. That Sunday night information was leaking out.

The BBC had the phone call of a sailor who said I had bailed out of the plane. Even worse than this news, they had hidden a microphone in the collar of my jumpsuit. That's why they gave me the jumpsuit. They were listening to me all the time!

"She got out of the plane somehow. They heard her breathing after the bomb went off. She fell for three and a half minutes. When she was in the cold water she screamed her head off. But she never said a word. She was tough! Everybody was crying."

What must Steve have felt when he heard this! My parents must have gone nuts. I cried to think about it.

The BBC hurried along. The next presentation was a Senate hearing about the A-bomb explosion. The Senate Armed Services Committee convened on Tuesday morning. The BBC had videos of this hearing for me to watch.

The first witness was the Director of the little known Defense Intelligence Agency. He talked about how his watchers had been keeping an eye on me since I was ten years old. "She claimed the alien jumped out at her from a fox. We still don't know if this was true or a little girl's imagination. We do know something remarkable happened to her." After describing how I came to their attention, he testified there had been up to four hundred people at a time assigned to watching me. He explained it was very difficult to follow somebody for years without being detected. People had to be changed frequently or be noticed. Then he got to the part that I found most interesting.

"The most difficult kind of tailing is following somebody around a college campus. A stranger is easily recognized. But we knew her schedule and where she should be every hour. We'd have somebody walk by at a distance of a hundred feet to confirm her movements except that she might not arrive somewhere at exactly the same time every day and we had to keep our people moving. We'd send twenty or more people by a spot in thirty second intervals. One or two of them would spot her."

"All these people walked around the college and were never noticed?"

"Actually, they were, but never by the students. The first week Theresa was in BC, the campus police saw two of them, and took them to the station. Theresa Hartley was called in. She told them to call their supervisor who called me and I called the President. The President called the campus police and told them to keep it quiet. We made an agreement with the police. We told them our people were there to protect a matter of national security. We told them no more than that. Our people all had DIA credentials. The police accepted them."

"That seems unusual, their accepting your people's invasion."

"Not at all. We pointed out to the police that our agents would be on the lookout for suspicious characters. They were helping the campus police. The two forces were very friendly about it."

"And did none of these hundreds of watchers tell the police why they were watching Theresa Hartley?"

"They didn't know. They were told not to speculate."

"That's incredible. At least one of them should have talked to the press."

"That's the interesting part, Senator. If we had only twenty watchers, some of them would think that the taxpayer's money was being wasted on something not that important. But since we had up to four hundred watchers, they believed this operation was a life or death matter for the United States. None of them broke rank."

"How much did this surveillance cost over eight years?"

"Approximately half a billion dollars."

There wasn't much more for the DIA Director to say except that he hadn't known about President Martin's operation. So Jan Struthers was not part of it! The Director was soon dismissed.

The next witness was the CIA Director. It was his men that had taken me to the carrier. He said the Defense Intelligence Agency had briefed him about the alien and Theresa Hartley four months ago. Then the President ordered him to organize a team of agents to abduct me and bring me to the aircraft carrier. The Director said it had been difficult to assemble a team. Most men refused to participate.

"But you had no qualms, sir?" asked the Chairman.

"Of course I did. But I tended to agree with the President. The situation could not be ignored."

"Were we in danger?"

"Who can know, Senator? Can you tell me whether or not we are in danger now?"

"We have learned she escaped the plane. How could that happen?"

"We don't know."

"Could she open the canopy?"

"No. It was locked down. The release was disabled. Two sailors at the scene will testify to that."

"Could she break it open?"

"Impossible. It's a three quarter inch sheet of high tensile strength plastic. Unbreakable. Bullets bounce off it."

"Could she push it out?"

"Not possible. It was held in by many steel pins. An elephant couldn't push it out."

"How did she live through the fall?"

"There are cases of people falling into water from great heights and surviving. It's rare. The mistake people make is thinking they should enter the water head first or feet first. Wrong. That will kill you. You need to go in spread out horizontally to let the entire body absorb the shock. It happened recently. An American woman fell 1,500 feet into a lake when her parachute backpack failed to open. She suffered no injuries."

"How far did Theresa Hartley fall?"

"The canopy opened at 57,900 feet. That's eleven miles. It took three and a half minutes to reach the water."

"Why did she scream in the water?"

"It was partly panic. All jumpers scream. But she never made a sound on the way down. We can't explain that."

"What about the cold water?"

"Definitely painful. Mostly in the bones of the extremities. It's not like they show you in the movies."

"Do you have a recording of the woman?"

"There was one. Admiral Ruck threw it in the ocean."

"Just as well" said the Chairman.

The BBC said the Committee milked this witness for one and a half hours. They asked the most detailed questions about things that were not important. The BBC said this was probably of no interest to me and it was all skipped.

The hearing broke for a late lunch and a committee aide told Steve he would be called to testify at two o'clock.

Steve's testimony had been anxiously awaited. Who better to tell the world what I had been doing with the alien than my husband? He was sworn in. The Committee began on an apologetic note.

"We know you were called in quickly during a difficult time. We hope you understand how urgently we need to know about the recent event."

Steve waved his hand without saying anything.

"Now then, sir. Can you tell us what your wife said about the alien?"

"She said nothing about it."

A groan of surprise and disappointment arose from the crowd.

"Nothing? She never told you anything?"

"Nothing. Not a word."

"Did she give hints that you didn't understand at the time?"

"No."

"Did she talk about the possibility of aliens?"

"No."

"Are you saying you knew and suspected nothing?"

"That's what I'm saying."

The Committee Chairman didn't know what else to say. He looked from left to right offering other Committee members a chance to jump in. None would touch this one.

"Well, sir. We are very surprised. Is there anything you want to say?"

"Yes. Theresa hasn't been dead forty-eight hours, and I have eight messages from Hollywood offering to make a movie about her. There won't be any movie. People like to see somebody get in trouble. I have bad news for you. Theresa never got in trouble. She was perfect in every way. Live with it!"

"That's a remarkable assessment."

"Theresa was a remarkable person. She became an adult before she became a woman. Other girls worried about diets and hairstyles. She worried about being the mediator between the alien and the world. That's what her major and MISSION IMPOSSIBLE file were about. Theresa was different from the rest of us. We won't see her kind again."

The Chairman obviously thought it was time to get rid of this witness.

"Thank you for coming in, sir."

Steve automatically got up and walked to the door with swarms of reporters hounding him as he walked from the Senate office building to a government car. He went back to his hotel room.

The next section of the montage was about early Wednesday morning. The Ronald Reagan had arrived in Florida during the night. That young female officer who made a video of my "last words" was 26 year old Lieutenant Junior Grade Virginia Connor who was sure to be remembered. The BBC showed her video.

I was waiting on the Ronald Reagan deck while the jet fighter was being brought into place. Yours truly was on screen with my wild mane of hair blowing in the wind. Connor's voice was heard asking if I had anything to say. "This is the most stupid thing ever done. I'm glad I won't be here to see what happens." Connor asked if that was all I wanted to say. "If people grieve your passing rejoice in the good you did and die like a hero going home. I feel good about who I was."

I hoped Steve and my parents got some comfort from that.

The screen changed to four talking heads on an American news talk show who debated the meaning of my remarks. What did I mean by something happening? Did I know what it was? Was I making it happen? Was it serious? Who would be affected? Could it be stopped?

Their discussion was futile at this point.

The video was bad news for President Martin. "Now they'll make a movie about her," the talking heads agreed.

The next hearing witness was a big surprise. My priest, Father Richard Donoughty, was extensively documented in the files on me maintained by the DIA. He was called in as a witness. He walked into the Senate Office Building chamber carrying a heavy briefcase and was sworn in.

"Now, Father" began the Chairman, "you have previously advised this Committee by phone that as Theresa Hartley's priest you cannot discuss her character except in general terms known to her acquaintances. What was she like?"

"Everybody will tell you she was a good girl, a brilliant girl, the pride and joy of her family. If this alien's arrival was an inevitable event of the natural world, God saw to it that it associated itself with an exceptional girl."

"For what purpose, Father?"

"That remains a mystery. We deal with many mysteries in my line of work. We wait for answers with trust."

"How long have you known her?"

"Eight years. She first came to the rectory when she was ten."

"Our records show you managed to be assigned to her parish church for those eight years. It is the norm for priests to be reassigned every two or three years. Was this a coincidence?"

"It was arranged by Cardinal Rook. The Holy Father was interested in her case and wanted me to stay close to her. It was the Holy Father who arranged her full scholarship at Boston College. Theresa couldn't turn that down."

"He wanted her to go to BC because it's rigidly Catholic?"

"It isn't rigidly Catholic. One third of its students are non-Catholics from all over the world. If you want to operate a large, diverse university you can't do it with a heavy hand. It was important for Theresa to get a truly worldly educational experience. She might have had some role in dealing with the alien in the name of humanity. She had to have wisdom."

"How did the Holy Father become interested in her?"

"Cardinal Rook and I told him about how Theresa was being followed by government watchers. We saw them ourselves. We were sure she wasn't possessed. The government watchers proved her story about HAL."

"HAL?"

"That's what she called him. It's from a movie you probably remember."

"What did she say about HAL?"

"Not much. She knew nothing about him."

"Did you have contact with her 'watchers' as they're called?"

"Only once. A woman followed her to the rectory. She didn't give her name."

"What did this woman tell you?"

"Nothing except that many people were watching Theresa."

"For what reason?"

"She didn't say. She assumed I knew."

"You only had Theresa's word there was a HAL?"

"That's correct."

"How did you become convinced there was a HAL?"

Father Donoughty opened his briefcase and took out three playground horseshoes which had been bent into twisted shapes.

"Certain statements have been made in this hearing about how Theresa got out of the plane. Do you think anybody could bend one of these, Senator?"

"I doubt it."

Father Donoughty stacked the three horseshoes together. Despite their twists they fit precisely on top of each other.

"When Theresa was ten years old, I watched her bend all three at once. She did even more amazing feats of strength for Cardinal Rook and myself. She could hold a heavy book in one hand and squeeze until her fingertips pierced the book from cover to cover. There seemed to be no limit to her strength. She was a baseball pitcher in high school. She could have been an NFL quarterback and scored a touchdown on every play."

"Are you implying she had enough strength to push out the canopy?"

"With HAL's power but her own initiative, yes."

The room was silent. Father Donoughty enjoyed watching the bug-eyed expressions on the Committee's faces. I'll bet no one was more surprised than Steve. All that time I had seemed to have the delicacy of a petite female. I could have broken his back with a single blow.

The priest had an afterthought. "When she was

abducted she must have known she could fight her way out. She could have killed everybody around her. She went to her death without a fight. She's a martyr. I think God's purpose in choosing her was to show HAL there are good people and we are worth saving."

The Chairman had the political savvy to give this idea a respectful moment of silence. It was the finest thing that could be said about a person. He couldn't fail to note the sad expressions on people's faces.

"How did she explain this super strength, Father?"

"She couldn't. It was as much a mystery to her as us."

"What else could she do?"

"She could throw things with perfect accuracy. She threw coins into a glass twenty feet away and never missed."

"Anything else?"

"That's it."

"Did she communicate with HAL?"

"She always denied there was any communication, but clearly they were aware of each other."

"Clearly, yes. Well, Father! This has been the strangest story I've ever heard. Have we all lost our minds?"

"I hope not," he grinned.

The BBC talked about the next development in this weird week.

A small freighter carrying grain from Argentina to Africa was nine hundred miles out to sea. The Captain and his first mate were looking out at the water. The wind had been noted to die out during the night. Now there was a dead calm. The water was motionless. A bridge video cam had recorded these two men's brief exchange. In words that were much discussed, the first mate asked, "You ever see a calm like this?"

"Not this time of year."

The small steamer was crossing the area where I'd fallen from the fighter jet. Word got out quickly. Commercial airplanes passing over the area were asked to note the location and extent of the calm seas. It appeared that the calm area was spreading out at eighteen miles an hour on the edge, broadening the width of the area thirty-six miles per hour. It was already thousands of miles wide. Soon it would lock up the entire Earth's weather pattern and stop the wind everywhere. Without wind there was no way for the water vapor from the oceans to get to land fast enough to provide the rain needed to grow anything. World famine would follow. There was no way to prevent it.

The BBC said Prime Minister Peter Blair sent ships to the South Atlantic to look for me. This was considered the most ridiculous naval mission of all time. "Blair's Folly," said the newspaper headlines. "Blair's Search for the Holy Grail". Anybody who had been to sea knew the impossibility of finding a body in that vast nothingness, even if it was floating on the surface.

The next part of the BBC program was a real shock.

That Friday night, President Martin suddenly resigned in the middle of the night and left the White House to go to his Indiana home. The Secretary of Defense was rushed to the White House because according to the 'Two Man Rule' he had to confirm the President's identity before the nuclear missile launch codes could be activated, but for an hour the

United States had no President while Vice-President Veronica Stinson was asleep and unaware.

Did I have any responsibility for this mess for not telling people about HAL when I was ten? You decide.

Chapter 6

I was getting depressed. This BBC program had been giving me nothing but bad news. Did anything go right in this world?

The United States was also in a terrible mood. It had always been assumed a man with the will power to become President would never suddenly resign without a fight. President Nixon had resigned after being under tremendous pressure for two years. President Martin simply walked away. Commentators agreed it was another shock in a horrible week, but we shouldn't be so surprised. The poor guy had condemned the world to a slow, miserable death. There was no chance he would be allowed to stay in office.

President Martin's unprecedented sudden resignation with no warning was another indicator that the world was in a real mess.

I must have made some of my trademarked funny faces because Nancy laughed. I told her, "I wish I could walk away from his mess. An eighteen year old girl with no experience in anything has to save the world from extermination. Good luck, everybody!"

Vice-President Veronica Stinson was sworn in as President at four o'clock in the morning. Her first televised statement showed she was shaken. She said something about how we all had to pull together and do what we could. It was something like that. I didn't pay much attention. I was shook up myself.

Somehow all this disastrous mess had something to do with me. If I had told people about HAL years ago, would any of this have happened? That was my burden.

The program wasn't over. There were more surprises.

The Captain of the ship that found me in the South Atlantic had given a statement last night when I arrived in England. His statement was taped while I was being driven by ambulance to London, a fair distance from shore. His ship was the newest British aircraft carrier.

As the BBC announcer explained, the program was quickly put together for me. I needed to know everything so that I could guess what HAL might be thinking all this time and why he did what he did. The Captain's detailed statement was given in its entirety along with videos.

"We sailed with partial crews. Many sailors were visiting their homes all over England and couldn't be called back in time for this panicked rush to the South Atlantic.

"It was a fool's mission. It had taken seventy years to find the Titanic, although it was known where it sank. Now, we were being asked to find a tiny body, which almost certainly sank, that may have been moved a hundred miles or more by ocean currents in any direction. Madness, I thought.

"In the beginning of the voyage we had to plow through ten to fifteen foot swells typical of the North Atlantic in June. The ship's rolling motion was comforting to sailors who loved the rock-a-bye baby sensation, but in the last two days the ship felt virtually motionless as it skimmed on water as smooth as plate glass. It was unnerving. The Queen Elizabeth was a hundred and twenty miles from target at dawn when the radar screen operator said, 'Something unusual ahead, sir'.

"I looked at the radar screen. An indistinct horizontal smudge could be seen.

"'How wide is it?' I asked.

"'A mile, sir. Can only be birds. There must be a million of them.'

"I considered how this could come about. Perhaps nuclear radiation killed a lot of fish. If so and Theresa's body was floating, she drifted with the fish. We might find her after all!

"'Lay a course for that flock of birds' I said.

"An hour later the sun was several diameters above the horizon. It was full light. On every ship sailors not on duty were on deck to see this once in a lifetime sight. Some passed around small, cheap binoculars bought in department stores, and some had video cameras waiting for a remarkable recording opportunity.

"Two more hours passed. I ordered a helicopter to fly ahead and take a closer look. It was soon close to the scene but not close enough to have its blades fouled by the birds. The helicopter crew looked down with binoculars and saw something never beheld by human eyes.

"'Captain. It's a school of sharks. There are tens of thousands of them. The water is red.'

"It was a massive feeding frenzy. As we came nearer shark fins appeared briefly on the surface. They were all swimming toward the frenzy's bloody waters which had spread out for many miles. It had been going on for days and the sharks could smell the blood from a great distance. I recognized the cursed white tips on the rounded dorsal fins. Bloody ocean whitetips. The scourge of seamen. Unlike the great white shark that stayed close to coastlines, the oceanic whitetip shark spanned the oceans. It killed more people than all other types of sharks combined.

"A mile from the frenzy we slowed down to lower speeds until we reached the frenzy where we stopped to consider our next strategy. The frenzy was about four hundred yards wide and the carrier was stopped on the edge. The sea was red with blood everywhere and around the ship. Through binoculars I could see sharks fighting over pieces of dead sharks. They were eating each other.

"I searched the center of the frenzy where the activity was greatest.

"'God in Heaven have mercy on us!' I shouted. 'Theresa Hartley is in the middle of it!'

"Sharks were lunging at the unconscious Theresa but were being killed before they could get a bite of her. Other sharks fed on the bleeding dead. This nightmare had been going on for days.

"I ordered a launch be lowered and twenty machine gunners to the deck.

"The launch was lowered with six sailors. It set off towards Theresa, but it would not be safe to pull her out of the water with a crowd of sharks lunging at them. I ordered the machine gunners to fire at the sharks. Officers kept them firing to the left and right of Theresa, but no closer than fifty yards from her lest they hit her or the launch. It was only necessary to wound one of the monsters and its blood drew attack from others. Thousands of rounds were fired per minute but only a small fraction of the sharks were being killed. Many times as many sharks swimming deeper down were coming up to the surface to join the frenzy. The slaughter was working. There were two areas of mayhem safe distances from Theresa. By the time the launch got to her there were only a few confused sharks nearby and they weren't attacking.

"Theresa was unconscious. Her head and shoulders were above water. Two men pulled her into the boat and they headed back to the ship. She was placed in a large basket on a cable and hauled up to the deck as quickly as possible. She was rushed inside the carrier to sickbay. The jumpsuit was unzipped. Two electro-cardio leads were placed on her to see if there was any cardiac activity at all. There was no activity, no signs of life.

"The doctor pronounced her dead."

The screen returned to a BBC announcer. "Next we hear Prime Minister Blair."

Peter Blair came on the screen. He was reading from notes.

"Good evening, Mrs. Hartley. You asked to be told everything related to HAL. What I have to present involves his activity. I'll be complete.

"When I heard you were dead the tears leaked from my eyes. So much hope crushed. As a staff member said, 'It was a heroic effort, Prime Minister. Her family will be grateful.' I said, 'Thank you. We are all lost, ladies and gentlemen.' Without you there was no possibility of communicating with the alien.

"The ships set off for home. Your empty bottles

were found in your suit and we learned how you remained afloat. Of course, when you were on the Ronald Reagan nobody would have believed you could escape the plane, so nobody was suspicious of anything you carried on board. You were allowed to carry the garbage bag of bottles without anybody giving it a thought. The reason for wanting to remain afloat was easy to guess. A woman doesn't mind dying so much if she knows her body will be preserved.

"Your Senate Committee called in the Ronald Reagan commander, Admiral Ruck, who had been told to stay in the Virginia area in case he was needed. Here is his testimony after you were found."

The scene changed to a video of a large Senate hearing room.

Admiral Ruck was nervous when he sat at the Senate hearing's witness table. In the eyes of many he was largely responsible for my death.

Senator Clay began.

"Admiral, we already know the circumstances of June 13. Before we go into the details, I would like to ask if Theresa Hartley could have been rescued after she entered the ocean water?"

Admiral Ruck held up a piece of paper. "I have a written answer to that question which I believe will clarify the situation. May I read it?"

"Go ahead."

"There is a remote possibility Theresa Hartley could have been saved if we had immediately sent out a fighter jet. The pilot could have reached her in ten minutes, and, in the unlikely event he saw her while flying low at two hundred miles an hour, he could have bailed out with a small raft, put her in the raft to get her out of the cold water, and she might have been revived when the helicopters came.

"But all this would have required my knowing that she was still afloat. I did not know that HAL had stopped the wind and waves around her, causing the radio to go silent, and leading me to believe she had sunk, as any unconscious person in turbulent waters would have to do. I did not know that HAL had gotten her out of the plane and might be doing more to keep her alive. I could only believe the government had arranged for the fighter jet canopy to open up and let her get out of the plane, although what reason they had to do this was unknowable to me. I did not know about Theresa Hartley's connection to HAL until one and a half hours later, when the President spoke on television. By then it was long too late to save her. Because I didn't know all these things at the time it mattered, I have to say it was not possible to save her."

He looked up at the Chairman to give a heartbreaking remark.

"When I saw it was a girl, it was too late to change my mind. What could I do with her with six thousand people on the ship?"

I hate using clichés, but in this case there really wasn't a dry eye in the room. It was a pitiful scene.

A long list of questions followed about how Admiral Ruck was given this assignment, what President Martin said to him, and who else knew about the operation. The Admiral looked like a broken man.

Finally, the Chairman said, "Thank you for testifying, Admiral."

Prime Minister Blair came back on screen.

"Your death made most people give up hope. Universal starvation could not be prevented. The end times had come."

Nancy had mentioned that Blair majored in literature in college, and it showed. He spoke dramatically. Nancy said he always talked like he was in a Shakespearean play. Maybe he was grandstanding. These days would be remembered for a long time. Grandstanding is hard to resist, I guess, and maybe I'd do it myself before all this was over.

"The world settled in for the long wait for the HMS Queen Elizabeth to return to England. Somber music was played on radio day and night. A favorite selection was Saint-Saens's *The Swan* for cello and piano made famous by Russian ballet as *The Dying Swan*. But the most appropriate piece for the girl descended from the Irish was a soulful instrumental version of Danny Boy. It was perfect. Great Britain was proud to bring one of its own back home for a final visit.

"But for most of the world there was no consolation. Dreams of a good future were gone. There was nothing to look forward to but misery or death. Parents spent all the time they could with their children. Mothers held their children and cried, wondering why this horror was happening.

"The HMS Queen Elizabeth anchored near the coast of Southern England while you were moved to shore by helicopter. You were put in an ambulance for the long ride to London.

"I waited in a London hospital to receive you. I had to be there, it would be an insult to America if I wasn't, but I wanted to be there. I felt it was my duty to pay respects to this important personage. I was also curious to see you.

"When the ambulance was two miles from the hospital I went down to the morgue where doctors and nurses waited. There would not be an autopsy; that was left to the Americans. But the English did want to make a 'careful examination'.

"From somewhere in London, American soldiers had been found to carry the casket in. An American flag covered the casket as it was rolled into the morgue. The honor guard of U.S. soldiers removed the flag and took it away. The doctors moved you from the casket to an exam table.

"'It's been nearly fourteen days, Prime Minister' said the chief doctor. 'This won't be pleasant.'

"'I've seen it before,' I said.

"A plastic waterproof bag covered a velvet body bag. The plastic bag was removed. The body bag was unzipped and slipped off. There you lay on the table still dressed in the clothes you wore when abducted fifteen days earlier. Your clothes were full of coagulated shark blood. It was a frightening sight.

"Everybody moved closer. You were remarkably well preserved. In fact you were in great shape. It soon dawned on us.

"You were perfectly preserved. You might have died 30 seconds ago.

"We looked at each other. Every person was afraid to say it. Could Theresa be alive?

"The chief doctor seized an ophthalmoscope to look at your retina, the only place where blood vessels could be seen directly. There was no breakdown.

"You were in absolutely perfect condition.

"Everybody looked at the doctor in expectant silence. What were we to do with you?

"The ranking doctor protested. 'I don't care how advanced these beings are. No technology can keep her alive this way.'

"I waited a moment to give the doctor's comment due respect. Then I said, 'Why not?'

"'Every atom needs to be kept in its proper place. Her body uses all the space available. There's no way to get to the atoms.'

"'Quite right, doctor, but if she dies we are all lost.'

"Everybody stared at the doctor. He knew he'd lost.

"'Put her in a patient room.'

"The room was heated to 105 degrees. The theory was that if your body temperature returned to normal your heart would automatically start beating. Much argument ensued among the doctors about what resuscitation procedures to use. It was decided to use none except as a desperate last resort. They didn't know what HAL was doing. Any interference on their part might be harmful.

"The doctor in charge explained. 'We're not even going to take a blood sample. If anything is wrong with it there's nothing we can do. There's no circulation.'

"I nodded my understanding.

"'There is one more concern, Prime Minister. Some molecules of the body become denatured when subjected to low temperatures. It's irreversible. She may revive briefly only to die later.'

"'When will we know?'

"'Very quickly. It would be like radiation sickness. She will become nauseous within the hour, weaken and die. We could do nothing to stop it.'

"'Thank you for informing me.'

"If such were the case I'd have to get as much information out of you as possible in a short time. It would be a very unpleasant situation.

"The room was filled with every kind of diagnostic and monitoring equipment I could imagine and some whose purpose I couldn't guess. Wires from your body led to a monitor to display temperature, an electrocardiogram machine to detect heartbeat, and an electroencephalogram machine to monitor brainwaves. All these machines registered nil.

"Your temperature was 56 degrees, up from 48 when you arrived at the hospital. It would take many hours to reach 98 degrees.

"Something had to be told to the people in the morning. But first I had to deal with the husband. 'Get Steve Hartley on the phone,' I ordered. The connection was made after a representative at Steve's apartment told him to put the phone on the hook.

"'Mr. Hartley. This is Prime Minister Blair. We have some rather startling news. Your wife arrived in absolutely perfect physical condition. It has been suggested that she is still alive and can be revived.'

"'When will this happen?'

"'If it happens, and we're not sure it will, it will happen in twelve or more hours. Her temperature is 58 degrees. The room is heated to 105 degrees to raise her temperature naturally. The doctors don't want to do anything unless she doesn't revive by herself.

Resuscitation techniques will only be used as a final measure if all else fails.'

"'Will she be the same Theresa?'

"'That, sir, is unpredictable.'

"'It would be sad to see her a vegetable.'

"'Yes.'

"'Would you do me a favor? Ask people to pray for her. God can't ignore a hundred million people.'

"'He can't. We shall be insistent.'

"In many hours your temperature reached 93 degrees. I had been visiting your room only twenty minutes at a time because of the heat, but now I remained. A nurse gave me a glass of ice water to sip.

"You reached 94.2 degrees. The cardiac monitor registered a single heartbeat and returned to a flatline.

"The seconds ticked off. Twenty-two seconds, and there was another solitary heartbeat. The count resumed. Twelve more seconds and a third heartbeat registered followed two seconds later by a steady heartbeat. Your heart was functioning.

"A minute went by. Your chest heaved in what looked like the breath of death, a final reflexive breath before the body gives up. After a delay of a few seconds your breathing resumed normally. All attention was now on the electroencephalograph monitor. If your brain didn't work there was no artificial way to resuscitate it. It was all up to you.

"And there it was! Two of the twelve monitor lines were wiggling. Soon, all lines were wiggling. Everything seemed to be working.

"A few minutes later you started squirming like somebody in a dream. Your eyes opened and you started loudly crying. I understood. You were remembering that terrible ordeal of freezing in the water. Well of course! To you it seemed a moment before. How had we failed to anticipate this?

"I left you for a few minutes and went to another room. Colleagues congratulated me. I was greatly excited. This was the Olympic gold medal of politics, the possible saving of the nation. Nothing could equal this."

Blair stopped for a moment and then said, "The rest you know. I know you're the right person. I'll see you in twenty minutes."

So what had HAL done? I hoped the BBC presentation would show what HAL did, but I didn't see anything except his saving me from the sharks.

"What did HAL do?" I asked Nancy. "He just let me revive myself. Does HAL even know what happened? He acts like a jellyfish."

Nancy looked at me with that doe's eyes in the headlights expression.

Commentators took over on the television screen. One said, "How does the Prime Minister know Mrs. Hartley is the right person to restore the wind? Does she have communication with the alien? What haven't we been told?"

It was a good question. Blair already knew from the way I acted on the hospital balcony that I didn't even know about the wind business. He could not be sure I could do something about it.

Then I remembered something. When I woke up in the hospital Blair said I was the right kind of person to do what was needed. This made no sense if he meant restoring the wind. Anybody could do that if it could be done. What he meant was I would be the right kind of person after the wind situation was fixed. If I could influence HAL to restore the wind, I could influence him to do other things later. What kind of person I was would be very important.

I told Nancy, "He's not talking about the wind. He's talking about what I'll do later. He knows I won't mess up the world like a world dictator."

"I see" said the suddenly aware Nancy. "It's an amazing concept."

"Your Prime Minister knew it one minute after I woke up. He's a smart man."

Blair's job was to guide me in assuming great responsibilities without messing things up. He had to be very worried. How could a forty-something Englishman connect with an eighteen year old American girl? It was like I was the alien from space.

I thought this was funny and repeated it to Nancy.

"Poor Blair. Dealing with me must be like dealing with a space alien."

She laughed.

Yeah, well, poor me! I had to deal with a real alien who was destroying the world. And everybody expected me to save them.

The situation was becoming maddeningly complex. HAL helped me in several ways, then stopped the wind which any child could see could only hurt me. He was doing something all the time but never spoke. Sherlock Holmes said everything becomes simple in the explanation. Good luck with this one, Sherlock! I was expected to come up with the answers, but judging from what Jan said, the U.S. Government with all its experts, didn't have a clue what was going on.

I hung around for a few minutes and went

downstairs. When I got out of the elevator, some government men pointed the way to the meeting room.

All of humanity had been sweating blood all day waiting to hear what I had to say. The Earth stood still. Baseball games in America had been postponed. Highways were deserted. Plane flights were canceled for lack of passengers. Every person, who could by any means stay home watching television, did.

This was the critical meeting. If nothing came out of it, "we are all lost".

Chapter 7

I walked into a small meeting room on the ground floor. Four television cameras placed at different angles were pointing at a small table with two chairs. The table held a large loose leaf binder, a pitcher of water, glasses, notepads and pens. Besides the camera crew, there were twelve government people and two hotel staffers. There were no other guests, although thousands of highly placed people had called, asking to be invited. The meeting was too important to risk interruptions.

I was early and Blair was not there. He was probably caught in the bathroom. The meeting could last for hours and he didn't want to be knocking his knees with billions of people watching. Well, I was glad to be alone, to get people used to seeing me standing there without talking. One of my BC professors was commenting one day about this and that. He mentioned how it annoyed him to see the talking heads on television keep talking all the time like they had something important to say. They just lowered their credibility. I was determined not to speak unless necessary. Then when I did, people would know I was saying what I believed.

I walked up to the table and stood there. After a moment I opened the loose leaf binder. It contained my MISSION IMPOSSIBLE file. My eyebrows went up in surprise. Then I resumed my gaze at the entrance I thought the Prime Minister would use.

The whole world was watching. My hair had dried and flared out in that magnificent mane that ooh'ed and ahh'ed everybody. My green outfit was modest, only five inches above the knees and with not much cleavage, but didn't hide my well-turned figure. All right, my chest and butt were well outlined. There. I said it. So call the police. Was I conscious of the effect I had on viewers? Everybody knew I was or I would be sitting down! I could imagine Steve grinning from ear to ear.

I glanced at a TV screen. It showed my magnificence in full length profile. The technicians started grinning. They knew, and knew that I knew they knew etcetera. I struggled to maintain an innocent expression, but the grin worked its way out.

I couldn't help myself. I had to say it.

"You should see the little black nothing dress I had on the first time Steve entered my dorm room!"

The technicians and government men all laughed.

Who could blame me for taking a once in a lifetime opportunity to flaunt it to the world!

While I posed Blair came in the same entrance I'd used and walked to the other side of the table.

"Good evening. How are you?" he asked.

"Fine" I answered with a warm smile.

Blair indicated my seat with his hand and we both sat down. He waited a few seconds to let me settle my stuff in. I spoke first.

"We made it to the big leagues. Think they're watching in China?"

"Most likely. I am told four billion people are watching this."

"Too bad we can't sell tickets. It must drive

celebrities crazy."

"You say?"

"They would kill for an audience like this. I don't even care."

He laughed and so did I. He was relieved. My personality was coming out and it was something he could work with.

"I called your room but you were on the way down. I don't think you're a space alien." He said it with a smile to show he was kidding.

"I'm not so hard to get along with." It was a weak thing to say, but I couldn't think of anything clever.

"I talked with President Stinson. Her people know much about you and assure her you can be trusted.

"I would like to talk about HAL. The first question is of what is he made? Not matter?"

"I've believed for a long time he's made of dark matter."

"What is dark matter?"

"Nobody knows, but there's a lot of it."

"How do we know it exists?"

"We only know about it from its effect on gravity. Galaxies don't rotate at the right speed for the amount of visible matter they have. I think they found out dark matter made galaxies get together in the first place."

"Can anything be made of this dark matter?"

"Why not? Think of a dark matter universe with dark matter people. They can't see our universe. They can't know matter has ninety-two elements that organize in a million ways. How could they guess we have planets with millions of kinds of creatures? We find new things in nature all the time. The dark matter world should have lots of surprises for us."

"What keeps HAL together?"

"His own gravity, and some dark matter particles may have some kind of stickiness."

Interestingly, he didn't pursue that line, probably because it was outside his field and he didn't want to look dumb.

"Let's talk about what HAL does. He seems to do things for you. You should have had broken bones when you fell in the water. Did HAL prevent that?"

"Maybe. When I played baseball with the boys the kids had a betting pool on how many games I'd play before I broke an arm or leg when I crashed into basemen. They were sure I'd wipe out. Nobody believed I'd last four years without an injury. HAL takes care of my bones."

"More. He protected you from the sharks."

"I'm grateful for that. I don't want to sleep with the fishes."

"HAL gives you extraordinary strength. This helps you?"

"It's useful."

"He gives you accuracy in throwing things. Useful?"

"It helped in pitching baseball. Father Donoughty told you that. I didn't tell him one other thing. When HAL merged with me my hair started growing thicker. I looked at it under the microscope. It's nearly twice as thick as other girls' hair. I guess HAL keeps it full of water."

"This has helped you?"

"It looks good" I smiled.

"How does stopping the wind help you?"

"It doesn't. I've been thinking about that. HAL is beginning to sound pretty dumb."

"Ah! We have HAL the stupid?" The desperately hoped for progress!

"He's never shown me any brains. He doesn't talk and he does this dumb thing."

"He does complicated things."

"Animals do complicated things."

"He came to Earth exactly when we developed high technology after our presence here for millions of years."

"He could have arrived here before the dinosaurs."

"He was seen coming down to Earth as a white ball."

"Could have been something he needed. Maybe he called it down."

Blair stopped. To each of his points I had given a perfectly legitimate counterpoint. I shot down every idea people had had about HAL. I wasn't arguing. I was pointing out that nothing certain was known about HAL. We knew some of the things he did, but nothing about HAL himself. Poor Blair looked confused. Where could he go with this?

"The pressure is pretty high on both of us," I said to help him rally.

"It is." He resumed. "Perhaps if we study what HAL does, we'll better understand what he is."

"I'm game."

"HAL thickens your hair, gives you throwing accuracy, gives you great strength, and defended you from sharks. Putting aside their individual effects, what is the purpose of these behaviors?"

"It's either to defend me or our merger."

"HAL might be defending your merger?" he asked, clutching at straws.

"He must get something out of it."

Now we were getting somewhere!

"Let's review. HAL is made of dark matter, he's stupid, he defends you and your merger with him. What does he get from the merger?"

That was a tough question. I thought about it for twenty seconds.

"He becomes something more than he would be on his own. It must be pretty dull in the dark matter universe."

"Ah! A stupid HAL who has a need. A fox walked up to your mother before you were born and HAL merged with you ten years later. Are there two HALs?"

"I never heard that story. What happened?"

"A fox walked up to her and watched her for a few minutes. This happened eighteen and a half years ago. You were expected."

"The BBC didn't mention that."

"Your father told the story. Is it important?"

"It could be. What was my mother doing?"

"She was raking leaves in the backyard."

Raking leaves. Something HAL probably never saw before!

"Don't you see? HAL might have been in North America a hundred million years, but he never saw anybody raking leaves before."

"But HAL was seen coming to Earth three years later."

"There's only one HAL. Jan Struthers told me Doppler radar shows a column of disturbed air above me. They sent up a satellite to look for more HALs. They never found one. He was interested in my mother, but not ready to make a transfer. What you saw was something he needed."

"Why did he want to transfer to your mother?"

"Mom was holding a rake! HAL thought it was an extra appendage. That's what made her different."

Blair's face showed he sensed I was getting close to the goal.

"Trees have many appendages."

"Trees don't do anything."

"HAL needs something that moves?"

"I wouldn't call it a need. Something made of dark matter couldn't evolve in its own world. We make it evolve."

"Remarkable!"

"What's remarkable?"

"You're remarkable. What of that difference of the rake made HAL interested in your mother?"

I thought about that. And I thought. I thought a full minute.

I asked, "Can we take a break?"

"Yes."

He looked shocked. I wanted to take a break now?

The government people felt the same way. They rolled their eyes as I got up and walked out. A dozen security guards escorted me through the lobby to the elevators. Hotel guests were caught by surprise watching television in their rooms and didn't have time to come down and see me in the flesh. Outsiders were kept out.

I got back to my suite and asked Nancy to turn off the TV. I needed silence to think things out.

It was an hour and fifteen minutes later when Prime Minister Blair knocked on the door. Nancy let him in. I was sitting at a table.

"Oh, hi!" I said cheerfully and took another look at my notepad. "I guess I have enough."

I got up to leave.

"Enough?" asked the PM.

"Enough notes. I figured out what HAL is about."

He looked doubtful. From such scanty evidence could anything be deduced?

We got back to the meeting room and sat down. I ripped off six pages from my notepad and arranged them on the table left to right, but I would never refer to them. I waited for Blair to start.

"You have something to announce?" he suggested gently.

"HAL has nothing to do with any alien civilization. He has no more brains than a jellyfish. He's a natural thing left over from the Big Bang. There must be trillions of HALs all over the universe. After spending time on one planet they reproduce somehow and travel to other stars.

"The HALs cling to objects made of matter. Think of syrup on pancakes. The HALs are the syrup and they assume the shape of the pancakes. Most of the HALs clung to rocks billions of years ago. They'll be there forever. A few HALs wandered into planets with living creatures. An animal has a more complicated shape than a rock, so when HAL slipped off a rock during a landslide or something, there was a good chance he'd cling to an animal and stay there.

"An animal has appendages that act like grappling hooks. HAL won't slip off. The animal grows old and dies. But now the animal's shape is imprinted in HAL like the pancakes in syrup. The next thing he clings to will be similar. Does this make sense?"

"Yes," he said without adding something to interrupt my thoughts. God forbid he knock me off course now!

"HAL will cling to a more complicated animal if he finds one. When he saw my mother holding the rake that triggered the transfer response. It probably took years to do this, but time means nothing to HAL. By the time the transfer was ready to do, I was ten years old. Instead of my mother holding the rake with both hands, I was on the deck holding a book with both hands. HAL was too dumb to know the difference and transferred to me.

"Now we have to talk about why HALs do anything. They merge with creatures on a hundred planets to have something to cling to. Animals move around and do things. The HALs' structures modify to keep up with these movements. They work together.

"Here's the critical point. This is where HAL becomes what looks like an active agent.

"Everything an animal does is a reflex. HAL's structure is doing reflexes to keep up with its host animal. HAL's own structural organization depends on the structural organization of material things. That's why he clings to things.

"What you have to understand is HAL doesn't operate like we do. He acts because he taps into momentum of something else. He moves because he's always moving in some way, not because he needs anything. He has no needs."

By this time I'll bet nobody could follow my

reasoning. The technicians showed their confusion. Peter Blair was too smart to give any hint he didn't understand either. He was letting me talk myself out.

I continued.

"This becomes so imprinted in his structure he will do the reflex ahead of the animal when the stimulus is present. For instance, if the animal is attacked HAL will do the defense reflexes before the animal does. That's what the shark attack was about. HAL was fighting off sharks while I was unconscious. It's a good thing no human tried to hurt me. They would be hamburger.

"There's one more step to take and we get to the fully evolved HAL. After billions of years of merging with thousands of kinds of creatures on a hundred worlds, HAL's reflex systems become so complicated he will generate new reflexes to help the animal that the animal itself doesn't do. Hair is an example. It's useful. It protects from the cold. It can be a kind of armor. HAL makes my hair grow thick or keeps it thick by keeping the water in."

I took a deep breath and smiled. "I am getting to the end."

He gave a smile to encourage me.

"Strength is useful to any animal. It's a no-brainer why HAL gives me strength. It was probably the first reflex he developed.

"Some animals hunt by throwing things. Snakes spit venom. There's a little fish in New Zealand that squirts water at insects crawling on leaves to make them fall in the water. Accuracy is important. It shows how brainless HAL is that he doesn't know I don't throw a baseball to kill somebody. I guess it's lucky he didn't kill the players for me.

"About the wind. Birds, bats and who knows what else on other planets make their living by flying around. The air has to be calm. A high wind can knock the creature to the ground. When I fell out of the plane HAL stopped the wind so that I could go back to flying. I can't ask him how he does it. There's nobody to talk to. We may never know how he stops the wind. The problem is, he never developed a reflex to bring the wind back. There was no reason to."

I stopped. Blair remained still.

Could that be all? Was there nothing to be done? No. The tone of my voice was not expressing hopelessness. I was calm. I was expectant. I was waiting for him to say something. He smiled and so did I.

"But that's not the end of the story?" he suggested.

"No. The bad news is HAL is brainless. I can't communicate with him. The good news is he has no resistance to change. It might be possible to control HAL by manipulating his reflexes. It would be very difficult."

"If you can do that what could you do?"

"I don't know. There may be no limit to what I can do."

That was not what the PM wanted to hear. He was silent. I could see his concern.

The situation had changed. Up to this point it was about what HAL did. Now it was about what I did.

I suggested, "Or we could set up a committee to take over."

He liked that even less. I said, "You want to take a

break?"

"Yes."

Neither of us moved, he because it was up to the lady to move first, and me because there was something wrong.

I thought, *Shouldn't he be satisfied with the way the meeting turned out? What the heck does he want from me?*

I said, "We came into this meeting hoping to get an alien to give us a break. It's in human hands. That sounds a lot better to me. After what happened to me two weeks ago, most people would give up. I'm still here."

I got up and left before he responded.

I got back to the television in my suite to see people's reaction to what we discussed, a talk that had been nearly a monologue on my part. Many people couldn't follow the train of my thoughts. They were interviewed in bars and meeting halls, anywhere reporters could easily get lots of comments. "What did she say about growing hair?" "Why did HAL come here?" "How does HAL get reflexes without a brain?" "Did HAL merge with Samson?"

News network anchormen tried to explain my theory but showed they didn't understand much better than the public.

"Theresa Hartley said HAL develops reflexes by clinging to animals and adapting their behavior. She did not make clear how something made of alien substance would even want to adapt our world's behaviors. Nor did she explain why she was chosen by HAL out of the world's billions."

That's not what I said. HAL didn't "want" anything. He didn't "choose". I shook my head.

"It's their fault if they don't get it" I said to Nancy. "Everything has been explained. Nothing is understood."

People didn't understand because they didn't get what they wanted, an intelligent alien that could communicate and negotiate with them. They got me after I survived an assassination attempt by my own President. No wonder they didn't get it! They were afraid of me and the power I might get.

As I surfed through the channels, discussion changed from what HAL did to what I was going to do. I was going to use HAL's reflexes to control him somehow. From that it followed that I would become a powerful person. Finally, they got to the part that really interested reporters: my offer to share power with a committee.

The media loved political controversy and speculated in detail. All it did was add to the confusion.

"How do you organize a committee?" asked an anchor. "Do we have one representative from each country like the United Nations? Then we have paralysis. The small nation majority will favor small nation actions. The larger nations won't help out. A Security Council would disenfranchise smaller nations. You can't equalize unequals."

"The committee will presumably meet with Theresa Hartley who is an American. Many nations will object. It's not like the United Nations that meets in New York with no government presence. Theresa and the committee will be the government. With

Hartley the most important member, it will be an American government. That will be unacceptable to many."

Complications and complexity! Even I was near confusion with all being discussed. It soon got much worse.

I changed to the biggest international media circus of all: CNN.

CNN said it was doing an unscientific telephone call poll inviting people to vote on whether they wanted a committee in charge of HAL or me alone. Telephone numbers were posted on the screen, one number for "Theresa Hartley alone", another for "Committee". The voting was tabulated according to the country of the phone call's origin. Voting numbers were also shown on the screen. As CNN continued to promote the poll, numbers rapidly climbed.

"We have 368,000 votes from the United States with 76% in favor of Hartley going alone. No surprise there; they trust one of their own. In Europe we have most of the Western Europeans leaning towards a committee with the interesting exception of Italy going for Hartley. The East European countries, formerly dominated by the Soviet Union, want Hartley, while Russia leans towards a committee. In Moslem countries, we see overwhelming preference for committee, while African countries South of the Sahara want Hartley. Japan is voting for Hartley....."

I changed the channel.

"You know what's wrong with these people?" I said to Nancy. "They have no heart. They don't talk about who I am. I'm an 18 year old girl. All I want is to be with my husband and go to my quiet little job.

They don't care. They see me as a threat."

I found another channel giving news. At the bottom of the screen a banner streamed by with the latest breaking news: *French President says committee is impractical.* I waited a minute while they finished talking about something else. Then the President of France was shown being questioned by reporters as he left a social function. A translator's voice was heard providing the English.

"Monsieur President, do you approve Madame Hartley's committee?"

"It is not practical. We are not talking of the United Nations where thousands of people are needed to do something. HAL can do something alone. This is power on a new level. A committee in control of HAL would be a target for every terrorist organization. I believe nobody will want to be on the committee. We would need to surround each member with an army."

"Then how can Madame Hartley control HAL alone?"

"She will have to be hidden where a thousand assassins can't find her."

My heart sank. The world no longer made any sense at all.

The French President was right. There was a new order coming into the world that would bring a new response. All power-hungry groups would combine their efforts to either bring me under their control or kill me. It was madness, but terrorists were not known for rationality.

I changed back to CNN. The anchorman was interviewing a guest about the French President's pessimistic thought. The anchorman interrupted.

"We take you live to the meeting."

Prime Minister Blair was seen sitting at the table where we met. He sat rigidly with a frown. He was angry.

"The Prime Minister appears to be upset. It may be he did not appreciate the remarks of the French President."

I knew that had to be it. An hour and a half had passed since our last break began, and there he sat madder than a mama bear protecting cubs.

He wanted me to return. I got up and went to the elevator. I wished it would go below the ground floor and sideways to some place where I could forget all this insanity.

I walked through the lobby, past the security people, hotel guests, and the one permitted television crew. Most of them looked as sad as I was. I got to the meeting room and dropped my bottom in the chair. The PM wore the most sympathetic look he could muster. He let me speak first.

"It's rough in the big leagues! I didn't do anything and people want me dead. It's wrong. Why do people do the wrong thing?"

"People who have no conscience think everybody lacks one. They fear you."

"You can kill me if you want. HAL will just move to somebody else. It could be anybody. HAL wouldn't know the difference between Joan of Arc and Adolf Hitler. You want to try your luck?"

"Lord no!"

"I feel like that girl in *The Hunger Games*, except that she only had twenty-three assassins to worry about. What are my chances?"

"There is a good chance. Every nation will surround you with its best security people. I assure you we will."

"Yeah, well, if I don't get results soon I'll be first to go."

"What will you do?"

"I'll go on as long as I can. Maybe they'll give me two months."

"Courageously spoken!"

At that moment I won the world.

"Will you try to control HAL?"

"Sure. It's only the most impossible, burdensome, insane task ever imposed on a human being."

"We will render any assistance you need."

"I need a place where I can work undisturbed. Atom bombs break my concentration."

"We will find you a place."

"I need to stay alive."

"All the armed forces of the United Kingdom will defend you."

I relaxed and took a deep breath.

"Did you see the Prince William and Kate Middleton wedding they showed this week?"

"I did. Magnificent."

"Kate was so nervous before the wedding she couldn't eat. She went from size ten to size four. After exchanging vows they sat on the side for the sermon. The cameras showed her breathing rapidly. Nothing could have prepared her for a wedding in front of two billion people. It's a miracle she didn't faint."

"She was twenty-nine I believe. And you?"

"Eighteen."

"How are you doing?"

"I'm all right if I don't drop on the way to the elevator."

"You are under the most extreme pressure. I'm so sorry."

I smiled, and so did the PM. His admission of my pressure made me feel better. Of course, he was under pressure too. Letting me take over HAL was gambling the world I would do what was needed.

"I'm surprised I have the nerve to try controlling HAL. It's a heck of a challenge, you know."

"You have no model for what you're doing. Your parents didn't do it. Nobody you know did it. Nobody told you it can't be done. You believe it can."

"What does Mr. Blair need after I take care of HAL?"

"I need Mrs. Hartley to do nothing."

"I won't change anything. You have four billion witnesses."

As if to make amends for suggesting I keep my greedy hands off the world, Blair changed subject.

"In his book *On War*, the eminent authority Karl von Klauswitz said there are two kinds of courage, the courage to face danger, and the courage to assume responsibility. You demonstrate both."

I smiled and joked, "If I pull this job off call me Bond. Jane Bond."

Blair picked up on that and started singing the James Bond theme.

"Tum tum da rum tum tah da dum ta ta da da da dum ta rum ta dahhh dah dum de dum...."

I laughed. A silly moment was just what we

needed.

We looked at each other for a moment. It was intense with mutual feelings. We had achieved something besides a fruitful meeting. We had become good friends.

I immortalized him with a simple remark that would be carved in granite all over England.

"You did a good job, Mr. Blair."

I got up. He rose as I walked around the table to meet him. I gave him a warm hug. His eyes moistened. His emotion was shared by a newly hopeful world.

Chapter 8

I returned to my hotel room and looked out the window for the first time. The 58th floor gave a spectacular view of a city that seemed to stretch out to infinity. I could see millions of lights and figured no city could be this big. The furthest lights had to be far beyond London. I had to save all these people and a thousand times as many in the rest of the world.

I looked up to Heaven and prayed.

"Our Father in Heaven, take this away from me, but if you don't want to take it away at least help me get through it."

What the heck was I doing here! Does an eighteen year old American girl belong in London with a mission to save humanity? It was crazy.

Blair did do a good job. He didn't mention the disasters to come and kept me thinking about HAL. But now, alone in my room, I had nothing to think about but the job ahead of me.

But it worked both ways. What must people be thinking about an eighteen year old girl getting HAL's awesome power? There were probably already assassins down there staking out the hotel for a chance to get to me.

I felt tired and went to bed.

I woke with a dread of the day. The PM had put me at ease during our talk and helped guide me to the thrill of solving the HAL mystery that weighed heavily on me for eight years. Now, lying alone in the hotel bedroom, the significance of the challenges facing me, unfiltered by the smiles of Peter Blair, was depressing. How could I get through it?

I called room service for a breakfast delivered in only fifteen minutes. I watched television while eating. All the media people on all channels were talking exclusively about me. The whole world had stopped what it was doing to avoid creating news that might interrupt my story. People on the street were questioned for their opinions of me. They were universally supportive. "Theresa is awesome." "Theresa is a darling." "We think she'll do the job." "Good luck, Theresa." While observing the comments of the media I came to realize something. The crazy terrorists would come after me, but no politician who depended on public support would ever take me on. It would be political suicide. The people would storm his government building and throw him in the street.

The television switched to some remarks President Veronica Stinson made to the press hours earlier, shortly after I went to bed.

"When we face invincible threats to our lives and well-being, we feel a loss of influence to what happens to us. We're helpless and impotent. In desperation we support a hero who promises to save us. For some it was Napoleon, for others Lenin, Hitler, or Senator McCarthy. Now we look at Theresa Hartley. But while the four men I mentioned had their own agenda, Theresa is working for a higher cause. She will submit her will to a higher will. Let us look forward with confidence and trust. Theresa is fighting for us."

It didn't rival the Gettysburg Address, President Stinson was no Lincoln, but it said what was needed.

Apparently the hotel told the Prime Minister I was awake, because while I was eating, he called to ask if he could come by to take me to the "place" I had asked for.

"Sure. Anytime. I need some luggage."

Luggage was brought up from the hotel shops in ten minutes.

The television showed Steve arriving at Logan Airport for a flight to London. He'd had trouble getting one. Everybody wanted to fly home to wait for Armageddon. Then he had the bright idea of giving them his name first and then asking for a flight. A limousine was sent to him in ninety minutes.

What did he think of me now? A wife should not keep secrets that involved her, and I didn't tell him about HAL. Would he be mad? Could he forgive? Was he coming to London with divorce papers for me to sign?

The television showed something else. Somebody had started a "Doomsday Clock". They estimated the total amount of food reserves in the world and subtracted the number of tons people were eating every second. Nobody could know the exact amount of food in storage in every corner of the world. Somebody had estimated a reasonable number of 800,000,000 tons and started counting from there. The number was dropping 40 tons a second. We had 228 days to go. Thanks for reminding me!

The PM arrived in mid-morning and we left in his Bentley.

"Where are we going?" I asked.

"A friend of mine has a considerably large estate not far from here. He called me and offered to shelter you. I think you'll like it. His name is Edmund Parker. He has a charming family, a wife and four children."

I was satisfied with that. A family environment would be nice.

"I was watching television this morning. The dummies are saying all kinds of stupid things. They say HAL can't be made of dark matter. They say dark matter can't stick together, can't use energy, and can't do anything with matter. They say I've been communicating with HAL, and stopping the wind was a plot to make me look like a hero. They say when the government grabbed, me HAL promised to get me out of the plane and keep me alive until a ship came. Sounds like a cheap made for TV movie. "

"I heard all that. It is disgraceful."

"It's more than disgraceful. It's stupid."

"They wasted no time. We only talked a few hours ago."

"I will never talk to reporters. I can't waste time on idiots."

"They tell lies to build up viewership. They will be exposed as liars. This is building sandcastles as the tide comes in."

"'Those who ignore the conscience will kill it.' One of my teachers said that. The more I see of the world the less I like it. People are unpredictable. They don't act according to their professed beliefs. You can't find enough trustworthy people to fill an elevator. I think people have stopped thinking about morality altogether."

Blair was silent a long time after that. I sensed that he worried about keeping me in control.

"I'm making you worry. Why?"

"Those who adhere to a system of morality, admirable as that may be, are often the most unyielding in their endeavors."

"Like who?"

"Radical Islamic terrorists for example."

"Why do they do that?"

"The promise of changing yourself from nobody to somebody is irresistible to terrorists and to cults of all kinds. It draws in the alienated and disaffected."

"I won't try to set up a religious movement if that's what you mean."

"The best inspiration is good example."

"Father Donoughty said that. He taught me a lot."

I changed the subject.

"Remember when you asked if anything could be made out of dark matter? I asked Steve the same question. He was talking with some physics majors and he mentioned dark matter. I never heard of the stuff and asked him if anything could be made from it. Sure, he said. It would hold itself together by its own gravity. Atomic nuclei never get close enough to feel each other's gravity. If an atom was the size of the United States, the nucleus would be a baseball in Kansas where Dorothy lived."

He laughed.

"If you have two atoms the size of the United States you have two baseballs as far apart as New York and California. They can't feel each other's gravity. But dark matter particles can touch each other and atomic nuclei too. The gravity gets very strong. HAL uses gravity to hold together. Some dark matter particles may have a kind of stickiness too. It doesn't take much to hold stuff together. DNA is held together by hydrogen bonds that are very weak, but there's millions of them so DNA is strong.

"Later, Steve changed his story a little. He said a dark matter body couldn't hold itself together by itself. It would need a piece of solid matter to act as an anchor for its organization. Matter only needs itself to stay together. HAL needs to cling to something in our visible universe or he would fall apart. And there's one more thing. A rock is too rigid. HAL needs his host to have some fluidity. The logical choice is water. We think of rocks being dry but they always have lots of water. Water molecules have some attraction for each other which is why it's liquid instead of gas, and they can move around. The rigid rock provides the lattice HAL needs, the sticky water molecules provide fluidity, gravity lets HAL keep his own particles together while clinging to the rock and water, and momentum from something gives HAL his version of energy. A living host like me provides the rigidity and fluidity HAL needs. "

"You did say something about HAL needing matter to hold his order together last night. I didn't know what you meant."

"I didn't think it was the time to go into it deeply last night. Who would understand it?"

"Can HAL act in extended space beyond his host?"

"Yeah. Think of a computer. A fifty pound desktop computer is all controlled by a chip no larger than a fingernail. The Earth's atmosphere has a certain kind of rigidity too. It's fluid but it takes hours or days for air masses to move around much. HAL does things in a fraction of a second. The air changes slowly enough for HAL to use it as a lattice."

"You refer to HAL as he instead of it. Is there a reason?"

"I thought he was an alien for a long time. It's males who go out seeking adventure. I don't know why. It's like the guys who climb Mount Everest. A quarter of them are killed or permanently injured. A surgeon lost the use of his hands from frostbite. What's the point?"

This might not be a safe topic to pursue. He returned to HAL.

"How does HAL use energy?"

I smiled. "You're getting a lot of heat?"

"I am."

He didn't catch the weak pun.

"Steve said something made of dark matter can use momentum instead of energy. A mass of matter colliding with HAL would transfer its momentum to him by gravity. This momentum passes through HAL and he pushes matter on the other side. Think of a train with the locomotive in the rear. The locomotive pushes the train, and the car in front flattens the car of some idiot trying to beat the signal lights."

"Your husband explained this without knowing about HAL?"

"He could see I was interested but not why."

"How important was he to developing your theory of HAL?"

"Without Steve, I wouldn't have a clue what to think about HAL. I think I would have told you I can't do anything and gone home. You might drop Steve a thank you note."

There was a silent pause. Then I said, "If President

Martin hadn't tried to kill me, I would have taken the secret of HAL to my grave. What did he think of this wind thing?"

"He made no statement. He is in seclusion. Rumor has it he had a mental breakdown. His family protects him from the public eye."

"The poor guy. If he had destroyed HAL he'd be a hero. Steve would say he overreached himself. You can only be what you know you can be. You can only do what you know to do. That sums up who we are."

"Ah! Like Shakespeare. Macbeth, Richard III, King Lear, Julius Caesar, Hamlet, Romeo and Juliet all reached for something beyond their reach."

"I wanted a quiet life. That was out of my reach. This is like 'The Caine Mutiny'. Do you know that story?"

"Yes. It's required reading for all leaders."

"If the Navy had thoroughly investigated things before the trial, maybe the trial and all its embarrassment could have been avoided."

"I believe you're right."

"If President Martin had invited me to the White House to talk things over, maybe this mess could have been avoided. Now I have to take on a ton of responsibility like Queen Victoria except that she only had England to worry about."

Blair's earlier references to Shakespeare's characters hadn't gotten the message across to me. He tried again.

"Let's not miss another literary allegory. In Joseph Conrad's 'Heart of Darkness', a man named Kurtz goes deep into the heart of Africa. He's hired to find ivory, but his own personal ambition is to civilize the natives. It worked in reverse. The natives made him a savage. It takes a thousand years to change a culture. His efforts to do it in a short time ruined him."

I got the message. "In other words, you want me to save the world but not try to change it."

"Quite right."

"Don't worry. I'm not a social worker."

Yeah, well, you have to believe in something or your mind shuts off. This Kurtz guy believed in the wrong thing. He believed in the impossible. His mind shut down. My job was simple: just save the world!

I turned my mind to happier times while I still had a mind.

When Steve and I first started dating, the girls said we were naturals for each other. They were right. We hit if off immediately.

Neither of us were great talkers. There were periods of silence. But that was all right. We were bored by the constant chattering other kids felt they had to keep up all the time. It was good to know you didn't have to do that with your companion.

Neither of us was on the inside crowd in high school. Steve had dates with only three girls and the relationships didn't get very far. He didn't even go to his Senior prom. When he was a teenager he lived only a mile from a small university. He visited the campus many times and saw the beautiful girls. He knew the best was yet to come when he got to college and did not worry that much about high school dating. I had dated only one boy in high school, Jeff Winslow, a geeky kid with red hair and glasses. A nice kid. A cheerful kid. Someone fun to be with. A boy who took me to all the school events including the Senior prom.

Jeff was the only high school boy who ever had the nerve to ask me out—partly the price of being a female baseball star—but also because I was so beautiful boys were afraid of being put down. Jeff would probably marry an average girl, but for the rest of his life he would remember he had once dated a drop dead gorgeous woman. He helped me through the teen years
and showed me a boy could be a friend. He made me feel I was worth something. I owed him a lot.

Neither of us had a large circle of friends in college. Steve wasn't heavily into sports or the party scene, although he wasn't a misanthrope either. He talked easily to anybody. He just didn't seek them out. He concentrated on his major because he actually wanted to get a job when he graduated, not move back in with his parents as so many graduates did. I was not that popular with the girls. I wasn't interested in their gossipy talk and they thought I was a snob. In fact, the years of worrying about my situation with HAL had made me serious at an early age. I left the usual teenaged girl's concerns behind me long ago. I skipped over the thirteen year old girl's obsessions with makeup, hairstyles, rock music stars, designer clothes, and boys. I worried about what HAL would mean in my future. As a result, girls talked about me being of indeterminate gender orientation. Not a word of truth in it, but perhaps this also kept the boys away. I was not willing to talk about the scandals of people not present. In college I heard talk of girls doing incredibly bad things they read about in magazines. They didn't seem aware they had eternity to worry about. The first being was not a composite because nothing preceded him and he could get nothing from something else. Nor could anything be taken away from him since he had no parts. Something that is not a composite has to be its own essence, which was that which makes it what it is. God's existence is his essence because he has nothing else, and existence, if there is any, can have no beginning or end. Therefore, he is eternal.

Catholic students at BC had to take some religion or philosophy courses. Two weeks into my philosophy course, the instructor was replaced by somebody who was heavy into Aquinas. I was sure this was done for my benefit. Somebody wanted me to have a solid grounding in theology. It was likely the Holy Father. After BC, I found the sermons of prosperity religion televangelists infantile. God as Santa Claus? No, God as Father.

Steve and I did have things in common that attracted each other. We ran through the whole list of positive qualities in well balanced personalities. A whole bookshelf of books would have to be written to say everything that could be said about us. We both had respect for the truth in ourselves and in all things, and that was important in finding out what each other was about; neither could have gotten away with faking good points and neither would try. But perhaps the most fundamental characteristic we shared was simplicity. We were not complicated by the internal contradictions that made Hollywood celebrities fodder for the tabloids. Our hearts were built on the best moral standards that thousands of years of human experiment had developed. We were simply good people, and if the tabloids would find us boring then so be it.

After a seventy minute ride we arrived at Edmund Parker's magnificent estate. The house was three hundred feet from the road with a perfectly flat lawn in front. It was built in the old English post-and-beam style, sometimes called Tudor. This palace, for that's what it looked like to me, was a hundred and twenty feet long and three stories high. To the sides and rear of the house was a forest where thousands of British soldiers were moving in.

My car door was opened by a maid and I got out. A fifty-ish butler with a broad, smiling face opened the Prime Minister's door. The chauffeur and two maids took care of the luggage. No words were spoken as the butler guided the group through the front door. I thought this was odd.

Edmund Parker and his family stood to the side next to the door to one of the living rooms. Peter Blair walked over to them immediately.

"This way, madam" said the butler leading me to the side of a grand staircase. We went into an elevator. I thought not being introduced to the family was odd too.

"Why didn't I meet the family?"

"The British respect for privacy, madam. They understand why you're here and won't speak to you unless you speak first."

"I can't imagine that happening in the States."

"It doesn't here either in normal times. Every moment of your time is the world's treasure."

"Can I ask your name?"

"Arthur Bemming at your service. Everybody calls me Arthur."

We had arrived at a third floor bedroom. It was more like an apartment with a sitting room, dressing room, and bathroom. This would be considered the master bedroom of an expensive American home. I wondered how many of these bedrooms there were in this palace.

"Susan will attend to your needs," said Arthur. "She will go shopping for you if you wish."

Susan was a twenty-something maid with the same enthusiastic attitude of Nancy back at the hotel. I was overwhelmed by the luxury of this home, but I managed a smile for Susan.

I turned on the television to check on Steve's progress. It showed a huge crowd in St. Peter's Square. The Pope had asked all humanity to pray for me every day, and he was leading them in saying the rosary. The scene switched to other churches all over the world. The churches were packed with people. In one day, I had inspired a larger religious revival then all the television evangelists in history.

Steve's plane landed in London. The Prime Minister sent people to greet him and drive him to the Parker estate. Arthur guided him straight up to the door of the third floor bedroom and discreetly made himself vanish. Steve came in.

I was just inside the door and wrapped my arms around his neck immediately.

"Oh God! I'm so glad you came."

"When I thought you were dead I wanted to die too. What would I do without my Theresa?"

"I should have told you about HAL."

"No. I would have needed to marry you to prove

something instead of for yourself. HAL has nothing to do with us."

I smiled. The issue was dead that quickly. No tears. No histrionics. No complaints. It was always so simple with Steve. Anybody who was hoping to see our marriage break up and fill the talk shows with drivel would be disappointed.

"How are my parents?"

"Your mother is having a rough time. First you were dead. Then you were invaded by an alien. Then they said you fell out of the plane. Then they said you were screaming in the water, then they found you in the water and declared you dead again. Then you came back to life. Now it's your job to save the world. That's a lot for a mother to take."

"How is she doing?"

"She's confused. The doctor says she's always thought of herself as your mom. She was supposed to take care of you. There's nothing she can do to help you. She's lost her purpose. She'll get used to it. Your father told me to come take care of you."

"He was right."

We had a lot to talk about. Steve described what he was doing in those two weeks and how people we knew were reacting. I added interesting details not previously revealed in the news. After fifty minutes of this we decided to finish later and went downstairs to meet the household.

We went to the foyer. The Edmund Parker family could be seen sitting quietly in a huge living room. They looked like they'd wait there weeks for us.

"Who are those people?" Steve asked.

"I'm not sure. I think they live here. Arthur said

they won't bother us unless we speak first."

"Who's Arthur?"

"The butler."

"Oh yeah. Shall we meet the folks?"

We lumbered into the living room with as much dignity as unpolished Americans could muster. The Parker family stood up and gave welcoming smiles.

"How do you do, sir" said Steve. "Steve Hartley. You probably know Theresa."

"Edmund Parker, sir. This is Helen." The wife extended her hand and we shook it in turn. "My sixteen year old, John..." The son shook hands enthusiastically. "Stephanie, twelve years....." The girl was thrilled to meet the guests. The top rock stars would not have seen a wider smile. "Jennifer, ten years..." The younger girl was shy but excited. "We have an older son in the military."

Edmund Parker waved his hand to invite everybody to sit down. We made small talk followed by a tour of the house. I was dazzled by its opulence. There were more objects in it than could be discussed in a day. It reminded me of the Boston Museum of Fine Arts. You couldn't get a good look at everything in less than a week. This house was a palace! I joked, "I may never go home."

Steve and I could have eaten by ourselves, but we ate with the Parkers. After an excellent dinner, Steve became very drowsy

"When did you sleep last?" I asked.

"Saturday, I think."

I pointed a finger to the ceiling. "Off to bed with you, young man!"

Steve went upstairs.

Helen Parker and I drifted to the family room which was on the right of the foyer unlike the living room on the left, and we did some female bonding. Finally, I felt sleepy too and excused myself. Steve was fast asleep. I quietly slipped into bed.

Tuesday was a day of settling in. I was not ready to tackle the difficult work of cracking the HAL communication code that I would have to invent myself.

EarlyWednesday morning Steve and I walked around the Parker estate to unwind. The woods began about 150 feet behind the house. The edge was mostly a small number of widely separated large old trees. This cultivated edge extended some one hundred feet in. Beyond that, the woods had a more natural density. It was here that the soldiers could be seen. They were assembled in small groups of about a dozen. No more than a hundred feet separated these groups, sometimes less if the brush was too thick to see far. As we walked within sight of hundreds of these soldiers, it was obvious they made an impenetrable wall around the Parker house. I waved to the soldiers who happily waved back. But actually walking up to the soldiers and talking with them didn't seem like a good idea at the moment. As Steve said, "Anything we say will leak to the press. They'll try to twist it around."

We returned to the house to eat lunch. After that I decided it was time to start organizing a strategy for breaking through to HAL. I'd use a third floor den the Parkers had offered to me to do my work. Steve knew he couldn't do much to help me. I was the mathematician. He left me alone and went downstairs.

The first thing Thursday morning, an agent from

Scotland Yard called to ask if he could come to the Parker estate and talk with me. The SY agent arrived, and we sat down with him in the living room. He explained.

"As we expected, you are getting an enormous quantity of mail from all over the world. Our concern is attempts on Mrs. Hartley's life. Letters may contain poisonous substances. Packages may contain bombs. We suggest that our people screen this mail before it's delivered to you."

"Sure" said Steve.

"Sure" I agreed.

"It will also help our work. Any threatening mail could give us information about terrorist groups and other dangerous people."

"Absolutely. Go ahead," Steve said.

This was all the visit was about. It could have been done by phone. Everybody wanted to see me in person.

The first delivery of mail arrived Thursday afternoon. There were six thousand letters and two hundred packages large and small. The man driving the delivery truck said this was a small beginning. There would be a lot more Friday.

While I was busy upstairs Steve started going through the letters which were already opened. There was no possibility of reading so much mail—never mind answering it. So he asked Arthur for some cardboard boxes and planned to trash any letters that didn't appear to have anything worth reading. He skimmed through a letter every ten seconds.

After a couple dozen letters, he hit on one that had a check in it. It was from France and the check was for fifty Euros, roughly fifty American dollars. He put that letter aside and continued.

A couple of minutes later he found another letter with a check in it, this time for a hundred Euros. He had barely begun going through the huge pile of mail and already had two checks. He read this letter which was in English and found that the writer was sending the money as a kind of payment to Madame Theresa for saving his life.

Steve kept working through the mail all afternoon and found that about one in sixty letters contained checks. There was something about people's mentality that made them think paying me to save their lives would get me to do it. He'd kept a list of the check amounts and now he added them up. The Euros came to 1,800. There was around 1,000 in American dollars and a few hundred in various other denominations. This was from one afternoon's work, and far more mail was promised for tomorrow. The Hartley family financial situation had taken a new turn.

I came down for supper.

"You're getting a lot of money in the mail," Steve said.

"Oh yeah? How come?"

"They want to thank you for saving their necks."

He showed me the amounts he'd found that afternoon. I raised my eyebrows.

"You think I should keep it?"

"Why not? You're earning it."

As the week went on we settled into a routine. Three hours was about all I could take doing the intense work I was doing. So after working from 8 to

11 in the morning, I'd take a walk around the estate with Steve. Then it was lunch. Then work from 1 to 4 in the afternoon and a couple of hours of reading or television before dinner. Finally, maybe an hour or two of work in the evening before winding down to bedtime.

By Monday I was getting homesick for my parents. Using the telephone was out. So was email and snail mail. It was sure to be intercepted. Steve asked Arthur to go to the Prime Minister and ask if some kind of courier service could be set up to move mail between me and my parents. "Easily done" answered the PM.

I wrote to mom.

Dear Mom,

I know a lot of things are going on right now and you feel helpless. Don't worry about me. You raised me right. You taught me to care about people, to think things out, to react to things without being a drama queen, and to have a positive outlook.

I don't know what the future will bring but Steve is here with me and we will get through this. Remember how I told you that when a baseball game was being lost I said it's not going to end this way? This won't.

Take care of dad. I know fathers worry over their daughters too.

I love you both,
Theresa

Every Wednesday the Prime Minister appeared in the House of Commons in a duty called "Questions to the Prime Minister". This week hard questions were expected about me. How could I be trusted with my burden if even I didn't know what I was going to do?

I was the world's worst nightmare. An ordinary girl was about to take control of the world. The implications even terrified me. Could I handle so much power?

The world worried about my character. Pundits said nobody with the power I was on the road to acquiring could remain humble. I would go mad with my self-importance and fame. I would blackmail the world into doing what I wanted. I would become a power-mad dictator.

Others thought there was no reason to think I would behave that way. My past indicated nothing in my personality to make me change. It was the question of the day, and when Prime Minister Blair walked into the House, you could see in the eyes of the members they couldn't wait to have at him.

My BC philosophy professor warned us not to get into long-winded arguments with atheists. Those who don't understand what they're talking about will talk all day. If you do understand what you're talking about, you can express it in a few simple words, like Abraham Lincoln in his Gettysburg Address. Prime Minister Blair brought out a hundred points about me I hadn't thought of myself. This was his Gettysburg Address.

A member from the opposition stood up and asked, "Can the Honorable Prime Minister assure this House that by his lonely decision, our esteemed friend Mrs. Hartley can be trusted with this arduous task, which she herself described the most impossible ever imposed on a human being, without abundant assistance from His Majesty's government?"

Blair jumped up to the table with his book of notes to answer.

"The time factor was crucial to my decision. Mrs. Hartley has been working on the problem for years. A team of assistants might take months to understand her theories and reach consensus on strategy. Let us give her a chance to make progress."

He stalled and became pensive to get full control of his audience.

"We should consider how it came to be that Theresa Hartley was chosen to be host to HAL. Her character is impeccable. Her intellect is of the finest quality. No more perfect choice could be found for her task. HAL merged with her when she was ten. A few years earlier and she would have told everybody about HAL with most unfortunate results for herself and us. A few years later and she might not have developed the skills needed for the challenge. But she received HAL at age ten, old enough to know to keep HAL a secret, but young enough to set herself on that path of intellectual development to enable her to address the HAL problem. Did all these happy circumstances happen by chance, or by design?"

Now he really had their attention. They sat in stony silence wondering where he was going.

"Mrs. Hartley is not vindictive. You saw she had not said a word about the assassination attempt in our long discussion. Not a reprobating word from her for the man who tried to kill her. The morning after I drove her to Mr. Parker's. She expressed sorrow for, in her words, 'the poor guy'. This is Theresa Hartley. This is the woman chosen to save us all. This is Saint

Theresa among us now."

The House stood up as one to cheer his answer. But the leader of the opposition wouldn't let it rest. He stood up and was recognized.

"Is the Prime Minister aware it may come to pass Mrs. Hartley, acting alone, can do anything she wants no matter how outrageous, and the whole world can't stop her?"

The PM jumped back up.

"Who will trust a committee? We know Theresa well enough. The only thing that can stop Theresa is her own conscience, and it will."

The opposition leader kept at it.

"Does the Prime Minister agree a person with good conscience in ordinary circumstances can be overwhelmed in the extraordinary and be changed for the worse?"

"There is only one version of the truth. Theresa knows it and lives by it. I spoke with President Stinson last evening. She said everything is known about Theresa. Their intelligence agency has a room full of reports and tapes on every moment of her life for eight years. Teams of psychologists have studied these documents. There is nothing to suggest a fault in the steadiness of her character despite her youth. She is grounded on rock, not sand."

And again!

"Does the Prime Minister agree a person with conscience should not be a physician if he has not been so trained, or one in a position of power without adequate education and experience?"

"My honorable friend points to jobs requiring skills. But Theresa does not set out to manipulate organs or people. Theresa's job only requires cleverness and a good heart."

And another question!

"Does the Prime Minister agree it may come to pass we have a person in power without democratic representation?"

"President Stinson's people have studied Theresa and agree she supports democratic principles, but how do you make control of HAL democratic? I do not believe she will do anything contrary to people's wishes. Have courage. She will ask nothing from us."

One more shot.

"Is the Prime Minister aware it is written 'As the heavens in height, and the earth in depth, the heart of kings is unfathomable'?"

"It is also written, 'By patience is a ruler persuaded, and a soft tongue will break a bone'. The story of man is that the individual must deal with the world. In this case it works both ways. The world must deal with Theresa. She and we must deal with each other reasonably. Better to be alone in the jungle than in a dictatorship, but also better to be a fisherman than a governor of men if the people speak ill of you. Theresa will return kindness given to her."

A woman rose to pose a question no American politician would get away with. But this was not America.

"Does the Prime Minister agree a man's reaction to criticism is laughter, while a woman's reaction is unpredictable?"

The House burst out in laughter. It liked nothing better than a loaded question and this one was a minefield. Blair milked the moment looking around like he was afraid to answer. His expression was hilarious. Even Steve and I watching at the Parker residence were laughing. Finally, the PM got serious and paused. The sense of the moment was that he was about to deliver an ultimatum of some kind, a 'here it is whether you like it or not and live with it!'. The world held its breath for twenty-seven seconds.

"I understand your fears. What human being can bear the responsibilities demanded of this woman? It hardly seems possible. We've seen many strong men broken from lesser challenges, men trained thirty or forty years for their tasks.

"What shall we do if a child leads us? And make no mistake, Theresa is younger than many of the children and grandchildren of the members of this House. Who are we dealing with? Will she change?

"I say, Theresa's interests and endeavors may change, but not her heart. It is too well-considered. It is written 'worse than death is the life of a fool', but we saw in my talk with her Theresa is no fool. 'Woe to thee when your king is a child' says the Good Book, but Theresa shows lack of response to recent ill events. It is also written, 'You are the light of the world. A city set on a mountain cannot be hidden'. Theresa's works will be seen by all. She can only do good works if she cares at all what we think of her, and we've seen she does. A philosopher who lived a few miles from Theresa's home wrote, 'In dealing with truth we are immortal, and need fear no change nor accident'. A woman who puts her trust in a higher power will be unchanged. Theresa will remain Theresa."

Chapter 9

I went over the ideas I put in the MISSION IMPOSSIBLE file. They had been for communicating with a non-verbal alien, a machine or something, but I thought the MI ideas could be adapted to HAL. But before I used these math theories I would have to get some response from HAL. This became the first priority. I had to get him to respond to something I did, in effect, get him to develop a new reflex that I could gradually modify in small steps to do something else. Animal trainers did this. Somebody had once taught a rhinoceros to walk a tight rope. I should be able to get HAL to do something.

My real work began. I tried to get HAL to respond in four ways. One was to slide a small coin between two glasses on a table. I'd place a coin next to one glass, leave it there a moment, then put my finger on it to slide it to the other glass. After doing this a few times, I'd place the coin at the first glass and wait a while to see if HAL would move it for me.

The second thing I did was a takeoff on the throwing accuracy skill that HAL gave me. I tossed a coin in a small metal can a few feet away. Keeping my eyes on the can's opening got the coin inside the can every time. Then I'd toss a coin with my eyes shut. Once in while the coin would go into the can by pure chance, but generally it missed. HAL hadn't caught on to the idea yet.

The third thing I did was stand up and drop a coin on the floor besides the can while keeping my eyes on the can's opening. If HAL got the idea he would move the coin into the can. I was not throwing the coin; I was dropping it. If HAL guided the coin to the can it was a new reflex using elements of an old one. I could then try changing it by dropping the coin with my eyes shut. HAL's response to this would be a radical jump of some sort. I'd be on the way to changing one of his reflexes "step by step".

The fourth thing I did was entirely different. I suspended a one foot ruler on a piece of string. The string was attached to the end of a yardstick held in place with a book on top of a bookshelf. After steadying the foot ruler, I pointed to its end for a moment to give HAL a chance, then I pushed the ruler's end to make it rotate a hundred degrees or so. This maneuver had nothing to do with coins, or throwing, and would seem to require very little of HAL, just a tiny push.

HAL didn't respond. I tried all day the first day on the job but HAL didn't respond. How long would I have to try these stupid things before getting results? Would it drive me crazy first?

Meanwhile, Steve was going over the mail that had been pre-selected by the Scotland Yard people for checks. At one night's supper he said, "People are sending larger checks. We already have a million dollars."

"Really! In one week?"

"One week. The checks are getting really big."

"That will help. We can't get regular jobs."

We could not. The idea of going out and getting

jobs after all this was over was out of the question. We would be pestered by crowds of curious people wherever we went. No employer would want a thousand reporters camped out in front of his building.

Days went by. I did my coin and measuring stick tricks with no response from HAL. It was incredibly boring work. Added to the boredom was the tremendous pressure I was under. To fail would mean the death of everybody. Nobody could know what I went through.

It wasn't much easier on Steve who felt he was supposed to be taking care of me but could do little. He felt that he should be giving some useful ideas, but he had none.

Steve soon realized that when I broke the code to HAL, if ever, I would need advice about the mechanics of motion in order to control HAL. Any movement of matter required consideration of many parameters. This was the realm of physics and he was a physics major. He missed his college textbooks but instead of arranging to have them sent from home he decided to make a trip to Cambridge University and buy some. He and Arthur drove to Cambridge to visit the bookstore.

He quickly found the physics section and selected fifteen books. Somebody recognized him while he was on his way to the checkout and he was soon followed by a crowd. "Hello," said several people. Steve merely smiled politely without speaking to show he wasn't interested in conversation. They respectfully didn't push the point.

Somebody who looked like a college professor said, "Why doesn't your wife appear on television?"

He answered, "People wouldn't like her. She's too perfect."

The people who heard this remark got the idea. Thousands of newspaper and magazine articles about me had failed to uncover a single flaw in my character. There was nothing controversial to hold people's interest. It would be like interviewing a nun.

When the remark reached the press, it opened the door to talking about my morality. Anybody who'd known me since birth was considered fair game for questioning about my sexuality, religious beliefs, and social opinions. Reporters cornered Father Richard Donoughty and asked him to comment on my personality. He had a memorized answer.

"Let's hear atheists explain a miracle like Theresa! She is a very bright girl but she has a simple personality. She knows there is evil in the world. It doesn't affect her. She has simple needs. She doesn't seek what is not hers. She accepts what God gives her. She has borne a great burden for eight years with no complaints. She is the sanest person I know. We will see if a good girl with no unreasonable ambitions can do good in the world. We believe what we know. We know Theresa. Believe in her also. The lesson is anybody can be as fine a person as Theresa if only they'll try. Someone who wants to do God's will has an invincible ally. Theresa can't be defeated. I have hope she succeeds. I have hope she is a benevolent power. I hope."

He told me hope is never giving up.

How many people noticed Father Donoughty's statement didn't identify my religion? I learned something from him. Don't try too hard selling your agenda and you will sell your agenda. If I wanted to lead the world I would do it by waiting for people to ask me to lead.

The day after Father Donoughty's statement, President Stinson said something that gave people a new focus on my story. She was at a press conference. After the usual questions one would expect from reporters about the current state of the world, someone asked her to characterize the 'Theresa Hartley situation'. President Stinson seemed to speak spontaneously which made it stick.

"We're all trying to understand what's going on. This is new territory. We're not being invaded by an alien race or attacked by an unexplained force. HAL is neither an alien nor a force. From now on whatever happens will be one hundred percent Theresa's responsibility. This is a story like none we've ever heard. An eighteen year old girl is single-handedly driving world events. Heaven help us all!"

Ten days had gone by since I arrived at the Parker place. The constant games I played with the coins and hanging ruler were becoming oppressive.

The Prime Minister came around to talk to Steve.

"She hasn't made any progress" Steve told him. "The theory is HAL adapts his structure to the host's activity and it becomes a reflex. There's no other way to explain what HAL does. There's one problem with that. How long will it take? HAL has been around for billions of years. How long does it take before he picks up a new reflex?"

"The matter is urgent. She may succeed but too late."

"That's the problem."

"HAL stopped the wind when she fell from the plane. Have you considered asking her to take another plane ride?"

"We have and we'll try it when the time is right. We don't have much hope for that idea. HAL may have a reflex to respond to something but how do you get him to reverse that reflex? How do you tell him to undo it? He stopped the wind. Case closed."

Steve checked the mail almost every day. Packages had been sent through to him after the British security people checked them for bombs or poisons. A tube came in. He opened it and found a life size poster of me. It was a photograph taken of me at the hotel where I met with the Prime Minister. It showed me walking from the elevators to the meeting room for the first of our three sessions. I wore my famous Irish green outfit copied by women all over the world. At this point the full frontal image showed me calm and thoughtful. I appeared to be looking straight into the camera although I never noticed it. It was a great photo. He taped it to the wall of the bedroom. When I saw it, I asked, "Where did you get this?"

"A poster company sent it. They're going to put it on sale next week. I'll bet it's a hit."

"So now I'm a pinup girl," I smiled.

More days passed with no progress in getting HAL to develop a new reflex. Word came over the airways that farmers' crops planted only a few weeks before had stopped growing. Plants that should have been a foot tall were only a few inches. Without rain soon the crops would be a failure.

On one of our walks around the property I said,

"Do you know how long I've been here?"

"Three weeks isn't it?"

"That's twenty days in this place."

"Want to go for a ride, little girl?"

"I have to get out of here for a few days."

"All right. We'll go somewhere. Where do you want to go?"

"Paris."

A trip to Paris without being recognized seemed an impossibility for us, but a phone call to the Prime Minister made it feasible.

First, some government security people in unmarked cars drove us from London down to the coast. Then a fifty foot Royal Navy boat, with no markings to distinguish it from a private yacht, snuck us across the English Channel. Another pair of cars drove us to Paris where we were registered under false names in a small, quiet hotel two hundred feet from the Champs-Elysees. With dark glasses, my hair piled up on my head, and Steve wearing floppy hats to change his profile, we would be free to walk out of the hotel and roam the streets. We arrived late at night and went to bed, thinking that everything would be closed after nine o'clock.

After a continental breakfast, coffee, a muffin, and one piece of toast, which helped explain why French girls were so skinny, we set out to see the Champs-Elysees. This was a broad avenue about one and a quarter miles long with the Arch of Triumph at one end and the Louvre not far from the other end. It was lined with fine restaurants, movie theatres and expensive shops. French "anti-banalization" laws made it difficult for a foreign chain store to open anything here; it was nearly all French. Or, more accurately, it was nearly all Parisian, for the Champs-Elysees was the most expensive strip of land in Europe and the Parisians wanted it to remain so.

We walked casually down the avenue. Surprisingly, there were not that many people. We would have thought there would be no breathing room on this famous street. Where was everybody? Perhaps the people were all in the shops and restaurants. We'd check it out later.

Near the end of the avenue the buildings stopped and the street was lined with trees and lawns. Just a short distance away to the left was the famous Louvre, the world's most visited art museum. Immediately inside the door was the world famous Venus de Milo and the almost as famous Winged Victory of Samothrace, a headless statue of the winged goddess Nike. These were just in the entrance foyer!

We entered the main museum and wandered. Often we recognized a painting. In one large gallery were huge paintings including the huge one by David, *The Coronation of Emperor Napoleon,* which at a length of thirty feet would not fit well in your living room. There were some one hundred and fifty people standing in a church in this painting.

A museum map showed the way to the Mona Lisa. We'd expected a large painting but it was only thirty inches tall. Furthermore, it was in a recess in the wall covered over by a light absorbing darkened glass to protect it from flash cameras. It was not impressive, and there were only a few people looking at it, not a crowd as you'd think the world's most famous painting would attract.

We continued wandering around the museum until about noon. By then we'd had enough and went outside to take the short walk down to the Notre Dame Cathedral. It was smaller than we expected. It was basically a pile of stone erected around 1200 and the huge pillars holding up the roof didn't leave much room for the people. There were no pews; everybody had to stand. The artwork was pre-Renaissance and rather unspectacular after our visit to the Louvre. It was disappointing.

We left and found the subway system to go to the Eiffel Tower. The subway didn't drop us off at the tower, however, but a half mile away. By the time we walked up to the Tower we had already seen enough of it. But here we were, so we went up to the lower observation platform for a decent look at the city— which, however, was not much to look at. It was just unrecognizable buildings extending to the horizon. By now both of us were beginning to wonder what was the allure of Paris.

"Why do Americans visit Paris?" I asked.

"I don't know. Hype, I guess."

It was only a tired old city. American cities offered as much.

"I miss chipmunks," I said.

"Let's go find some."

"There aren't any in Europe. I checked."

"People must be crazy to live here without chipmunks."

"Exactly."

We returned to the Champs-Elysees and wandered around. After this we went to the hotel to cool off and wait for the nightlife. Maybe this disastrous trip could be saved yet. We were learning that when you go somewhere make sure there's something to do when you arrive.

We went out at nine. Now the Champs-Elysees was crammed with people. Crowds of the beautiful people filled the avenue. Paris, or at least this part of it, was a night town. We were looking for a nightclub of some kind but didn't find one, which made us wonder what these beautiful people did down here.

We found a second floor restaurant and went in. It was a large room, but instead of wrapping up supper, people were only now arriving. Many tables were still empty but filling up. This was what the Parisians did at night. They met friends and acquaintances at the restaurants for meals and conversation that lasted hours. The Champs-Elysees had just begun its evening. These people would not get home until three in the morning.

"Look at that," I said. "It's almost ten and they're just getting here."

"When do they sleep?"

We stood twenty feet from the door and waited politely to be conducted to a table. Four of the beautiful Parisians walked by us and without their even breaking stride a waitress met them as if by previous arrangement and led them to a table. We waited. Two minutes later another Parisian couple walked by us and were immediately led to a table. I noticed that all the women in the room were dressed in beautiful clothes while me and Steve were dressed in American casual, which these Parisians probably considered no better than potato sacks. Even Steve was beginning to notice this. "Don't worry, Myrtle" he said. "I'm sure Uncle Homer is feeding the cows while we're gone."

I noticed a man in tie and daytime jacket standing along the far wall. He was fully alert. Not a patron, apparently. When he saw me looking at him he looked away.

I looked around the room. There was another man standing discretely in a far corner, and another standing next to an emergency exit.

"There's security people all over the place" I said.

"I noticed. Looks like they don't get fed either."

"They must have followed us all day. How do they get in here?"

The minutes ticked by as other Parisians walked around us and were seated. Steve suggested, "Maybe American slobs are supposed to seat themselves."

"Let's try it."

We walked out on the floor passing twenty tables to arrive at an empty one close to the middle of the room. "Bonjours" said Steve to people next to us. We sat down.

The waitresses did not come. We smiled as we waited ten minutes, fifteen minutes, twenty minutes. The well-dressed patrons gave us frequent looks. We didn't feel welcome but we didn't care. This was an interesting and funny experiment in human psychology.

"Think they'd agree to throwing us a hot dog?" said Steve.

I looked around and thought I saw many more security people. I waved to one to invite him over. After a moment's hesitation he came to the secret Hartley table. "Yes, ma'am?"

"We want to fly to Dublin, Ireland in the morning. Ask them to have somebody who can show us around the city. We want to see people having fun."

The man left without a word.

"You know," Steve said, "I'm getting tired of this disguise." He took off his dark glasses and floppy hat.

"Me too," I said, and took off my dark glasses and let my hair down, shaking my head to make the famous mane spread out.

Yelps of astonishment and excitement came from around the room. The secret was out.

It was now impossible to remain in the restaurant. We would be mobbed. Steve took hold of my hand and said, "Come, my dear. We shall not dine here."

We got up and walked to the door giving friendly waves all the way. Steve said, "You all come visit us on the farm. Bring the kids. Bring your banjo. Take your shoes off. You hear?"

Ten security men met us at the door. There was no longer a reason to avoid getting ourselves noticed. We walked back to the hotel followed by a growing crowd of people. At the hotel the crowd had no excuse to go inside. They dispersed.

Early the next morning we were driven out to Charles de Gaulle Airport for an Aer Lingus flight to Dublin, Ireland. There was a crowd of gawking French to see us off. The curious kept quiet because they were embarrassed by our restaurant experience described by sullen broadcasters on French television. In Dublin we were met by Kathleen who would show us around town. This time I wanted to see people instead of museums and historical sights. Kathleen took us to wherever there were people: public parks, a street festival of sorts that was going on that day, and an afternoon outdoor concert of folk song groups. We were accompanied by a dozen security people wherever we went. The Irish got the idea. I wanted to see the old country without being mobbed. The crowds kept nearby but didn't crowd us.

Kathleen took us to a dancehall with large Irish folk singing groups dressed in traditional costumes. A part of the floor was kept clear for dancers. We tried out the Irish steps and a male and female couple from the singing group came down to give us lessons. People laughed at Steve's clumsiness. It was a fun evening.

By the third day in Ireland the crowds were getting too large to keep under control, so we had to go back to England. But the trip was a success. I had unwound. Now it would be back to work.

We got back to the Parker mansion around breakfast time. Mr. Parker and his family took me out in back of the house. Colonel James' soldiers were putting the finishing touches on a large animal enclosure. It was square shaped, eighty feet on the edge, with half inch metal screening on most of the walls and glass on some parts, vertical sheet metal on top of the walls to keep out small animals, a small tree in the center, piles of logs here and there, and little birdhouses on the ground with doors cut into them at ground level. Some parts of the walls had a roof to protect from sun and rain. There was an entrance consisting of an outer door and inner door. Opening and closing one at a time would prevent the animals' escape.

"What's this all about?" I asked Parker.

"Steve called when you were in Paris. He said you wanted chipmunks. They should arrive from America today."

That afternoon a courier brought in twenty-five chipmunks in ten cat transportation cages. They were released into the enclosure and they immediately disappeared into the piles of logs. I understood. Piles of logs made ideal winter homes for chipmunks. Deep inside there, they had a warm home in the winter, and they were safe from cats and dogs. It was their 'safe zone'. Somebody in America had lots of good advice.

"This is terrific, Mr. Parker. Thank-you a million times."

"It was Steve's idea, my dear."

I was very happy.

It was over three weeks since I told Mr. Blair I'd try to save everybody.

Chapter 10

I returned to the torture chamber to play the coin and hanging ruler games with HAL. This was definitely the most boring and frustrating thing I had ever done. It was like factory work, only especially irritating in that I was making no progress in a project of so much importance. Once more I was reminded of how my ambitions had been thwarted by events. It was not how I planned to spend my life.

After a morning of intense ennui, I walked to the bedroom to chill out. I stood in front of my life sized poster taped to the wall and stared at it. If I could have known what was ahead of me when I walked out of that elevator...........

I let myself collapse on the bed and stared at the ceiling for a moment. Then I closed my eyes. For a few minutes I lay there quietly. I opened my eyes.

There was a black thing halfway between my bed and the poster on the wall. It was an upright ill-shaped form about my height and width. It slowly undulated along its length as if trying to assume a more definite shape. I got up and fearfully looked at it. Recent experience taught my anything could happen with HAL. He might harm me unintentionally.

Looking at the form I realized HAL was trying to duplicate my appearance. He was doing a poor job of it. There was a knob on top which I assumed was supposed to be my head. Some protrusions on the sides might be my arms. The legs were wavy columns on the bottom. HAL might please an abstract painter but not a surrealist. There was no face; HAL wasn't that good an artist.

My fear was diminishing. HAL had never harmed me. His reflexes weren't designed to harm the host creature. However, there was no telling the bizarre situations on other worlds. Translated here they might be dangerous.

Suddenly the black shape moved forward and disappeared into me. It happened too fast for me to react.

Something was happening to my eyesight. The room blurred until I couldn't see it. Instead, I saw vague shapes. They changed in size and number. They were too indistinct to be recognizable. And then I noticed they were in black and white.

They looked like things I would see if I was in motion. I understood. HAL was showing me something. But what?

The vague shapes abruptly changed to sharp images of a building viewed from above. It was the roof of the Parker mansion. HAL had been showing me the underground rock formations but now had brought my view into the sky. The view continued to climb in the air. The Parker mansion became smaller and I could see the surrounding features. The view continued climbing in the air as if I were in a rocket going up to orbit. There were now hundreds of buildings and other features in view but getting too small to make out. I was, in a sense, far above the ground. The climbing continued. I made out the shape of England, then Europe, and finally the Western Hemisphere. I was looking at the Earth. HAL must have extended out to an enormous distance.

A new thought restored my fear. What if HAL did this forever? I'd be blind!

This horrible possibility made me unconsciously put my hands to my closed eyes. "My God! What will happen to me?"

I removed my hands and opened my eyes. I could see the room again! The black and white view of Earth was gone.

I thought about that. Yeah, this was another reflex. It made sense that if HAL had done this for creatures on other planets, he wouldn't have made it permanent, or they'd be blind too and starve to death for failing to find a meal.

Then I remembered the fall from the fighter jet. The first thing I'd done on getting out of the cockpit was cover my face with my arms to protect my eyes from the fast wind. I'd just taken two more plane rides in the last 48 hours. HAL was being prompted to adapt a new reflex. Putting my hands to my face completed this adaptation.

What would happen if I put my hands to my face again? I tried it. Upon opening my eyes I saw the black and white view of the Earth again. Once more I put my hands over my eyes. My normal vision of the bedroom returned.

That made sense too. But of what use was a view of the planet to a stupid creature on another world? Could the black and white view be modified?

I imagined a ten legged creature crawling around on another world. The only way it could get HAL to modify the view was by doing something with its front legs.

I put my hands to my eyes again and the black and white view of the world returned. Now I held my hands in front of my face and moved them around. The black and white view moved back and forth. Moving my hands closer brought the world closer. I dropped my hands and raised them again to move them close to my face. The view took off where it had left off, bringing me closer to the Earth. I repeated this procedure several times and found myself "coming down" so to speak to the coast of France. But I started over the Parker mansion. Why the lateral movement?

I moved my hands sideways and the view moved around. By many manipulations over several minutes I found myself looking at the roof of the Parker mansion again.

It did not seem like an overview would be of much use to a creature on another world. He wouldn't recognize what he was looking at. I tried twisting my hands until the angle of the black and white view changed. By lots more manipulation I got a view of the front of the house. An animal might take months to learn all this. I'd figured it out in a few minutes.

What if I moved the view closer to the mansion? I did more hand manipulations and the view seemed to penetrate the wall and show the interior. I could spy on anybody anywhere.

The usefulness of this thing was obvious. A hunting animal could more easily find food if it could see around trees and hills. It would be in HAL's basic repertoire of reflexes for helping out host creatures.

Steve had to hear about this. I went looking for

him.

"HAL is a lot more sophisticated than we thought" said Steve after I explained everything that happened in the bedroom.

"You'd expect that. HAL was evolving for billions of years before the Earth was formed. Think of how many kinds of eyes Earth creatures have."

"This started when you dropped on the bed?"

"Yeah."

"It's like when you dropped in the ocean. Let's see what we can do with that."

We went to the torture chamber to get the simple equipment I had been using and returned to the bedroom.

I sat on the bed and threw a coin at the can on the floor with my eyes open. The coin went in the can because the orange dot in my eye field was on the can. Then I threw a coin with my eyes shut. The coin missed the can. Next, I threw a coin with my eyes open to give HAL the idea. Now, I dropped back on the bed and threw a coin with my eyes shut. It went in the can.

"A new reflex" I said.

"Try it in the hall without the bed."

I moved the can to the hall and threw a coin at it with my eyes shut. The coin went in.

"Can you use that reflex to get HAL to do another one?"

I moved back in the bedroom and set up the table with the two glasses. I put a coin next to a glass and slid it towards the other glass while at the same time throwing a coin at the can with my eyes open. Then I repeated the procedure except that I let go of the coin at the glass while I threw a coin with my eyes shut. One coin went in the can and the other slid from one glass to the other. HAL moved it. Finally, I forgot about throwing a coin at the can and placed a coin next to the glass and let go. It slid to the other glass.

I looked at Steve triumphantly. "Did it!"

Steve could not have been prouder if I'd won the Miss Universe contest. "I'm writing a letter to Blair."

Peter Blair called an assembly of the House of Commons to give the announcement.

"I have received a letter from Mr. Steve Hartley containing important news. I will read it.

"'Dear Mr. Blair. I don't want anybody to get excited. There's still a long way to go. Theresa has made a major breakthrough with HAL today. He's responding. She's getting him to do new reflexes that have nothing to do with another world. She is controlling HAL at a simple level. This is only the first step in a long journey. There are a lot of details to work out. But the journey has begun. I don't want to talk about what she's doing in detail because someday somebody might want to take control. But I'm confident that she will succeed in solving our problem. By the way, this proves her theory about HAL was right on. Respectfully yours, Steve Hartley.'"

The members of the House stood up and cheered. Blair looked more relaxed than he'd been in a month. A lot had been said in the media about my mental state upon which the world's fate depended. It appeared to be in good condition. The trip to France and Ireland was a good sign, indicating I was still interested in things outside myself. Blair had talked to Edmund Parker about how Steve was bearing up to the pressure. He was doing well, reported Parker. It was clear that Steve's loyal support gave me emotional stability. "Thank God for Steve!" Blair told Parker.

The work of training HAL was now an exciting adventure instead of drudgery and I would have worked on it twenty hours a day if Steve didn't drag me away for some R&R.

I got HAL to perform a few more reflexes. Now there were new obstacles to overcome. One big one was that HAL couldn't read a clock. Time meant nothing to him. When I threw a baseball, the baseball's own speed through the air determined when and how fast he guided the ball to its target. Similarly for the other reflexes he'd done so far. But what if I were to get him to do something in another place, something I wasn't doing myself? How could I get him to do it at the right speed?

Steve drew a diagram and asked Arthur to have the object on the paper made by government workers. A few days later the object was delivered to the Parker place. It was a kind of clock, but instead of a fixed round face with moving hands, this clock had no moving hands and the two foot wide face spun around. A circle of one hundred pieces of one eighth inch thick wooden dowels were glued to the border of the face. Another piece of dowel was fixed on a mounting. When the pieces of dowel on the face passed the fixed dowel and were in alignment for an instant it was an event which I would get HAL to recognize. An electric motor turned the clock face once a second to divide a second into one hundred intervals. If I wanted HAL to move some large object I would get him to move it a hundred times a second over a period of time. I would get him to move it each time there was a "click' on the clock, one hundred times a second. This would continue until I told it to stop. Now I had to get HAL to respond to the thing. That would take some work.

Two other problems were related: identifying an object and identifying its location. The object in mind would be something some distance away from me, perhaps on the other side of the world. This was different from the reflexes I had gotten him to do up to now. Then the object and location was myself or something with which I was in physical contact. It would be necessary to get HAL to fool around with things in other places. To do this it would be necessary to set up a "tag" system so I'd identify the object and get HAL to manipulate it when I wanted.

Steve got to work gathering the equipment for a preliminary tag system. It would have to be simple. I might develop far more complicated tag systems later, but I had to begin somewhere.

Steve and Arthur drove to a nearby hardware store to buy dowels, electric drills, drill bits, four by four foot sheets of plywood, glue, small nails, large amounts of the little metal numerals used on home street number signs, and a circular saw. Arthur could go back some other time to get more supplies if needed. Then they went to a department store to buy wooden chess sets.

When Steve got back to the estate he went to work on the few supplies he'd carried out of the store. He put wooden chess pieces in the vise and drilled holes in their bottoms. He drilled similar holes in the middle of the squares of the chess board. He glued short pieces of dowel into the chess pieces. Now the chess pieces could be placed on the boards securely. The "tags" would be numbers glued along one edge of the chess board. HAL would have to be trained to feel these three dimensional numbers and associate them with an object somewhere.

As for identifying the location of the objects associated with the tags I would have to use triangulation. Another thing HAL couldn't do was count. I couldn't tell him to go 23 miles north and 14 miles east. I would have to get the government to drop markers at specific places around the world. HAL would be made to watch these markers. Knowing where these markers were, I could then use simple geometry to triangulate between these markers to specify an exact location. I could draw the geometric pattern needed on a piece of paper and HAL would match this pattern to the markers around the world.

These plans were all theories for the moment. Implementing them would be very difficult, but I had told the Prime Minister at our broadcast meeting that it would be. "I hope I don't die of old age before this job is done," I told Steve.

What about the chipmunks? I soon gained enough of their trust to feed them from my hand. What I did was lay a small rug on the ground in case there were little chipmunk poos I couldn't see, then I lay myself down on the rug with my forearms on the ground. This was a non-threatening position. The chipmunks came near out of curiosity and I finger snapped some nuts or pieces of cheese at them. In time I got them to eat out of my hand.

The Parkers had never seen this done and thought it was charming. They took videos of me feeding the little guys by hand and put them on several social media websites having the effect of ruling out copyrights. The videos were shown in every corner of the planet, especially on kid's programs which showed them every day.

I suppose people found the videos comforting. If I took care of little rodents, much more would I take care of people.

It had been seven weeks since I started working on the HAL problem. I had reached the point where it was necessary to more thoroughly address the twin problems of timing HAL's actions and identifying distance objects and their locations. Steve and Arthur drove to Number 10 Downing Street to show Peter Blair the simple rotating wheel he'd had made to serve as HAL's clock.

"We need four larger versions of this thing" Steve explained to Blair. "This little one doesn't divide a second into enough parts. HAL's motions are too choppy. We need clocks to divide a second into milliseconds."

"Why four?" asked the PM.

"We need at least one of them moving at all times. If all four stopped at once while HAL was doing something the results are unpredictable. We don't want to find out what happens."

"Must they be in synchronization?"

"In perfect synchronization. HAL needs only one of them at a time but there has to be at least one running at all times. I know this is a tough problem."

"I will have a large team work on it immediately."

Blair's scientists and engineers threw together the four clocks in two weeks. Steve went to look at them and was satisfied.

The problem of locating places anywhere in the world turned out to be simpler than Steve thought. At first, he thought we'd have to get the Navy to dump markers all over the oceans to allow me to triangulate them. It turned out I could just use my black and white vision and the tag system to fix HAL on immovable landmarks, the Golden Gate Bridge, Empire State Building, St. Peters, the Taj Mahal, Mount Fuji and anything else anywhere in the world I wanted HAL to do something.

We were making a lot of progress. Soon the world would see results.

By late July farmers all over the world were saying their crops were dying for lack of water. Irrigation alone wouldn't save them. There had to be some rain. The media never stopped talking about it. The pressure took its toll on me, but at least I now had the tools I needed to get HAL doing something larger and more interesting.

Chapter 11

It was nearly a month since our trip to Paris and Dublin and the oppression of being trapped in this luxurious prison was getting to me again. If people could see what I was doing here every day, manipulating HAL to spin a plate in the air, juggle four balls in the air, squirt water from a dish, they would think I was crazy. They wouldn't understand that I had to develop the parameters for controlling HAL one by one. As I explained it to Steve, I was trying to shoot an arrow without the bow. An archer aims the bow, not the arrow. The bow's rigid structure and the tension of the string determine where the arrow will go. I had to arrange for the arrow's movement by listing out all the parameters involved in three dimensions, in magnitude, and in time. Besides that, when I'd do something on a grand scale I'd have to factor in the curvature of the Earth's surface. Besides that, I'd have to take into consideration the speed of the Earth's rotation at the place I was doing something, a speed that differed for each latitude. And all that with a thing that couldn't count and couldn't read a clock. People had no idea of the complexity.

I missed Framingham. I remembered walking around town and out to the countryside. Even a simple thing like seeing a chipmunk by the road was a treat when you were young and had no responsibilities or worries. Why did I have to grow up?

I'd heard it said: life is what you think about all day. My life was getting pretty lousy. All I could think about was developing one more parameter for controlling HAL and the unthinkable consequences if I failed.

Even worse, I was conscious of how Steve suffered too. He wanted so much to help me. There was nothing for him to do except leave me alone. HAL was coming between us. I began to cry.

"If I don't get out of here I'll lose my mind."

Now I was talking to myself! That was it. It was time to get out of the house before I went completely loony.

I walked down the grand staircase to the ground floor. Nobody was in sight. I went through the backdoor behind the staircase and headed straight for the rear forest. The soldiers hidden in the woods recognized me immediately and alerted Colonel James.

Steve and I had visited the headquarters in the woods. There were twelve television screens and the woods had hundreds of cameras covering every square inch. The headquarters people could switch the cameras' views to watch somebody's movements through the woods. Colonel James said a squirrel couldn't move through tree branches without headquarters seeing it.

I went deeper and deeper into the woods. Headquarters must have wondered if I was going to go straight through the forest and head for the nearby village. That's exactly what I was doing, and when this was realized there must have been panic at headquarters.

I reached the edge of the woods and walked out onto the open fields. A collection of four hundred homes were a half mile away. The surrounding land was bare fields. That's how the Europeans did things. Houses were gathered close together and large tracts of open land were a two minute walk away.

I heard vehicles behind me. I saw what looked like Humvee convertibles filled with soldiers. So much for getting off alone! They moved slowly in time with my walking but kept a hundred yards back.

A few minutes later I reached the village and walked down a street. The homes' architecture had a startling similarity. Perhaps this was a development. The colors were muted beige earthy tones with red shingle roofs. There were no American style wooden houses. The Europeans built homes out of masonry to last for centuries.

A couple of people were on their front lawns. At first they didn't recognize me and I continued walking down the street. When I'd gone by a dozen homes I heard somebody yell, "Mother! Come quickly! Look who's out here." I looked in the direction of the voice. It was a teenage girl looking at me with wide open eyes. The mother came out and also recognized me. She ran to the neighbor's house.

As I walked slowly along the street more people came out onto their small front lawns. I didn't have any destination in mind. I was simply exploring the village. Now, people were running over from distant houses. Word was spreading quickly. A crowd followed me at a respectful distance at my sides. I noticed one of the British Army's Humvees parked at a corner of a street connecting to the street I walked on. There was another one parked down the opposite street. And, there were two more vehicles moving slowly behind me a short distance behind the crowd. The British Army was taking no chances with the world's most important citizen. As I continued along I saw more and more army vehicles. The village was full of soldiers.

This safari was interrupted. A sixty-ish but vigorous woman came out to the street and shouted, "We're having a picnic. Mrs. Hartley is guest of honor."

People cheered and went off in different directions. Odd they did that!

"I'm Juliet Graham, dear," the grand dame said to me. "Won't you join us?" She showed the way with her hands. I smiled and walked in the indicated direction. I entered the woman's backyard. There was a kind of picnic table there, a long table with benches placed alongside. I was invited to sit down next to people Mrs. Graham's age. I sat, wondering what would develop from this.

About a dozen of the townspeople gathered around the table. Mrs. Graham said, "They'll all be here soon. Eat up while there's plenty, dear."

I helped myself to some chicken, potato salad and soda. More people were arriving. Then someone brought in a folding card table and placed it at the end of the picnic table. Another folding table was brought in. I got it. This was not a spontaneous community response to my visit but a routine. Mrs. Graham shouted "picnic" and the people came. Food was brought in from parts unknown and spread on the tables. People freely grabbed whatever they wanted. In ten minutes there were over a hundred people crowded into the Graham backyard.

I did no talking. The community sensed that that was not why I came. They didn't try to draw anything out of me.

I noticed a mid-thirties man standing to my right at the outskirts of the crowd. He was fully alert and all business, not someone here to enjoy the society. He wore a loose fitting jacket despite the heat. I was sure he had an Uzi machine gun under his jacket. I spotted another guard to my left. And another was in front of me at a discreet distance. All these guys kept a clear view of me. If anybody made a sudden move in my direction it might be his last.

Of course the villagers could recognize strangers. They knew these men were gunmen ready to shoot in an instant. They said nothing about it. I noticed that mothers were keeping their children away from these men.

This would be my life from now on. I'd be kept alive only as long as government people could keep the assassins away. I had done nothing to anyone, but a lot of crackpots wanted to kill me for whatever it gave them.

When the eating slowed down the impromptu entertainment began. Mrs. Graham went through her repertoire of stories collected over forty years.

"I bought an antique car. Mr. Graham said I paid too much for it. I spent my money foolishly. We drove it on a holiday to Plymouth. Holiday means vacation trip in American." That was intended for me. I laughed along with everybody. "A man there liked my car. He made me an offer I couldn't resist and I sold the car. I told Mr. Graham the profit paid for the holiday twice over."

The people laughed on cue. They'd heard all these homely stories before but that wasn't important.

When Mrs. Graham's repertoire ran out a ten year old girl was invited to sing *The Sun Will Come Out Tomorrow*. Then a couple of college aged girls with guitars sang *Greensleaves*. Six ladies in their sixties had their own little glee club of sorts and sang *Nearer My God To Thee* and other old fashioned tunes. This was cliché upon cliché. But unlike snobs who would look down on this small-town conviviality, I understood that what they were doing didn't matter as much as the fact they were doing it. These people were a community. They got together for no other reason than being a community. It was exactly what I needed today.

There was one woman who actually was a semi-professional singer. She made occasional appearances at nearby theatres and nightspots. She sang an Academy Award winning song called *Morning After* from a 1972 movie about a shipwreck disaster.

"There's got to be a morning after
If we can hold on through the night……..."

I didn't remember hearing this song before. It greatly affected me. The semi-pro singer knew her audience.

After two hours of this casual socializing Colonel James walked into the yard and spoke to me.

"Mrs. Hartley. We've been keeping the television cameras away at your husband's request, but the traffic is becoming too much to manage. Many people are trying to see you. They abandon their cars to walk here. We can't hold them all back. The area will be overrun."

I got the message. "Okay. I'll go."

I got up and waved to all. "Good-by everybody. Thanks for a wonderful time. The work I do all day is inhuman. I was going nuts. You reminded me of what it's about."

I got into the Colonel's vehicle and returned to the Parker house. Steve met me at the door. He smiled. My experience in the town had been reported back to the Parker house and Steve was kept informed of the proceedings.

"You know what you've done, don't you?" he said. "You made that Mrs. Graham a national hero."

"You didn't want to come over?"

"I guessed that's not what you wanted."

"That's why I love you."

It was August 30, over two months since my televised talk with the Prime Minister. President Stinson called her cabinet together to assess the situation. Right after that the Secretary of Agriculture announced that the year's crop was a ninety percent failure. Since most of the rest of the world had less irrigation technology than the United States, it had to be as bad for them too. Without adequate food stores hundreds of millions of people would die before next year's harvest.

Conscious of what was at stake, people around the world were still filling the churches, synagogues, mosques, and temples. There was a feeling of calm in the world. Yes, the future was full of danger, but the word was out. Millions of people held posters repeating something Prime Minister Blair had said to another session of Questions to the Prime Minister. He'd said, "Theresa is at work and God is in control". Somehow this quote resonated with the people. "God is in control" became the universal mantra. I couldn't agree more. Maybe God answered the prayer I made after the Sunday night meeting with Blair asking God to help me get through this. We'd soon learn how much help he gave me.

Of course, atheists said nobody was in charge. They were materialists. There was nothing supernatural. Yeah, well, if their thoughts were nothing more than the chance interactions of atoms going back to the Big Bang, then their own thoughts couldn't be trusted. They couldn't believe their own opinions. One of my BC teachers told me that.

I was ready to attempt my first large manipulation of HAL. I set up all the parameters on a four by four foot piece of plywood. HAL could "read" symbols that had three dimensions. I twisted pieces of wire into the shapes of the HAL parameter codes I had devised. I was gradually replacing the little metal street numbers with wires which worked as well. The code was triplets made of three characters: AB2, AB3, AB4, CAA, DBB, and so on. Only I knew the code. It couldn't be broken by all the intelligence agencies in the world because they represented actions and locations, not words. Besides that, I threw in some useless dummy parameters to confuse anybody looking over my shoulder. To pound the final nail in the coffin, I randomly surrounded the parameter codes with tiny circles, squares, rectangles, and arrows that meant nothing. There was no way the code could be broken because much of the stuff was junk and position meant nothing as it did in other code systems. Each triplet represented a single parameter. Each was placed on a square on the plywood. Some parameters could be quantified by rows of short pieces of wire placed near the parameter triplet. There was also a tag number made of the metal street numbers. This task was tagged 00000187. To Steve and Arthur these instructions looked like gobblygook.

Steve watched me move my hands along the borders of the plywood starting at the middle of the top and working my way down to the bottom. This was the signal to HAL to carry out the task described by the 255 parameter symbols on the board. He did so immediately.

In my experimentation with HAL I'd found out that it was easier to get HAL to pull something than push it. It was analogous to pulling a string rather than pushing. I got the idea when Steve mentioned that gravity doesn't pull things down. Rather, it pushed things down from above. If gravity pushed instead of pulled then HAL could pull instead of push. With the task initiated HAL moved his "stuff", whatever that was, to a spot thirty miles off Gloucester, Massachusetts. This historic fishing city was on a peninsula jutting out from the Northern part of Massachusetts. I used the Prudential Center in Boston and two other landmarks on Cape Cod and Long Island to triangulate on this spot. I did this by drawing the triangle to scale on a piece of plywood, drawing lines between the three landmarks and sticking a pin on the exact spot within this triangle to correspond to the target area. I had trained HAL to match this diagram on the actual full sized triangle on the Earth. Using the black and white view HAL provided, I confirmed HAL had zeroed in on the right area and assigned a tag number to it. Finally, I arranged the wire parameter symbols on a plywood board to have HAL zero in on the target, and initiated the action by tracing my fingers around the board's borders.

Fishing boats off the Gloucester coast were startled to see a ten foot wide column of water rising from the ocean. This water column was rising two hundred miles an hour. Word spread quickly, and people on land with good eyesight could see the column rising from thirty miles away. When the column reached a height of ten miles it wouldn't go up any further. The water poured out and fell under the influence of gravity. Water falling from such a height was soon torn apart by air resistance into fine mist. A cloud formed around the top. Other than this cloud, it looked like any vertical fountain in a European castle's gardens but it was a giant.

This was really spectacular, and the media splashed it onscreen. Crowds jammed Gloucester. Thousands of boats went out to see the fountain close up. There was little danger because the fountain stayed in one place and the water came down as a light rain. Of course, some fools wanted to get close enough to touch the water column. The Coast Guard positioned small boats around the column to keep the thrill seekers away. Adding to their foolishness some shot arrows into the column of water to see what happened. The arrows were taken up into the ascending water and eventually fell back down somewhere. The Coast Guard had to stop this nonsense too before somebody was hurt.

The world's gloom and doom of the last two months turned to optimism. "Theresa is delivering on her promise in spades" said President Stinson at a press conference, forgetting that I had promised nothing. "I believe she will solve the rain problem soon."

A week passed with nothing new happening. I was working on my most ambitious project yet.

To do this I used one of Steve's wooden chessboards. Holes had been drilled in each square of the board. Quarter inch pieces of dowel were glued in holes drilled in the bottoms of chess pieces. I placed six chess pieces in the middle of the board and glued a tag number on one edge of the board. The number matched an identical number on a sheet of plywood on which I had attached over three hundred parameters. Now I selected a location: the Pacific equator directly South of Hawaii. I did the triangulation routine to fix the place to the tag number. I traced the plywood borders with my hands to start it off.

In the center of the Pacific six water columns rose up. They were not ten feet wide but each one hundred feet wide and located a hundred yards apart. They rose at two hundred miles an hour.

These fountains were large enough to be seen a thousand miles away by commercial jets. Pilots plotted courses to stay a safe distance and radioed the news to airports. The U.S. Navy immediately launched a plane from Hawaii to investigate. Before long, a live long distance shot of these six water columns was on television. I couldn't be blamed for being proud enough of myself to wear a big smile. "Not bad," said Steve.

The water columns climbed for 45 minutes to reach a height of 150 miles. At that point the water fell off the columns and started a free fall. The water dropped rapidly through a near perfect vacuum. A few minutes later it hit the denser atmosphere at thirty-eight miles. The impact instantly turned the water to steam which spread out rapidly. The steam thinned out and disappeared from view some eight miles from the columns. Immense quantities of water were being put into the atmosphere.

The media brought in scientific consultants who said I was using more energy every few hours than the human race had used since Adam and Eve.

"Look at what's happening" said a scientist. "The weight of five million Boeing 747s moving straight up two hundred miles an hour. The power requirement is almost beyond calculation."

President Veronica Stinson was reported as saying, "My God! How do we deal with a person like that?"

The Secretary of State told her, "You don't say a word and hope she doesn't notice you".

Peter Blair was just coming back from his weekly meeting with the King at Buckingham Palace when he heard of the Pacific fountains and what it took to make them work. He cheerfully told reporters, "We all work for Empress Theresa now. The new Jupiter throws thunderbolts". The reporters laughed.

Not everybody was so easily amused. The talking heads warned about what would happen if all the water in the six Pacific water columns was to suddenly fall back to Earth. A scientist said, "If these water columns collapsed the crash would be tremendous. We'd see tsunamis rolling over the coastlines all around the Pacific. It would be far worse than anything we've seen with tsunamis caused by earthquakes. A hundred million people could die."

I raised my eyebrows. "They're not going to fall."

"Bunch of worrywarts!" said Steve.

More negative reactions came from China. The Chinese President gave a speech condemning the water columns as too little too late. They were not introducing that much water into the atmosphere. Furthermore, China faced the coming winter with inadequate food stocks. He demanded to know my plans. He demanded that I go to the United Nations and give an official statement for the record.

The Chinese President's demand was repeated throughout the media over the next 24 hours. Everybody was asking, "What is Theresa planning?"

"Maybe I should go to the United Nations and give them the program" Steve suggested to me.

"Might be a good idea" I agreed. "Everything seems to be working."

Steve got up and found Arthur.

"Arthur. I want to fly to New York tonight. I'm speaking at the UN."

This might have been a little grandstanding on Steve's part, but that was forgivable. This could be his last chance to hold the spotlight.

Chapter 12

With the Prime Minister's help Steve got a seat on a British Airlines flight to New York. He was driven by an Army sedan to Heathrow Airport for the 11:17 p.m. flight. Television cameras followed his every move through the airport and reporters asked for details of my plans. Steve smiled and didn't answer.

I went to bed still filled with anxiety. I'd gotten one set of water columns up. My plan called for two hundred sets all over the world. Could HAL handle that much? If not, then kiss your butt good by, everybody. I had no backup plan.

Sometime in the night I heard Arthur pounding frantically on my bedroom door.

"Madam! Awake! Awake!"

He knocked again and repeated the message.

I became alert. "What is it?"

"The North Koreans are bombing your water columns. The President wants to speak to you."

"Holy crap! I'm going to my work room. Transfer the President there."

Arthur raced to my third floor work room where I did my manipulation of HAL. A phone had many preset push buttons one of which tied into the house line. Arthur pushed.

"Are you there, Madam President?"

"Yes."

"Madam Hartley is here."

I arrived only two seconds after he connected to the President. I grabbed the phone.

"What the hell is going on?"

"The North Koreans launched a missile at your water columns. We must assume it's nuclear. What will happen if it hits HAL?"

"I don't know."

I didn't know. What would happen if HAL suffered a direct hit by a nuclear weapon? Would he be destroyed? Would he have the wind knocked out of him for a while?

The President added, "You've heard what will happen if those water columns fall?"

"Yeah. We lose a hundred million people."

"Can you stop the missile?"

"No."

"Can you get HAL out of there?"

"Yeah. All I have to do is make him withdraw his support of the columns."

"Can you keep the water from falling if you get HAL out of there?"

"No."

"We're running out of options, Theresa."

"How much time before the bomb hits?"

"Four minutes."

Four minutes to make an impossible decision! I looked around as if there were help somewhere.

"What do you think, Arthur?"

"We can't afford to lose HAL, madam."

The truth was simple. I could not allow HAL to be destroyed or damaged. But that meant condemning millions. My hand would be the instrument of mass destruction.

"Arthur says get HAL out of there" I told the President.

"Then we lose a hundred million people?"

"Might beat the alternative."

"How do you know HAL would be harmed?"

"I don't."

"A tough decision, Theresa!"

It was, and the President was leaving it up to me.

"She left it up to me, Arthur."

"She leaves you room to think, madam."

"Think about what?"

"Three minutes" said the President.

My eyes winced and I started to cry. Try as I might I couldn't think of anything. There were no more options. There was nothing to be done. It was hopeless. Panic was setting in. I was losing it.

"Of all times for this to happen" I wailed. "Steve's not here."

Arthur said, "They did that to unnerve you, madam. Hah!" He pulled his shoulders back in the British manner and gave me a wide confident smile. It worked. I calmed down and let my mind clear itself.

"Two minutes."

I looked at the chessboard used to control this task. If I removed the six chess pieces, the water columns would stop beginning from the bottom, while the water that had already risen into the air would continue to go up to an altitude of 150 miles. But would HAL still be in the missile's path? I didn't know. After considering for a while I rejected the idea.

"One minute."

I thought. What if I laid the plywood board flat

and removed one of the metal street address numbers making up the tag number? Then HAL might stop the task immediately. Maybe. Or maybe not. Then if I replaced the numeral............?

"I have an idea. If it doesn't work we can say the butler did it. Give me a countdown."

I handed the phone to Arthur who understood he was to pass on the countdown. I raced to my desk to get a metal letter opener. Then I laid the plywood board flat and got ready to pry up the last numeral of the tag number glued to the board. The glue was weak; it would be easy to remove the numeral.

"Thirty seconds" said Arthur.

I was ready for the most desperate act of my life whose success I couldn't guess.

"Twenty-five seconds."

"Tell her to give me individual seconds."

"Twenty, nineteen, eighteen, seventeen, sixteen, fifteen, fourteen, thirteen, twelve, eleven,...."

I pried up the last numeral.

HAL stopped pulling up the water columns. The rising water slowed down. In ten seconds it had decelerated its 200 hundred miles an hour uprising to nothing and started to fall.

"Zero seconds" said Arthur.

The bomb exploded. A cloud of steam hundreds of yards wide was visible to the Navy ship near the scene.

I put the numeral back on the board.

HAL started raising six new water columns. In a few seconds they collided with the water falling down. The force HAL was using was much greater than needed and the new water columns continued rising even into the collision with the falling water. There was no stopping them.

The point of collision of the two opposing watery forces rose up at 200 mph. The splash turned all of the falling water to the side at high speed. The falling water was spread out to a large area in the form of a heavy rain. It looked like a liquid umbrella reaching down to the ocean. Spread out as drops in this way the water did not have the calamitous impact that the water columns would have had. There were trillions of tiny drop impacts rather than one big slam of a massive quantity.

"How's it going?" I asked the President. I couldn't see what was happening.

"I'm not sure I understand what the Navy is saying. The water stopped rising and now it's rising again."

"All of it?"

"No. Some is going up and some coming down. There's a big splash where they meet."

"That's what I wanted. How long before the tsunami gets to Hawaii?"

"Less than an hour."

"Call me."

I hung up.

There was nothing to do but wait. I simply stared into space. Arthur loyally sat nearby. It took a little less than ten minutes for the last of the falling water to reach the ocean. Time had never passed so slowly.

The phone rang fifty minutes later. It was President Stinson.

"Good news, Theresa. No tsunami came to Hawaii. The rest of the Pacific must be safe. How did you do it?"

"I stopped the water columns for a moment and restarted them after the bomb. The collision broke the fall of the earlier water. It was a rainfall."

"That's what the Navy is saying. Congratulations. It was brilliant."

"Yeah, well, I'm taking a day off. This night killed me."

I hung up. Arthur was proudly beaming.

"You're off the hook, Arthur" I smiled.

There was one more task. I removed the six chess pieces from the board. HAL stopped raising the water columns from the bottom. The Navy got the strange experience of seeing the bottomless columns rising up in the air.

In 45 minutes the task would be closed down. North Korea could send all the bombs they wanted.

I was still trying to fall back to sleep an hour later when Arthur knocked on the door again. He said Prime Minister Blair was coming to talk to me.

What? Blair at four o'clock in the morning?

I got dressed and went downstairs where Mr. and Mrs. Parker were waiting with Arthur in the living room. We said nothing until Blair arrived.

The Prime Minister explained North Korea's insane action.

"From the viewpoint of the North Koreans their action made perfect sense. Destroying HAL and causing a tsunami of all the Pacific coasts would severely damage the economies of its enemies, South Korea, Japan, and the United States. It can be predicted that the United States would not destroy the North Korean people it being a humanitarian nation. The United States might wash its hands of foreign involvements and abandon its long-time defense of South Korea. The North would then be in a position to conquer the South. They also thought the bomb would destroy HAL and restore the wind. They would appear heroes. This would cancel out blame for the effects of the tsunami."

I pondered this for a few moments. The hunger for gain destroyed common sense.

"Too bad I can't wash my hands of foreign involvement. I didn't want this job."

"We do understand your position. It's grossly unfair."

I had blocked it out of my mind earlier, but now it hit me.

"I was planning on raising a thousand water columns all over the world. It would put enough water in the air to cause rain. Now I can't do that. If somebody sent off ten missiles at once I couldn't keep up. A bomb might kill HAL and the columns would send tsunami waves everywhere. We could lose two billion people."

I was already starting to cry when the Prime Minister asked, "What will you do?"

"There's nothing I can do. There's no other way to make rain. All that worrying for nothing. The idiots won't let me save them."

With that I really broke down. Mrs. Parker rushed over to hold me as I had a meltdown. She took me upstairs and consoled me until I calmed down.

I slept a few hours and woke up still miserable. The feeling of failure and all that meant weighed on me.

I checked the tube. Prime Minister Blair had given

a statement to the press hours ago.

"Early this morning I spoke with Mrs. Hartley about last night's incident. She was very upset. I suggest our main concern is Mrs. Hartley now. I urge the world's leaders to say nothing until we see what Mrs. Hartley does or doesn't do. President Stinson has assured me she will not speak of this matter."

In other words, everybody was afraid of what I would do next. That's why Blair came to see me in the middle of the night.

It was kind of amusing in a strange way to watch the media commentators nervously talk about the North Korean bomb and how I foiled it. They were very grim faced and carefully avoided speculating about what I would do. HAL had not been destroyed. I still had the power. Don't piss me off!

When Steve arrived in New York he grabbed the next flight back to London. He got back to the Parker mansion nearly twenty hours after leaving. It was already evening. I was waiting with a glum face when he strutted into the room very proud of himself.

"I have a new plan" he said with obvious pride. "You'll really love this one."

It took me five days to throw together a new plywood sheet with all the needed parameters of a new task. Then I started the first of two tasks.

Two hours before dawn the British people heard a very faint rumbling sound. Barely audible, it sounded like the movement of a large amount of earth. It didn't go away.

The news channel jumped on the story. Seismologists said there was much ground vibration around the North Pole. It wasn't an earthquake; there were no waves in the bedrock radiating outward. Instead, there was some kind of disturbance in the bedrock around the Pole. No effects had yet been seen on land.

Blair sent Royal Air Force planes to the North Pole.

A few hours went by. The Air Force arrived at the scene and sent back live video. The ice in a thin one hundred and fifty mile wide circle surrounding the Pole was being cracked and broken up by some submarine force. In time the circle of disrupted ice became two concentric circles approximately twenty miles from each other.

The Americans also sent out their planes and the White House said President Stinson watched the screen constantly.

Early in the afternoon something rose up from the fractured ice. It was a mound of rocks broken up into enormous pieces larger than houses, some breaking up even as they rose. It soon became apparent that these mounds of rocks were rising up completely around the two concentric circles. Nobody could guess how many trillions of tons of rock were rising up. No wonder there was a rumbling in the Earth. I was pushing up the rock by using HAL as a bulldozer as I had once referred to him. Making HAL apply pressure at many points along the circles automatically broke the rock up into house sized pieces because the pressure was applied to curvatures, not straight lines.

Planes from several nations flew here and there and established that the concentric circles of rock mounds were not complete. They were made of curved sections some five miles long with one mile gaps between them. Soon, it was noticed that the inner and outer curved rock mounds were placed so that the one mile gaps in one circle faced the center of the rock mounds in the other circle. A ship that wanted to sail to the North Pole would have to enter through a gap in the outer circle, turn 90 degrees to sail a couple miles between the circles, and find an inner circle gap to get to the Pole.

The curved rock mounds continued to rise until they reached a half mile above the ocean. Commentators pointed out that the Arctic Ocean was only a half mile deep which made this piling up of rock easier for me to do then it would be in the three mile deep Atlantic. Then the process changed somewhat. The outer incomplete circle thickened outward and the inner circle mounds thickened inwards. This required HAL's applying his forces from a greater distance. This fascinating process continued for four more hours until the rock mounds were half a mile above the water and five miles thick from inside to outside. The surface of the mounds were very rough like granite stone levies built to protect shore lines. Planes and helicopters could never land there. Then, everything stopped.

What were these rock mounds for? everybody wondered.

"They're barriers to absorb tsunamis" said the PM to the press. "Look how any wave that gets through the inner circle gaps will be absorbed by the outer circle. Theresa will raise water columns at the North Pole."

He was right. It was clear to everyone. For once they knew what I would do ahead of time. Everybody was relieved that I wasn't doing something dangerous like going after the North Koreans.

Steve found the butler.

"Arthur. Call the Prime Minister and tell him to get everybody out of there. Anybody foolish enough to stay within seventy-five miles of the North Pole does so at his own risk. Theresa can't save their miserable necks. She's too busy to play nursemaid to fools."

"Very good, sir."

The PM passed the word and all weather station scientists were evacuated. Two days were required to do this.

In the morning when the last of the North Pole scientists were being flown out in ski planes, I went to work on a new phase of the project. Steve set up one of his chessboards with a tag number. I placed four chess pieces in the middle of the board and moved my hands along the borders of a sheet of plywood with the three dimensional parameters associated with the chessboard tag number. HAL began raising four water columns, each three hundred feet wide and rising two hundred miles an hour. This event was immediately detected by the planes.

It was quickly pointed out that four columns weren't enough to bring rain to the world. I was doing something else. Everybody had to wait.

Five hours went by. The water columns reached a height of one thousand miles. At this point I removed the last digit of the tag number on the chessboard. As he had done in the North Korean bomb incident, HAL stopped his support of the water columns.

The water columns fell. For the first few minutes

there was an enormous splash in the ocean as the water crashed down at ever increasing speed. Huge waves spread out but settled down as their impulses were translated into rapidly moving tsunami forces. As the highest parts of the water columns fell their greater speeds caused them to be broken up into mist, and then finally heated to steam, so that there was no longer a giant splashing at the ocean surface. About the time all the water had fallen the first impulses reached the insides of the inner rock circle. The waves climbed high up the side of the inner rock mounds to nearly the top, but did not spill over. The waves settled back down to nearly nothing; the first impulses were bouncing back to counteract with and cancel out the newer impulses still radiating from the Pole. In eighteen minutes it was all over. Everything was quiet.

The experiment was a success. The rock circles had suffered no damage. I knew they could take a much harder hit.

The world's anxiety about the Korean missile fiasco dissipated. I had not declared war on North Korea. I had turned my attention to the North Pole.

Steve's promise that when I got control of HAL I'd do giant actions had been fulfilled. In only a few weeks I'd done four spectacular feats: the small water column near Gloucester, Massachusetts, the six larger columns in the Pacific, the North Pole rock mound circles, and the four 1,000 mile high water columns.

The world waited for my next move.

Chapter 13

We woke up at eight. Since this was the big one, the action that would bring rain to the world and save everybody's lives, I felt the event should be shared with the Parker household. We brought the chessboard and related sheet of plywood down to the living room and invited the Parker family and Arthur to watch history in the making.

The chessboard I used to control the North Pole water columns had sixty-four squares. The tag number on one edge of the board used up eight squares leaving fifty-six squares vacant. I put chess pieces on all fifty-six squares. Then I replaced the last digit of the tag number that matched the parameters on the plywood sheet. The last step was to move my hands along the borders of the plywood to initiate the process. I did so.

We watched the television screen showing the North Pole where the water columns would rise. A minute went by.

Nothing happened.

Steve and I looked at each other with puzzled expressions. Always another surprise we didn't want!

A second minute passed and there was still nothing. Steve said, "This is very annoying."

It was a standard expression of his which he used when there was some outrage on the news. He was trying to put humor in a situation far worse than annoying. This was alarming.

"What should I do?" I asked.

"Nothing. Wait a while."

There was nothing wrong with the parameters I laid out on the plywood sheet. I used the same parameters the day before to raise the four experimental columns. The only change I made was to the maximum height the fifty-six columns would reach. That should have no negative effect.

The Parkers looked embarrassed but said nothing. Arthur kept a stiff upper lip. I was becoming depressed again. HAL drove me crazy.

"I did everything correctly," I claimed. "In this world perfection isn't good enough."

A half hour had gone by with no water columns. Steve broke the horrible silence. "We'll try again tomorrow" he said and got up to remove the fifty-six chess pieces from the board. He looked at Edmund Parker and managed a little smile. "Back to the drawing board."

I asked one of those questions that make the heart stop.

"Could HAL know what I'm doing?"

Steve's eyes opened wide. What I said was terrifying. At the moment when I asked HAL to do something that would fix the problem I'd been working on all summer, the rain problem, HAL failed to perform. He'd never failed to perform anything before.

A shaken Steve addressed Edmund Parker.

"If this gets out it will cause global panic."

Edmund Parker understood. "We will be silent."

The chess set and plywood sheet went back upstairs to my workroom where I double checked all the parameters. There was nothing wrong with them. Something had been overlooked.

That evening Peter Blair called Mr. Parker to ask if there had been any developments in the Parker household. He said he couldn't speak on the phone. Blair asked if he could visit in the morning.

Shortly after ten the following morning, Peter Blair arrived in his limousine. His visit to the Parker mansion had been noted on the news and Steve and I were told he was coming.

Edmund Parker took Blair into his private first floor den and explained what happened the previous day. The PM was very worried. If HAL was refusing to cooperate there was no hope.

"All may be lost," he said to Parker.

A few minutes before eleven we brought the chessboard and plywood back down to the living room. Steve thought that perhaps HAL would initiate something new only from the third floor workroom where I had done all my work with HAL. This possibility had to be ruled out, so we went back to the living room.

There was no talking. The atmosphere was too oppressive. Steve signaled to Arthur to have a seat nearby. He thought it was rude to expect Arthur to leave. He'd been a loyal supporter.

The television was turned on to the view of the North Pole constantly being provided by military planes. I put fifty-six chess pieces on the chessboard. Then I traced the borders of the plywood with my hands.

HAL began raising fifty-six water columns at the North Pole. The observers in the planes were surprised enough to exclaim the rudest expletives. Seeing the fifty-six columns in person was far more thrilling than seeing them on the television screen.

We all smiled with relief. HAL was cooperating.

We sat down as the columns continued to rise. We watched this exciting scene for a few minutes. Then, Steve gave his theory.

"This requires a lot more force than HAL has ever used. He wasn't ready to do it yesterday. He had to go get more power."

"From where?" asked the PM.

"The sun. I've suspected it for some time. HAL couldn't get it from Earth. There's nothing on Earth large enough to give HAL the momentum he needs. It can't be the moon's momentum because HAL has been raising that small water column near Gloucester, Massachusetts. That should use enough power to change the moon's orbit a tiny amount. Astronomers haven't noticed that. It can't be other planets because the planets are on the wrong side of the sun half the time. It can only be the sun. You have giant hurricanes racing around there all the time. They're big enough to blow away the Earth in a minute. Plenty of power for HAL"

"This is most remarkable!"

"If you think about it, you can see it can't work any other way. A lot of stars have no planets. HALs that wandered into a system like that would be trapped there forever unless they could use the star's power to send themselves back out into space. They couldn't spread through the universe and get to Earth."

"HAL must have infinite power."

"You bet. The sun converts five million tons of

matter to energy every second. That's like burning a million Saudi Arabian oil reserves every few minutes."

But I needed to unwind. "I'm going for a walk in the woods."

"I'll join you," said Steve.

The North Pole water columns reached a height of a thousand miles at four o'clock. People thought I'd let them pour off at that point. Nope! They continued going higher.

At nine o'clock they reached two thousand miles and kept rising. Steve and I went to bed at eleven. Mr. Parker called Blair to note this fact and Blair leaked out that nothing would happen tonight. Everybody could go to bed.

At seven the next morning the water columns reached four thousand miles and kept rising up. The media was going nuts wondering how long this would go on.

Noon was coming near. We sat in the living room with the entire Parker family waiting for the columns to reach five thousand miles. Steve mentioned that would be the maximum height. Mr. Parker asked if he could call PM Blair and tell him. "Sure. Why not?" Steve said. Within minutes the news was on the air.

The water columns were actually ice columns. A hundred miles above the Earth there was only a trace of air molecules. The temperature was—actually, there was no temperature—because there was no matter to hold heat. Infrared radiation poured out of the columns. The water quickly froze solid.

Noon arrived. According to the banner at the bottom of the television screen, the height was five thousand miles. This could not be measured exactly.

In addition, the manner in which I had to pass parameters to HAL was not precise so that even I didn't know the true height.

The television banner soon read 5,012 miles. The ice in the columns was as hard as rock, and beyond the point at which HAL stopped providing support, the columns might stand up on their own for up to a mile. Finally, telescopes provided a faint image of the top of the column complex spreading apart. The ice columns could stand up no more on their own and were breaking apart.

"Approximately twenty-four minutes for the water to reach the Earth" noted one of the media's scientific consultants.

"How fast will the water be falling when it reaches Earth?" he was asked.

"Seven and a half miles a second."

"Doesn't that exceed the Earth's escape velocity?"

"Escape velocity and falling velocity work differently. Meteors come in at twenty miles a second."

"That should be an interesting spectacle."

"Very much so. No missile travels anywhere near that fast. Think of getting hit by a mountain moving faster that the fastest missile."

The military planes had telescopes that could barely capture the widening of the column complex falling down. This was the shower of fractured ice falling parallel to the columns. As the ice fell it was possible to estimate its height more and more accurately.

Only minutes remained until the re-entry of the ice into the atmosphere. I felt a tingle in my spine.

Time was up. A voice from one of the English planes patrolling the North Pole gave the height of the falling ice.

"Sixty miles.... fifty-five miles.... fifty miles....forty-five miles....forty miles...."

A blinding flash whitened the television screen. There was only a whiteout to look at. It was a titanic explosion.

Steve quipped, "It's not every day you see white hot water."

I elbowed him in the ribs.

After fourteen seconds the white flash faded away to reveal a sixteen mile wide yellow ball. This ball expanded rapidly and gradually turned an intense crimson red.

Someone on a plane in the area said, *"This is insane. It's a hydrogen bomb exploding every second."*

Mr. Parker asked, "Is that true, Steve?"

"It's about right. I calculated eight million tons of TNT every second."

"Good Lord!"

Adding to the eeriness of this event was the silence. The fire ball was far from the planes and the delay of the sound's arrival was startling. The planes were what was thought a safe eighty miles away.

Two minutes after the explosion began, an airplane crewman said, *"Doppler radar indicates blast wave coming in at Mach 3. I hope we make it."*

The blast wave reached the plane. It was a very loud low rumbling. The voice in the plane could barely be heard shouting something. Television viewers couldn't make him out. People began realizing this was not a momentary explosion but a continuous one which would last as long as the ice kept falling. It was an astonishing concept: a continuous explosion!

The initial noise was the front wall of the blast wave. After that passed we could hear the plane's pilot. *"It almost finished us. The plane dropped twenty thousand feet."*

The red blasting ball had increased to thirty miles in diameter at which point the matter cooled down to invisible infrared. Soon, a new phenomenon began. White steam coalesced seemingly from nothing some miles from and around the bottom third of the red ball. These steam clouds fell at a steep angle to form what looked like a giant umbrella. Then as the steam reached lower altitudes, it diverted more horizontally to spread out over the ocean. This cloud blanket was very thick, and meteorologists predicted it would spread out for hundreds of miles.

The spectacle had reached a steady state. There was nothing new to see.

The media talking heads turned to general discussion.

How would this give the world rain? Wouldn't it just cause useless rain at the North Pole? It was agreed that's all it would do.

"Has Theresa failed?" asked the commentators.

Nope. Steve and I had one more surprise for them.

Two hours after the North Pole explosion began people all over the United States and Europe noticed a rainbow forming in the sky. It didn't matter how little cloud cover there was or even if there was a clear blue sky. The rainbow was visible everywhere in the United States.

How could this be happening? It was Steve's idea. He was a physics major, and realized when the water hit the atmosphere, it would heat up to thousands of degrees. Hydrogen atoms would be stripped of their electrons and scattered in all directions at thousands of miles an hour. They would be spread out over most of the Earth and when they came back down they'd combine with oxygen to make water. The rainbow came from tiny ice crystals high up in the atmosphere.

The first tiny rain droplets were seen on windshields five hours after the North Pole columns first started exploding. It was a very slow and light rain. Very tiny drops were falling like a mist. But the important point was that it would be continuous, lasting as long as the water columns went up and down. The weather service said the rain would amount to a quarter inch a day which was nearly a hundred inches a year. That was enough to grow any kind of crop.

There was one more problem to deal with. A whole year's food crop had been lost and it was September. Winter was coming. The West was in fair shape but Asia couldn't make it through the winter. They would have famines unseen in all history.

I went to my work room to start my last surprise.

I had another chessboard and plywood sheet with parameters for a new HAL task. I put one chess piece on the board. This would tell HAL to exert a five billion ton force on the Poles. More pieces could be put on the board later to exert more force if needed. Finally, I moved my hands along the borders of the plywood to get HAL started. With that there was nothing to do but wait and see what happened.

Prime Minister Blair showed up shortly before ten p.m. He was very anxious to talk to me. Steve and I went down to the living room. I mentioned to the Parkers they were invited to watch us. Arthur was there too.

The PM began. "Greenwich Observatory reports the Earth poles are moving. Is this true?"

Steve answered while I had the fun of watching their talk.

"Yes, sir. Theresa is turning the Earth pole over pole. The Earth declines twenty-three degrees and twenty-seven minutes from the plane of its orbit. This causes the seasons. Theresa wants to decrease the declination to five degrees to give everybody summer weather all year long. The farmers can grow three crops a year. They can start planting now."

"How does she do this?"

"She has HAL push rock under the North Pole with billions of tons of pressure in one direction and the same force on the South Pole in the opposite direction. To counteract this torque she exerts the opposite torque on the moon, but you'll see no change on the moon. As it revolves around Earth its torque cancels out."

"When will it reach five degrees?"

"Theresa wants to do it by Christmas, but we don't know how much force to exert. The Earth isn't a solid ball. If you could have the daily change in declination reported on television she can adjust the pressure."

"It will be done. Mrs. Hartley is trying to eliminate winter?"

"Yeah. She figures we don't need it."

"Good Lord!" he said looking at me. "You'll be

remembered for a million years."

Looking back at Steve he asked, "May one inquire what other plans Mrs. Hartley has?"

"She has no other plans. When you think about it, HAL is not very useful for anything unless you want to move the Matterhorn to Texas which is a tempting idea. What else can she do with HAL? Nothing."

"Good Lord! So much power and she can't do anything practical?"

"Pretty weird, hunh?" smiled Steve. "We'll probably become professional college students. We can't get jobs."

"Thank you for the information. I'll leave you now. It's late."

"Are you going to tell people about this?"

"This moment. The astronomers already question. Edmund, your telephone?"

"Of course, old boy."

You could see how excited the Prime Minister was.

"Now it will hit the fan," said Steve.

Chapter 14

Edmund Parker invited the Prime Minister to stay a while and Blair accepted. We all watched the television as the news broke out.

The reporters talked excitedly about how I had saved seven billion lives. There wouldn't even be a famine in Asia. I was the biggest hero in history. Steve was so proud of me he almost popped the buttons off his shirt.

It was still light in America. Early evening baseball games were going on and the crowds were jumping up and down screaming my name. The scoreboards showed series of my pictures. New Yorkers were pouring into Times Square for a New Year's Eve kind of celebration. Church bells all over Europe were constantly ringing as they had at the end of World War II. St. Peter's Square was filled with people in an emotional display. Next, television showed Tokyo. The Japanese enjoyed demonstrating on happy occasions, and millions of them were on the streets. But all this was nothing. It was morning in Beijing, China. Millions of people had been collecting in the Forbidden City, anticipating that something important was about to happen. Part of this area was the famous Tiananmen Square, equal in size to the Vatican. Camera scans showed the huge spaces and wide boulevards filled with people for a mile around.

It was estimated that twenty-five million people were gathered there, making it the largest crowd in history. The sound of their voices was one continuous, unwavering roar. They were holding my photograph in their hands and yelling Tah-ee-sah! Tah-ee-sah! I was smiling and tearing up at the same time. This was my greatest moment.

Most touching were the shots showing mothers and fathers holding their children and crying joyfully. I wish I could put words together as eloquently as Blair. I can't. But I think you can guess how I felt on seeing all this. I was crying. Steve held me closely and Mrs. Parker came over to hug me too.

This was what all the inhuman, infinitely boring work had been for. That immense crowd in Beijing was not even one percent of all the people I saved. If there was justice, what would my reward be?

The worldwide celebration went on endlessly. Watching all the crowds gathered everywhere numbed the senses, and reporters resorted to testimonials of individual people in the street. Politicians tried to get some television time too. They struggled to outdo each other praising me.

Shortly after midnight Steve and I went upstairs while Blair continued his visit with his old friend. It was a delicious moment and he didn't want it to end.

We woke at seven fifteen and turned on the news. Church bells were still ringing everywhere and would continue to do so all day. The 'big bell' in St. Peter's Square was ringing along with all the smaller bells and the crowd filling the Square cheered. All Europe was celebrating the latest miracle. The crowds in the now dark Beijing were still incomprehensibly large. I had brought out a "new and better world", the tube said. It was a "new era" and a "new dawn". For once, these tired old clichés were really true!

We got dressed and went down to the dining room for breakfast. We watched the dining room television. Now, people were getting into their cars and driving towards the Parker mansion. A TV helicopter showed views of the roads loaded with far more cars than usual heading in the direction of the Parker house. This spontaneous vehicular demonstration took the public's fancy and grew. It was reported that a hundred thousand cars were trying to get to me.

Arthur appeared in the dining room.

"Madam, Colonel James wishes to speak to you."

"Please have him come in here, Arthur."

We were still munching breakfast when Colonel James came in.

"Trouble with the crowds again?" I asked.

"Yes, ma'am. We believe a half million people will try to visit the house by day's end. It's an impossible situation for us."

"Yup, yup, yup," I said nodding my head. "I get it. You want me to get out of here. We'll go to London until this blows over. Give us half an hour."

We packed some bags and got in an unmarked sedan driven by a soldier in civilian clothes. Colonel James was in the front seat. We were followed by five military vehicles loaded with armed soldiers. As we drove down the relatively empty southbound left lane we saw the heavy traffic on the right lane. In some places it had simply stopped dead on the pavement as the road could not handle so many cars.

I made no attempt to hide my face. The idea was

to keep the crowds away from the Parker estate. It worked. Reports came in that the cars were turning around to go back home.

All right. Everybody was in a festive mood and I was happy about that. But I couldn't let myself be mobbed by the grateful masses for the rest of my life. This had to stop.

We arrived in the outskirts of London.

"Now what?" asked Steve.

"Let's go see Mr. Blair."

Colonel James got on his cell phone. In two minutes he said, "The PM is in Parliament today. Do you wish to go there?"

"Yes," I answered.

The Palace of Westminster, or the British Parliament building, was an imposing structure on the Thames River. Big Ben was on the northern end and ringing constantly like all the church bells.

We were led through a series of hallways. Inevitably we were noticed and the press was alerted to our visit. We finally arrived at somebody's office where the Prime Minister waited. He got up to enthusiastically welcome us.

"So glad to see you again. Won't you sit down? What can I do for you?"

I said, "We're worried about the crowds. We can't hide out forever. Look at what's going on in Beijing. Twenty-five million people on the streets. Think if I showed up there."

"What do you hope for?"

"I just want to walk in public without being mobbed."

"Something we all want but must give up when we

become famous."

"I didn't want to become famous."

"I see your point. It is unfair. Perhaps an appeal to the public will yield results."

"Can I speak to Parliament? I won't have reporters screaming at me."

"I'll arrange it. I'm sure they'll attend."

Prime Minister Blair spread the word that I would appear in the House of Commons, and as he predicted, 'announce it and they will come'. The House was packed. Blair walked in first closely followed by me and then Steve. On seeing me, the House members stood up and cheered loudly. I kept an impassive face. That was to be my message. Thanks but no thanks. Steve and I sat.

Blair stood up to the table and waited for the clamor to play out.

"My friends. Mrs. Hartley has a request. I hope it won't be denied her."

He indicated I had the floor. I got up and nervously walked forward.

"I'm not a public speaker. I never wanted to be. I'm talking to the media and the people on the street. Excuse this little piece of paper. It reminds me of the points I've been thinking about for a long time.

"I've seen the world's reaction to what I did. Parents are going wild because their children won't die. Everybody is grateful. Believe me, I am aware of all this and I am happy about it. Let's not talk about it.

"Like everybody else I've watched a lot of television. Everybody you see on television is there because they wanted to be. Movie stars, singers, dancers, politicians, reporters, they all wanted to get on television. They want the attention. I don't."

"Why are you here?" somebody asked.

I could single him out because he had stood up when he said that. I suppose it was a House rule. I stared at him with no attempt to hide my contempt. How dare he interrupt me! In answer to his own question, why had he spoken if not to attract attention to himself? This hypocrisy had to become plain to everyone as I stared his political career into oblivion.

"You interrupted me," I said. "Nobody interrupts me. I don't need you."

You could almost see the miserable man's political career melting down to his feet. He had dared to interrupt the world saver. There would be rioting in his hometown.

I looked over the crowd. "Reporters are the same way. They don't let you complete a sentence. I didn't even have a chance to open my mouth and they were telling lies about me the night I talked with Mr. Blair on television. They don't know crap but they won't shut up. I told Mr. Blair the next morning I would never talk to reporters. I didn't ask for this and I won't take garbage from anybody."

A chill was felt around the room. The old rules were out. There was a new sheriff in town.

I resumed. "In high school I saw kids anxious to grow up. What's the big deal about the adult world? Everybody drives themselves crazy trying to get a piece of the pie. They want more than they can get. I just want to fool around and enjoy watching the world. People forget I'm a kid. I don't want to be anything else."

At that, everybody stood up to applaud and cheer. I

struck some kind of nerve with them. I'd have to work out why later. They settled down.

"I did the things I did because it was the decent thing to do. That's all. I wasn't looking to become famous. I didn't seek publicity. I don't want to be queen of the tabloids. I don't want to be asked what's my favorite food.

"I won't answer reporters' questions. Nobody elected you. I'll talk with elected heads of state when necessary for the public good.

"Reporters say they want to interview me to find out what I'm like. Steve already told you at the Senate that I was perfect in every way. He may have exaggerated, but a thousand interviews won't tell you more than that.

"Reporters want to find out what I plan to do. They say imagine the temptations that come with unlimited power! Who could resist changing things? I can resist temptation. I'm not going to tell anybody what to do. People know best what to do with their lives. When I was a little girl, baby chipmunks walked around my feet when I stood still. Mom taught me they need our protection. I was not to try to pick them up. Leave them alone and they'll be all right. I'm still that little girl."

A woman House member directly opposite me started crying. I saw similar sad faces around the room like somebody had died. I looked back at Steve who only shrugged. Blair said, "All is well". I resumed.

"Reporters want to interview me because I did remarkable things. I'm not remarkable. Millions of girls are just like me. Go interview them!

"If I went around making speeches, somebody would find something I said that wasn't correct. Then people would say I lie. That's not going to happen. People need to know Theresa Hartley always tells the truth. I won't go around making speeches.

"There is another important point. My work isn't done. I still have to watch what HAL is doing. Some people will want me to do this or that with him. They will demonstrate for their pet project when it will benefit them at the cost to others. I cannot allow myself to be influenced by demonstrations. I have a responsibility to be fair to everybody.

"And finally this. I saved your lives. All I want in return is the right to walk on the street without being mobbed by a crowd of curiosity seekers and hounded by the paparazzi. You owe me that much."

I waited a few seconds to let that last remark sink in. Then Steve and I walked out of the room.

Neither the House members nor any of the millions watching could believe it. They had never heard of any person with any kind of achievement no matter how small not seeking some kind of recognition for it. Nobody was immune. Even Medal of Honor winners, whose aura depended on a show of humility, at least gave one interview to one reporter. Here I'd just saved the world, and I wanted nothing to do with them. The all-powerful World Empress wouldn't make the rounds of the talk shows and political meetings. I wanted a private life.

"Do you think it worked?" I asked the PM when he came out.

"I believe it will. They are fundamentally fair people."

"People must be disappointed. They expected a bubbly, gushy airhead like the movie actresses who spit out every line like it's an announcement of the Second Coming. They got Robot Girl."

"Do not concern yourself with the masses. You are exactly what we need. Many heads in high places will sleep well tonight after seeing what you're like."

I turned to Steve. "Let's go to that hotel where I talked to Mr. Blair."

"In the middle of London?"

"Yeah. That will be the supreme test."

We returned to the hotel where I had the historic Sunday night talk with Blair. In an hour a crowd did gather in front of the hotel, but it was quiet.

Blair leaked my remarks to the press, and the British media commentators rallied to my side in a mad dash to jump on the bandwagon of my sudden popularity. One noted:

"Did you see her talk with the Prime Minister? Did she sound like an actor or television personality? No! I dare say no actress could play her. She is a real person with no attempts to convince, fool, impress, charm, or ingratiate herself with people. She is your neighbor's daughter, exceptionally gifted as we have seen, but otherwise a very ordinary girl. She wants privacy. She earned it."

Minutes later, a BC philosophy professor was interviewed on television. Many BC people had been questioned by the press for the simple reason that I attended the school for a year. The man said, "It's not just that she wants privacy, or doesn't want to be bothered with us all the time. Theresa wants to maintain integrity with her real self. Talking to people she doesn't know about subjects she doesn't want to discuss will change who she is. You must compromise yourself to accommodate others. She doesn't want to do that. The great saints and philosophers remained so by guarding their private lives."

Well, yeah, that's what I intended although I hadn't thought it out in words.

By early evening there was no crowd in front of the hotel.

The next morning we tried out the new arrangement. Instead of eating breakfast at the hotel, we wandered out to the street. Immediately, we noticed that we were being followed by government security dressed in plain clothes. We weren't mobbed. The few people walking around recognized us but didn't crowd us. Instead they smiled and waved. Of course, there were a few publicity seekers who tried to immortalize themselves by walking right up to my face and trying to start a conversation. The security people pulled them away. There were certain to be more aggressive intruders later. Security would have to wrestle them to the ground. This was how it would have to be.

There was a scuffle in back of us. A half dozen security people wrestled a man to the ground. That was how it would be from now on, too!

We walked along the street until we found a small restaurant that advertised breakfast. We went inside where we were instantly recognized by everybody. A hostess quickly got us seated. The whole restaurant crowd was staring at us but kept its distance.

"Well, that's better," said Steve.

"If we can get out the front door."

The food arrived quickly. The kitchen had been operating on panic mode to get us our breakfast in good time lest it be told throughout Western civilization that the humble restaurant had kept *these* people waiting.

With food in my stomach I said, "You know what? We've been spending too much time in the house. We need to go into society and live a little."

"You want to throw a party?"

"That's empty. I mean go where people are living their daily life. Let's travel around, stay in small hotels in small towns, go to Irish pubs, county fairs, and that kind of thing. We'll skip Paris. We weren't sophisticated enough for them."

"They weren't sophisticated enough to know how to save the world."

He jumped to another subject.

"Whatever happened to Jan Struthers?"

"I don't know. I asked Mr. Blair to look her up but I never heard from him."

"She was on your side?"

"Yup. That information package she sent to Canada last year was a call for help. It got Mr. Blair involved and he sent the ships to find me. The world owes Jan a lot."

"I have an idea."

As usual, the restaurant has been infiltrated by government security people who stood rather obviously around the room. Steve looked at one and waved him over.

"Sir?" said the man.

"We want to find out about Jan Struthers. Ask the Prime Minister to announce her name and have her report to the British Ambassador in the United States. If she wants to be found she'll show up."

"Her name again, sir?"

Steve pulled out a scrap of paper and a pen to write her name. "Here" he said giving it to the man who walked away.

"Takes care of that. What do you want to do today, my dear?"

"Let's get a London guidebook and walk around."

"The security people will love that!"

Jan Struthers had not had a good summer. Her eight years of managing my watchers did nothing for her. She couldn't tell anybody about it; nobody would believe her. That left an eight year hole in her resume. Now in her thirties, her college education wasted, unemployable, unmarried, and living with her aging parents, her life was a ruin.

Glum with lack of purpose and ennui, she turned on Channel 24, the "all Theresa all the time" station. They talked about how the Hartleys had spent their day in London. We walked to Buckingham Palace and through the nearby St. James Park with its peaceful pond with the ducks and swans. We taxied to St. Paul's Cathedral, to Westminster Abby where poets and kings were buried, and way out of town to the famous London Zoo. There were television cameras all along the trip, but as they showed on the tube the government security men kept them from getting too close to us. Ditto with the paparazzi who were continually being pulled away.

Would it work in the United States? Probably not. Freedom of speech and information and all that junk gave the curious a license to kill privacy. America could be rough on the famous.

The scene switched to Prime Minister Blair at a press conference. Jan wasn't really listening until Blair mentioned her own name. Then she was all attention.

"Theresa Hartley has asked me to notify Jan Struthers to call the British Ambassador to the United States at the embassy in Washington. All is well. Mrs. Hartley knows about the material Miss Struthers sent to Canada. She believes if Miss Struthers wants to be found she will call the embassy."

Theresa wanted to see her! All this time she worried I believed she'd cooperated in President Martin's mad plot to bring me and HAL down.

Jan cried loudly. Her parents came in the room to ask what was wrong.

"Nothing" Jan said. "Theresa still likes me. It's wonderful."

I talked with Jan on the phone. When President Martin came to office and found out about me and HAL, he didn't like the arrangement. He disbanded Jan's watchers, replaced them with a smaller group of professional agents he could trust, and issued an Executive Order warning Jan to never talk about me to anybody and to never contact me. This had the force of law; you did not disobey an Executive Order.

Jan didn't like the President's arrangement either. She suspected he was up to no good. But she had anticipated this kind of development for years and assembled the package she sent to the Canadian Prime Minister. It was in her father's house. All she had to do was call him with a coded message and he'd send it.

Jan gambled that if I was arrested or disappeared the Canadian Prime Minister would make a big stink about it. As it turned out, I was put into the jet fighter too fast for the Canadian PM to find out I was missing. When President Martin said my name on television, Prime Minister Blair remembered Jan's package and a few days later sent the ships to find me.

Chapter 15

What happened to President Martin?

After I brought rain and eliminated winter to allow a twelve month a year farming season all over the world, people were saying the world was much better off than before Martin tried to get rid of me and HAL. What Martin did was wrong, but things turned out all right after all.

President Martin was seen appearing in public to go to a restaurant or theater. He didn't answer reporters' questions shouted at him on the street, but he did smile and wave. It looked like he was doing okay.

Steve came down to breakfast while I caught a few extra minutes of sleep upstairs. He hardly reached the foyer before Arthur intercepted him.

"Excuse me, sir. The Prime Minister wishes to visit Mrs. Hartley this morning. He says it's urgent."

"OK. Tell him we'll be here."

Now what? We thought everything was going fine.

The Prime Minister arrived at quarter to ten. Arthur led him into the living room where we waited. Blair sat down and got straight to the business at hand.

"A group of oceanographers have informed me that the oceans will rise due to thermal expansion.

They believe it is already up a sixteenth of an inch. They say it will rise two or three feet in a year."

"What's causing it?" asked Steve.

"It is the reduction in the Earth's declination. Normally water is heated in the summer months and cooled in the winter to maintain a constant average temperature. With the reduction in declination this process is frustrated. The oceans are not losing their heat normally. Sunlight is coming into the Northern Hemisphere at a more vertical angle than normal for this time of year. The Northern oceans will not lose their heat even as the Southern oceans are gaining it. This causes the water to expand above normal volume."

"All right but up to three feet in a year sounds like a lot."

"Parts of the ocean are three miles deep. Three feet is only two hundredths of one percent. Recall that the water on the ocean floor has been around zero degrees Fahrenheit because of winter cooling. Now it will climb up to ten or fifteen degrees. That's a huge difference."

"What will this expansion do?"

"It will cause horrible damage along our coastlines. Beach levels are maintained by a delicate balance. A three foot rise in water will erode many beaches to the point of endangering valuable real estate. You are aware of our problems in London?"

"Yes. You have these giant gates to block off the Thames River."

"Your Miami Beach is also perilously close to water. There are many such cities. Potential losses over the world amount to catastrophic amounts."

I had been listening patiently to all this.

"I thought I could retire from all these problems."

"The world is a very complicated mechanism" answered the PM.   "You can't change one thing without affecting others."

"What happens after a year?"

"The rise will continue more slowly.   Eventually we will see a rise of about six feet."

"Un hunh. How much water is that?"

"They put it in interesting terms. It's enough water to cover the United States to a depth of two hundred and twenty-one feet."

I slapped my forehead in astonishment.

"You want me to get rid of all that in one year?"

"It would be appreciated," he said with a touch of embarrassment.

I looked at Steve. "Do you believe this?"

"No, but it'll have to be done."

Steve rose and the PM automatically rose too.

"Thank you for your help," said Blair. "I know this is most annoying."

Steve smiled.   The PM was close to using an expression he used himself when something went wrong.

Arthur escorted Blair back to his limo. Steve said, "I'll go make some calculations".

He went upstairs to hit the computer. He returned twenty minutes later.

"You need to get rid of one cubic mile of water every three minutes for a year."

"Is that all?"

"That's all."

"Will they ever leave us alone?"

"No. Face it, my dear, you're stuck with HAL and there'll be one problem after another. I know it's not fair. Who said life is fair? We struggle and then we die."

"After this we take a real vacation before we croak."

I got to work on a new HAL program. It was a complicated one and I needed eight days to finish it. Then I moved my fingers along a plywood sheet to get HAL started.

HAL lifted a cubic mile of water out of the South Pacific a few hundred miles from Antarctica on the Pacific side. It rose at forty miles an hour bringing it completely out of the ocean surface in one and a half minutes. After three minutes another cubic mile of water started rising.

These one mile to the edge cubes rose slowly up to a height of ten miles where the air was very thin. At that point the complicated HAL program increased their speed to a hundred miles per hour but in a direction ahead of the Earth's orbital motion. In a short time they reached the threshold of outer space and kept going. I increased their speed to a thousand miles an hour and then two thousand and finally three thousand. Powerful radar systems monitored their rise. In one day they were well above the Earth's orbit. They would never return.

"Where will they go?" a science consultant was asked on television.

"They will go into orbit around the sun well outside the Earth's orbit. They can never get back down low enough to collide with us. To add to the affect, the solar wind will give them comet tails all over the sky. They should put on a spectacular show. I can't wait to see it."

We set out on a leisurely tour of the British Isles. Certain famous places were obligatory destinations. Stratford-upon-Avon, Shakespeare's hometown, the Blarney Stone in Ireland, and castles where kings and queens had lived were all quick visits, but most of the time we drifted from one small unknown town to another, not to see famous sights, which were few, but simply to check into a small hotel or inn, eat and drink at the local pubs, and see whatever it was the local people were doing. We were never crowded. Everybody wanted the Hartleys to visit their little town and put it on the map. To get this exciting experience they understood they had to give us some space.

We had a little fun on this trip. When Steve came up with the North Pole water column idea we realized there would be a light rain all day. The head and neck could get drenched if you spent a lot of time outdoors as we intended. We foresaw that millions of people would be walking the streets with umbrellas all the time. This would not do.

Steve found an American firemen's apparel website. They sold authentic American firemen's helmets. These helmets had brims all around that caught water and guided it in back of your head to fall on the ground. No more perfect headgear had ever been designed to keep your head dry. Steve ordered three helmets, one white one for me, and two black ones for himself and Mr. Blair. There were optional shields with the names of major American cities. I chose a New York shield for my helmet in honor of the 220 firefighters who died in the 9/11 disaster. Steve ordered my white helmet's New York shield with the word CHIEF on it! His and Blair's helmets would not have the shields. There was also an optional and very ugly leather neck cover which I guess was supposed to protect you from a fire's heat. We didn't order those. Finally, there were plastic face protectors something like some football players used except that they could be raised up over the front brim. These made the helmets authentic, all business helmets. We ordered them.

The first day of our England tour we wore the helmets. They were a smash hit. The English people had never seen them in real life and oohed and ahhed. Prime Minister Blair was soon seen wearing his helmet too. Many companies had already been making cheap, light knockoffs of American firemen's helmets and now they all went into frantic production. In a week, it looked like every young person in the world was wearing a ten dollar plastic knockoff. Our genuine helmets each cost over five hundred dollars.

After two weeks we'd seen about as much English culture as we could absorb. We went to Italy.

The Italians like the English knew they were not to crowd the Hartleys or the famous couple would leave. Occasionally somebody tried to get himself on television by approaching us. Security quickly blockaded these characters or wrestled them to the ground. This had been expected. The media had fun showing these intruders.

We visited the immense St. Peter's Baselica, the Sistine Chapel, the Colosseum, Pompeii, and Venice which had the world's best pizza. We did not visit museums; that was too tourist and security in these crowded places would be a nightmare. We spent time in night spots with the people in many small forgotten towns. Sometimes we stayed in people's homes making the families therein nationally famous. The Italians were a very friendly people; we never got tired of them.

Traveling can be exhausting. After a week of traveling around Italy we returned to Edmund Parker's place to rest up. There was a little bit of business to take care of.

Steve brought Arthur over to the chessboard with the fifty-six pieces that controlled the North Pole water columns. It had been raining lightly all over the world for three weeks, not a steady rainfall, but an occasional drop that added up to a quarter inch every twenty-four hours. Not all this water was from my columns; some was normal ocean evaporate encouraged to fall out by "my" water. Steve explained what he wanted Arthur to do.

"It's not good having it rain all the time. The world will turn into a fungus garden."

"It will, sir. Many have discussed it."

"Take this chessboard to the Prime Minister and tell him he can control the number of columns by removing chess pieces. We'll see if it works when the board is away from here. It should. We have to make sure before Theresa and I hit the road again."

"I will go immediately, sir."

Arthur happily went to Number 10 to give the PM the chessboard. Blair alerted a military plane keeping an eye on the North Pole columns and took off five chess pieces. The plane soon reported that five water columns had been cut off at the bottom while continuing to rise up.

"Remarkable!" said the PM.

"Most extraordinary, sir" replied Arthur who had hung around.

"I shall set up an advisory committee to determine the proper amount of rain to maintain at all times. As Mr. Hartley suggested it will be necessary to let the world dry out sometimes."

"It will be a political matter, sir. Nations will disagree on how much rain to make. You'll have a sticky time of it."

Blair laughed. "This is Theresa's revenge for my putting so much responsibility on her."

We waited for another week while the Prime Minister and his people experimented with the chess board. It was working. We felt free to hit the road again.

Edmund Parker recommended we visit the Southern part of Germany. We visited the Neuschwanstein castle near the German-Austrian border. This was the "Walt Disney" castle that inspired the plastic castles at Disneyland and Disney World. It was on a steep hill and had the high watch towers made obligatory in cartoons. The insides were elaborately decorated to a ridiculous degree. The walls were all covered with paintings painted on the walls themselves. The throne room had a large floor covered with designs made of two and a half million small colored pieces of tile individually cut to shape, and fitting together so close, the edges couldn't be found with a fingernail. The "Mad King" Ludwig II had built this and two other useless castles to recall stories from German folklore. Officials met with him and told him he was bankrupting Bavaria with these projects. His older brother had died in an insane asylum and Ludwig had to think they would put him away too. Three days later, Ludwig's dead body was found in a nearby stream.

We headed back north and passed a vast open space covered with thousands of oil tanks extending beyond the horizon. We learned that Germany kept a two year supply of oil on hand in case the supply was cut off by war or international trouble.

Still drifting slowly, stopping at small towns along the way, we arrived at Nuremburg just in time for Oktoberfest. This annual festival at most large cities was a carnival set up in a large open space. There were rides for kids of all ages and all the other attractions of carnivals, but the real reason people went to these things was for the beer tents. Huge tents were set up with tables and seats for thousands. There was a stage with bands dressed in traditional German costumes playing peppy old oomph-pah-pah songs. Everybody drank beer from one liter mugs. Waitresses with fingers like the car crash jaws-of-life carried six of these mugs in each hand. This beer had twice as much alcohol as American beer. It was brewed fresh daily at local breweries and the taste was wonderful. Steve had six mugs but somehow managed to stay on his feet when he took his innumerable "breaks". I had two mugs myself and laughed hysterically when Steve slurred out, "Are we sophisticated yet?"

The next morning there was a knock on the hotel

door. Steve answered. It was a security man.

"Excuse me, sir. Prime Minister Blair requests that you return to the Parker residence today."

It struck us like a lightning bolt. Something was wrong. Again! Would there be no end of it?

"The party is over" said Steve.

The news gave no hint of anything happening. We had to sweat it out on the rushed trip back to the Parker mansion. The Prime Minister's limousine was parked in front of the house when we arrived. Arthur conducted us to the living room and quietly walked out of sight. Peter Blair greeted us and asked how was our trip. Great, we answered. Some man stood next to the PM. We all sat down. The PM began.

"This is Doctor Harold, an expert in meteorology." He nodded his head for Doctor Harold to begin.

"We have speculated on how HAL stopped the wind. He had to add something to the air, something that would increase the air's viscosity to drain away the effect of pressure differentials. Perhaps these were strings of dark matter particles too small to detect but large enough to entangle with each other and increase air viscosity. We now have evidence that HAL put something like this in the air."

Steve had already guessed much of this. His face was puzzled. What was the evidence? Doctor Harold continued.

"The wind is slowly returning. We believe whatever HAL put in the atmosphere is sinking into the Earth where it has no effect, or it may be breaking up. We have been cataloging air movements. It seems the wind will be ten percent restored by February. We think the process has been going on since June."

"So Theresa didn't save the world after all?" Steve suggested.

"Oh but she did, sir! We could have lost two billion people next year along with all animals. The world couldn't survive such trauma. It was the end of all."

"Then what are we talking about?"

"With the Earth's declination being reduced to five degrees by January the oceans will overheat causing constant hurricanes all over the planet. While the return of ordinary wind is slow, the effect on formation of hurricanes will be much greater for reasons too complicated to get into. These hurricanes will be horrific, sir."

Prime Minister Blair took over.

"We can't tolerate these hurricanes. They will destroy everything within a hundred miles of the coasts. Even repairs will be impossible because of the constant winds. This will be as bad as nuclear war."

"That figures" said Steve. "Just when everything is going fine we get a new problem."

"What am I supposed to do," I complained, "change the laws of physics? This is the most impossible problem yet."

Blair said, "You have to return the Earth's declination to the original."

"I thought the Asians couldn't get through the winter."

"It will be hard on them."

"How hard?"

"We may lose half a billion people."

Steve protested, "You can't be serious!"

"We politicians are necessary evils. The matter must be addressed politically, not sentimentally. In politics there are no men, only ideas, no feelings, only goals. Order must be preserved or we are all lost."

My heart raced. I could not kill half a billion people! I looked at Steve miserably and shook my head.

He told Blair, "Let us think it over a few days."

Blair and the meteorologist got up without a word. Conversation was useless. They walked out to the foyer where Arthur opened the door for them.

I think this was my bottom. Despite all my efforts millions of people were going to die. The misery and pointlessness of it shook me. I even wondered why God was letting this happen.

Doctor Harold did not have a monopoly on the weather service. Word of the next imminent disaster leaked out as Blair drove back to London. One of Doctor Harold's colleagues talked.

Peter Blair felt terrible about dumping this problem on me after my spectacular success with the rain problem. Reporters were waiting for him when he got back to London. After reviewing the problem he said, "I am reminded of King Lear. 'Before such sacrifices the gods themselves burn incense.' She won't sleep well. 'Uneasy lies the head that wears a crown.' Poor Theresa! When her story is written, it will be said her adversary was not people in the world, but the world itself."

Chapter 16

I spent a sleepless night. The unfairness of my position kept the tears flowing. "What have I done to deserve this?" I thought. It was like when I was ten years old and HAL first merged with me. I thought of the unfairness of having this thing intrude in my life.

Now the thought was oppressive. The consequences of HAL was upon me, and I couldn't escape. No matter what I did, whether I returned the declination to the original or not, millions of people would die, and their families would blame me for not doing the opposite. Why did God choose me for these trials?

People interviewed on television said they envied me my glamorous power and importance. Oh really? Who would trade places with me now?

I was learning something new about remorse. You can feel guilty about doing something wrong, or not doing something you should have. You can also have remorse for doing something good the wrong way. I shouldn't have let Blair lead me to handling HAL alone. I should have invited a committee to share power. Things might have turned out better, or at least I wouldn't be taking all the blame alone. I guess that is the regret of a lot of old people when they look back and realize too late what might have been.

This was what President Martin regretted. He thought he was doing something good. It was a disaster. How can anybody know what is the right thing to do?

Steve and I lay awake on our backs until the early hours. There was nothing to say.

Around four in the morning Steve got up and walked out of the room. It wasn't his usual hour for a pit stop. In a moment I got up to see where he'd gone. He was sitting at the computer in my work room. I watched him for a while from the door without his noticing me. Steve came up with the weirdest ideas in the world. If he had something to fix this problem, I didn't want to disturb him. I went back to bed. If he came up with something, he'd tell me all about it in the morning.

Here's what Steve was doing. He booted the computer to do internet research. He had figured out that there was no earthly solution to this problem. He needed to look elsewhere.

What was the elemental composition of the sun? He found the answer quickly. The sun was 73.4% hydrogen and 25.0% helium. That left 1.6% of the sun made up of other stuff, and 1.6% was a lot. It was equal to four thousand Earths.

He found a list of the most abundant solar elements. The sun was 0.2% carbon. That was surprising. The sun was a dirty place. The article mentioned that there were 67 elements in the sun in sufficient quantities to be measurable by spectrometry. That would include virtually every common element found on Earth.

Steve thought about it. Which of these elements would be useful to prevent hurricanes? It would be a gas, one that was heavier than air, that would stay near the ground and make the updrafts of hurricanes impossible or at least much less severe. It was a simple idea.

But which gas? As a physics major he knew a little chemistry. There was a family of elements called inert gases that would not react with anything and poison the atmosphere. He went through the list. Xenon, second from the bottom of the list, was nearly four times as dense as air and had no radioactive isotopes. It was perfect.

After breakfast Steve and I went for a walk in the woods. I was still visibly shaken and he gently introduced me to his idea. He knew I was close to the brink. He knew nobody could endure the pressures I'd been having without some effect on the mind. Even the media was talking about the state of my mental health. Somebody, Blair or Parker, must have said something to him. Now he was trying to introduce me to the wildest idea he'd come up with yet.

"I've been thinking. Do you know what xenon gas is?"

"Yeah. It's used in lights."

"It's an inert element. It's nearly four times as heavy as air. If there was a lot of it in the atmosphere there wouldn't be hurricanes because the warm air on the ground couldn't go up fast."

"Where is there a lot of xenon?"

"On the sun. The sun has all the elements. They can be separated by their melting points."

He didn't push further than that but let me think about it as we slowly walked through the woods. Thirty minutes later we got back to the mansion and I gave my opinion.

"It might be possible. I'll need Mr. Blair to build something that will take a temperature measuring device to the sun so I can watch the temperatures. We'll call it Sky Spy. There's no landmarks in space and I can't triangulate the sun's position to HAL, but if they put cameras on Sky Spy I can see where the sun is and give orders to HAL."

"I'll call Blair."

Prime Minister Blair arrived that afternoon with thirty-six scientists and engineers. There was also a Royal Air Force general. Steve was the physics major and he did most of the negotiating with these guys while I stood by. It was fun watching their surprised faces.

After explaining about the need for xenon, Steve went into how to get it. One thing I couldn't do was triangulate a position in space. I would have to be told where Sky Spy was.

The scientists were very excited. They came up with a scheme of sixteen satellites orbiting the sun to serve as a GPS system. They proposed a set of simple levers on Sky Spy that their satellites would control for automatically relaying information about Sky Spy's position and what changes were needed. Could I get HAL to respond automatically to these levers? Yes.

They asked another question. "When you manipulate the gas masses, could you do it some distance away from Sky Spy instead of directly underneath?"

"I guess. Why?"

"You'll be dumping unwanted material back down to the sun. We want to see what happens. We can learn a lot about the sun."

"OK."

They were pleased with that. I saw of couple of them shaking each other's hands. It was an astronomer's dream come true, a close up look at disturbances in the sun's surface. It would generate a thousand scientific papers.

The Royal Air Force general now spoke up.

"Could you also bring in helium?"

Steve looked puzzled. "I guess. What good is it?"

"If helium was plentiful we could send up thousands of miniature dirigibles over territory invaded by terrorists groups. They would be lighter than air drones surveying the land for weeks at a time. We could put the terrorist organizations out of business."

Steve and I looked at each other. What a great idea this was!

"I'll do it" I said.

A team of twelve hundred experts from all over the West was assembled in London. They quickly threw together the GPS satellites from pre-existing components. These satellites were ridiculous looking assemblies resembling high school science fair projects, but appearance didn't count, They only had to work. They had small rockets to precisely adjust their solar orbits. I sent them off to the sun.

I wasn't interested in mechanical devices and didn't pay much attention to the Sky Spy monstrosity they made. Describing details would get me arrested as a public nuisance. Basically, it was a 36 foot wide platform with every kind of scientific device the scientists could think of. All I needed was the temperature and a visual of what was happening.

I moved Sky Spy to four million miles above the sun's North Pole and went to work. The principle was simple enough. HAL grabbed a gigantic mass of solar gas and raised it to high altitudes where it cooled off. This made it possible to separate the elements.

After HAL grabbed a handful of xenon I had him rush it to Earth at really super high speed. As it got close to Earth I had HAL slow it down to a safer speed and stretch it out into a long thin stream.

The stream reached the North Pole. By now it was frozen solid. I let go of the end a few hundred feet at a time giving it a last second squeeze to break the brittle crystal into countless harmless small pieces. The xenon showered down all over the top of the world. At night millions of people stood outside watching what looked like a dense meteor shower raining down in every direction. It was the xenon entering the atmosphere.

A month went by. Xenon was now accounting for two ounces of atmospheric pressure. Tropical hurricanes attempted to stir themselves up but were only storms with forty mile per hour gusts and were infrequent. The power to raise up billions of tons of xenon heavy air per second didn't exist. It was soon pointed out that warm air was breaking through thermal layers and rising slowly in hundreds of places over the entire ocean instead of rapidly in a small area resulting in a thousand mile wide hurricane system.

It was nice that I wouldn't have to kill half a billion Asians. So much for that problem.

I hadn't forgotten about the helium that Air Force general wanted. Three weeks after the xenon arrived so did the helium. The military had something to play with. It was a sad day for the terrorists. The atmosphere was soon a tenth of a percent helium which didn't sound like much, but it was a million times what it had been. It could easily be separated out by centrifuges.

The wind, rain, thermal expansion of water, food, and heat problems were permanently fixed. This was the end of my problems with the natural world.

I wasn't so naïve as to think all my problems were over. A lot of people in the world were jealous of my power. They were sure to come after me. Many statesmen predicted it.

Blair visited with four guys from NASA. They had interesting questions.

Could I put a large telescope on the moon?

"Yup. I can do that. Throw something together and I'll deliver it."

Could I put a roving robot on Mars?

"Er..... no. The problem is the time delay. I can't give HAL instructions exact enough to keep it from crashing. Put together a package and I'll put it in orbit around Mars. You take over from there."

How big could this Mars package be?

"Any size. A million tons. It doesn't matter to HAL."

"We hesitate to ask. Europa is a moon of Jupiter. It has an ocean covered with ice and we think it has a chance of harboring life, but it's far away and the ice is thick. It may take two hundred years to get a sample. Could you get a sample?"

"How big is Europa?"

"It's slightly smaller than the Moon."

"I'll put Europa in orbit around Mars."

The visitors were astonished. Then they laughed and gushed with exuberant thank-yous.

That left them plenty to brag about back home. Meanwhile, I was working on a really interesting project.

Fort Knox, Kentucky was the site of the United States Gold Depository. It contained 147,000,000 ounces of gold and was protected by hundreds of feet of open space surrounding it in all directions. The property had many secret security systems to prevent anybody from stepping on the land. In addition, it was surrounded by an Army base of 40,000 soldiers. The rarely used front entrance was on the eastern side of the building, and the most open field and the closest to Army facilities was the western field.

NORAD's radar detected something coming down to Earth over the North Pole. It was moving at a steady 120 miles per hour and it seemed to be a narrow line some hundreds of miles long. As the night went by it lowered to an altitude of 100 miles and then curved to the horizontal heading south. There was no alarm; this obviously had something to do with me. President Stinson was awakened and advised of the situation.

Military planes with telescopes flew to Northern Canada to get a visual. It was not a steady line but rather a stream of small yellow objects.

The yellow stream, excuse the expression, continued due south at high altitude. By 2:00 pm it was directly over Fort Knox, Kentucky. The stream made a sharp turn and headed straight down. In less than two hours it reached ground. A two foot wide almost perfectly spherical ball of gold hit the middle of the large field west of the Gold Depository. A half second later another ball of gold hit the ground. And another. And another. By now people on the ground had been alerted the gold was coming and thousands lined the fence surrounding the Depository.

The gold balls stacked up in a very shallow pyramid. In an half an hour there was easily more gold on the field than inside the Depository and it kept coming down. The gold balls made a loud thump as they landed on the growing pile; they weighed about four tons apiece. In twenty-two hours the last of the gold balls came down. The mountain of gold was hundreds of feet wide and much higher than the Depository. It was worth trillions of dollars at current prices.

"And there's a lot more where that came from" said Steve who watched the spectacle on television with me. There was. I could bring down any amount.

Prime Minister Blair called me and asked what the price would be.

"Fifty dollars an ounce" I said.

"I am relieved. Your President said if I didn't get the price down to one hundred dollars the United States would declare war on England."

"Now you tell me!" We both laughed.

He said plentiful, low priced gold had a thousand uses in industry besides being a monetary stabilizer and basic material for jewelry.

I pleased him again by saying I'd bring millions of tons of silver down to a British Army base and sell it for five dollars an ounce as long as people were willing to buy the stuff. British silversmiths could have fun working the metal. Blair thanked me for providing thousands of jobs.

The media jumped on the story. The silver would provide stable pocket money for all the people on Earth. The common people could have real money to spend, money that was exchangeable across all borders. The benefits to nations' economies was unimaginable.

I hired Jan Struthers as my financial manager and sent her to Kentucky to set up the gold business. She found a small iron foundry in Lexington and made them an offer to buy the place. They quickly accepted. It was infinitely more interesting to work with gold than iron! Gold from the Fort Knox field was melted down into gold ingots a little over three inches square and an inch thick. These little ingots weighed what Jan thought was an amazing 6.85 pounds. They were worth $5,000 dollars apiece. She had them put in Brink's trucks for transport to New York City where they were sold through banks. Corporations were already blabbering about all the things they could do with the metal. Within a month I was a billionaire.

I wondered what my old BC boyfriend Jack Koster was thinking of all this!

Chapter 17

Thirty-two year old lawyer Connie McKesson worked for the old New York law firm Kent, Stein, O'Connor, and Farley. I soon learned about her. Steve and I watched the news with Mr. and Mrs. Parker. Once again I was the lead story.

"A class action suit is being filed against Theresa Hartley for damages to owners of gold. Attorney Connie McKesson spoke to reporters a short while ago."

The scene switched to Connie McKesson standing at a podium with eight older lawyers standing behind her. "We are filing a class action suit against Theresa Hartley for suddenly and callously ruining the fortunes of thousands of gold bullion owners. Many people put most or all of their retirement funds in gold thinking it was the safest of all investments only to be wiped out when Mrs. Hartley caused the price to collapse. Her failure to make some kind of arrangement with the victims has lead us to ask for thirty-five billion dollars in damages which is far less than she will get from her gold sales."

The scene switched to a reporter interviewing a Yale law professor.

"Does Connie McKesson have a case?"

"In most districts, no. But with the amount of money involved they will file in every district in the country until they find a judge who will take on the case. They do have an argument although a weak one. She did not discover a gold mine on Earth which would be a legitimate basis for competition in sales. Lawyers will argue she changed the rules of the game during halftime, switching an alien commodity for a domestic one, and that's not fair to her competitors who had no way to defend themselves."

"A thousand corporations have said they need that gold."

"They won't be on the jury."

"Will we see Theresa Hartley testify on camera?"

"Yes. This is only the beginning. There will be more class action suits here and abroad. She may spend most of her life in court."

"Those scumbags!" exclaimed Steve. "You save their worthless butts and this is the thanks you get."

But I was not ready to hear that. It was Steve's idea to get gold and I suffered from it. I was so angry the tears came to me eyes.

"Getting gold was your idea," I said and got up to run upstairs.

Stunned, Steve watched me walk away. This was not like me. He was getting angry too.

Instead of following me upstairs he went down to the recreation room. He had to do something physical to let off steam. He walked to the pool table and started practicing shots. In a moment Edmund Parker came down to join him.

"May I play a game, old boy?"

"Sure" Steve said and racked the balls.

I lay on my bed fighting back the tears. The horrible unfairness of it! I had done nothing wrong. The dogs were barking again like that annoying dog I had to walk by on my way to school.

Was I being unfair to Steve? It was his idea. I hadn't wanted to do it. People had sent me fifty-six million dollars in the mail which was enough to last a lifetime. Had I done nothing after bringing down the xenon, people would have forgotten me.

I calmed down a little. What did I have now? I had a marriage to a great guy, and while he had an occasional lapse from perfection, perhaps I did too. Steve was a good man. Before he realized I could outwrestle King Kong, he treated me as gently as if I were made of brittle glass. There was a kindness in this man few women would find. And he thought a lot of me, too. I could see it in how he looked at me.

While I juggled this flurry of confusing, juvenile thoughts, there was a knock on the door. Steve wouldn't knock. "Who's there?"

"Mrs. Parker. May I come in?"

I got up and let the lady in. She sat on the bed next to me.

"Long ago Mr. Parker and I had our little tiffs. It was his fault, it was my fault, it was both our faults. Marriage partners share responsibility for all that follows because everything they do affects each other. All they try to do is get by in this world. When something goes wrong, they're both to blame and neither is to blame. The world is to blame."

Steve and Mr. Parker were still playing pool when I came down the stairs to the rec room. Mr. Parker immediately put his cue stick down on the table and went back upstairs to leave us alone.

"I need help," I said.

"Don't worry. We'll get this lawyer bitch."

Prime Minister Blair called to say he'd talked with President Stinson. There was nothing the President could do because it was not a criminal matter. Both the President and Blair wanted to know what I'd do.

"I'm going to force her to drop the suit," I told him. "I can't allow myself to be bullied."

"You wouldn't do her harm?"

"Of course not."

"Or damage her property?"

"Won't have to do that either."

"What else is there?"

"Sorry, Mr. Blair. The surprise is the fun of it."

The night of Connie McKesson's lawsuit announcement, a U.S. Senator was interviewed on CNN. He said, "This is the most harebrained idea I've ever heard. Every person on Earth owes his life to Theresa. If she is summoned to court, we'll see a million people demonstrating outside the courthouse."

That's all he had to say to start the avalanche.

The next morning 300,000 people gathered in front of the New York County Courthouse. This beautiful building that looked like an ancient Greek temple and was used at a backdrop in countless movies was probably not where the civil case would be heard, but that didn't matter. It was a visual symbol and the crowd gathered there. They were chanting, "Free Theresa and drop the suit. Kill the lawyers. Give them the boot."

The next morning there were 800,000 people at the Courthouse. I was still in England. A date for the suit hearing hadn't even been set.

What would happen if I actually did show up at

the Courthouse? Holy smokes!

Things were getting out of control and President Stinson called a hasty press conference at three o'clock Washington time.

"Our intelligence services inform me of increased terrorist traffic on telephone and computer networks. A terrorist attack seems imminent in New York. A crowd edging up close to a million is an irresistible target for terrorists. I appeal to everybody to disperse and not return to the Courthouse. The police cannot protect crowds this large."

It was nine o'clock in London. Steve jumped up and went to the phone.

"This is Steve Hartley. Get me the BBC" he said to the operator. The connection was made in a minute.

"Good evening, Mr. Hartley."

"Are you recording this?"

"If you wish. It's being recorded."

"Tell the American people to stop demonstrating. Theresa will never go to the Courthouse. She's going to make the lawyers drop the suit. That's official. Good night, sir."

The next day there were only a few thousand curiosity seekers at the Courthouse. The police could handle that.

A week went by. I was ready to get Connie McKesson.

A little research on the internet revealed that the law firm of Kent, Stein, O'Connor, and Farley was on the sixth floor of the Lamper Building in upper Manhattan. I found a picture of the building and printed it out to commit it to memory. Next, I went to

MapQuest to get and print out a map of that part of the city. With that done I could zero in on Connie McKesson.

I put my hands over my eyes to start HAL's black and white vision. I located the Eastern Coast of the United States, zeroed in on New York, Manhattan Island, Upper Manhattan, and the street on which the map said the Lamper Building was located. With a few minutes' search I found the Lamper Building. I zeroed in on the sixth floor and found bitch Connie McKesson in an office talking on the phone. It was nearly five p.m. New York time.

"I have her. Tag her."

Steve was sitting next to me waiting for this word. He had a two and a half by fifteen inch strip of artist's mat board in his lap. The number 00000451 was written on it in thick acrylic paint. This number matched a number on a mat board containing the McKesson program. I had stopped using wire on plywood. Thick acrylic paint on artist's mat board worked as well for HAL and was much faster and easier. Next to the number Steve added a T painted on an inch wide piece of mat board. This "tagged" Connie McKesson. HAL would keep track of her until the T was removed.

I watched the woman. After a while Connie put on a jacket and left the office. She was going home for the day. She went down an elevator, out the front door to the street and walked to a parking garage next to the Lamper Building. She got into her car and hit the streets. I followed her car.

Connie drove down many city streets ending up on a highway. She headed north for miles and turned off the highway onto a residential street. A few more turns and she arrived at her house.

"She lives in a single family home" I informed Steve.

"I hope she likes it" Steve said and I laughed.

Connie parked in the garage and walked around the back of the car. She had become a celebrity for taking on the World Empress and a television crew stationed across the street yelled "Hi, Connie" or something to her. She waved back. She was a ham. Who isn't?

Connie went into the living room where two young children waited with a baby sitter. After exchanging a few words with her employer the baby sitter left.

"Yup. She lives there" I said. "I think she's in for the night. Hit her."

Steve put an X next to the T. Connie McKesson was in for an unpleasant surprise in the morning.

I switched back to my normal vision. "We got her" I said triumphantly.

Connie McKesson had to get up at 5:00 a.m. in order to get the house going and still make it to work on time. After the babysitter arrived she walked out to the garage. The television crew shouted morning greetings at her. The ham waved and smiled at them. She started the car, put the transmission in reverse and hit the gas. The engine stalled. She tried again pressing further down on the gas pedal. The front drive wheels spun on the slick garage floor throwing up smoke, but the car didn't move at all.

She got out to check the front of the car. It wasn't tied down in any way. She got on her knees to look under the car. There were no tire blocks or anything she could see. She walked to the garage entrance with no particular purpose. She was simply mystified.

"Need help?" yelled the television crew.

"Yes. Come over."

Three men came over. One pointed a camera at the proceedings.

"Can you guys push the car out?"

One man set the shift stick to neutral and they both pushed the car out to the driveway with little effort. Connie got back in and pushed the gas pedal, but despite the drive wheels smoking the car didn't budge.

She got out again. "You guys try it."

One of the men got in and had no trouble driving the car out to the street.

Connie looked alarmed.

"Can you guys give me a ride?"

They all went to the television van and got in. It was the same result. No amount of pressure on the gas pedal could make the van move. Connie got out. The driver got the van to move forward. She got back in. It didn't move.

The reality hit her. Any vehicle she entered would not move. I wasn't going to allow her to go anywhere except on foot. It was horrible. Nobody in New York could live any kind of life without transportation.

She returned to her house to ponder the idea.

The media discussed this development all day. A lawyer said, "Theresa Hartley is committing a felony. Restricting someone's movements without due process is kidnapping. She could get twenty-five years."

Another lawyer on the panel replied, "What evidence do we have against her?"

"What do you mean what evidence? We all know it's her."

"Of course, but there's not a shred of evidence. You can't go into criminal court without evidence. Anyway, who's going to arrest her?"

So! I could do anything I wanted to anybody and nobody would dare do anything about it! I kind of liked that.

This was the first time I had done anything to influence somebody's activity. Some people said this was a sign that I had a bad streak in me and I would eventually tell everybody what to do. Oh really? When had I told anybody what to do? I couldn't even lead by example because nobody could do what I did. The most I could do was give an example of the right attitude to have about life, God, and myself.

The law firm Kent, Stein, O'Connor, and Farley didn't issue a statement all day. I went back to work because the greedy sharks needed more convincing. The scene of Connie McKesson making her announcement about the lawsuit was shown repeatedly. There were different camera angles showing all eight of the lawyers standing behind her. Steve found these scenes on the internet and printed them out. Now I could find them too.

I zeroed in on the Lamper Building and found the eight lawyers. They were all men, so the crybaby media couldn't say I was making it hard for mommies to take care of their kids as they said about Connie McKesson. I found them, and Steve 'tagged' them with T's, and 'hit' them with X's while they were at work. When they left the building to go home they found out one by one that no vehicle would move with their butts inside. They were forced to walk to a nearby hotel.

The effect was electric. I could do this vehicular immobility trick with anybody and in any numbers. No one was safe.

"Imagine not being able to go anywhere" said an astonished President Stinson to her cabinet. "Forget about trying to charge her with kidnapping. Who's going to arrest her?" That was the exact phrase being used by the media.

The next day, the law firm Kent, Stein, O'Connor, and Farley announced they were withdrawing the lawsuit. I took the X's off the nine strips of mat board and the nine lawyers could use vehicles.

Nobody would ever dare to sue me again.

"Don't mess around with Empress Theresa," Steve smirked.

"Madam," said Arthur, "the Prime Minister wishes to make a visit accompanied by the American Ambassador."

There had been many such requests for visits by people other than Blair, but I'd refused them all. I couldn't waste my time with people who wanted to advance their careers by being photographed with the World Empress. But this was different. Blair wanted me to meet someone.

"I'll see them", I answered.

Steve, Peter Blair, the Ambassador, Mr. and Mrs. Parker and I were soon seated in the living room. The Parkers were there at my invitation. I thought they had the right to know what was going on in their own house.

Blair started it off. "Ambassador Fox has a request. Mr. Ambassador?"

"We were greatly impressed by your grounding of the lawyers. That was quite a trick."

"I don't know what you're talking about, but thank you anyway."

Ambassador Fox smiled. He saw I was no fool!

"You have nothing to worry about. Who would be crazy enough to arrest you?"

I smiled in turn. "OK. What's up?"

"We have the idea this grounding trick can put terrorists out of business. If you could do that to thousands of them, the terrorist movement will die out. They may hope to be martyrs and go to Paradise, but there's no glamour in having to walk everywhere all your life."

Steve and I had suspected that he would say something like that. I looked at Edmund Parker. "What do you think, Mr. Parker?"

"This is Caesar crossing the Rubicon. Once you are involved in international politics there is no turning back."

Mrs. Parker shook her head to indicate 'no'.

These two people had a lot more experience than me. They were advising me to drop the idea. I could see where "grounding" as the Ambassador called it would get the terrorists mad as hell, but they were killing innocent people. Could I ignore that?

I took Steve's hand and stood up.

"Will you excuse us a minute?"

We crossed the foyer to enter the family room.

"What do you think?" I asked.

"Parker is right. Governments will come after you."

"They're already after me. Look. I'm not going to

drag you into something you didn't ask for. If you say no I'll say no."

Steve agonized over that silently for a full minute.

"I'm thinking of all those innocent people being slaughtered. I can't say no but I don't like it."

"Me neither. All right. We'll go for it. So much for retirement."

We returned to the living room.

"I'll do it."

"Excellent! I'll have some people come in a week."

The Parkers made no effort to hide their disappointment. Their darling Theresa was more important to them than nameless bombing victims.

"When I was a little girl mom tried to find me toys that would teach me to figure things out, like toys the boys had before there were video games. Now you want me to play games with the world. If this leads to war I want the President to take responsibility. I want it in writing with her signature this week."

"Fair enough."

We went for a walk through the forests to ponder whether this was a giant leap for mankind or a step into quicksand.

Ambassador Fox returned in three days with President Stinson's signed statement.

"I take full responsibility for the grounding of international terrorists by Theresa Elizabeth Sullivan Hartley who is acting as my agent.

Veronica Stinson
President of the United States"

Chapter 18

Did I know what I was doing? Heck no! I admit it. I was just an eighteen year old kid who tried to accommodate people's needs. I didn't know what it would lead to. Mr. Parker told me you can't do something right the first time you do it. Any change in routine is sure to cause problems every single time. There are no exceptions. Yeah, well, not doing something can be a mistake too.

Four men sent by Ambassador Fox arrived at the Parker estate. I was amused as they introduced themselves as Bob, Jack, Harry, and Chuck. These were probably all fake names.

"I get it. You guys work on the Thanksgiving Day parade organizing committee."

"How did you guess?" laughed Bob who was the leader and the jovial diplomat.

Bob did all the talking for this group and he might as well have been talking about the philosophical theories of the Three Stooges for all the lightness of his speech. Did this clown really work for the CIA? He had to be faking his demeanor.

"The first thing we need to know is can you find any particular person you want after you've grounded him?"

"Oh yeah. I had to set it up like that. The lawyers might have tried to trick me by saying they needed an ambulance. I'd need to look at the person quickly to see if he really needed an ambulance. Then, if I did turn off the grounding and turned it on again, I'd have to look at the person to make sure he wasn't in an airplane."

"Hoo boy! What would happen then?"

"HAL would stop the plane instantly. The passengers would be crushed like apple sauce."

"Ouch! Cancel my reservation!"

Bob would be a little tiring after a while.

"How can you find the person if his grounding has been turned off?"

"Each person has a number. Once I tag him HAL will always keep track of him grounded or not. Why does it matter if I can find a person again?"

"If you can do that, you can use one terrorist to find many others."

"I didn't think of that. Maybe we shouldn't ground them right away, just tag them and see where they go."

"It depends on the place you find them. In the Middle East we want them to lead us to others. In an Afghan training camp we just ground everybody except somebody who looks like he's visiting. He'll lead us to others."

"I get it."

We got down to work. Bob would show me maps of places where intelligence said there were terrorists. I'd memorize the maps as well as I could, then switch to my black and white vision to find the location. I gave descriptions of what I saw and Bob told me to move left, right, up, or down until I found the target. Sometimes it was a camp in an isolated place. There might be dozens or hundreds of terrorists training there. I'd look at tents to find the ones who looked like the leaders. They were tagged but not grounded right away. They would eventually travel and lead us to other terrorist groups. One strategy was not to ground anybody in the camp for a couple of days. Then when there was a visitor who'd already left for other locations, he wouldn't realize that he had been found at the same time as the rest of the camp. This way the terrorists wouldn't know what was going on.

Meeting three days a week the team could find and tag, or tag and ground, two or three hundred terrorists a week. In two weeks the press was filing stories that terrorists were being grounded. Everybody knew it was me. The news brought praise from nearly all politicians in Europe, the Americas, Africa and Asia. My name was being mentioned for the Nobel Peace Prize.

The effectiveness of the program was not yet known. Bombings are often planned months or years ahead. Presumably, at some future time bombings would decrease in number.

In the midst of all this I found time to turn my attention back to the sun where I raised huge cylinders of gas for the fractional separation of silver. This precious metal was a more practical element for coinage as it could be made in small coins of low value for everyday exchange in retail stores. People in undeveloped countries where the national currency was of questionable worth would now have a medium of exchange that was accepted everywhere. President Stinson promised that the U. S. Mint would issue silver coins in twenty cents, one dollar and five dollar denominations with my picture on them in numbers too huge to be absorbed in the American economy.

The excess would spill over into the third world in the interest of international prosperity and peace.

I dumped a pile of silver twenty times as large as the Fort Knox gold pile on a British Army base. More would come when needed. The old English trade of silversmith was restored. Tradesmen bought the silver to make silver tea sets, mugs and silverware. Everybody could afford to have a king's dinner set.

Total sales of my gold and silver reached more than a billion dollars a week, and was climbing fast. This might taper off after a while, but in less than a year I would be richer than some small countries. Theresa calling Jack. How are you doing with Ginny?

Now began the most complicated political mess I'd ever get into. Khaled bin Azad was the charismatic and worldly Secretary General of the Organization of the Petroleum Exporting Countries, OPEC, a cartel of oil producing countries that met at its Vienna, Austria headquarters to set policies for the safeguarding of member nation interests and stabilization of oil prices from harmful fluctuations. It had thirteen member nations in the Middle East, Africa, and South America.

There were other countries that exported oil but were not part of OPEC, seeing no reason to have to protect their interests or simply not wanting to be dependent on the Organization's policies. Secretary General Azad set out to recruit their membership.

Unlike on previous trips abroad, when the handsome forty-two year old pandered to the press, Azad kept a low profile. He traveled without announcements, usually escaping the media, and when he talked to people in the countries he visited it was done behind closed doors. He sometimes slipped in and out of a country without being noticed.

I was aware of all this because the media was talking about it day and night. OPEC had been largely the equivalent of an old ladies' quilting club for many years. Now they were stirring themselves up. The world didn't like it. OPEC no longer had the near monopoly of oil it had before very deep ocean drilling came on, but they still controlled enough of the oil supply to cause a lot of mischief. The United States didn't depend on OPEC much anymore, but Europe and most of the world did. There was only one world price for oil. We all had to pay the same price even if we produced the stuff.

The White House announced the President would make a courtesy visit to London to acknowledge the friendship and value of its longtime ally Great Britain. Nobody was fooled. President Stinson could only be going to London to meet me in the "summit of summits" as it was being called. Why President Stinson didn't call me ahead of time is still a mystery. Maybe she was afraid I would say no to a meeting on the phone, but couldn't say no if she showed up in London.

She had come under a lot of criticism for doing nothing when I was trying to get control of HAL and restore the rain. She might have invited me back to the United States, or she might have come to London to help me. She did neither. Supporters said she was preparing the country to cope with the worst possible scenario, which was true, but that's not how things turned out. I solved the problems under Blair's wing and critics were slamming her. This visit was partly to repair her image.

She was taking a big risk. If I snubbed her she would be a political lame duck. This was also explained on the news, as if to make sure I understood it. So,……… how loyal was I to my President?

Air Force One, and the identical backup plane, were ready for the President's boarding. We watched the crowd waiting for Veronica Stinson's arrival and Air Force One's departure. With the press having little else to yap about they made a big issue about what kind of reception the President would get from me. Would I be waiting at the airport? Would I snub the President because of what President Martin did?

"What do you think I should do?" I asked Steve.

"Meet her at the airport. I'll stay here."

"Are you sure?"

"Yeah. She's our President."

"I mean are you sure you want to stay home?"

"I'll just get in the way. The President's husband isn't coming. They'll have to find ways to entertain me somewhere while you talk with the Prez. It would be embarrassing. Besides, I have a cute French maid waiting for you to leave."

"I knew it!"

I understood. Steve wasn't sure what he'd say to Stinson who was part of the administration of President Martin.

To make it short, Prime Minister Blair waited at the airport for President Stinson, Arthur and I showed up just before the President came down the stairs of Air Force One, and we agreed to a meeting in the U.S. Embassy, with Blair present as a representative of the rest of the world at my insistence.

President Stinson asked me, "How much do you know about OPEC?"

"Not much. They used their oil to blackmail us in 1973. Why do they get worked up now after all that time?"

"Power was distributed among many nations. We had some, the British had some, everybody had some. They couldn't take on the whole world. Now you have all the power. They think they can make you cave in and turn you into a slave. That will give them the power they always wanted."

"Yeah, well, Steve and I have a plan that will take care of them. The sun has lots of carbon. We're going to bring trillions of tons of it to Earth. It can be used to generate electricity at very low cost. Everybody will switch to electric cars. Driving will be almost free."

"Who gets this carbon?"

"Anybody who wants it, even nations that don't like us. The idea is to reduce the need for oil."

"How much will you charge for this carbon?"

"Not a penny. It's free."

"My goodness! That's very generous."

"I'm not going to be anyone's slave. They can drop dead."

"Of course, we don't know what they're planning. It may be nothing, but your plan should limit any damage if they do. I just wonder if you can deliver this carbon quickly in case they turn off the spigots right away?"

"I can have it here in two months. I'm working on it now."

Blair jumped in. "I understand it would take years

to change the transportation system from fuel power to electricity. If there is an embargo there will be hardship."

"We do have our own limited oil supply" answered the President. "Offshore drilling technology is advancing more and more quickly every day. We're drilling in two mile deep water. An embargo would accelerate drilling ten times, I think. But you're right. A severe embargo would cause hardship. But Theresa's carbon will calm the public nerves."

"Indeed it will. As always public confidence is the main concern."

"Why's that?" I asked.

"The people must believe things will work out well or their fears will make the situation much worse. During the '73 embargo there were absurdly long lines at the petrol stations but in reality there was always enough petrol for everyone's needs. It was public fear that caused the long lines and other problems."

The President added, "The need for importing oil is far greater today. The problems would be worse."

"Don't we have plenty of offshore oil?" I asked.

"Yes but it's in deep water."

"I can bring the land up to the surface."

"You can?"

"Sure. I did it at the South Pole."

"That would help. How do you raise land?"

"I slip crushed rock under the land I want to lift up. HAL is nothing but a bulldozer but he's an awful big one. I read we're drilling ten thousand foot wells in the Caribbean. I could raise the Caribbean floor to the surface. Of course, you understand raising that much ocean floor will take a few months."

"Good Lord!" exclaimed Peter Blair. "Shall we announce this?"

"And force them to do something? Let's see what OPEC does first. Let the bastards shoot themselves in the foot."

There was a personal matter I wanted to discuss.

"If I provide a cheap source of oil, it will save people a heck of a lot of money, don't you think?"

"Trillions of dollars a year" Stinson agreed.

"More than the gold people lost?"

"Many times more I would think."

"Then I don't want any more lawsuits about gold or anything else. I can't be sitting in courtrooms all the time because some people are greedy. I could ignore whatever OPEC does, you know."

"Understood. You play hardball, Theresa."

She said it with a smile. I think she was proud of me.

"Yeah, well, I didn't ask for any of this. I don't deserve to be bullied. Ninety percent of the gold in the world was dug up centuries ago at very low prices. Now people want me to buy it all back at trillions of dollars nobody ever paid for it? They can all drop dead."

"I'll see what I can do. Congress could pass laws exempting your from suits. The government can't be sued. I think you could be included. It wouldn't take a Constitutional amendment."

Blair added, "I'll attempt the same with my European friends. That should settle the matter."

No more detailed ideas about the OPEC situation were possible because we didn't know what OPEC would do if anything. Discussion drifted off into general topics. President Stinson asked many questions about what I could do with HAL. I had to tell her not much. I was still in the early stages of breaking the code to control HAL. I was developing new parameters all the time, but couldn't predict all future needs.

The meeting eventually ended. I returned to the Parker house, President Stinson went back to the States, she told people in vague terms that I was preparing unspecified actions, the stock market calmed down and everybody waited for OPEC's move.

President Stinson called in several dozen Senators and Representatives to explain the gold situation and why I wanted exemption from lawsuits. Like President Martin with the BC campus police, President Stinson read the Congressional representatives the riot act. They went back to the Capitol Building swinging bats and asked Congress to pass laws exempting me from lawsuits. Not many people were against it except the lawyers and nobody cared what they thought.

President Stinson summed it up at a press conference.

"Theresa is a tough little lady. If she plays hardball with her own government, she'll be Godzilla to OPEC."

OPEC met in secret session. It lasted three days indicating to the outside world that there was difficulty in reaching any kind of agreement. Members understood that taking me on was a high risk gamble. Finally, a public statement was announced.

Secretary General Khaled bin Azad droned on for an hour complaining about alleged insults and attacks his OPEC countries and their people had suffered over the years. Steve pretended to fall asleep on the sofa listening to this harangue and snored. I jabbed my elbow into his rib cage.

Finally, Azad got down to the nitty-gritty.

"We seek justice on the world stage. If it is not given to us we will take it. We demand the operation known as grounding be removed from all freedom fighters." The phrase 'freedom fighters' was his term for the murderous terrorists. "We demand that Theresa Hartley put ten billion dollars every month into a fund for the world's poor. We demand the land known to the West as Israel be returned to the people who lived there before 1947. If these demands are not met we will sell no oil to the United States or the European Union."

I was near tears at these outrageous demands.

"I saved their lives, I turned their deserts into gardens, and they do this to me?"

Steve stared at the television with a fierce frown. He was livid.

"This is the world we live in. We're going to kill the bastards!"

Steve started up the computer and did research. He was looking for offshore oil deposits. Raising the Caribbean floor was an option but came with loads of political questions as to who owned the Caribbean. He wanted a neater solution.

After looking up a list of known or suspected underwater oil reserves he read that there was more oil under the gap between Africa and Madagascar than there was in the Middle East, but not a single oil well had ever been drilled there because the oil companies didn't trust the leftist Madagascan government. So much for that solution!

He looked up how this oil had been created. It seemed that millions of years ago Madagascar had broken off from the eastern side of Africa. The growing gap between the two land masses was what created the submarine oil deposits. Well, that was interesting. Where else had this happened?

He turned to plate tectonics. Soon, he found something startling. Antarctica was originally connected to Africa right next to Madagascar. Antarctica drifted south and was just beginning to cross the South Pole. The Antarctic coastline on the Atlantic side with the tip of Africa pointed right at the middle was the part of Antarctica that had once been joined to Africa just below where Madagascar had been similarly attached. The coastline of that section of Antarctica still matched the African coastline from which it moved. The two continents were separated by a distance equal to the width of Antarctica which was a lot of room to play in. Except for one tiny, uninhabited, ice covered island called Bouvet Island belonging to Norway, there wasn't a single square foot of land in this immense expanse of ocean. I could pay off the Norwegians later. Maybe I'd raise another island for them. He printed out a map and drew an elongated ellipse along this coastline. He showed it to me and explained why he thought there was oil. I agreed it was worth trying to raise the ocean floor to the surface. But this presented problems. What to do with all that water that would be displaced? Where was the rock under the island to come from? After two hours I developed a plan.

I drew a rectangle on the map Steve gave me. It was parallel to the Antarctic coastline that had once been connected to Africa. The rectangle began two hundred miles inland from the coast and extended five hundred miles further inland towards the Pole. It was fifteen hundred miles long. This had to be the most useless real estate in the world; nobody would miss it. After thinking about it for a while I drew a thick line from the southwestern corner of the rectangle all the way to the Ross Ice Shelf. This would be a spillway to bring in water. Steve copied the map and showed it to Arthur.

"Arthur, take this map to the Prime Minister." He pointed to the rectangle I had drawn. "Tell him if there are any people in this rectangle or this line from the corner they have to evacuate immediately. Theresa will destroy this area in a week and she doesn't care who's in the way."

"Very good, sir."

"And no planes overhead either. They'll be destroyed."

Arthur nodded his understanding. He took it to Blair and before you could burp the map was on television. There was a raging controversy about the line I had drawn out to the Ross Ice Shelf. Some BBC commentators talked about it.

"As the map shows" said one of them to his associates, "most of Antarctica is in the Atlantic with only a small amount in the Pacific. A line drawn from the rectangle to the Atlantic would only be two hundred miles long, but the line Theresa drew goes thirteen hundred miles across the continent to the Ross Ice Shelf. Why does she prefer the Ross Ice Shelf?"

"Consider the differences between the Atlantic coast and the Ross Ice Shelf. The Atlantic coast has whales, seals, penguins and nearby boat traffic. There are cruise ships. Much the same can be said for ninety percent of the Antarctic coastline. The coast around the Ross Ice Shelf has none of these. There is nothing there."

"Why is that important?"

"I must say it is an intriguing mystery."

I was enjoying this!

The next morning Prime Minister Blair called. Arthur handed the phone to me. I assumed it was about Antarctica. It wasn't

"This is Theresa. What's up?"

"Israeli Prime Minister Benjamin Scherzer flies to London tomorrow morning. He is very concerned and wishes to meet with you."

I dropped the phone on the floor and sat on one of the living room sofas.

Steve picked up the phone and told the PM, "Hang on, Mr. Blair. We have a problem."

He put the phone down and sat next to me.

"What's the matter?" he asked.

"Everybody wants something from me" I said in shock. "I can't do everything."

Steve picked up the phone again. "Mr. Blair, did you hear that?"

"I did. Shall I call later?"

"Might be a good idea, sir."

He hung up the phone.

"Mr. Parker was right" I said. "I shouldn't have got involved in politics."

Parker replied, "I have reconsidered my statement.

It was inevitable you would be involved. You have power. Somebody was sure to try to get it from you. Now consider who could do this. Governments couldn't do it. The only hand they have to play is military. The United States and all Western countries would come to your aid if a government tried to blackmail you with military power. But OPEC had the oil card to play. There is no defense against that. OPEC would have challenged you even without the grounding of the terrorists."

We were enthralled by Parker's remarks. He was no fool.

But his assessment didn't help me and I said, "I read a short story. A Hindu god told a Prince, 'I will give you all wisdom and immortality if you come up my mountain and live with me forever'. The Prince agreed. People heard about him. For a thousand years they came up the mountain to ask his advice about their problems. Finally, he threw himself off a cliff and killed himself. He left a message behind. It read, 'Too late I learned the curse of having what others want'."

Steve and Mr. Parker wore frowns. They couldn't think of anything to console me. It was Mrs. Parker who saved the day.

"The Prince had nobody who loved him."

I smiled. Mrs. Parker said the right thing.

I looked at Steve. "What do I do about Israel?"

"I don't know. We don't have to come up with something in five minutes. Tell Blair you'll see the guy. He might have ideas."

"Arthur, would you get Mr. Blair back?"

"Happily, madam." He reached Blair.

"Mr. Blair? I don't know what I can do but I'll meet with him."

"He is also at a loss. Perhaps a meeting will inspire us."

"OK. We'll work on ideas."

Arthur drove us into London Wednesday morning so we could have a long leisurely lunch at a first class restaurant. Shortly before one we arrived at Number 10. We were ushered into the PM's residence where the two Prime Ministers waited in a nearby office. Arthur had to wait in another room. "Sorry, Arthur," I said. "This is very sensitive stuff."

"I fully understand, madam," he answered with his standard reassuring smile.

We were conducted into the meeting room. Steve carried a briefcase containing the 'sensitive stuff'. Typical greetings and handshakes were exchanged and we all sat down at a table.

Prime Minister Scherzer's face was grim. He'd all but given up finding a solution to the crisis. It would take a miracle. I noticed his mood and gave him a big smile to indicate things weren't so bad. His return smile indicated encouragement.

Blair began the discussion. "Prime Minister Scherzer graduated from your West Point."

"Really!" said Steve. "I thought it was only for Americans."

"There are international students. A classmate was a Saudi prince."

He spoke English like an American.

"Not your roommate, I hope. What can we do for you, sir?"

It was evident to everybody that Steve would do all

the talking. I stayed out of it to let old warrior Scherzer have a dignified male-to-male bull session with Steve, who was being deliberately deferential.

"We are surrounded by enemies. We fought them off many times but this new embargo looks like it will be a long one. I'm not sure we can depend on our friends to stand by us."

He stopped. That settled it. Scherzer had no ideas about what to do.

"Well, sir, I think we all agree your friends won't stay with you long if it means abandoning their cars and walking to work. But we can't give in to these bastards' demands.

"As we say in America, I have good news and bad news. The bad news is you can't stay where you are. Theresa is going to clobber these bastards. When they find out what's going on they'll be mad as killer bees. They'll swarm over you.

"The good news is Theresa can give you a new homeland. She has two plans, A and B. Plan A is moving Israel."

He pulled a map of Israel out of the brief case. Red lines drawn with a felt marker separated Israel into three parts. The middle part was trapezoid shaped.

"The trapezoid section is moved west into the Mediterranean. That makes it possible to move the northern part of Israel south for a few miles, then west into the Mediterranean. Finally, the southern part is moved north a hundred miles then west into the Mediterranean. The parts are put together again in between Italy and Greece here." He indicated the place on another map showing the entire

Mediterranean Sea. "The problem with this plan is it doesn't give you anything and fishermen will complain you're ruining their business."

"What's Plan B?"

Steve smiled. "I knew you wouldn't like A. Plan B is Theresa can raise an island for you out of the ocean floor."

He pulled out a crude drawing of an island. It was in the shape of the Star of David.

"This island will be five hundred miles wide which is something like twenty times the land area you have now and every square inch will be fertile soil. Each arm of the star has 20,000 foot mountains to catch the rain and give you fresh water. They will also be the greatest ski resorts in the world. Kids like ski slopes more than rocks in the desert. Your tourist trade will explode. The problem with this plan is it will be months before it's habitable. You may have to put up somewhere. Maybe your friends in New York and Florida can take you in."

"How can she raise an island?"

Apparently he liked this plan better!

"Very simple. She cuts out two slabs of bedrock, crushes one into gravel and packs it under the other slab. She's done it before underwater in the South Pacific close to the Pole. We have bets on how long oceanographers will take to find it."

Blair quietly listened as we explained that. He'd already heard it when President Stinson visited.

Scherzer said, "If OPEC had known of these powers they might not have made their demands."

Steve and I were shocked. Scherzer had made a good point. A little knowledge shared with the world might have prevented this mess. Were we to blame?

Blair intervened. "Mr. Prime Minister. These young people are not experienced in diplomacy."

Yeah, well, Blair had already known I could do something with the Earth's surface. Where was he when this mess started?

"Let's leave it behind" said Steve. "Where were we?"

"The island" Scherzer resumed. "Where is it?"

"Anywhere you want. I assume you're not interested in the Indian Ocean. We're betting you'll choose the North Atlantic."

"You'd be right."

Steve pulled out a map of the North Atlantic showing the lands around it.

"You have to avoid that red line down the center. That's where the volcanic thermal vents are. You might choose to be close to New York, but then you wouldn't be a refueling stop and transfer point for planes crossing the Atlantic. That could be a good business."

Blair added, "This is amazing, Mr. Prime Minister! A traveler from any city in the New World can go to any city in the Old World with only one stop on your island. The savings are tremendous. Existing airports can't do this because none is large enough to handle the planes."

Prime Minister Scherzer was sold. He thought a moment.

"I'm leaning toward Plan B, but I'm not sure my people will give up Israel."

Steve answered, "They have two choices: stay and be exterminated to the last man woman and child, or leave. I don't think there's a third alternative."

"There isn't. Can you move Jerusalem to the island?"

We were startled. We never thought of that. What an idea!

"Yeah. Easily. Right, Theresa?"

"It's a piece of cake."

Steve offered a felt pen for marking the spot. Before choosing a spot Scherzer asked, "Where will you get soil for all that land?"

"That's very interesting, sir. The ocean floor is covered with hundreds of feet of mud. It's millions of years of dust and micrometeorites, full of microbes, the most fertile soil on Earth. When Theresa raises the island she'll have to scrape most of it back into the sea leaving twenty feet."

"Are there mountains on the ocean floor?"

Steve smiled. "You don't miss a thing, do you, sir?"

"It's my job."

"There's tens of thousands of them everywhere. Extinct volcanoes from tectonic plate movement. Theresa will have to push most of them back into the sea."

Scherzer was satisfied with that. He moved the felt pen over the map and chose a spot near the middle of the Atlantic at a latitude matching New York. That would put it right in the center of many commercial airplane routes between the United States and lower Europe making air transport far more profitable.

"Good choice, sir. Theresa will start working on it today."

Prime Minister Scherzer was hesitating to respond.

He quietly said, "As much as the Star of David warms our hearts it's not the most practical design. Can we change it?"

"Sure. It was something we threw together overnight."

Steve turned the map of Israel upside down to the blank side and pulled a handful of writing instruments out of the briefcase.

"It's all yours, sir."

Blair was right on the ball with this one! "Hold on. I'll call for a piece of parchment." An aide was summoned with a piece of parchment and left. Blair pulled out his expensive fountain pen and said, "Use my pen, Mr. Prime Minister. It has India ink. It will never fade."

Scherzer took the pen and went to work designing his new country. He started with a circle and added features. He drew thirty projections along the perimeter.

"What are those, sir?"

"Peninsulas. Twenty miles long and five miles wide."

"Got it."

On the western side of the circle he drew two adjacent peninsulas in the shape of opposing Ls coming into each other out at sea.

"Protected harbor" he explained.

He drew a similar protected harbor on the eastern side. He indicated Jerusalem was to be next to the western harbor. He drew a cluster of mountains in the middle of the island. Using his topographical map knowledge, he indicated elevations in meters. "Elevations in meters" he said. In a large valley in the middle of the mountain cluster he indicated an area with a negative elevation, that is, it was below sea level. "A lake" he said. He drew circular contour lines here and there around the island to indicate hills of fifty meters in height. He drew two circles close to the harbors and noted they were to be flat as a billiard table. "Airports" he said.

He took a final look at the design and turned it around for Steve to look at. Steve didn't even study it. Instead, he handed it to me for my signature. I signed the map at the bottom using Blair's pen.

"Your signature to a historic document, sir?" Steve suggested to the Prime Minister.

Scherzer also signed with Blair's pen.

"You can send us a copy, sir. Keep the original. It'll be a good piece for a museum of Jewish history."

At this, the Prime Minister had trouble keeping control of his emotions. "Thank you" he said with a frog in his throat. "And thank you, Mrs. Hartley."

"You're welcome!" I said with a proud smile.

Prime Minister Blair jumped in.

"How will you clobber the bastards?"

"Well, sir, technically speaking Theresa won't do a thing to them. In seven days she will raise a large area of the ocean floor between Antarctica and Africa. We believe this area has trillions of barrels of oil. It will all belong to Theresa. She will sell the oil on the world market for twenty dollars a barrel. No limits. OPEC will still make a little money. They should thank her."

"I wonder if they will attack Israel at all. Why would they?"

"They may blackmail us with an attack on Israel if

Theresa's oil island brings their profits down. The funny thing is she has to supply oil to frustrate their oil embargo. They'll be clobbering themselves."

"Who knows about these plans?"

"Only the four of us in this room. Politicians are hiding under their desks. Theresa has to do it all."

"Can Mrs. Hartley raise other oil islands?"

"Sure. They'll all belong to her."

"Will the oil islands be protected?"

"Theresa is an American citizen. She'll say the islands are under the laws of the United States. Who's going to argue?"

"How can Israel be evacuated quickly enough so the Israelis are not attacked?"

"Theresa plans on raising a land bridge from Israel to Crete. They can move to Europe from there at their own pace."

"Mr. Scherzer will have to make plans to move all their valuable possessions quickly. Decisions must be made ahead of time."

"Yeah, but keep it secret until the last minute."

"Agreed. What can Prime Minister Scherzer tell his people?"

Wow! That was a tough one! What could people be told without precipitating an early attack? I watched Steve ponder it a minute.

"Theresa needs time to prepare for the evacuation. Tell them Theresa could destroy the world. Tell them as long as she's around they're safe. Tell them the bastards are crazy if they push her too far. There's no stopping her. Let them sweat for a change."

Blair asked a question that shook us.

"It will take many days to move millions of Israelis

across the bridge. It won't be possible to keep assassins from infiltrating the crowds. In the darkness of night they will shoot many thousands of Israelis."

Steve's face was frozen, but you could tell from his eyes he was stunned. Blair was right. Assassins couldn't be spotted in the dark. They'd have a field day with the Israelis.

Steve sat there thinking, but this was one problem that seemed really too difficult to solve.

"Are you saying Theresa needs to give the Israelis twenty-four hour daylight?"

"I merely stated the problem."

I said, "I would have to be God to do that."

It was a tense moment. The two Prime Ministers' eyes showed they were worried I might be being pushed too far. Would I walk out on them?

Scherzer eased the tension. "We're not asking for more miracles. What you've given us is miracle enough."

Blair tried to further distance everybody from the twenty-four daylight idea. He turned to Scherzer.

"Mr. Prime Minister. Are you satisfied with our meeting?"

"I am. Mrs. Hartley saves my people."

Chapter 19

Prime Minister Scherzer had not tried to hide his visit to London to see me. The Israelis needed to know he was trying to do something, whether or not he got anything out of me. When he returned to Tel Aviv he made a television broadcast to the nation. The usually stern PM allowed himself to emote.

"My beloved Israelis. This is a blessed day. I talked with Mr. and Mrs. Hartley hoping against all reason that Mrs. Hartley could help us. I am happy to announce that she and her husband were most helpful and sympathetic. No negotiation was necessary. No deals were made. The Hartleys walked into the meeting prepared to give us everything.

"Those who challenge Theresa Hartley's power are fools. She could destroy the world. Don't push her too far.

"I cannot tell you what agreements were made at this time, but let me assure you the future of the Israelis is secure. We will at last have our long awaited land of milk and honey. The young woman well deserves the title Empress Theresa."

As usual the media tried to stir up controversy. They said Scherzer was using doublespeak in saying there were no deals but we made agreements. The media could go to hell! Blair told reporters, "Theresa gave Scherzer everything unconditionally. Scherzer gave Theresa nothing. That's not a deal".

My Antarctica project took longer than expected. Several HAL programs had to be written. The first one I needed was also the simplest, and I initiated it two days after Steve's one week warning ran out and there were several dozen planes stationed at the tip of South America flying out one after the other to watch what I was doing. They saw the first task begin.

Along the southwestern corner of the rectangle where the line I had drawn began, the ice went straight up at two hundred miles an hours. This ten mile wide curtain of ice went merrily down the line I'd drawn at twenty miles an hour. The first plane to reach this activity went down into the 'channel' as it was soon called and noted that the bottom was a perfectly flat table of rock one thousand feet below sea level. The channel was already sixty miles long when this information was passed to the world. It was clear I was ripping up a lot of rock along with the ice to keep the channel bottom below sea level.

There was a lot of excitement in the American Station located at the exact South Pole. Officially called the Amundsen-Scott South Pole Station, it had around 150 scientists. I wondered what they had to do besides look at the three mile thick ice. The line I'd drawn passed less than a hundred miles from the Station and the rising ice curtain would be closest to them in two days. They planned to send out a dozen people on snowmobiles to get a close look.

Now came one of those surprises that complicated my life. You would think that people would appreciate my efforts to do something about the OPEC situation. You would think they would love what I was doing in Antarctica and appreciate everything I had done to save their lives. Nope. All forgotten.

A U.S. Senator who wanted to be a television celebrity made a speech saying that I was tearing up an area of land equal to New York City every fifteen minutes and I was the most dangerous person who had ever lived. Steve told me, "He's going to look like an idiot when you're done with Antarctica".

What had changed? Nothing I had done until then damaged land. Now I was ripping up three square miles of land every minute. That scared people. What if I did this in their backyard!

Within hours people demonstrated in the streets all over the world. And it wasn't just in big cities. There were demonstrations in small towns. Television showed mothers holding their kids and crying, complaining "Has Theresa gone insane, destroying land like that?"

How quickly people forgot my benevolence when fear took control of them!

The next morning, Steve and I were in the living room with the Parker family when the phone rang. Only a few people had access to that phone. Arthur came over and announced, "President Stinson calls Madame Hartley."

I took the phone. "Hello."

The President was in a nasty mood.

"Theresa, you have to stop everything until we find out what you're doing!"

Er, what? This was not the sweet lady she presented to the public. I kept silent for a while trying to control my own temper. It wouldn't do to have the World Empress blow her top. That would really make the world nervous. I selected a calm response.

"I can't tell you what I'm doing. People will get in the way and get themselves killed. I would be blamed. Forget that."

"That's not good enough, Theresa. I want you to stop everything and come to Washington tomorrow!"

Holy smokes, Batman! Was she worked up! They had to be pelting her with crap over there.

"Are you leading the crowd or following, Madam President?"

"I'm trying to calm a thousand riots. Get on the next plane to Washington!"

Well, this was going nowhere. "Tell the people I'm still waiting for an apology for the attempt on my life, but I haven't done anything to anybody, have I?"

I hung up on her and went back to sit by Steve.

"That went well," I said sarcastically.

"What did she want?"

"She told me to stop everything and go to Washington to explain what I was doing."

"You can't do that."

"I explained that but she didn't listen."

The phone rang again. Arthur answered and then walked up to Mr. Parker.

"The Prime Minister calls you, sir."

Eyebrows went up all over the room. Parker went to the phone and listened to Blair for a couple minutes. He returned to us and sat down.

"The Prime Minister will order soldiers and anti-aircraft weapons moved up to the house."

I looked at Steve who was equally amazed. "I'm going to write a book," he said.

I asked, "Mr. Parker, would the President try to stop me?"

"There are many unfriendly countries. The Prime Minister's message is a two edged sword intended to calm world fears. You will be defended, but if you start to harm people the guns could be turned on you."

Steve jumped up and headed for the phone. Mr. Parker also jumped up and intercepted him.

"Wait, Steve. Whatever you say will be interpreted as Theresa's anger. Silence may speak loudest."

Steve yielded and came back to my side.

Early that evening the soldiers started moving in. By dawn's early light they'd set up Gatling guns and small anti-aircraft missiles on all four sides of the house. The Gatling guns were mainly for the small drones everybody had now. The missiles were for planes and helicopters. The soldiers had rifles to take down anybody who approached on foot.

All this was shown on television. It encouraged people to continue their demonstrations. They felt they were fighting me.

Two days had gone by and the American Station scientists were waiting next to the line of the coming channel. They had to stay a few miles away because a lot of ice was falling in. The rising ice and rock curtain passed by. It was a thrilling scene. The scientists had a ground view and captured the ground level noise. Bug-eyed people around the world watched in stony silence.

A little after midnight on the third day, the channel reached the Ross Ice Shelf. Water from underneath the Ice Shelf rushed in at a hundred miles an hour. The water was from a thousand feet below sea level and the 400 pounds per square inch pressure made the water move very fast. I needed a lot of water coming in quickly. Some ice had fallen into the channel. The violence of the rushing water broke the ice down into a slurry. I had worried about an ice jam but it didn't happen.

After waiting a few minutes to make sure the water didn't stop rushing in for some reason, I changed a parameter on the HAL program to stop tearing up more ice and rock but keep on pushing the material already raised to beyond the Earth's gravitational influence. Steve called the BBC to tell them to watch the western edge of the rectangle in the morning at nine o'clock London time. Then we went to bed.

We woke up at seven to get ready for the next phase of my Antarctica spectacular. The week's warning about the destruction in Antarctica ran out a few days late because of the complicated HAL programs I needed to write first. It was time to initiate three programs at once. Long range propeller driven airplanes were slowly cruising around Antarctica outside the rectangle indicated on the map we sent to Blair. What I had done with the channel to the Ross Ice Shelf was nothing. The pilots were not prepared for what happened next.

Along the western edge of the rectangle a curtain of ice flew straight up in the air. The ice went up at my standard two hundred miles per hour, but so huge was the rectangle the ice appeared to rise in a barely perceptible motion. The western edge of the rectangle was five hundred miles long. This operation was similar to my channel digging, but it was fifty times wider. A plane pilot connected to a television network said, "This is ten thousand times larger than what she's doing at the North Pole. Forget the pictures. You have to be here to understand the size of this thing."

Even Steve and I watching television in England had underestimated the impression this sight would have. It made your spine tingle. One plane got sight of another with the ice curtain behind. Zooming away made this second plane disappear into an insignificant dot compared to the ice. Now people could get an idea of the size of this thing.

In a couple of minutes the ice was higher than the highest plane and then it became visually clear it was going out to space just like the material from the channel. I was going to empty the rectangle of ice.

The ice curtain moved east. Planes moved in for a closer look. The curtain had moved over a few miles leaving a hole in the two mile thick ice cover. A two mile high sheer wall of ice could not stand under its own weight, and the ice walls were collapsing section by section in spectacular crashes on the ground far below.

Having HAL hold up all that ice in the air within the Earth's gravity field would be too dangerous. As soon as the ice reached a height of twenty miles, I had HAL start accelerating it towards escape velocity. We would never see it again.

The street demonstrations had just started organizing in Europe when the ice flew up. They quickly dissipated and everybody rushed home to watch television.

In a while the ice curtain had moved a few miles further away and more planes felt safe to fly down and inside the ice hole. Flying close but at a safe distance from the collapsing ice walls was a thrill for the pilots who tended to be daredevils. They could see that the floor of the de-iced space was flat and at sea level. Again, it was clear I was tearing up rock along with the ice.

An hour went by and only ten miles of the fifteen hundred mile long rectangular area had been cleaned out of ice. President Stinson came on live television at four a.m. Washington time to address the nation. Yes, that's right. She came on at 4 a.m.

"I'll be brief. This is not the time to talk about Theresa. We don't want to distract her. We want her to fully concentrate on whatever it is she's doing."

That's all she said. She was really saying, *"Shut the hell up about Theresa! We don't want to get her upset. Let her forget about us"*.

This was evidently going to take six days at the rate it was going and after three hours the networks reduced the image to a corner of the television screen as they moved to other subjects.

But minutes later the television screen returned to full screen views of the rectangular area. The planes had noticed that the ground that was being denuded of ice cover was sinking. The rock was going down!

"Where is it going?" exclaimed President Stinson to some people in the White House.

At least two operations were going on at once. I was stripping off the ice and rock down to sea level and at the same time lowering the rock underneath.

What was I doing, everybody wanted to know? Why was the rock in the rectangle going down? Where was it going?

We and the Parkers were having a good time

watching all this on television. The chattering of the anchors helplessly speculating on my intentions were funny. They didn't have a clue. Only Prime Ministers Blair and Scherzer knew parts of the plan. Each of these gentlemen, sitting in his capitol city, must have enjoyed the show.

Meanwhile, lest we forget, the water in the channel to the Ross Ice Shelf had been rushing down the channel for thirteen hours. It reached the rectangle and water was seen falling a hundred feet into it. It was like a ten mile wide waterfall.

By bedtime the rectangle's rock had descended over three hundred feet. We called it a night.

In the morning the rectangle had dropped 1700 feet. Rock and ice were visibly collapsing along the western half of the rectangle while the eastern half, still waiting for the uprising ice curtain, was sinking still covered with the ice that had been there for eons.

The news anchors had figured out that I had to be moving water into the rectangle to maintain world ocean levels. There could be no other reason, especially as no changes in ocean levels had yet been detected. Not even an inch. From this, and the fact that the rectangle's rock was disappearing into the Earth, it necessarily followed that I was doing something that would increase the ocean's volume if not for the spillway moving water to the rectangle. Therefore, I had to be moving rock deep below the Antarctic continent out to the ocean. They were right. That's what I was doing.

On the third day, it was announced that the Atlantic Ocean had risen by four feet. This made me worry. The ice and rock removal was happening faster than the inrushing channel water could replace it. This showed in the channel's waterfall; it was 800 feet high. A little thought provided the explanation. The bottom of the channel was a thousand feet below sea level, but the water in the rectangle was higher than that. Therefore, the channel's water supply wasn't operating at one hundred percent efficiency.

A little while later and some really surprising news reassured me. Scientists said the Pacific Ocean had dropped a foot! This was because the channel to the Ross Ice Shelf was draining water from the Pacific side of Antarctica. As the day dragged on the Atlantic rose to five feet above normal and stopped there. Coastlines could handle that if there were no hurricanes.

President Stinson's not so subtle hint took effect. The street demonstrations stopped. Newscasters were careful what they said. The world was nervous. Nobody wanted to breathe a word against me for fear I would run amok.

By noon of the fourth day it became clear where the unseen moving rock was going. The surface of the ocean between Antarctica and Africa was flowing outward in all directions. Something was rising. A day later the outline of this flowing water could be made out. It exactly mirrored the Antarctic rectangle. And so all the mysteries were solved. I was moving incredible amounts of rock from under Antarctica northward and raising the ocean floor.

Why I told President Stinson people would get in the way and get themselves killed was now obvious. If the world had known I was going to raise the ocean floor between Africa and Antarctica, boats full of people would have rushed to the area for various reasons. It would have been a disaster. Boats would be crushed against each other or overturned by the outrushing water. Now it was too late to go in. The outrushing water would push them away.

By the sixth day, the mirroring rectangle of ocean floor finally broke through the surface. The water flowing out of the way had washed away most of the ocean floor mud leaving some small mounds of rock exposed. We had not expected this washing away of the ocean floor mud. But no matter. The effect would be helpful when I raised the Jewish island.

When the complete outline of the new Antarctic Ocean island had broken through the surface and reached a hundred feet above the sea, I stopped everything except for pushing out the ice and rock already stripped off Antarctica farther and farther out to space.

We went to bed. Prime Minister Blair called Edmund Parker to ask if he could visit in the morning, and of course Parker said yes.

The soldiers and their weapons were withdrawn from the Parker house during the night. Nobody apologized to me.

Blair arrived at ten. Arthur told us the PM was visiting. We took the hint and went downstairs.

Blair and Edmund Parker were chatting in the living room as we entered. We exchanged the usual pleasantries. This time Steve opened the discussion.

"Theresa has turned off the part of the HAL program that tore up the land. When the ice and rock escapes Earth's gravity she'll dismantle the program."

"But doesn't HAL now have a reflex to destroy

land?"

"No. The program is made up of hundreds of reflexes she's given to HAL, but the program isn't a reflex."

"That is a considerable relief."

"Here's good news. Theresa has been working on bringing a large amount of carbon to Earth. We decided that it's not needed for electric power. We think the new island will give us all the energy we need. Theresa changed the program. The carbon she's isolating is close to the sun's heavy gravity and it's around eight thousand degrees. The gravity there is twenty-two times what we feel on Earth. It occurred to us that if Theresa stretched out this mass of carbon to a cylinder a hundred miles high the pressure at the bottom will be way over a million pounds per square inch. The carbon will turn to diamond. If it works Theresa will throw a ring of diamonds in orbit and give the Israelis twenty-four hour daylight."

I was surprised that Blair didn't get very excited at this news. He seemed not to notice. Maybe he didn't believe Steve or understand him.

I added, "I'll dump a pile of diamonds in England. You'll all go into the diamond cutting business. I can see it now. We walk into McDonald's and teenaged girls are wearing diamond necklaces and tiaras with real diamonds."

Blair's eyes were wide open. Then he became emotional and had to clear his throat. Apparently he'd finally understood what Steve said.

"Thank you. You have no idea what this will mean to Israel and England."

"Why England?"

"It will provide thousands of diamond cutting jobs for our people. At least fifty thousand, I would say."

"Oh. Yeah. I guess if the price goes down women will buy them a hundred at a time."

Blair went on. "I came to ask what should be announced about the new island raised yesterday?"

"It's Theresa's island" said Steve. "Nobody has any rights to it. If any ship lands there without her permission she'll destroy the engines. The sailors can row a rowboat back home."

"And if there's oil there?"

"Theresa bought an office building in New York next to Central Park. Jan Struthers is setting up business there. If anybody wants to make a deal drilling on Theresa's island or just want to buy the oil, they can contact Jan Struthers."

"Her price is....?"

"Twenty dollars a barrel. She's not greedy ."

"May I announce these plans?"

"You bet. I can't wait to see OPEC's face. I wouldn't mention the diamond business. Israel's enemies might find a way to get around it."

"Quite right."

Blair now assumed that anguished frowning expression of someone who was about to ask a really big favor.

"I hesitate to make this request. You're already doing so much."

"Go ahead" I said to encourage him.

"Prime Minister Scherzer points out that when you raise the land bridge to Crete it will all be mud. It will be impossible to drive and walk through it. Could you raise the bridge soon to give the mud time to dry out and harden?"

"Sure. I can do it in three weeks. Soon enough?"

"Yes. It will take Israel's enemies much longer to prepare an attack. We detect no preparations."

"Won't raising the bridge now tell everybody what's going on including Israel's enemies?"

"Yes, but the benefits outweigh the risks. The Israeli people must be prepared for an evacuation if one is necessary. It's not something people can adjust to in one day. Imagine an evacuation is needed and the people panic at the idea. They need time to think about it. Also, the Prime Minister needs to see if the Israelis are willing to move."

"They'll need to understand it's leave or die."

"If the situation deteriorates to that level. The Israelis will thoroughly discuss their options in all eventualities."

"Tell Scherzer it's in three weeks."

Prime Minister Blair returned to London and made the announcement about my 'oil island'. Of course, nobody actually knew if there was oil there, but oil company spokesmen said it was almost certain there was or all theories about oil formation would have to be thrown out. It looked very promising. They had never explored the area because it was so inaccessible.

A period of tension followed. OPEC assembled an emergency meeting of its members. The organization had not set a deadline for its demands. Now it was feared it would start the embargo immediately. For two days the OPEC leaders met in secret. Then the conference broke up and everybody went home without making an official statement.

Gradually, details leaked out. The members feared

that if they started an embargo there would be a mad rush on the part of every oil company in the world to get their drilling equipment to my island. Then, if there did turn out to be a lot of oil there, I could drop the price to ten dollars a barrel and OPEC would be out of business. Their wells were too expensive to drill and maintain at that price and still make a profit. At a world market price of twenty dollars a barrel as I proposed, they could still make a little money.

When this explanation came out worldwide esteem for yours truly Empress Theresa reached hysterical levels. President Stinson, speaking at a veterans' dinner, said, "Theresa is either the smartest woman who ever lived or the luckiest."

My dream of early retirement after the rain restoration was replaced by enough projects to keep a dozen people busy. The next task was to raise the Jewish island. I carved out the needed slab of rock in the ocean bottom, carved the specified mountains from adjacent rock as well as the small hills Prime Minister Scherzer had drawn on his map, slid the mountains and hills up onto the rock slab, scraped off the numerous small volcanic mountains, and scraped some rock off the center of the slab for the lake's depression. The mountains I'd put on the slab were twenty thousand feet tall and stuck up a mile into the air even before I started raising the island. It took a day to move them to the center of the slab. It was a startling sight. What was I doing, the world wondered?

Then, I pushed crushed rock under the slab. This was a dangerous operation to do in the middle of the North Atlantic with Europe on one side and America on the other. If HAL failed at this time the island would crash down causing a deadly tsunami. To minimize the potential disaster I raised the slab only five feet at a time and filled the space with rock before raising it another five feet. When the island reached the desired height I let out a sigh of relief. I hoped to never have to do this again on such a large scale.

Meanwhile, work was begun to get oil from my island near Antarctica. Jan Struthers told oil companies to go explore the island immediately and financial details could be worked out later. Within two days of this island's rising to the surface, an ExxonMobil service ship set off with exploratory crews, and all the basic needs that human beings would need in that primitive place.

The ship reached the island in six days. Two helicopters stored on the ship's deck shuttled back and forth from the mooring to the island's shore. Vehicles with large tires for traveling over inhospitable terrain were taken to the island by powered rafts. In twenty-four hours a camp had been set up near the shore. Exploratory teams set out into the island.

One of the helicopters' functions was to photograph the land contours to see where oil deposits were most likely. Armed with this information, the exploratory teams drove to the likely sites and set up their equipment. They sank sensitive microphones into the ground. A couple of men a hundred yards away set off a dynamite charge. The shock wave traveled into the ground and bounced back up to the microphones feeding the information into computers. Three such men studied the computer screen. Reporters recorded their activity.

"Bingo!" said one of them. "A hit the first time."

"Yup" said a second. "This is a hole."

Other exploratory teams miles away made similar hits.

The foreman of the teams said, "If the whole island is like this we have oil for a thousand years."

There's an expression in the rich people's circles: "What are you worth on paper?"

On paper, I was a multi-trillionaire. I was still eighteen.

As for OPEC, Steve and Parker were watching me innocently hand-feeding my innocent little chipmunks when Steve told Parker, "They tried to blackmail something out of Theresa. They're guilty of criminal stupidity. It's their fault they're going to lose everything. It's incredible how stupid people are."

Chapter 20

Three very busy weeks had passed and it was time to raise the land bridge to Crete. It was going to be a mile wide and six hundred and twenty miles long.

When Steve and I met Blair and Scherzer in London, I thought raising the land bridge would be simple. Have you seen those films where divers retrieve ancient Greek treasures from sunken ships? I assumed the Mediterranean's depth was only a hundred feet. It turned out that was only along the coasts. Further research showed the Mediterranean was mostly a mile deep. "Raising" the land bridge at that depth would cause too much disturbance to the Sea's floor. Something more complicated was needed.

I'd already used a HAL program to move a snake-like string of gold from the North Pole over North America down to Fort Knox, and modified the program to bring silver to a British Army post. Now I modified the program to build the land bridge.

I started the HAL program. I didn't want to catch some boat by surprise so I programmed HAL to raise it starting at the Israeli end and gradually move out to Crete. Scherzer and his people crowded on the shore watching the bridge build up to fifty feet above the Mediterranean Sea.

Here's how the program worked.

HAL grabbed some of the limitless mud on the floor of the Atlantic, flattened a stream of it a mile wide, and moved the stream in the air from the Atlantic over the Mediterranean to Israel. At first the water was shallow and the bridge broke the surface quickly. As the water got deeper it took longer to break the surface and I changed the program's parameter to slow down the flying stream's progress. The media had helicopters and boats watching the bridge's progress and kept me informed how much to speed up or slow down the program to build a nice evenly high bridge all the way to Crete. The whole process took two weeks. There was enough room on the bridge for all the Israelis within hours if they'd needed to evacuate immediately. Because the mud above the Sea surface was fifty feet deep, the water's pressure made the water move to the lower mud pile very quickly. Finally, another program I'd written scraped the top of this mud pile into a flat surface.

Some of the Israelis cheered. Others weren't so happy. Not all of them wanted to leave no matter what the OPEC situation descended to. Yeah, well, when they saw a gun pointing at their children's heads they would change their minds. If they wanted to sacrifice their own lives for a hopeless cause, fine, but they had children to worry about. The only alternative was for me to kill millions of their enemies. I wasn't going to do that.

With the new Jewish island in the North Atlantic and the land bridge to Crete in place, there was no longer hiding the plans I made with Prime Minister Scherzer. It was obvious that we were preparing for evacuation. Politicians in the Israeli Parliament and people in the streets vigorously debated the issue. I didn't follow it much. When the choice had to be made people would do what they had to to stay alive.

The next day Blair showed up at the Parker estate with a really big surprise.

"A representative from Saudi Arabia wants to meet you in Geneva, Switzerland."

I was frozen for a moment. The idea of negotiating with these blackmailers had never occurred to me.

"Will you be there?"

"No. It will be you and the Saudi alone except for a neutral Swiss official there in consideration of your gender and age."

"You can't be serious, Mr. Blair. I'm only eighteen. I'm supposed to negotiate with this expert?"

"You don't have to agree to anything the first day. These meetings occur in many sessions over several days. We will be there with you between sessions. Tell us the latest proposal and we will advise you."

"Why am I talking to a Saudi Arabian instead of OPEC?"

"Saudi Arabia is considered a friend of the United States. The two countries cooperated fully in the Persian Gulf War. Mind you they're not close friends. There are serious disagreements. Saudi Arabia has some influence in the Arab world but it's limited. Some Arab countries hate each other more than the United States, but all agree they are in the same lifeboat on the global stage. This is all very vague, I'm sure, but the Saudi will come to Geneva hoping to get something. I point out that if what he suggests is agreeable to us then he is our friend."

"What will he ask for?"

"We believe it will begin with the oil island. We

think he will propose that the oil island be administered by a consortium of nations. To make this acceptable to you he will suggest it be administered by all countries that drill oil whether or not they export it. This would include the United States, Canada, Mexico, England, Brazil, Russia, China and many others. The purpose is to control the supply so as to keep the price at a fairly profitable level. Every country will want to do this, obviously."

"But I lose control of the island?"

"Yes."

"What will they give me?"

"We think the first thing they offer is to cancel your donations to the world poor fund."

"That doesn't cost them anything."

"It doesn't. If this offer isn't enough we believe they will abandon their demand that Israel be turned over to the 1947 occupants. The truth is many of the common people over there don't care that much about Israel. It's largely an issue for political posturing."

"That doesn't cost them anything either."

"True. However, we don't believe they will yield their insistence that you remove the grounding of the terrorists. Terrorists are not universally supported over there. Indeed, there have been terrorist bombings inside Saudi Arabia itself. However, most Arabs would not want to see the end of terrorist organizations. They are jealous of Western society and wealth and are amused to see the terrorists slap us in the face once in a while. The Saudi representative cannot ignore this popular support. Please understand that Saudi Arabia is not responsible for this quagmire. This man is trying to find a way to reduce tensions.

He is our friend."

"What does Prime Minister Scherzer think of all this?"

"Prime Minister Scherzer wants his people to move to the new island where they will be safe forever."

"That would take away OPEC's only bargaining chip. I could ignore everything else."

"Quite right. However, not all Israelis are sympathetic to his wish. To many of them the Holy Land, especially Jerusalem, is sacred and they couldn't conceive leaving. Many have already said they will fight to the death before leaving."

"Don't these diehards have wives and kids to worry about?"

"That is the big question. If there is a crisis and certain death seems imminent, will these traditionalists stay regardless of loss, or will they leave? Such questions are not decided ahead of time but on the day of crisis."

"So in the end, whether there is a crisis or not may be up to me?"

"Prime Minister Scherzer is aware of that. He understands your power and your challenges."

"What does he want me to do?"

"He doesn't want you to give away anything. Any agreement would leave danger in place indefinitely. He wants the situation to play itself out whatever the outcome."

"Do his people agree with him?"

"Probably not, but it's not up to them."

"Doesn't sound very democratic."

"It never is. What can the masses do but wait for

the leaders to decide? Your Congress did not decide the conduct of World War II. Neither did your President Roosevelt. The military decided strategy."

"And in this case Scherzer has to go along with me."

"Right."

"Great! Scherzer doesn't want me to make any deal to prod his people to the new island, and it's his people's lives at stake. Everybody else wants me to make a deal to keep their oil."

"Hard as it may be that is the situation."

"I want a television camera in that room. I want everybody to see what's going on."

"We shall insist."

What was my young head supposed to think of all this? Why should I negotiate at all since Blair and others could do the job better than I could? Then I realized the Saudi negotiator probably thought he could get me to agree to a deal Blair and the others wouldn't like. Maybe he was right. Maybe he'd convince me Blair's gang was just looking after their own butts and didn't prioritize my interests. Blair and Scherzer must have been aware of these possibilities, but had no choice but to let me negotiate. I had the power.

I talked everything over with Steve, but he understood no more about this political Chinese puzzle than I did.

We arrived in Geneva in the early evening and checked into a hotel. Blair didn't talk to us that night. I think he knew I needed to get my mind on something else or I might become overwrought.

The meeting was to begin early in the morning. I

must have been the only person in the world who didn't know the name of the Saudi negotiator I was going to meet. I hadn't paid attention. It didn't matter to me what his name was. And to be honest, what he had to say didn't matter much to me either unless he was prepared to give up all his demands.

As we drove to the building where the meeting would take place I had three thoughts in mind. Blair and most of the world wanted the oil from my island at giveaway prices, Scherzer wanted the Israelis on the new North Atlantic island where they'd live better than they ever had since Abraham, and the poor Israelis themselves didn't know what they wanted.

Steve and I walked into the building accompanied by Blair and his six advisors. Steve carried a large manila envelope. There were far more people inside. I estimate there were over a hundred representatives from many countries. Scherzer was there keeping a careful eye on me. Poor man. He was powerless to affect events.

Blair asked me, "What is your final strategy?"

"I can't answer because my strategy depends on the common people to hear it from me first. As I see it, we're really dealing with two groups. One is the governments of OPEC. The other is the terrorists and the people who support them. But not all the people support the terrorists. This Saudi has two groups to deal with too, us and the terrorists. Somehow he has to keep everybody happy while some of his people are working against him. I'll deal with the governments and forget about the terrorists. I have a surprise."

This was all very mysterious to everybody who heard it, but my intention was that it get back to the

Saudi negotiator so that he'd know I had a surprise for him. It would make him listen instead of snowballing me.

A television camera showed the meeting room. A fifty year old woman was seated at the end of a table like she was the chairwoman of a corporate board. She was the neutral Swiss official there to protect my virtue or something. Two chairs on either side of the table had been drawn back. That's where I and the Saudi would sit. I guess if we started throwing knives at each other the Swiss woman was supposed to throw her body between us.

An official appeared and said it was time for the meeting to begin.

"Good luck" said Steve handing me the manila envelope.

I followed the official out to the meeting room door where the Saudi negotiator waited. I barely glanced at the Saudi. We walked into the room together. He walked around the Swiss woman to take the farthest seat and I sat in the nearest.

I opened, "We can clean this mess up fast if I speak first."

"Please," he said with a smile and a hand signal, inviting me to go ahead. He must have heard I had a surprise for him, and he could see my mysterious manila envelope.

"This mess was started by the Organization and you had to go along like a baseball team is expected to clear the dugout and run on the field when two players start a fight, but your heart wasn't in it. The only two players fighting are me and the Organization. You're here to calm things down. I understand that and appreciate you calling this meeting.

"Your oil will run out in forty years and then what will you have? Let's not talk about oil today. I have a fabulous treasure that will last you forever, that will make all your people richer than they ever dreamed of, that I will be glad to give you free if there's no attack on Israel."

I wasn't being extemporaneous. Every word and gesture was carefully planned. He knew I had a bombshell and waited.

I opened the manila envelope and took out a pile of computer printouts.

"Let's take a tour around the Mediterranean. Here's the desert of Algeria. Could you pass him this please?"

I slid a picture of the desert towards the Swiss woman to pass to the Saudi. The table was six feet wide and I didn't want to make paper airplanes. The Saudi glanced at the picture.

"The desert of Libya," I said passing another picture.

"The desert of Egypt.

"The desert of Iraq.

"The desert of Iran.

"The worst of all, your own Saudi Arabian desert. Not even bacteria grow there."

He was particularly interested in that picture.

"Your countries are all desert because the land is flat. You don't have mountains to make the air rise up and cool off. The air stays hot enough to evaporate rain before it hits the ground. You're all crowded in cities on the coast and the desert starts a few miles away. Now let's take a look at Europe."

I passed a beautiful picture of the Italian Alps. "Italy."

And a picture of the French Alps. "France."

And the Swiss mountains. "Switzerland. Some of their ski resorts stay open twelve months a year."

And Austria's mountains. "Austria."

And the beautiful hills of Germany with tiny villages surrounded by vast areas of green grass and trees. "Germany."

That was the end of my 'tour'.

"The land around the mountains I can raise in your country will be below sea level. It will become fresh water lakes. I will give you all the mountains you want if there's no military attack on Israel. I've been told you have no control of the terrorists. They even attack you. I don't see how we can talk about the other issues until some future time. Let's give the terrorists and the people a chance to prove they can behave. What you have to worry about is what the little shopkeeper, with a wife and four kids to feed, wants for the future. They have desert. I can give them France."

Did he get the message? I thought so and walked out of the room to rejoin Steve, Blair, Scherzer and all the others.

Blair said, "Very clever idea."

"I made him an offer he can't refuse. Right now he must be figuring out those mountains are ten times as valuable as his oil. Ninety-five percent of his land is totally useless desert. I can give him France. He can't risk losing that."

"Interesting he didn't say anything."

"He got the message. I could see it in his eyes.

The message is I can raise land and I can lower it too. Look what I did in Antarctica."

Blair rolled his eyes. "No wonder he said nothing."

Steve said, "Isn't she a bitch?"

We all laughed.

I wasn't giving away any secrets. It would only be a matter of minutes before the media figured out I could lower OPEC's land. It was reasonable to think I would only do this if there was a governmental military attack against Israel. I had said that the OPEC governments didn't control the terrorists. So they didn't have to panic about what I'd do in case terrorists attacked on their own without the government backing them.

The 'carbon', if that's what it was, arrived from the sun. It was an eighty-two mile wide red hot ball. I gently nudged it into orbit five thousand miles up. Scientists pointed out that because of its size it would stay red hot for centuries.

To see if it was diamonds or just carbon I programmed HAL to grab a small handful of the stuff and bring it down to a wide field on a British army base. They were diamonds, a three hundred feet high and eight hundred feet wide pile of them. The jewelry industry was thrown into a panic until it was realized women would buy one hundred times as many diamonds as before because of the cheaper price. A box of the diamonds was delivered to me. They were uncut stones from a quarter inch to three quarters of an inch wide in all kinds of shapes and rather dull in their raw condition, but it was still a thrill to hold a handful.

Reports came in that diamonds as large as three inches wide were being found. Officials were seizing these giants until it could be decided what to do with them. Letting these monsters out in the open would cause chaos in the jewelry business.

I went to work on the gigantic orbiting ball of diamonds. On the middle of the leading side of this ball a thin stream of diamonds advanced ahead at three hundred miles an hour. Released from the giant red hot ball, these diamonds rapidly cooled off and sparkled. The thin stream stretched out in front of the ball and assumed its own slightly higher orbit. Nobody noticed this stream for an hour until it and the giant ball orbited around the Earth's sun side and headed back to the shadow side. At that point the thin diamond stream reflected sunlight to the Earth's dark side. Wildlife used to settling in at dusk were stirred up by the unexpected light. People living in the country far from city lights were the first to notice the light from the thin diamond stream. The news flashed through the electronic media.

"Now what is she doing?" said President Stinson to her staff.

In ninety-five minutes the ball and stream complex came around the corner of the world again, this time giving off much more light. Everybody saw what I was doing. I was eliminating the darkness of night.

It took five days to form a complete ring. Even before that the partial ring was putting out enough light so that people could read a newspaper outdoors at two o'clock in the morning when the partial ring was in the right position. The world would have many changes to get used to. Crime would go down as criminals lost the cover of darkness. Everybody was joyful at the prospect having 24-hour daylight.

The ring came to completion. There was plenty of diamond left in the red ball so I continued generating the diamond stream adding to what was already in place. The diamond ring gave off many times the light of a full moon, not enough to play a baseball game without electric lighting, but more than enough to walk around without stumbling on something. Friends could easily recognize each other from a hundred yards away. It was truly a new world.

There was still another project related to the resettling of the Israelis. Along the shores of the Antarctic, where nobody was around to watch, I did experiments in raising water up into the air until I developed the exact technique I needed. This was for The Big Surprise. This project was so secret I didn't even tell Scherzer and Blair.

Oil exploration on what was being called Theresa's Island continued to be successful. It was believed there were forty-five trillion easily accessible barrels of oil there. My credit rating must have been good.

Four months after I raised the oil island tanker ships were being filled with oil using underwater pipelines leading out to the ships anchored half a mile offshore. The race was on to see which company would get its ship home first and, not surprising, it looked like ExxonMobil would win. The 210,000 ton Exxon Maria was filled with millions of gallons of crude and set sail for New Jersey.

The crews on oil tankers were surprisingly small. It really only took one person to drive them over the open sea. With the various functions on the ship, cooking, laundry, maintenance, and sleeping shifts, the Exxon Maria had a crew of 27 men.

As the Exxon Maria approached Jersey shores a 55 foot sports fisherman's power boat headed straight for the tanker's side at high speed. The boat hit the tanker with a titanic explosion. The flash momentarily hid half the tanker's length. Flaming oil poured out of a sixty foot wide hole in the tanker's side. Burning oil spread out over the water. The heat was so intense, other pleasure boats in the vicinity had to back off half a mile. A black cloud of smoke obscured much of the disastrous scene, but flames could be seen.

In only nineteen minutes the giant tanker sank out of sight.

Chapter 21

Steve and I were upstairs when the television flashed the news of the Exxon Maria's sinking. At first all the reporters knew was that the ship sank probably, they thought, because it had caught fire. Soon word came from witnesses that it had collided with a pleasure boat. Then the 'Anderson video' was shown and the world knew this had been a terrorist bombing.

The Coast Guard arrived minutes after the Maria sank. Michael Anderson steered his pleasure boat to intercept them and gave them the video tape he and his friends made. The Coast Guard immediately sent the images to shore electronically and the FBI went to work. They had already been watching the people responsible. They were from Middle East countries and suspected of being associated with the infamous Al-Qaeda terrorist organization. They bought the boat called Deep C Guy from an American millionaire a month before. Somehow they smuggled tons of explosives into the country and loaded it on the boat. They had succeeded. None of the twenty-seven men on the tanker could be found.

Finally, pictures were shown of the family of one of the dead sailors. It was a young family, a mother with three young kids and the man's mother and father. They were all crying and complaining that their husband-son-father was a good man who never hurt anybody. I cried on thinking this sad scene was being repeated twenty-six more times somewhere.

Commentators speculated that no tanker would ever again go to Theresa's Island. If true, then OPEC had won.

After covering the American scene, the media turned to scenes in the Middle East countries.

I was never so shocked. The people were dancing in the streets to celebrate the tanker disaster. Scene after scene showed these mindless people celebrating in one country after another. I found it incomprehensible. Could whole populations support the terrorist monsters?

I ran into the bedroom. Steve followed and found me crying on the bed.

"They're animals!" I wailed. "I'm trying to do good and they kill. I didn't ask for this. I want to go home."

"You can't do that."

"Leave me alone."

Steve knew his limits. He couldn't help me now. I needed time to mull over the disaster until my senses dulled to it. He went downstairs.

A few minutes later Mrs. Parker knocked on the bedroom door and I let her in. She gave me a hug.

"You poor dear. You share the lot of all women. We worry about those we are responsible for. We hope the world will treat them well. We send our sons to war and pray they come back. We see our daughters marry strangers. Our lot is to worry until death."

Mrs. Parker calmed me down. We went downstairs to the living room to join the rest of the

Parkers, Arthur, and Steve. I looked at Steve and held up my hands with all fingers extended.

"Ten dollars a barrel" I said.

Steve shrugged. "So you only make a few trillion."

"It's time to get to work."

"Are we going to the mattresses?"

"You bet!"

"Mr. Parker, Theresa is declaring war on OPEC."

"Good show!"

It was not exactly war on OPEC. It was the terrorists who sank the tanker. But I had to respond. This couldn't be tolerated. At ten dollars a barrel OPEC couldn't make any money to speak of. Too bad! They should have made a vigorous public education campaign to eliminate people's support of the terrorists. They didn't. They didn't care enough to do the right thing. Now they would pay.

"Mr. Parker, I need to use the secure phone."

The secure phone had recently been installed by the British government. It would get me through to Prime Minister Blair at a moment's notice.

Parker got up. "Come along, everybody." All the Parker people went to the family room on the other side of the foyer.

I picked up the secure phone and was automatically connected to Blair's office. He had been waiting.

"PM, here."

"I need to talk to President Stinson."

"One moment."

The President was also on the alert. "What's up, Theresa?"

"All hell will break loose. I need our parents' house surrounded by the Army."

"I'll invite them to West Point."

"Why West Point?"

"They have sixteen thousand acres and it's the most secure place in the world. There's never been a terrorist attack there. Your parents will have plenty to do. New York City is only twenty-six miles away."

"That's a good idea."

"What are you doing?"

"I'm going to evacuate Israel."

"Why?"

"I haven't even told Prime Minister Scherzer yet. He should be first, I think."

I hung up the phone and picked it up again to get back to Blair.

"Mr. Blair, I have to talk to Prime Minister Scherzer."

"I'll see if he's available," the PM laughed.

Not more than twelve seconds later, "This is Scherzer."

"Prime Minister, you will have to evacuate."

"Why is it necessary?"

"I'm going to lower the price of oil to ten dollars a barrel."

"That will do it."

Scherzer actually wanted the Israelis to move to the new island where they would be safe forever. He saw no reason to talk me out of my ten dollar price for oil. The people all over the Middle East could be expected to demonstrate in the streets by the tens of millions when they learned their free lunch was over. This might give Scherzer the argument he needed to get the Israelis to move.

"When can you begin the evacuation, sir?"

"In thirty-six hours. It will take a day to get my people to understand the situation."

"I'll raise a mountain in the middle of the Saudi Arabian desert tonight to remind them of my offer. I can't believe they would throw it away with an attack."

"We can't take the chance. We'll evacuate."

"Good night, sir."

I hung up. Steve went across the foyer to retrieve the Parkers. I heard what they said.

"Come watch the fun" Steve said. "Theresa is out for blood."

"Our quiet schoolteacher?" remarked Edmund.

"I hardly recognize her."

They returned to the living room where I said, "Mr. Parker, I'm afraid we have to turn this into a war room. Steve and I won't be getting much sleep for a few days. Do you have some tables we can bring in here?"

Steve and Edmund Parker smiled at each other.

"We have folding tables in the lower floor for lawn parties. We'll get them."

Mr. and Mrs. Parker and Arthur went downstairs to fetch the folding tables while Steve and I went upstairs to get a pile of mat boards used to control HAL. The Parkers set up the lightweight tables in the living room. When we returned they arranged the tables around the room's periphery.

"Can we borrow some books?" Steve asked. "We need them to prop up these boards."

The Parkers retrieved dozens of books from around

the house. Piles of books were set up on all the tables and I leaned my mat boards against them in the order I thought they would be needed.

"The room looks like a yard sale" quipped Steve.

"Yeah, well, wait 'til they see what we're selling!"

I had recovered quickly from the tanker disaster. I was thoroughly immersed in this exciting challenge. Steve and the Parkers were visibly amused to see the change in me. The girl who wanted nothing more than to be a high school teacher was acting like Genghis Khan, leading an army in battle. I was enjoying this!

The time was right for raising the mountain. I put an X on a parameter filled mat board.

Saudi Arabia had a vast sand desert called the Rub'al-Khali. It was a horrible, uninhabitable place. Countless travelers had died trying to cross it.

I had refined my technique for raising land with one more feature. In the exact center of the Rub'al-Khali desert, HAL began raising a circular piece of land ten miles wide, only this time he didn't do it all at the sáme time. I programmed him to raise the central one hundred yard wide part first to a height of 70 yards. Then HAL raised a ring of land around this central piece with the side of the ring a hundred yards wide up 70 yards with the central piece also raised another 70 yards. Then, HAL raised another ring on the periphery and all the land inside 70 yards. This process was repeated again and again. Over the next three hours it rose up to a height of four miles after much of the rock broke off and slid downhill.

Seismologists detected ground vibrations in the remote area. A commercial jet of a European country was asked to fly over the area and they saw the new mountain. The obvious message was: 'DON'T FORGET OUR DEAL'.

Midnight passed and the Parkers retired for the night. Arthur said he wanted to stay with the Hartleys for the duration to give them whatever service we needed.

"Let's go make the announcement," said Prime Minister Scherzer to his confidants.

They walked to a meeting room where over a hundred top government officials had been summoned in the early hours to wait for 'an announcement'. Everybody guessed it had something to do with an evacuation. The Prime Minister walked to a microphone and didn't waste a word.

"Theresa told me a few hours ago she will drop the price of oil to ten dollars a barrel. Our neighbors will react violently. We will begin leaving Israel at eight a.m. tomorrow morning.

"When we arrive in Crete, I believe the Europeans will help us ferry up to the mainland, where we fly to America until the new Atlantic island Theresa raised for us is ready."

His audience sat in stoic silence. They'd been through crises before.

"My friends. We had a long journey and many hardships, but finally we go to the promised land. Theresa has given us a new Paradise free from the menaces of this world. Our children will know no other Israel but the new island because Israel is where the Israeli people are. Don't look back. Look to the future of ourselves and our children. Go make preparations. God be with you."

Steve and I lived in the Parker living room for the next day and a half in case there was some crisis that had to be resolved quickly. I had written a couple of HAL programs to counteract some enemy activities. For example, if a bunch of tanks were moving towards Israel I had a HAL program to push up a mound of dirt to stop them.

The time for the evacuation arrived. Prime Minister Scherzer was standing with a huge crowd close to the Israeli end of the land bridge. People had not been allowed on the bridge prematurely because the army hadn't yet moved onto the bridge to secure it from enemy attack. If any enemy assassins were on the bridge somewhere, they would easily be identified as such.

It was six a.m. in London. There were thousands of ships and boats along the land bridge waiting for the evacuation as were the entire Parker household in the living room. Steve went to the phone.

"Get me the BBC."

Some BBC official answered.

"Are you recording this?" Steve asked.

"Yes, sir."

"This is a warning. All boats and ships have to move two miles away from the land bridge or they'll be destroyed. You have one hour. This is your final warning. Have a good day."

All along the land bridge boats and ships moved away. They had no reason not to take Steve at his word, but what was going to happen?

The hour dragged by at a snail's pace. It ran out.

It was time for The Big Surprise.

"Wait 'til you see this, Arthur!" I said and made a silly funny face.

I put an X on another mat board program to start the task.

I didn't expect the wind. Nobody had been nearby when the North Pole water columns rose up so nobody had felt the wind. It seemed obvious now. HAL couldn't rev up his engines without moving some air around what he was doing.

After eight seconds of wind sheets of water rose up on both sides of the land bridge starting at the Israeli shoreline. They were rising up at 87 degree angles away from each other. Their ascent was at my standard two hundred miles an hour.

Starting at the Israeli shore the water walls extended toward Crete at fifty miles per hour. It would take all day for the walls to reach the length of the land bridge. The visual effect of watching the ever lengthening walls go down the bridge was heart-stopping. In one minute the leaning walls of water extended out nearly a mile.

This was overwhelming for some of the older people in the crowd who had been through too much. They fell to their knees and extended arms towards Heaven to praise God.

Scherzer's top general said, "A tank couldn't get through that. Did you know about this?"

"No" said Scherzer, and then he made a soon to be famous comment.

"Theresa is the right hand of God!"

This comment was captured on television cameras. When I saw and heard it moments later, I cried openly.

The opposing four foot thick water sheets diverged a total of six degrees from each other as minute after minute they got further down the land bridge. It was a breathtaking sight. Finally, the water rising up from the shore reached a height of nine miles and HAL let it go. It fell down, splayed about by air resistance into trillions of droplets like the water falling from Angel Falls, the world's tallest waterfall. At the moment only the planes and news helicopters could see this water falling if they were to the side of the bridge. The helicopters broadcast images to the television networks. In three minutes the water walls approached the sea several hundred yards from the land bridge. When the water finally returned to the Mediterranean Sea the noise was thunderous. This would not be a problem to the people crossing the bridge between the walls.

The Army had been lined up along the shore to prevent people from wandering onto the bridge prematurely. As it turned out this would be their only task. Obviously, no terrorists could get on the bridge from the sides. This was the reason I raised the water, but people suspected there was a little showboating in me, too! Can we say 'Exodus'?

Scherzer's top general noted something else. He said, "If our enemies want to launch missiles on us while we're crossing the bridge, they'd have to send them right down that line between the water walls. They'd have to be launched from a thin line in Jordan or Saudi Arabia. I don't think they can do it. They'd have to attack us here."

"Jordan and Saudi Arabia won't attack us" said Scherzer. "We can keep the others in line with our planes."

"Do you think Theresa thought of all this?"

"She thought of a way to keep out the terrorist snipers. I wouldn't put anything beyond her reach."

Nobody had ever believed the moderate countries of Saudi Arabia and Jordan would participate in a military attack on Israel. However, in certain political developments, they might allow countries to cross their land to get to Israel. To prevent this possibility a quick evacuation was necessary.

I had promised Scherzer he could evacuate in one day, and I gave him the means. But the need for such hurry seemed to be vanishing. Scherzer saw that my water walls along the land bridge was relieving the army from pressure to safeguard the bridge. They could be deployed elsewhere. The enemy had been caught by surprise and could not respond for a day or two. This was the reason I made The Big Surprise the ultimate secret even from Scherzer himself.

"Let's not cause a panic by hurrying" Scherzer told his top people. "We can take a few days to leave. Our people need time to get used to the idea."

Twenty-four hours before the Big Surprise the sun rose in the United States and Americans got caught up in the excitement. Television evangelists, who were on a Christian network twenty-four hours a day in some parts of the country, screamed for America's support. People rushed to schools and churches to sign lists volunteering to take in a Jewish family. Millions of Americans had a summer cabin somewhere, or a mobile home, or an empty apartment, and everybody had a garage that could be converted into a bedroom. The Jews were welcome to use them.

President Stinson told the Europeans America would take in the Jews if only the Europeans would help the Jews get across the Atlantic. The Europeans quickly realized a huge number of people would have to be moved out of Crete in a matter of days. They scrambled to find ships to ferry the Israelis from Crete to Greece, France, and Italy where the railroad systems could take them to airports for flying to America's vast spaces. Plans were made to fly or ship water, fuel and necessities to Crete to take care of the Israelis. All of this spontaneous cooperation was based on everybody's realization that this was what I wanted. They owed me their lives; whatever the Empress wanted I'd get.

"Begin the evacuation," Scherzer declared.

A loud roar of voices and vehicle horns rose from the assembled crowd and they started moving.

The land bridge was a mile wide but still it was a slow process to move such a vast gathering. Many Israelis, mostly the young, were determined to walk the entire distance out of some religious, historic or personal motive. Traffic lanes had to be established. The Israeli Army tried to get vehicles to travel in the center of the bridge while people on foot were urged to stay on the side. The fine grained mud in the center had dried out the most in recent weeks and was packed hard enough to support vehicles.

On the Cretan end trucks loaded with supplies from the Europeans set off to meet the Israelis. The day passed uneventfully. There was no attack. The first relief trucks from Crete met the advancing Israelis. Tent cities were set up every few miles on the southeastern half of the bridge. By nightfall there were relief stations all the way to Israel. Two million Israelis were on the bridge. My orbital diamond ring provided plenty of light.

The next day nearly 4,500,000 Israelis were on the bridge with another million still at home preparing to leave and only a quarter million diehard people planning to remain behind. Watching the spectacle on television, my heart raced with the emotions I felt. Proud that I'd saved the Israelis, humbled by recognition of my own mortality, I smiled while holding back the tears. Surely I could never experience anything like this again. Steve and the Parker household looked at me proudly.

There had perhaps never been a more stirring sight than that in the news helicopter video shots of this immense crowd walking along the land bridge between the walls of water. The line of people and vehicles extended to the horizon. All superlatives failed. There was a mixture of sadness that they had to give up the old land, and of triumph that they had escaped with their lives and were going to a new world. That I had made possible this latter-day Exodus assured my treasured place in Jewish history.

While I was proud of what I'd done about the rain, there was not an event with people that could be recorded on television. This Exodus was all about people. Can you imagine how proud I was? No. You can't. I can't describe it, so nobody can imagine it.

Steve and I finally managed to get some sleep in the living room, while the loyal Arthur, who had been with us throughout the ordeal, kept watch for news on television. The Parkers walked in quietly once in a while to ask him how the Hartleys were doing. It was a moving experience to see the immensely powerful World Empress and her husband asleep on the sofas like babies.

It was predictable. Stupid people in the media were jumping all over Scherzer for his remark about my being the right hand of God. They said he was blasphemous and made me out to be a goddess. They could all drop dead! I knew what Scherzer meant. God never did anything Himself if He could get somebody else to do it. He got me to do it. Scherzer never called me in the months since our London meeting. That's not how you treat a goddess.

A week had passed while Scherzer waited for stragglers to finally start moving onto the bridge. When he thought just about everybody who would move had done so he told his band of top government officials, "Let's head for the new land".

Many thousands of Israelis had already been ferried out of Crete to European coastlines where they traveled to airports and waited for flights to America. Millions of homes waited for them. Their comforts were assured until the new island was ready.

Even now, there was a handful of people still leaving. I had to leave the bridge in place until it was clear anybody on it was just there as tourists. At that point I could stop the rising walls of water one mile at a time so as not to cause flooding around the Mediterranean. The land bridge was a pile of mud. The Mediterranean waves would eventually wash the mud back underwater.

Scherzer visited the United States to talk with President Stinson. Details had to be worked out about what to do with the Israelis. It turned out money was not a problem. Plenty of groups and corporations issued loans and grants to ingratiate themselves with the Israelis. The new island with its mid-Atlantic location would be a financial gold mine for a hundred reasons. Ironically, Israel's former enemies would now become business partners in the tourism business. Scherzer found himself with many new cards to play.

There had been no attack on Israel. My deal with the Saudi negotiator was still on. I asked Prime Minister Blair to collect the information about where to raise the mountains and when. The countries were not likely to deal with me directly. It would be political suicide.

I reached my nineteenth birthday on May 8. Not wanting to start a second year in England we began thinking of going home.

There was one matter to clear up. I wrote a letter to Prime Minister Blair who read it to the House of Commons.

"Dear Mr. Blair, People say I should be given the Nobel Peace Prize for the Israel situation. It should be given to Prime Minister Scherzer. He's heroic. Anybody would have told him to stay in Israel and prepare for the fight. So what did he do? He came to London to see a girl who had no ties to Judaism, who couldn't find Israel on a map, who had no interest in politics or war, who might not be able to do anything at all about Israel, who might not even care what happened to Israel. Aren't politicians supposed to take care of those things? He threw all his chips in the pot and came away with a royal straight flush. Your friend, Theresa"

Prime Minister Blair called to say the American Ambassador to Great Britain had an interesting request from President Stinson. He said this would really be interesting, but would not tell it on the phone. It had to be kept secret until it was done. I agreed to meet the man.

Blair drove in with the Ambassador who was different from the man who got me to ground the terrorists. The mood was jovial when they arrived, so we all sat in the living room together with the Parkers and Arthur. The Ambassador got down to business.

"We know you'll be returning home soon. President Stinson asks if you will consider coming home on the Ronald Reagan? The ship has been a leper colony since last year. Nobody wants to serve on her. Your presence will restore the crew's pride."

He must have expected my enthusiastic approval to this idea, and his face fell as he watched me stare back at him in silence.

He followed up with a backup plan.

"Of course, a brief visit to the ship would also be helpful."

I continued staring and he lost hope. I said, "Will you excuse us a minute?" and got up. Steve got up too and accompanied me to the family room on the other side of the foyer. We were there at least five minutes while the Ambassador and Prime Minister waited in embarrassed silence with the Parkers. Steve and I went back to the living room and I gave the verdict.

"HAL is unpredictable. If I go back to the Ronald Reagan we can't predict what he might do. He could sink the ship."

The Ambassador shook his head. Now he'd really

given up hope. But as we'd planned, Steve spoke and saved the day.

"We're going to West Point. Send the crew to West Point on the Fourth of July and Theresa will play a football game with them. She'll be quarterback. We'll make it an Army-Navy game. To make it fair neither side can use regular Academy football players. The Ronald Reagan crew will be amateurs. The Army has to use amateurs too."

The Ambassador loved it. "What an exciting idea! It will be bigger than the Super Bowl."

"It will drive the odds makers nuts" Steve grinned. "The West Point amateurs will be in better condition than the Ronald Reagan crew, and they'll have more discipline, but the Ronald Reagan crew will be older and they'll have Theresa's super accurate throwing arm. Who will win?"

"There have been female high school quarterbacks but none at the college level. This is historic."

The Ronald Reagan had a few sailors who had been high school quarterbacks. They were sent to England along with ten offense teams to help me train to be a quarterback. We made up defense teams from the British soldiers assigned to the Parker estate. They loved the chance to help us out.

There were a couple of the sailors who unnecessarily groped at me. This had been expected, of course. I told their leader about it and he sent them home. They were easy to replace. There were far more sailors who wanted to play than could be put on the team.

The first anniversary of my world record eleven

mile drop without a parachute was coming up. It was inevitable. Somebody wanted to break my record. He was a Hollywood stuntman named Derek Eames who got some people to invest money in this harebrained project. At first the plan was he'd jump out of a high altitude helium balloon. This plan was too expensive. It was found that it would be cheaper to eject from a fighter jet. When these old planes become thirty years out of date, the military sells some of them to superrich millionaires who could afford the half million dollars a year needed to keep them in operating condition. A rich man agreed to rent out his plane.

Now the pressure was on me to tell all my secrets about how I survived the fall. What secrets? I didn't know how I survived.

I agreed to make a short video in the Parker living room. Edmund Parker operated the camera.

"People want me to give the secrets to how I survived the fall. You already know about the eleven Coke bottles in my jumpsuit," I said. "I fell face down in the spread eagle position. At the last second I covered my face like this." I demonstrated how I put my arms over my face. "My only advice to Derek Eames is that you take an oxygen mask with you at least for the first minute of the fall. Some people say your chances of surviving are better if you land on your back instead of your belly. I landed on my belly, but men and women are built differently. You make the choice and assume the responsibility. I did not actually see the position of my body when I entered the water. I have nothing more to say about this crazy stunt. If you kill yourself it's your own fault."

And now I read people the riot act.

"Shame on everybody for wanting to see this spectacle. I wash my hands of it.

"People ask why don't I stop Derek Eames? It's simple. If I stop him, other people will try it secretly — somewhere, sometime—without my knowledge. Maybe half a dozen guys will kill themselves before somebody survives and gets his television show. Derek Eames will either survive or fail. Either way it ends there, because even if he succeeds, people won't want to see it again, and if he dies, no network will show it again."

He went through with it, of course.

It was a highly publicized program lasting two hours. The stuntman was reportedly paid eight million dollars for the rights to his show. Finally, the two seat jet fighter was launched with the canopy removed to make it easy for the stuntman to jump out. He and the pilot who was to return the plane to the ground went up to sixty-two thousand feet to make sure my record was broken. He did use an oxygen mask at the beginning of the fall. Nearly four minutes later he landed in the water face down as I had done. Twelve boats were nearby to pick him up.

He was unconscious and not breathing. He was quickly moved to the largest boat where a team of medics were waiting. All attempts to revive him failed. He was dead.

What went wrong? How had I pulled off this miracle?

Experts now jumped in to analyze what would make it possible to survive a fall like that. There were countless factors to consider. For example, if my head entered the water before my lower body, then forces along the spine would be directed harmlessly towards my feet instead of my brain. There were many other considerations like that.

Two days after Derek's death, Edmund Parker and I made another short video. I said, "When I entered the water the ocean was covered with large waves. I could see them from miles above. My impact on hitting the water would have to vary depending on what part of a wave I hit. I noticed that the man fell in calm water. That was the difference. Somebody making a free fall can't control which part of a wave he'll fall on. I suggest that everybody stop trying this insane stunt.

Mr. Parker was a pretty smart guy. After a year in England, I developed an appreciation of English conservatism. They kept many old ways and institutions. Consider the royal family and all the rituals that go with it. What's that about? I asked Mr. Parker about that. He talked about prejudice as defined two hundred years ago by the English around the time of that complete breakdown of social order, the French Revolution. This was the kind of prejudice intended in Jane Austen's *Pride and Prejudice*. Prejudice, as Mr. Parker told me, was not racial prejudice but a preconceived traditional opinion or attitude about issues, whether it was for a proposed idea or against it. It was the wisdom of the species, an easy answer to confusion and emergency, and a steady source of knowledge gained though thousands of years of experiment. It was the capital of nations, he said, superior to individual reason, and made man's virtue his habit. It was like the Jewish idea of respect for tradition. A fool like Derek Eames wouldn't understand a word of this.

Mr. Parker was turning me into an old fashioned girl. That and my lack of the problems common to people my age would make me respected but not loved. Oh well. It's better to be yourself than other people's fantasy.

Chapter 22

The day came when Steve and I had to say good by to the Parkers. It was an emotional occasion. So much had happened in the last year it seemed like we'd been in the house most of our lives. Now the reality that we were leaving was very hard to bear.

We were all packed and the luggage had been sent ahead of us. Also, all the plywood and mat boards that I used to control HAL had been put in crates. They would be transported by the British navy under close guard. I couldn't let them fall in the wrong hands. They were as dangerous as a shipment of plutonium.

Steve went down first and asked Arthur to join him in the family room out of sight of the Parkers.

"Arthur, Theresa says you helped us a lot and she wants to reward you. Here's ten million dollars. Don't refuse to take it. It's nothing to Theresa. She wouldn't pick it up off the ground."

He showed Arthur a large suitcase full of hundred dollar bills.

Arthur was deeply moved. "Thank you, sir."

"I guess you'll hire your own butler now?" Steve joked.

"No, sir. You have made this house a shrine to the human spirit. I will never leave."

Steve returned to me and we took one last look around at the bedroom, and my work room where so much good had been done.

We went downstairs to say good by. The entire

Parker family and Arthur waited in the living room wearing brave smiles to cover their sorrow.

I went up to Edmund Parker to shake his hand. "Good by, Mr. Parker. Thanks for everything."

"Farewell, my dear. You will write?"

"I will."

Steve shook Parker's hand too. I went on to Mrs. Parker.

"Thank you for the use of your lovely home."

"You made it a true palace, Theresa."

Next was the 17 year old son John, and 13 year old Stephanie who could barely keep her eyes dry, and 11 year old Jennifer who was crying like she was losing everything she valued.

Most painful of all was saying good bye to Arthur, who was standing a respectful ten feet away. I walked up to him and shook my head side to side with a teary smile.

"I'll miss you most of all, Arthur."

I wrapped my arms around his neck in a tight hug. The normally imperturbable man came close to losing control. He could say nothing.

I walked away quickly. The Parkers and Arthur were left in mournful silence. Empress Theresa, the humble world saver and conqueror, the right hand of God, was no longer in their lives.

Colonel James gave us a ride in an unmarked car. Plane tickets had been arranged secretly thanks to Prime Minister Blair. The media knew we were planning to get home on July 1 but didn't know how we'd travel. When we got to Heathrow Airport we were rushed through staff doors and halls and loaded onto a Boeing 747 before anybody knew it. We were first on the plane. Other passengers came later and were surprised to see us. The ever present security men had the seats in front and in back of us to act as a buffer zone from the curious. People waved and shouted 'hi' to us but we ignored it. This was the way it had to be and if people didn't like it, too bad!

I'd never been in a 747 before and couldn't believe how big it was. Could this thing get off the ground? Well, it did. We took off. The plane crossed England and headed out over the Atlantic towards New York City.

There were two aisles. Stewardesses were coming down both aisles with their snack carts. One stewardess stood ahead of a cart and the other stood behind. We all watched them intently because we were like helpless children waiting for treats. The plane was so big there were several more sets of carts far behind us. Two carts were in front of us.

All four stewardesses fell to the floor.

Everybody else collapsed in their seats.

Steve was unconscious too.

"Steve! Steve!"

I felt his carotid and found no pulse. I was terrified that he was dead, but a slight hope kept me from panicking.

They'd once thought I was dead for two weeks. I was in what we were calling 'deep sleep'.

Could Steve only be in deep sleep? This thought kept me from losing it. But I was still scared for him.

Now was a time to think clearly if there ever was. Why would HAL be putting everybody into deep sleep? I was in a plane. I'd made several plane flights around Europe and nothing happened. What made this flight different? The size of the plane, maybe?

I was flying over the Atlantic! My government kidnappers put me in a plane and flew out with me to the carrier in the South Atlantic. This flight was getting HAL to rummage through his repertoire of reflexes. His mindless logic said something had to be done about this situation. There were four things to go after: the carrier, the Atlantic, the plane, and my kidnappers including Steve. HAL saw no carrier. He couldn't eliminate the Atlantic Ocean. The plane might be a part of me. The only thing left was eliminating my kidnappers. But I had never killed anybody and neither had HAL. He had put me into deep sleep last year. He put my kidnappers into deep sleep now.

Who was flying the plane?

I stepped into the aisle that was blocked by the snack cart. But they couldn't block both aisles at the same time. The center seat section had crossing aisles to use to get from one aisle to the other without crawling over four people. The carts were staggered in front and in back of these crossing aisles so that anybody could go to the front or back of the plane anytime. I went through a crossing aisle to the left and walked forward. The journey seemed like several miles.

The Boeing 747 had a circular staircase leading up to a lounge. Finally, I got to the cockpit, or flight cabin—whatever it was called now. The pilot, co-pilot and navigator were in deep sleep, I hoped. The pilot wore earphones. I didn't want to disturb those and carefully put them on a kind of shelf to his left. I pulled him out of his seat and lay him down on the floor. I assumed his seat and put on the earphones. They were silent. There were no adjusting knobs on them or anything like that. I looked over the control panel. Some lights were on. Some weren't. There were four computer monitors stacked two by two. They must be for displaying all kinds of data. They were all blank. The plane's electronics were dead.

I looked up at Heaven with an accusing look. Couldn't God give me a break once in a while? I mean really! This was going too far.

In a few seconds I remembered there had to be hundreds of cell phones on the plane. I could use them to communicate with the ground.

I went back downstairs to the passenger cabin. Virtually everybody in this plane had to have a cell phone. I quickly found one in a woman's handbag. It was dead. I found two more phones in men's shirt pockets but they were dead too. Why? I remembered something Steve said a few months back. He was talking about the deep sleep HAL put me in. "He put dark matter in you to hold your atom nuclei in place by gravity. But this wouldn't work if electrons could move around. You would turn to soup. There was enough dark matter to keep the electrons from wandering around."

I knew a little about physics. Computer chips used very low voltages. It wouldn't take much to interfere with the electrons. But electric lights and things like that used voltages ten thousand times higher. The sophisticated electronics I needed to learn how to fly this thing were dead. But this was not enough to bring down the plane. The earliest planes couldn't have had any electronics. They were all electrical. This plane had to have all kinds of backup systems, enough to let the pilot fly no matter what, if he knew how a plane works. I didn't.

I made an accusing look up to Heaven again, much longer this time to show Him how mad I was. I had reached the end of my patience and let Him have it.

"What's the purpose of this trial? Does it have a point? Didn't I prove my courage in the South Atlantic last year? What more do you want from me?"

I'd seen an old movie about a stewardess having to take over a plane. But she at least had some knowledge about flying and she had radio communication. I had neither. I think she flew an old fashioned propeller plane. I had this damn flying movie theatre to deal with.

There was nothing to do but go back upstairs. By the time I got up there I realized I needed to find manuals for how to fly the plane. There had to be some. There were storage lockers in the flight control cabin. I searched them and found a bunch of technical manuals. I pulled the co-pilot out to the floor too so I could use his seat for the manuals. I sat in the captain's seat and checked my watch. We were scheduled to land in New York in six and a quarter hours. I had that long to learn how to fly a Boeing 747. Real pilots probably took longer.

The technical manuals were about as useful as most of these things were. They were written for people who already knew everything. There was no "Flying For Dummies". Every page was filled with jargon that was defined in pilot's school back home. It was a mess. There was no way I could fly this damn thing.

"Staying alive for me is like surviving a train wreck."

It's a terrible thing to be alone and not have anybody to talk to about a serious problem. It would have been nice just to give up, lie down and forget everything. It was tempting. But something kept me going.

I allowed myself to luxuriate in this misery for a short while. It wasn't like losing valuable time. I couldn't concentrate on the manuals until my mood changed.

I saw a plane miles away. It was going in the same direction. Over several minutes it got closer. I wondered if they were aware of my plane. But they had to be. These big planes all had radar. They couldn't fly around without it.

The plane moved up to only a couple hundred yards away from us on my right and stayed in that position. It was a jet fighter. I understood. When my plane went off the air the airports must have noticed immediately. There must have been a lot of panic. 'Theresa Hartley's plane is missing!!!!!' Panicked calls were made to Prime Minister Blair who hustled his jet fighters out to find the Hartley plane. And there they were. They were checking us out. I bet the pilot was looking at me with binoculars. The world was finding out something happened to everybody else and I was flying the plane. They had to know I didn't know how to fly a kite. There must have been pandemonium at the airport. The media would go nuts over this.

His binoculars should be able to see my depressed

attitude. 'Theresa is giving up. Theresa has lost hope. Theresa wants to go back downstairs and wait for the end.'

The airport must have been screaming at him to stay with me. 'Don't let her quit. Keep her trying. Show her there's hope.'

They understood me better than I did myself. If it weren't for Steve I might have already given up. But I believed in something. And because I believed I didn't have the luxury of giving up. I couldn't abandon hope.

I waved to the plane and went back to the technical manuals.

I read for a while and learned a few things. I found the compass. It was scaled with two digit numbers. It currently was set on 23. What was that? I'd seen enough movies to know planes and ships used degrees for directions. Zero degrees was north. A hundred and eighty degrees was south. Two hundred and seventy degrees was west. 23 on the compass had to mean 230 degrees, or southwest, which made sense since we were going to New York and Europe was way up there level with Canada. There was one way to prove it. Change direction.

I did know there was something called the autopilot and with a little more research in the manual I found out how to turn the autopilot off and on. The steering wheel was a rectangular shaped thing. I turned off the autopilot and moved the wheel counterclockwise. The compass changed down to 21, 19, 17. That jived with the counterclockwise direction I was turning. That confirmed it. I returned the compass to 23 and let the autopilot take over.

The jet fighter was gone and replaced by a commercial airliner. That made sense too. Jet fighters were fast but couldn't carry enough fuel to cross the ocean.

I learned many things from the manuals. How to operate the speed of the jet engines which would also control altitude. How to use the rudder to turn the plane without using the wheel to lean the plane to the side. How to use the two large brake pedals. How to lower and raise the landing gear. Over the next four hours I did small experiments with all these things except for the brakes and landing gear. I thought lowering the landing gear at these altitudes might cause damage. Anyways I wasn't willing to take the chance. My little experiments caused small changes in the plane's position. The other plane stayed right next to us all the time.

I took a break and remembered that dramatic scene in the movie where Charles Lindbergh landed in Paris and two hundred thousand people pushed down the fences to run to his plane. It was known that what Lindbergh was trying was possible. It was only a question of whether Lindbergh would be the first or kill himself trying. Could I pull this off? The world had to be wondering. There would be a lot of people at the airport!

An hour later a small business jet approached from the direction of the United States. It made a wide turn and came up directly in front of us at a distance of several hundred yards. It clearly intended that I follow it. The commercial airliner backed away until I lost sight of it.

In a few minutes the business jet dropped altitude

by a hundred or so feet. I pulled back on the engine control lever to lower myself down to his level. He went down again at much lower altitude. I matched him again. A third time he went down and I followed him, staying as directly behind him as possible. We were communicating. I was telling him I would follow his movements which was what he wanted. I also was telling him I could maneuver the plane. The people on the ground must have stopped stampeding in circles. I might pull this off after all!

He moved slightly to the left. I understood he was doing a slight turn. I followed him. Now the compass arrow was on 22. It had been a ten degree course correction. I knew trans-Atlantic air traffic was crowded and planes had to be put into slots. One of these slots might not be a straight line all the way across the ocean. A plane might have to zigzag left and right all the way to stay away from other planes.

I found the phrase 'mechanical altimeter' in a technical manual and located it among the instruments. It said 29,000 feet. It did not depend on electronics and it worked. That was one more thing in my repertoire.

According to my watch we were eighty minutes from New York. There was a lot of cloud cover below and I wanted to see something. I turned off the autopilot and pulled back on the engine speed control lever gently. We started going down. The business jet ahead of me followed me down. We went down at a leisurely pace and in a few minutes reached the clouds at fifteen thousand feet. The cloud layer was a few thousand feet thick. We got under it at twelve thousand feet and I stopped there. The business jet was to my right. He repositioned in front of me and seemed satisfied with the altitude. He didn't try to make me change it.

Soon another small plane came towards us. It was a two engine propeller plane. It maneuvered over close to the business jet. Suddenly the jet veered off to the left leaving the two propeller plane as my guide.

You can see a long distance at twelve thousand feet. The horizon was probably four hundred miles away. Well, over two hundred anyways. I looked for land. A while later I could see some. I had a map of the New York airport at my right hand and also a map of the coast around New York. Long Island stuck out 118 miles from the city. Could I be looking at Long Island?

There was a large ship down there, and although at this altitude I couldn't see details, I could see from its shadow it was high above the water. It could only be a cruise ship with two or three thousand people on board. Where were they going? They had to be wondering the same thing about me. They could not fail to know those two planes overhead were my lead plane and my own plane. Safe on their ship, most of them must have pitied me and my fellow passengers. But maybe a few of them were envious. When their cruise was over what would be worth remembering about it other than seeing me fly overhead? An owner of a popular magazine had recently died. He was a bon vivant who had had many interesting experiences besides his magazine. The next issue showed a picture of him on one of his adventures. The caption read, "While alive, he lived!" I'll bet there were people on that ship who would gladly trade places with me now, even if it meant this was their last day.

"Sorry, folks. I wouldn't trade with you."

My lead plane had directed me to a compass heading of 27, due west. In a while I could see land on the right side. This had to be Long Island, Connecticut and Rhode Island. New Jersey would still be further away. A few minutes later I could see roughness over a small portion of the horizon. This was the skyscrapers of Manhattan.

The lead plane started lowering its altitude and I followed. We descended to three thousand feet and stayed there for a while.

I was starting to see pleasure boats far below. The tip of Long Island was no longer an amorphous blur, but I could see features, or rather, differences in how land was used, some green areas and some developed areas. It was still too far to see buildings and streets from my angle.

The lead plane led me down to eighteen hundred feet. They had some reason for this. I guessed that they wanted to see how I handled the plane at lower speeds or denser air. At this height I could clearly see the pleasure boats and people on board waving enthusiastically at me. We reached the tip of Long Island and I noticed something. Many hundreds of pleasure boats were going around the tip but all in a southward direction. They were trying to get to New York City to greet me, but they were too far away to make it in time.

As the next minutes passed I saw thousands of more boats heading for New York. This seemed odd. I was supposed to land at the airport and immediately fly out to West Point by helicopter. They would never see me. Then I realized they must know exactly where I was. The media would be informing them. They just wanted to see me flying over which was likely to be the closest they could get to me.

We were about twenty miles from New York and now the ocean seemed covered with pleasure boats. They spread out as far as I could see. How many of them were there? A half million? A million? I didn't know there were this many boats in the whole world.

My lead plane prompted me to go down to nine hundred feet. At this height the noise from my plane's engines had to be bursting the eardrums of the people on the boats. This was not a normal airplane approach. I thought they didn't want me to come down too quickly when we reached the airport. They were reducing the challenge of one of the three dimensions I had to worry about.

I had a map of New York and the airport in my right hand. The runway was two miles long and pointed straight at the Empire State Building. I would have no problem finding the runway even without the lead plane.

I lowered the landing gear. Lights indicated they were locked in place. Everything was set. But then my lead plane lowered its landing gear and immediately raised it again. What did that mean? The lead plane did it two more times. He lowered the wheels and raised them up. I got the hint and raised my landing gear too.

He now turned left and I followed. New York City was to my right. We were getting away from it! What the hell....?

He lowered his altitude and I followed him down

to five hundred feet. The ocean was really covered with boats around here, millions of them it looked like. Then I saw a clear space ahead. Two rows of ships were lined up in parallel and between them there wasn't a single boat. The clear water was a rectangle something like two miles long and we were going right down the middle of it.

They wanted me to land on water!

I nearly panicked but rallied. I had to make a decision. Something you saw in the news about once a year was a plane landing without its nose landing gear down. The plane would land with the nose scrapping the ground in a cloud of sparks. I'd seen this several times. What I had never heard of was a pilot deliberately landing on water.

The lead plane was going down closer to the water. I went down a little but not as far as him. We reached the beginning of the clear rectangle. He went down to just a few feet above water. I chickened out. I couldn't do it. I kept three or four hundred feet up. It took less than a minute to reach the end of the clear water and the lead plane suddenly turned off to the left much more sharply than the 747 could do. He abandoned me. I was on my own.

My heart must have been beating two hundred times a minute. What happened? What was wrong with landing at the airport? No pilot ever landed on water if he had a choice. It must be very dangerous. Why did they want me to do it?

I developed a theory. They didn't know how skillful I was at controlling the plane. Any mistake on my part would not be forgiven by the hard runway. The water might give me some slack.

Yeah, well, I'd been manipulating this plane for hours and I thought I was doing pretty good.

"I'm going to the airport! They can go to hell!"

I made a long slow turn to the left until I was finally pointed to New York. I kept checking the map of New York and the relationship of the beginning of the runway with the contour of the shoreline before it. Then I positioned the plane towards where the runway should be, and sure enough there it was in the distance. I lowered the landing gear. Lights indicated they were locked in place. I moved the plane some distance to the right and aimed it straight down the runway's throat. I stayed down at four hundred feet.

The little two propeller plane was positioned on my right to keep an eye on me. I went down to 250 feet. I felt sorry for the boaters below.

I was half a mile from the runway when I saw something. There were trucks parked on the runway. In twenty seconds I reached the beginning. There were hundreds of trucks on the runway blocking my way. I kept moving down the runway. It was the same the entire length, buses, fire engines, and trucks, trucks, and more trucks, large vehicles that I couldn't miss seeing.

The runway's end was in sight. I pushed forward on the engine speed lever. The plane started climbing slowly. Too slowly. The Empire State Building was straight ahead. I pushed the lever further forward. The plane climbed. There was something I wasn't doing right. The plane wasn't climbing fast enough. We were over developed areas. The altimeter read 340 feet. It had to be hell on the ground, storefront windows being blown out, people being knocked off their feet. I was getting to the end of Queens. The East River was coming up. I could see I wasn't going to get over the Empire State Building. I turned the wheel slightly to the left. Just to the left of the Empire State was a few hundred yards of buildings only a few hundred feet tall. Then the skyscrapers covered the rest of Manhattan. I aimed for this narrow gap of lower buildings. Seconds later I reached the eastern edge of Manhattan.

The plane passed a few hundred feet above the buildings in this gap but it was still far below the top of the Empire State Building which was not very far to my right, and below the tops of buildings to my left. For what seemed like an eternity I passed over the buildings of Manhattan, probably blowing out a million windows, and all the time I thought what a disaster it would be if I crashed this gigantic plane among those buildings. It would be worse than 9/11. It would take months to clean the mess.

Finally, I arrived over the river and into New Jersey where there were no tall buildings.

I screamed and shook my head. Then I broke down and cried. The unfairness and hopelessness of this situation! Even if I didn't crash this thing, Steve might already be dead. It was too much. I cried and cried.

The little two propeller plane was at my side again. It must have been there all along to document my crash into Manhattan killing forty thousand people. They had to have seen my breakdown. Well, what did they expect!

I stopped crying out loud and sniffled my way into calmness. There was still this colossal community coffin to land.

I made a U-turn and climbed higher as I went over Staten Island. The damned Atlantic Ocean was ahead.

The little two engine propeller plane stayed at my side but didn't try to lead me. They were leaving me alone. They didn't want to spook me anymore. But what did they want me to do?

I tried to think calmly. Pilots didn't want to land on water if they could avoid it. It must be dangerous. They were afraid to let me use the runway. Or were they? Might they have changed their minds?

I could imagine a bunch of people in a room reviewing the video of my aborted landing at the airport. "She didn't bob the nose up or down or side to side. She didn't lean the plane side to side. She didn't wander off the runway. She kept the plane at the same height. She has fair control. The landing gear looks good. I vote we let her land on the runway."

"I agree." "I agree." "I agree." "I agree." "I agree." "I agree."

That's what could be happening. Or not.

I reached the ocean. The rectangle was still clear of boats. They hadn't blocked it to force me back to the runway but neither did the lead plane get in front of me to choose a landing for me. Or else, they still wanted me to use the water. Or else, they didn't want me to use the water, but were afraid to block the rectangle because it might throw me into total panic. Or else, they wanted me to look for another airport where I wouldn't crash into skyscrapers. They hoped I'd figure out what they really wanted. There was only one way to find out.

I made another long U-turn and used the map to

zero in on the runway as before and lowered the plane to seven hundred feet. The runway was in sight. From a distance it looked clear.

I got close to it and it was clear! There wasn't a Matchbox toy on it anywhere. Whether they preferred me to land there or not they were leaving it up to me.

I noticed an enormous crowd a few hundred yards off the northern side of the runaway. I'd seen the crowd at Red Sox games. This one must have been a hundred times as big. There had to be two million people down there. Maybe three million. Aw, heck, everybody in North America was here. This situation had never happened before and would never happen again. It was the Hindenburg disaster multiplied a hundred times. They wanted to tell their grandchildren they were here.

"The restroom line must reach to Philadelphia."

I didn't go down. This high off the ground I felt safe to lean the plane slightly to the left to turn around again while pushing the engine control speed levers forward to increase altitude a little. The people on the ground had to be going nuts wondering what I'd do next.

I circled around over the bay, far back out to sea, then turned back to New York while lowering the altitude to two hundred feet. I wanted to simplify the landing. Already being barely off the ground, it would be easy to cut the engines a little and drop down. God help the thousands of boats below me! People were probably being knocked overboard.

The airport was in sight. The runway was still clear. I was only hundreds of yards from the runway. I pulled the levers back slightly until I thought I was very close to the ground.

I'd found that a big plane didn't react instantly. Just five seconds before reaching the beginning of the runway I pulled the engine speed control lever most of the way back. The landing gear hit the pavement hard and the plane bounced. I had anticipated this possibility and knew there was no changing my mind now. I pulled the engine speed control lever all the way back. The plane hit the pavement again but didn't bounce. We were rolling. I pushed down on the two large brake pedals. The plane was going towards the left of the runway. I turned the wheel right. The plane went slightly to the right. I turned the wheel slightly to the left. I'd gotten to know the feel of the wheel.

We were still rolling at high speed. I could hear the brakes screeching but we weren't slowing down much. What was wrong now? I'd used up a third of the runway and still we were going over a hundred miles an hour. I released the brakes for one second. The screeching stopped in that second so the brakes were working. I pressed down again. I could see the end of the runway because emergency vehicles were parked near it. We were still whizzing by vehicles on the side of the runway at high speed. The brakes never stopped screeching. What would happen if I ran out of runway? Finally, I could see that the plane was slowing down. The runway was only half a mile away. The plane kept slowing down. And slowing down. And slowing down. And slowing down. The end of the runway was maybe two hundred yards away when the plane stopped.

I released the brakes but the plane started creeping forward again. I pushed back down on the brakes.

I was exhausted. This was worse than falling from the jet fighter. At least then there was only one outcome to worry about. Tears streamed from my eyes. I was relieved but also very shaken up.

I got to thinking. The plane was safely on the ground with nobody at the wheel but a nineteen year old kid who knew nothing about flying. I could see the crowd of millions of people running towards the plane. "I can do anything!" I said out loud to myself. A few hours earlier I was ready to give up and wait for death.

All kinds of vehicles were surrounding the plane. They were all blasting their horns and sirens in celebration of my latest miracle. I noticed one of the fire trucks getting in place at my left. It wasn't a city fire truck but some kind of airport vehicle, but it did have a ladder. They extended the ladder towards the side of the plane.

In a minute I heard somebody coming up the stairs. He entered the cockpit. "I can't let go of the brakes" I told him.

He reached up to play with some switches on the ceiling panel. After a few seconds he said, "Now you can."

That was good enough for me. I jumped up leaving it all to him and went downstairs.

The passenger entrance door was open and airport workers poured through the door to scatter around the plane.

"What happened?" one of them asked.

"I hope HAL only put them to sleep, but I don't know."

I worked my way down the left aisle and across to

the right to rejoin Steve. He had a heartbeat! He was alive. Thank God!

In a moment he started breathing and slowly regained conscious. He saw me and the commotion in the cabin.

"What happened?"

"HAL put everybody to sleep except me. We were over the Atlantic."

He understood. "Don't tell me you landed the plane!"

"Yup. Not bad for a math major, hunh?"

"Not bad," he proudly grinned.

All doors were now open allowing sounds from outside to come in. The nearby vehicles were still blaring their horns and sirens. An immense crowd of people was cheering. And from the nearby water, thousands and thousands of boats were tooting their horns. How many millions of people had waited here to see me arrive?

The rest of the passengers and crew were awake. Some order was restored. Steve and I waited patiently until the powers that be told people to move out.

The captain, co-pilot, and three stewardesses came over to meet us. The captain said, "They told me you landed the plane without using the flaps and reverse thrusters. Do you know how amazing that is?"

"Not really. I don't know what you're talking about."

"You made history. They'll be talking about it for years."

I told Steve, "When I found out I had to land the plane without help I got angry with God. I asked Him what the heck the point of this was."

"What did He say?"

"He said, 'Look what you've done. You can do anything. Don't let people down.'"

The plane was inspected and towed to a terminal after the difficult task of clearing vehicles and crowds out of the way. We disembarked and were met by airport officials. They needed information to write reports to the National Transportation Safety Board. Why did everybody on the plane go to sleep? How much did I know about flying? What did I do with my time during the crossing over the Atlantic? Why did I refuse to land on water? Why did I try to land at the airport a second time?

When they had all the information they needed for reports nobody would read one of the officials said, "You left a real mess in Queens and Manhattan. The Boeing 747 generates a lot of energy and it has to be absorbed by something."

"What kind of mess?" Steve asked.

"Thousands of windows broken, some people injured."

"Who's going to be responsible? Not Theresa?"

"No. She can't be held responsible. I don't know who will take the fall. Nobody looks responsible."

I added, "If there had been a simple written procedure for how to fly the plane, things might have been different. All I had was a pile of technical manuals. They don't explain anything if you don't already know everything."

"I think the NTSB will consider that."

There was one more thing I wanted clarified. "What if I had gone straight to the airport?"

"Without knowing about the water landing

option?"

"Yeah."

"President Stinson would have ordered the runway cleared. She couldn't risk putting you in a panic."

We went out into the public area to get away and were surrounded by hundreds of reporters sticking microphones and cameras at us. Dozens of them were shouting questions all at the same time. Each reporter was desperate to get a response from me. It would make his career. When we got to the main room of the terminal it was wall to wall people cheering wildly. They wanted to be part of history. We would have been crushed to death if not for the team of government security people pushing outwards at this mob.

It had been decided to take us to West Point by car rather than helicopter as originally planned. We finally made it to a limousine and took off.

Chapter 23

A three bedroom ranch style house had been built for us on West Point less than a mile from headquarters. We could have had a house in the Point's large undeveloped areas, but Steve and I preferred to see some kind of Cadet activity from our windows. We were close to the campus. Before I got out of the limousine I saw my parents running out to meet me.

"Theresa! Theresa!" yelled my mother with great excitement.

"Mom!"

We met and hugged. There were the typical comments of missing each other and how-are-you. I observed that mom appeared to be mentally sharp. She was recovered from whatever problem she had a year ago. Dad hugged his daughter in turn. He and Steve shook hands.

We went into the simple three bedroom ranch style house. The furnishings were manufactured items from a chain store. There were no priceless antiques here like in the Parker mansion.

"You like it?" asked mom.

"It's nice. I don't have to worry about breaking anything."

We settled in to updating each other on the latest news. I could not say much that my parents didn't already know from the constant media coverage. Mom filled me in on the latest Sullivan marriages, funerals and scandals.

Our cross-Atlantic plane flight came up. I learned that President Stinson was called minutes after HAL put everybody into deep sleep. There was a raging controversy about what to do when I got to New York. Some people wanted to lower a telephone on a cable next to the cockpit on the chance that I would figure out how to open the pilot's side window which can be done at low altitudes. Other people said the telephone would be wildly whipping around in the wind and I might be knocked out, or I might fall out of the window reaching for the phone. The President said no to this idea, a brave decision on her part. What would she tell people if I crashed!

The water landing was almost certain to be a success. The plane was designed to do it. But nobody knew what I was thinking which could be any number of things, and President Stinson finally decided to let me use the runway rather than leave me in a state of complete panic. It was another gutsy decision on her part.

As unbelievable as it may seem, the media speculated that I had contrived this crisis to make myself look like a hero! Ridiculous! What about everything I had already done? The few people who suggested this stupid idea were getting a lot of criticism.

Mom announced that she and dad were returning to the Boston area to be with family and friends. They knew nobody in New York, and security said they had detected no threats. My enemies were not like the Mafia who go after families. It was considered safe for the Sullivans to go home, although they would still need bodyguards.

"You two need your privacy" mom added.

My parents stayed long enough to see the football game.

Like the Ambassador predicted, it was bigger than the Super Bowl. The whole world was interested. In America, baseball games had empty stadiums as people stayed home to watch the special Army-Navy game. Fourth of July parades were canceled. All networks were free to televise it and they did. Well really! What other programming did they have for the Fourth of July on a Thursday afternoon?

It was an unusual game. First of all, nobody wanted to see the game won by field goals and extra points. It was agreed that scoring would be by touchdowns only.

Films of my practice with the Ronald Reagan sailors on Mr. Parker's estate had been shown, and people thought no team could beat my super accurate throwing arm. Coaches spoke differently. They said the world's best quarterback couldn't win if he had lousy receivers, and both Army and Navy teams would be made up of amateurs, not regular Academy team players.

The newspaper had a shameless headline: "Can Cute Quarterback Coordinate Chaotic Club? Coaches Cautious, Crowd Convinced." Crazy cacophonous comments, crackhead! Corny crap.

There was one more interesting change in the usual procedures. Nobody wanted to see an embarrassing fiasco of amateurs tripping over each other. The two Academies agreed that they could have their regular teams at the sidelines coaching the amateur players. The effect was that every player had his own personal coach who knew all the fine points of that particular position.

It was the "Rednecks versus the Cream of Society", the "Underdogs versus the Elite". The Navy's Ronald Reagan team was drawn from all walks of life, but they had my throwing arm. The Army team was all disciplined cadets, but their quarterbacks couldn't hit a STOP sign at fifty yards like I could. Who had the advantage?

Army won 48-36. Oh well! At least people could see the game wasn't rigged to let me win.

So there we were living on West Point. Colonel Palin came by and invited us to eat with the Cadet Corps anytime we wanted. The 4,000 Cadets ate in a large mess hall. The seniors constantly pumped the underclassmen with technical questions while they ate. There was plenty of noise. Steve and I dropped by for lunch or dinner almost every day. When we did, the brass would allow the Cadets to walk over to us after eating and get to know us. Everybody wanted my autograph. Eventually they all got it.

After my parents left for Massachusetts, we drove to New York City which neither of us had ever seen. We were followed by a car filled with security people. In spite of this trip being kept secret, the paparazzi, ever vigilant at West Point's gates, spotted us and followed. There was an agreement among these parasites that information about celebrities' movements are to be shared to allow every photographer a chance to make a living, and so, when we arrived at my office building off Central Park, there was already a crowd of hundreds of people.

We got out of the car protected by security people.

The photographers and reporters carrying microphones crowded near. They shouted for our attention. We ignored them totally. It was like we were walking through the woods with nobody around for miles. This would make lousy television, which was what we wanted. So you see a famous person walk from their car to a door. So what? It they don't say anything, if they don't look at the camera, if nothing at all happens, do you want to tune into the news tomorrow to see them get out of a car and walk to a door again? Eventually these parasites would go away.

We went upstairs to talk to my financial manager Jan Struthers, who directed my oil, gold, silver, and base metal businesses. I had brought down a billion tons of rustproof nickel which had lots of uses. I was also bringing down copper, chromium, titanium and other metals.

Theresa's Island was now producing three million barrels of oil a day, with fifteen million a day expected in a year. Beyond that nobody dared predict the volume. I was going to be richer than most entire countries.

While I had said I'd sell the oil at ten dollars, I couldn't control the world price until I had a monopoly on the stuff. That would take a few years. The world price was down to thirty-two dollars and kept steady there. Jan told me something surprising. The oil companies were afraid that I might change my mind later and keep the price up. To lock in the ten dollar price they were offering me advanced payments at the ten dollar level for fifty-four billion barrels, a two year world supply. All I had to do was sign a piece of paper Jan held out to me to make it an official contract.

Steve nodded his approval. I agreed to do it. Jan brought in a bunch of oil company executives and photographers to witness the single greatest financial deal in history. I signed. I now had around half a trillion dollars in the bank.

After more pictures were taken, Jan told the executives, "Thank you gentlemen. We need privacy now." The executives left. Jan got on the phone again and said, "Send them in."

Five more executives came in. Jan explained.

"You have so much money you can't put more than a small amount of it in the stock market without driving stock prices crazy. There's an alternative. Buy out entire companies."

"What companies?"

"Boeing Aircraft, Ford Motor, General Electric, U.S. Steel, and Nucor Steel."

Like a hitchhiker, Jan crooked her thumb towards the five executives. One of them spoke.

"I'm CEO of U.S. Steel. After World War II, America dominated the world steel industry. Now, all large countries have steel works. Nobody makes a profit. You can get all the metals free and make America dominate again."

"I'm CEO of Ford. All our companies use metals. Combining our five companies into one privately held company will give us an unbeatable competitive advantage. There are certain synergies in cooperating with each other."

Steve said, "Countries are already talking about imposing import duties on the United States because Theresa has a monopoly on gold and oil. Now you want her to monopolize manufacturing too?"

The five executives looked like little boys who didn't get anything for Christmas. They had no answer to Steve's remarks. Taking over manufacturing could start a global trade war.

Steve and I got up to leave.

"Sorry, Theresa" said Jan Struthers who looked more embarrassed than anybody. As my financial manager she should have thought of these things.

"It's all right," I assured her.

Not long before we returned to the States Jan found us an apartment in downtown Manhattan. It was in an office building because we couldn't stay in the average apartment building. It would be too disrupting to the other tenants. We got back in the car to drive down Fifth Avenue. We had rented half a floor of an office building close to St. Patrick's Cathedral, Rockefeller Center, and Times Square. Our half was sealed off from the rest of the floor and converted into a living space. Here, we could stay for days or weeks at a time with frequent trips back to the West Point house for a more relaxing existence.

We visited the apartment and were very satisfied. Jan had done a great job getting it ready. The views of the city's activity were spectacular. The Empire State building was close by and we could see parts of the Hudson River over the lower West Side.

After an hour's rest we went down to the street. A team of security people appeared from nowhere.

"Our friends are here," said Steve.

"How do they know we're going out?"

"They watch the elevator."

We were instantly recognized by pedestrians. I

didn't return their waves or greetings. People had to learn I wanted to be left alone, and if they thought I was a snob, that couldn't be helped. I could not acknowledge every person I walked by and live normally.

There were few reporters trailing us. The word had gotten out quickly; there was no story to be gotten from Theresa on the street. Boring pictures of nothing happening was not enough to hold viewers.

Our first destination was the theatre district to buy tickets to a popular play for the next night. Then we curved around to get opera tickets at the Met for the night after that. Tonight we would just hang around in the apartment and cruise the local television stations to get acquainted with the city.

On the fifth day in New York we went downstairs to walk to a new restaurant written up in the New York Times. Just outside our front door was an unusual group of people. They were ten Asian men who looked to be in their twenties, although it was hard to tell. When they saw me they immediately started crying and lamenting. They held pictures of me, put their hands out and begged for something. I couldn't tell what they wanted; they spoke in some Asiatic language.

Normally I ignored all people on the street no matter what they said or shouted. This time I stopped and stared at them. Their crying, lamenting and begging was painful to see. We had never seen anything like it.

"Let's move on," Steve said, and we walked away. The crying Asian men stayed behind.

After dining at the restaurant, we took in a movie

and returned to the apartment. The Asian men were still there and went into the same crying and begging routine. I was moved.

"What the heck do they want?"

"Forget it. You help them and we'll have a million beggars at the door."

I knew Steve was right, but these men were so pitiable, they were either very desperate or really great actors.

The next morning we set out for breakfast to be followed by further touring of the city. Again the ten Asian men were outside the door and went into their begging routine as soon as they saw us. They had to be really desperate.

As we moved a hundred feet away I looked back to see the men still at it. I motioned to one of the security people tailing us. He came over.

"Find out who those men are," I said.

I ate my breakfast in silence. My mood was depressed after seeing the begging Asians. The day was ruined. Steve didn't even try to make conversation.

We went on to the Metropolitan Museum to get more sophisticated, but our hearts weren't in it. So we headed back to the apartment.

The Asians were there again and went into their crying, lamenting, begging routine. This time there was an eleventh Asian man who stood by calmly. A government security man had been waiting near the door and approached me.

"They're North Koreans who escaped their country. That quiet guy is South Korean. He can speak English."

"Call him over."

The quiet Asian man was motioned to come over. He said, "Please, Miss Theresa. See this tape and you will know how they suffer."

He handed me a videotape.

"I'll look at it."

We went upstairs to put the tape in a VCR. It was a documentary for a PBS channel. It began with an amazing sight. Millions of North Koreans were lined up on the sidewalk of some huge boulevard. The off screen commentator who spoke in English said the leader of North Korea had just died and his body was being carried down the boulevard in a convoy of army trucks. The people along the streets were crying and lamenting exactly like the ten men outside our office building. The camera panned down the sidewalk filled with these millions of crying North Koreans for what seemed like miles. They all behaved the same way without exception. It was unbelievable!

"The people mourn for the man they call 'our dear leader'" explained the commentator. "It is hard to know if their emotion is genuine or a display of what they are expected to do. They have been raised in this society since the nineteen-fifties."

There was no end to the hysterical North Koreans. This was personality cult worship carried to ridiculous extremes. There had never been anything like this elsewhere.

The scene changed to a hospital where patients were asked why they wanted to be cured of their illnesses. Every one of them said they wanted to go see 'our dear leader'.

Now this could not be the real reason they wanted

to be cured, because most of them were surrounded by family. But they knew to give the politically correct answer.

The scene switched to a small apartment the French team of reporters visited. A young family lived there with the grandparents. The commentator explained that a speaker blared out government propaganda twenty-four hours a day. The volume could be turned down but not entirely shut off. The French team interviewed the North Korean family. No matter what the subject the family managed to get in some kind of praise for 'our dear leader'.

The main terror weapon in North Korea was a system of prison camps. The government denied they existed but satellite images clearly showed them. Anybody who was suspected of the slightest lack of loyalty was sent to a prison camp along with all his family for life.

In another scene a young North Korean, who was one of the few people who had escaped one of these camps, was interviewed in the safety of the South. He told his story: "My father made a remark to a neighbor that could be interpreted as disloyal. The neighbor reported it. My father was executed and my mother, sister and myself were sent to the prison camp. I was an infant. When I was twenty, my mother and sister told me they planned an escape. This was against the camp rules. I knew nothing except the rules. I reported my mother and sister to a guard. He brought me to the interrogation room and tortured me with fire. He did this to tell his superior he had tortured the information out of me. I was forced to watch my mother and sister being hanged. Soon after, a guard who had been at the camp only a month came to me. He had an escape plan and needed my help. I agreed. We escaped and made it to South Korea. I will not tell you how we did it. This guard said when he arrived at the camp he was forced to beat prisoners for days to turn him into a beast. When the guards were sent to the prison camps, they were turned into animals."

I was shocked into immobility. I had never imagined there could be such a society among human beings. It was the devil's playground.

What could I do? Should I do anything?

As always, my conscience prodded me to do something if I could.

I stood up. "We have to do something about this. Let's go see them."

Steve followed me back down to the street. The unhappy Koreans were still there. I walked up to the South Korean.

"I will do everything I can for your people."

The man translated and the ten North Koreans showed body language signs that they were grateful. I went to each of them to shake their hands one by one. I was affected by the emotions myself. I was nearly crying.

I returned to the apartment and grabbed the phone to dial 0 for the operator. My mood had changed in the elevator. I was ready for a fight.

"This is Theresa Hartley. Get me the New York Times."

Moments passed. Clearly the operator wasn't putting me through to some answering service. Finally, somebody answered.

"John Maxwell, Editor in Chief. How may I help you, Mrs. Hartley?"

Steve smiled. He could imagine a hundred reporters gathered around the Editor's desk.

"I just found out what's going on in North Korea. It's disgusting. Send me information about what's happening there. I'm at the Fifth Avenue apartment."

"We'll do so. Will you speak to a reporter?"

"No. This business has to be secret."

"Can the right hand of God do something in North Korea?"

"God has to let evil men do what they want. I don't. Good by, sir."

What permitted me to mess around with North Korea? I didn't want anything for myself. Prime Minister Blair told me half of literature shows that desire and hate go together. Somebody goes after something, can't get it by legitimate means and turns evil. That wouldn't happen to me. I didn't want anything I didn't already have.

Chapter 24

The next morning's New York Times had an ominous headline: Theresa Hartley Eyes North Korea. Veronica Stinson called me.

"Theresa, President Stinson. How are you?"

"Fine. What's up?"

"We need to talk. Will you come to the White House?"

"Hold on."

I put my hand on the receiver and asked Steve, "What do you think?"

"Call me paranoid. I don't like it. Tell her to send a general to Colonel Palin's office."

"Mrs. Stinson, I'll meet a general in Colonel Palin's office at West Point tomorrow morning. That's as far as I go."

"I'll send General Walters."

"Who?"

"The Chairman of Joint Chiefs of Staff. Our top military man."

"That works. Good by."

General Walters arrived at nine a.m. Cadets couldn't fail to notice the presence of the top Army man, and speculation had it he was there to see me about North Korea. We walked over to headquarters confirming speculation.

Garrison Commander Colonel Palin, playing host to this meeting, had a hard time maintaining his military poise. The General exchanged greetings with us and we sat down to business.

The General asked, "What are you planning for North Korea?"

"I'm going to liberate the people from their monstrous oppressors. I've developed a technique to get HAL to find things when I've programmed the descriptions to him. I'm going to get HAL to destroy every weapon in North Korea. HAL works at lightning speed but even he can't search every square inch of a country without some kind of guidance. So I'll program him to pick out people at random and see if they're handling a weapon. If they are it's safe to assume there are other weapons nearby. HAL will search the area around that person until he finds no more weapons. Then he'll move on to the next person. This will take only seconds. Once all the weapons are destroyed the South Korean army can move in without resistance and take over the country."

"You're a good person, Mrs. Hartley, and I wouldn't expect you to think of how bad people can be. As soon as you said 'destroy all their weapons', I thought of the revolutions in Europe and other parts of the world. When the mobs take over their countries, they slaughter everyone perceived as oppressors. North Korea has two million people with government jobs, from the top leader, to the lowest city worker. They'll all be killed. The atrocities will make Nazi concentration camps look like vacation resorts."

I was stunned. I hadn't thought of that. I felt stupid and embarrassed at my incompetence.

"What do you suggest?"

"I suggest you think about it carefully. You're still

flush with helping the Israelis evacuate. I need to point out to you that the Israelis wanted to leave. You could sit in England and watch it happen from thousands of miles away. North Korea is a different situation. They will resist any efforts to change things. You can't accomplish anything from thousands of miles away."

And there it was. Despite my awesome power, I could do nothing without the North Koreans' cooperation.

"Give me a minute to think."

I stared at the floor and thought. Walters didn't believe I could get around these problems. When it came to human behavior, it is what it is, and it can't be changed. I could not eliminate the thirst for vengeance, nor could I get the North Koreans to change without violence, which I would not use.

It was another incredibly complex problem. This one wasn't just like raising an island or throwing water into space. I had to get millions of people to dump ideas that had been brainwashed into their heads since birth. How could I do that?

Did the General have an idea? He probably had ten of them, but he wasn't telling me. He wanted me to come up with an idea myself so I'd have the confidence to do it.

After a minute and a half I looked up at the General.

"Plan B. I'll destroy all their weapons in a fifty mile wide band across the country including their capitol city to show them what I can do. Then I'll fly in and take over the government myself."

"They'll kill you."

"Not after I tell them I programmed HAL to destroy all the weapons in the country in eight days and he can't be stopped even by me unless I fly back to South Korea once a week."

"You would go in there alone and assume the government yourself?"

"Why not? The information the New York Times gave says there's always a power struggle among the top leaders. Their jobs are not that secure. I think they'll rally around me knowing I'm not going to send anybody to the prison camps."

"That's not realistic. You'll walk in there and everybody will ignore your orders."

"All right. I'll destroy all weapons in a corridor from the border to the capitol city and go in with the South Korean Army. With the capitol city lost the North Korean leaders will have to give up. But I have to have absolute authority. The North Koreans will never accept South Koreans as their bosses. They hate each other. I'm a neutral third party."

It was a sketchy plan. So were the plans of all wars.

"That might work. I'll inform the President."

"Yeah, well, remember I only need the South Koreans. Do you think they'll accept me?"

"If it was only a military operation, they wouldn't. You have HAL and he's a powerful weapon. I think they'll go for it."

"I'm making an offer they can't refuse, the unification of their country."

It would take months to program HAL to seek out and destroy every kind of weapon used by the North Koreans. First, I needed full scale models of the weapons. "They don't have to be exact replicas," I told Colonel Palin at West Point. "You can make them out of wood. It's the size and shape that matters." The Army went to work making these models. Colonel Palin provided a warehouse on West Point grounds where I could go and program HAL.

Models of North Korean weapons were set up in the empty West Point building. It turned out full scale models were not needed for everything, fortunately, or the building would have needed to be many acres in size. Airplanes and artillery pieces could be represented by downscaled models. I had to give HAL the correct dimensions anyways.

One weapon needed special attention: the atom bomb. A nuclear expert showed me cutaway models and explained.

"There are two configurations. In this one you have a solid sphere of nuclear material in the center surrounded by hollow spheres of conventional explosives. There may be any number of layers of conventional explosive, but they'll all fit together tightly like a single solid sphere. The other configuration is a projectile that is fired like a bullet at the nuclear fuel. The compression of the fuel gets the fission reaction going. These are the only two possible designs for an atom bomb. There is no other way. Can HAL recognize them?"

"I think so. He doesn't feel something on the surface like we do. He feels throughout the thing. He'll see the mechanism."

I looked over the entire collection of weapon models. There were hundreds of items. There were so many ways to shoot people!

"It'll take months to describe these to HAL," I complained to Steve.

"You can give it up."

"Forget it. You can't go into North Korea with me. They might take you hostage and get me to do anything they want. If people don't understand that they can drop dead."

It was an ongoing issue. Steve felt embarrassed about staying back in the safety of the South while his wife went among twenty-four million enemies who wanted her dead. The media would make a lot of it.

Finally, everything was ready for the move to liberate the North Koreans. It was time for me to join the Army.

I insisted that I alone had to have full authority when we moved into the North, and it was hard to dispute my demands. North Korea had all the needs of a fairly modern country: food production and distribution, water supply, electric power, heating, transportation systems, hospitals, bureaucracies for every kind of activity, and infrastructure. It took hundreds of thousands of people with years of experience and knowledge of every square inch of the country to perform all the tasks needed. There was no way the South Koreans could handle everything. The North Koreans themselves would have to remain in their jobs as before. This would be politically unacceptable to the South Korean citizens. No politician would dare suggest it. Therefore, I would have to run the country dictatorially through the North Korean bureaucracy for a while with no backseat driving from the South.

To make this possible I had to have some

sensitivity to the North Koreans' pride. I couldn't strut around in jeans, or worse than that, a skirt. The North Koreans couldn't be expected to take that seriously. What they did take seriously was military authority; it's all they'd known for generations. It was agreed that I would be commissioned an officer in the United States Army.

But before anything was done to alert the public and the North Koreans that I was coming, some of the larger weapons had to be gotten rid of. I brought some of my HAL program mat boards to Colonel Palin's office and explained how they worked. Then I got down to business.

The first job was to get rid of North Korea's atom bombs. I put an X on the relevant mat board and HAL went to work.

Inspired by the little floating ball gauges used on old hospital oxygen tanks, Steve had contrived a simple device to monitor HAL's progress. It consisted of nothing but a ping pong ball in a glass tube. Whenever HAL hit upon an example of the weapon he was searching for and destroyed it, he raised the ping pong ball up to the one foot level of the two foot high glass tube. If he found many weapons in a short time the ball would stay at the one foot level more or less constantly. If hits were infrequent, the ball would have a chance to fall to the bottom.*

Eight minutes went by. The ball rose up in the glass tube for a second.

"There's a bomb" I said. "HAL cut it into a hundred pieces. He'll search the entire country for bombs."

Another twelve minutes went by before HAL

found another hit.

"It's taking longer than I hoped. We'll be back tomorrow. We have to make sure we get them all, you know."

"Absolutely."

The next morning Colonel Palin told us that HAL hadn't 'hit' on a bomb for six hours.

"That must be all of them" I said.

The next job was to get rid of North Korea's rockets and missiles so they wouldn't be able to attack across the border. For this task also I would have HAL scan the entire country, not just the corridor from the border to the capitol city. When he found a rocket or missile, which all had basically the same shape and therefore were easy to find, he'd slice it in two lengthwise. Repairs were impossible.

"Here we go," I said, as I applied an X to the center of the mat board.

Intelligence services would later say rockets and missiles were being sliced in two all over North Korea.

There weren't that many rockets and missiles. The ball rose up a foot and fell down again every half minute or so. It became a boring thing to watch.

"I have no way of knowing how long it will take," I explained. "We'll come back later."

We returned after lunch. The Colonel said the ball rose up about every five minutes.

"We want to get them all," I said. "We'll come back tomorrow."

We returned to Colonel Palin's office the next morning. The Colonel explained, "The ball hasn't moved for nearly an hour."

"HAL is faster than that. There can't be any

rockets and missiles left. Let's go after the jet fighters. They should be easy to find. They'll mostly be close together on airports."

I placed an X on another mat board. The ping pong ball started jumping up in half a minute. Airmen in North Korea were dismayed to see the rear eight feet of their jet fighters falling off. The engines were neatly cut through and the tail fins and rudders fell uselessly to the ground.

When all of North Korea's rockets, missiles and jet fighters had been destroyed the country no longer had the capability of a military strike outside the border. North Korea was left in a defensive situation only.

Next task was to go after the lesser weapons.

"I don't think this will take as long," I said.

The Colonel asked, "Why don't you go after all their weapons at once?"

"It's one of those peculiarities of mathematics. I couldn't find a way to make HAL do that. There might have been a way if I'd come up with a different control code system for him. I couldn't anticipate everything."

After we were satisfied all the fighters were ruined the next tasks were to go after artillery pieces, then mortars, then smaller caliber guns mounted on vehicles, then guns on ships, then tanks. It all took a week. North Korea could no longer carry out military maneuvers. All they had left was rifles and handguns. I'd take care of those later.

"Must be hell in our dear leader's office," noted Steve with a grin. "What do you do when the enemy is beaten?"

"I give up."

"You join the Army."

Next to Arlington National Cemetery was a little known Army post called Fort Myer. This was the honor guard company post. The company took care of ceremonial duties around Washington. Here was the old wooden horse drawn caisson used to carry President Kennedy's body to his burial. To the right of the entrance gate was a field where soldiers took the horses for a brisk ride in the morning to burn off their excess energy. To the left of the gate was a row of brick mansions. The Chairman of Joint Chiefs of Staff lived in one of them. Next door lived the Sergeant Major of the Army, the nation's highest ranking enlisted man.

The officers' club was on a curve right off the end of mansion row, and a little below that was the uniform shop.

We arrived at the mansion of Chairman of Joint Chiefs of Staff, General Walters. The General and several lesser officers present for the historic occasion greeted us. Handshakes were exchanged and we got down to the agenda.

Papers were signed. A Captain asked me to raise my right hand and led me through the commissioned officer's oath.

"I, Theresa Elizabeth Sullivan Hartley, having been appointed an officer in the Army of the United States, as indicated above in the grade of Second Lieutenant, do solemnly swear that I will support and defend the Constitution of the United States against all enemies, foreign or domestic, that I will bear true faith and allegiance to the same; that I take this obligation freely, without any mental reservations or purpose of evasion; and that I will well and faithfully discharge the duties of the office upon which I am about to enter. So help me God."

The group of officers enthusiastically applauded and cheered. I smiled with many emotions at what I was doing. I hugged Steve.

General Walters brought out a bottle of twelve year old Scotch and a bucket of ice. Glasses were passed around as Steve and I made small talk with the officers for half an hour. Then it was time to go down to the uniform shop.

I was scheduled to go to the White House sometime that afternoon.

Chapter 25

We were driven down the street to the Fort Myer uniform shop. A female clerk helped fit me in an Army uniform. I would only get the service uniform, the Army's equivalent of a business suit used whenever generals appeared at Congressional hearings or other such functions. I wouldn't bother getting the combat fatigues. I wanted to stand out from the South Korean soldiers.

There was another thing I wanted. I wanted a male uniform, not a female outfit. I wanted the authoritative aura of a male. There was precedence for deviating from uniform regulations. General George Patton stormed through Europe wearing a Wild West revolver and holster, and a young Douglas MacArthur wore a laughable 1920s raccoon coat over his uniform when he was garrison commander at West Point. Some personalities can get away with anything.

There was one more thing. A woman was supposed to wear long hair up while in uniform. I didn't. I assumed nobody would say anything.

Steve thought I looked awful cute in my little uniform.

"Hon, you never looked better. It turns me on."

"More than the first time you walked into my college room?"

"Not that much."

We had come a long way since that day. Then we were kids with an overabundance of hormones. Now we were dealing with global problems. Had we changed that much or were we still two kids called Theresa and Steve?

I bought six complete uniforms and three pairs of male shoes; female shoes would look silly with the male dress. Medals and insignia were displayed close to the door. I was entitled to wear the service medal and the armed services medal for being in the Army, but not any other medal yet. I got extra rank insignia and other uniform decorations and pins.

We ate at the nearby officers' club where I was watched by everybody. Then we went to the White House.

As I had pointed out in talks with Colonel Palin and General Walters back at West Point, I had to be in complete control of the expeditionary force going into North Korea, because the North and South had been technically at war with each other for generations, and the North Koreans could never trust the South Koreans. It was necessary for me to be in charge. I was a neutral third party, and a woman, who could be presumed to be kinder than the North Koreans' own insane leaders. In order for this to work I would need a high rank in the Army, the higher the better.

We were guided to the Oval Office where President Stinson greeted us. Then we walked to the East Room where a crowd of reporters waited. General Walters and an Asian man were there. President Stinson started the talking.

"As you all know, Theresa will lead the South Koreans into the North to liberate that long-suffering people. Sensitivity to the feelings of all involved, make it necessary that Theresa have the top military rank, so that her authority will be unquestioned. By act of Congress, Second Lieutenant Theresa Hartley is promoted to five star General of the Army."

The reporters cheered and applauded as General Walters replaced the Second Lieutenant gold bars on my shoulder epaulets with circles of five stars. I was the first five star general since the death of Omar Bradley.

General Walters saluted me and I returned the salute. It was a touching moment.

President Stinson spoke again.

"We never know what Theresa will do next. It seems just yesterday she said she had no interest in politics or war. Today she's planning to lead an army into North Korea. Who is Theresa? We all believed we had her figured out, but now we'll have to start over. Do you want to explain who you are, Theresa?"

"No."

The reporters and President Stinson laughed. Steve stared at me like he was displeased, but nobody was fooled. Anyone else on the planet would have jumped at the chance to talk about themselves, but not me. The moment was funny because it reflected a serious issue. It was still not known what I would do because the world didn't know me. What did I want? Why did I do the things I did? What would I not do? Who was I, really? How did I get that way?

The press now had its lead headline for the news: General Who?

President Stinson didn't give up. She smiled real friendly like and swung her head towards the podium inviting me to step up and say something. I had no choice. I stepped up to the podium.

"I'm very simple. I follow my conscience. I am what I do. If you think that's easy, try it for one day! We are saved or damned, not for what we think, but for what we do. If kids understood that they are what they do and they can change their identity today, there would be no street gangs and teenage prisoners. Personalities collapse if they have nothing good to do. What's within us? A person is defined by his intellect and will which drive his actions, but he can change his intellect and will at any time. We are what we do."

That seemed enough and I stepped aside.

The reporters gave me very loud and heartfelt applause. I'd said something they liked. It was like I had announced the discovery of alien life.

The New York Times said my tiny speech would be carved on my tombstone. I hoped it wouldn't be soon.

I was amazed at how this simple idea about being what you do is so completely ignored. It's implicit in everyday speech and human interaction, but nobody explicitly says the idea. Nearly every page of the Bible tells us what we should do, yet the Bible itself never explicitly states the idea. Or at least I haven't found it yet. Let's get with the program, people! Just keep saying "I am what I do" and you'll do the right thing. Nobody except a psychopath wants to be bad.

I hadn't wanted to talk about myself because whatever I said would be twisted around by somebody trying to get media attention. There had already been dozens of false stories about me, the price of maintaining a dignified silence. If people hadn't figured me out by now, they never would. I just followed my conscience. What's to explain about that? But as it turned out, what I said made me look good.

We spent a quiet night together in a hotel. The next morning Steve saw me off on an Air Force plane to South Korea. He stayed home.

I was trained in flying the Air Force plane in case HAL pulled his trick of putting everybody in deep sleep. As I expected he didn't. We weren't flying over the Atlantic.

Pyongyang, the capitol city of North Korea, was on the southwestern corner of the country a short distance from the sea. It was about 130 miles from the border. Capturing Pyongyang was the key to taking over North Korea. The dictatorial leaders, whose support among the people was shaky at best, would fight among themselves if the city was taken and their entire political system would collapse.

"I'll destroy all their small arms in this area" I said to the room full of South Korean generals as I pointed to a map. The area outlined by a red magic marker was a rectangle fifty miles wide west to east extending one hundred and sixty miles north. Pyongyang was in this area. "After that I'll keep HAL destroying the small weapons in an upside down U shape ten miles in from the coast going up and around Pyongyang and down the ten miles on the other side. We'll have our weapons but the North Koreans won't be able to smuggle small weapons through the ten mile barrier without being destroyed. Their larger weapons are already gone."

I placed one of my HAL program mat boards on a table with Steve's glass tube and ping pong ball indicator device.

"But before that we have to make sure they don't have an atom bomb. I've destroyed them already but my advisors said they might put another one together with components off the shelf."

I placed an X on the mat board.

"If this ball rises up the tube it means HAL found and destroyed a nuclear device. This takes time. We'll wait one day. Assign some soldiers to watch the ball and keep a record."

The meeting broke up. Twenty-four hours later, we returned and I was informed the ball had risen once.

"So they did put a bomb together! They must be very frustrated."

I removed the X from the atom bomb mat board, took out another mat board and put an X on it. The ball immediately rose up a foot and stayed there.

"This program is destroying their small weapons in the area around Pyongyang. HAL is finding rifles, handguns and small field guns and splitting them in two lengthwise. This is going to take some time. HAL finds people randomly and checks to see if there are small weapons near them. He works very fast. When most of the weapons are destroyed he'll find them less frequently and we'll see the ball moving up and down. We'll wait four hours."

We returned four hours later. As I predicted the ball was jerking up and down rapidly but generally staying up about nine or ten inches.

"He's still finding a lot. We better come back tomorrow."

The next day the ping pong ball was resting on the

bottom of the glass tube most of the time. Every few minutes it rose up and jerked up and down several times before falling to the bottom.

"They're trying to get small weapons into the area. HAL is destroying them almost as quickly. They don't have larger weapons to bring in. I think it's safe to say there are no weapons around Pyongyang. Now I'll turn on the ten mile barrier program."

In a moment the ball jumped up rapidly again.

"They're trying to get small weapons across the ten mile barrier. They can't get them across fast enough."

A two star South Korean General named Sonwu had been assigned to me as my aide. The man's primary value was that he could speak English better than most Americans. All the other Generals in the room could understand some English as they had associated with the American troops since the 1950s. Sonwu said, "What about airplanes? They are fast."

"Not as fast as HAL. I programmed him to put a priority on airplanes for this task. A plane won't get a mile into the area before HAL finds it and destroys the small weapons."

"When can we move into the North?"

"Let's wait until tomorrow morning and see how their leadership reacts."

I woke up refreshed and confidant everything was going smoothly. I joined General Sonwu for breakfast. He didn't look happy.

"I have bad news. The North Koreans leaders have ordered the people of Pyongyang to attack us when we enter the city."

"Without weapons?"

"Without weapons. A million active duty soldiers are being rushed to Pyongyang and another million reservists. With the civilians there will be five million people attacking us. We will be outnumbered a hundred to one. I believe we will be defeated."

"You mean slaughtered."

"Yes, but we will take many of them with us."

"How many?"

"Many of them. Two or three million. The civilians will be forced to attack first. Then the soldiers will come."

"But will they attack us like that?"

"They will. There was a war between Iraq and Iran in the eighties. Iran ordered hundreds of thousands of their citizens to attack the Iraqis without weapons. They were mowed down. The North is more fanatical."

I lost interest in breakfast. My hopes for the liberation were gone. My promise to the ten men outside my apartment would not be kept. I could not accept responsibility for massive slaughter.

"I'll be in my room," I said and got up to leave.

I stretched out on the bed with a feeling of utter defeat. Here, finally, was a problem I could not solve. Mother Nature left room for maneuvering but not madmen who would go to any lengths to keep their power. The North Korean leaders knew I wouldn't allow millions of people to be killed.

I wished Steve was here. I wished I was back home with him. I wished HAL had invaded someone else. He had brought me nothing but problems and anxieties. Now I had a new one.

U.S. armed forces stationed in South Korea

maintained their own television station to serve American soldiers. CNN programs, among others, were piped in and broadcast on this station. I watched the news. A political expert was called in to talk about the latest development.

"History shows us what happens when revolutions fail. The dictators purge their people. Hundreds of thousands of North Koreans suspected of not being fully enthusiastic about defending the country will be tortured and killed. They will die cursing the name of Theresa Hartley."

This was the low. There is an ultimate crisis in many people's lives. I had met mine.

I lay on my bed crying. I thought of what Dorothy said in the witch's castle: "I'm frightened, Auntie Em! I'm frightened!" This horrible place was no less a hell.

I slept fitfully. I fantasized about just leaving without a word, going back home and forgetting about the world. I couldn't do that. I couldn't do anything. I was giving up hope.

I was awakened by an insistent knock at the door.

"Who is it?"

"General Sonwu. Prime Minister Scherzer is calling. He says it's urgent."

I rushed to the phone.

"Prime Minister?"

"Do you remember what we discussed about Jerusalem?"

I did remember. I was going to move the city to the new Jewish island. The plan was put on hold. Nobody except Peter Blair had ever been told about the idea.

"I remember! Pyongyang, hunh?"

"Pyongyang."

"What a great idea! Is this payback time, Mr. Scherzer?"

"I hope so."

"You saved millions of lives. I'll tell the world about it. Good by, sir."

I hung up. The seven South Korean generals in the room looked at me with a lot of anticipation.

"I'm going to move Pyongyang to the West a few miles into the sea. The leaders will have to give up when they lose the capitol, don't you think?"

"Can you move Pyongyang?" asked the incredulous General Sonwu.

"Yes. I've already done it to a small piece of land in Antarctica. It's easy if you control HAL."

"The North Korean Army will be ordered to the mainland. They will spread over the country. We will meet them everywhere. Can you destroy their weapons without destroying ours?"

"No."

"Then moving Pyongyang will not give us victory."

I saw his point. With the North Korean Army spread out over the country and free to fight another day, the people in Pyongyang would assume they were to remain enslaved and obediently attack the South Korean task force. Was this the end of the line in what I could do?

One of the generals screamed out something in Korean. He was very angry.

"What did he say?" I asked Sonwu.

"I prefer not to translate."

The generals looked at me with a variety of

expressions. Some looked sympathetic, some annoyed, all looked like they were thinking I was an amateur general who didn't know what she was doing. The angry general probably said I was a stupid girl who should be home baking cookies. I was losing command fast. They'd walk out on me any minute.

"I need time to think," I said and looked at a map of the China-Korea-Japan region.

Most of the border between China and Korea was along the Yalu River which was a natural border. By drawing three or four straight lines along the border it was possible to include practically all of the Korean Peninsula below it except for a few tiny pieces of North Korea that were locked in like pieces of a jigsaw puzzle. These tiny pieces made up no more than two percent of the country. Between South Korea and Japan were two islands, Jesu on the left and Tsuchima on the right. Jesu could be moved straight down, but Tsuchima was in the way. If I moved Tsuchima just fifty miles to the East to rest next to the Japan mainland, I could move the entire Korean Peninsula seventy miles south.

"Who owns these islands?" I asked Sonwu.

"Jesu is Korean. Tsuchima is Japanese."

"Get me Prime Minister Blair," I ordered.

Sonwu made the difficult connection in a few minutes.

"Mrs. Hartley?"

"Did Mr. Scherzer tell you about Jerusalem?"

"He did. He's here with me in London. We thought you might need help."

"The Pyongyang move is out. It's not enough. Are there any island nations that are dictatorships?"

The Prime Minister was silent for a moment. He must have suspected what I was up to.

"Hold on, Mrs. Hartley. I need to discuss this with my advisors."

I held on for eight minutes before Blair got back to me. I wished I'd been a fly on the wall to watch Blair and his friends screaming at each other.

"There are two or three leftist island nation governments, all backward nations, but no modern nations with severe dictatorships as we see in North Korea. It is our consensus that such a government cannot long survive in the modern world. It's an economic phenomenon. Suffering both political and geographic isolations at the same time carries a heavy price."

"If I moved Korea out to sea, would the government collapse?"

"There is an excellent chance. The people will see there is a greater power than their leaders, and their leaders will fight among themselves. I should add the only reason China supports North Korea is they don't want a democracy on their border. Their own people would flood into a free Korea. If you move Korea away from the mainland, China's support will dissolve."

"Thank you, Mr. Blair!"

I hung up and said to Sonwu, "Not bad for a dumb girl, hunh?"

"Will you move Korea?"

"Sure. Why not?"

"What about earthquakes?"

"The Earth's mantle is forty miles thick. I only move the top mile. Don't worry. I know what I'm doing."

I went back to my room. Not being a dumbbell like that general thought, I'd brought dozens of my most valuable HAL program boards with me. I found the 'move Jerusalem' program. I had never used it, but seeing the utility of this program in other parts of the world I had made it much more sophisticated in recent months. The parameters could be changed quickly with the little detachable pieces of mat board I was using.

Before moving the land I had to move underwater rock to give the land a place to slide into. I had a separate HAL program to do that. HAL crushed the rock and moved it like gravel to a much wider area under the sea. In examining marine maps I noticed the waters around Korea were only a few hundred feet deep. This simplified things. I'd only move rock going down two thousand feet which was a safety margin. The ocean floor might have a few hundred feet of mud and a solid rock table was needed. I started HAL to moving this rock.

I examined my personal maps of the Korea region to mark the coordinates of Tsuchima Island. In a few hours it was done. I put the X in place on the board to start the move.

The rumbling started in minutes. The procedure was that the underwater bedrock HAL scraped was rapidly moved northeast into the Sea of Japan. For the Korean move I'd dump this rock into the Yellow Sea between Korea and China. It was all done underwater where nobody could see it. The rumbling from Tsuchima was from the top two thousand feet of the island below sea level, dragging along the billiard table smooth plane of rock adjusted for the Earth's curvature I had scraped away. There was no bumping up and down, but the friction was unimaginable. This was a good week to be a Japanese seismologist.

The program started the move at a gentle twenty-five feet per minute. After a few seconds of that I changed the parameter on the fly to fifty feet a minute, and continued increasing speed every few seconds. When I was satisfied with where the land was I'd reverse the procedure to slow it down again. Buildings would not topple over.

I turned on my TV and news announcers on the American station were already talking excitedly. The Korean generals had leaked the story out.

I followed the story for a while and then went to the lunchroom for supper. It would take until the next day before Tsuchima was where I wanted it.

The Korean generals were in the lunchroom too. This time they looked at me with wonder and respect. No words were exchanged. You did not bother the World Empress!

The next day Tsuchima Island was within two miles of Japan and I adjusted parameters to slow it down and stop it there. I planned to raise a land bridge from the island to the mainland with a four hundred foot gap for boats. The Japanese might built a bridge over the gap.

Then I began modifying the program for the Korean peninsula. This would be done more slowly over several days because of the delicate cities there. I drew lines along the North Korean border with China and Russia leaving out those tiny pieces of locked in land. China and Russia were almost certain to take over these pieces of land.

I started the program to move the underwater bedrock out to the Yellow Sea and gave Sonwu a map with lines showing where the Korean ground was going to divide.

"I only need to move rock two thousand feet below sea level" I told him. "I can't predict exactly where the ground will separate. Programming HAL is not an exact science. The ground along the crack might collapse. Tell people they have to get at least one mile away from it. It will begin at ten o'clock tomorrow morning."

With that I retired to my room to wait for my most spectacular action yet.

Word flashed on the television about tomorrow's exciting event. Commentators talked about many things. One was the question of whether I had asked anybody's permission to move two countries. Er, well, the Korean generals knew about it but didn't say anything. I just went ahead with it.

I smiled at the commentators' talk.

How did I come so far?

When I had just reached my tenth birthday in the fourth grade, mom and I met one of my teachers. The school system sometimes gave standardized intellectual potential tests to see if kids were meeting their full potential. It was not one of those old IQ tests which had gone out of fashion long ago, but an evaluation of a kid's thinking and learning abilities in many categories. The test was given two hours a day for a week. The teacher gave us the good news.

"Theresa did wonderfully. She scored in the 98th percentile across the board. She should be at the top of her class. Someday she could do anything."

Really? I didn't have a clue about anything then. Now still in my teens I was moving countries without permission.

Everything in the last nine years pushed me in this direction. HAL made me serious minded at ten. The kids called me the world's champion tomboy because I soon lost interest in girl things, and there was playing baseball on the boys' team. I think I even detected some worry in mom's face. Was I getting weird?

No, I was developing confidence to do anything. The intellectual potential test, good family support, the attention I got from Jan Struthers' watchers, being careful to keep myself out of trouble when so many kids around me were ruining their lives, the steady dating with Jeff Winslow, my quick early acceptance to BC, and Steve, all combined to build my psyche to where I could step up as Empress Theresa.

I slept well. Morning came. At ten o'clock Sonwu was in my room to confirm that I started the move. I put an X on the mat board.

The little pieces of mat I used to control numeric parameters fit on tiny shelves on the full board. I could change parameters in half a second. I started the move at five feet per minute. Every ten seconds I'd increase it five feet a minute. I aimed at a top speed of sixty-five feet a minute, or three quarters of a mile an hour. That seemed safe.

China and Russia had scores of helicopters in the air to watch for the crack to start opening. Some had television cameras and fed live pictures to stations in the region. Sonwu and I watched.

One clever helicopter crew had a camera aimed at

a paved road. We could see the crack opening in the road immediately. The asphalt bowed down and opened up. I was creating two thousand foot high sheer cliffs in the crack. No rock could stand up under the pressure and the ground quickly fell down a foot or so to fill the crack. When the crack was a few feet wider the land still collapsed slowly. People had plenty of time to get out.

We went out to the conference room to join the generals and anybody else watching television there. It was standing room only. Anybody who had rank or an excuse to be there had squeezed himself in.

After an hour the crack had opened up into a below sea level valley and that valley had reached its greatest depth of two thousand feet. It was three quarters of a mile wide at the top. Very little ground was going to collapse after that. Now, it really got interesting. The valley was below sea level and of course sea water was pouring in. A helicopter gave the first shot of it. A wall of water six hundred feet high was rushing in at around a hundred miles an hour! The bottom of it was crashing into piles of broken rock and abandoned buildings wiping them away in an instant.

A general said something. Sonwu translated.

"There must be water coming from the opposite direction."

Holy smokes! I hadn't thought of that!

Should I do something? The top of the wall of water was still three or four hundred feet below sea level. That was reasonable. There would be a long, gradual 'hill' so to speak in the advancing water. When the two walls crashed together they should not overflow on the undisturbed land still occupied by people. There was nothing I could do at this point anyways. It took days to program HAL for a new task.

The television screen bottom displayed a trailer showing the progress of the two walls. They were 375 kilometers apart, roughly a little over two hundred miles, and closing fast. Their combined speeds added up to around two hundred miles an hour. Cecil B Demille couldn't have dreamed up a scene like what would soon happen.

With an hour to go the stations needed something besides talking heads to fill time. The screen switched to a soccer stadium in Seoul. The crowd was mostly young people gathered to watch the move. Kids loved public events like this. It turned out this was a video replay. The giant screens around the stadium were showing the wall of water rushing forward and told the crowd there was an opposing wall coming in too. The crowd stood and wildly cheered.

The hour was running out. The gap between the water walls was closing at over three hundred feet a second. The screen showed ten kilometers, six miles. It would take two minutes.

I joked, "I hope they don't break for a commercial."

Nobody in the conference said a word in these final tense moments. The long helicopter shot and the immense amounts of water gave the optical illusion we were watching a slow motion film. In fact, the walls were converging at the speed of Indianapolis 500 racing cars.

The water walls met with a noise unheard since Krakatoa. Water, or water spray, was thrown up a thousand feet straight up and to the sides of the crash site. It looked like a giant, thick Japanese fan. It took a half minute for this water to settle back down to a mound of water filling up the valley to sea level or above. There was an immovable body of water at the crash site, but a trillion tons of water was still moving in from both directions. Spray continued to be thrown up at the two points where the incoming water hit. As these two rivers crashed with the immovable mound they piled up water to the top of the valley. This phenomenon was moving back two hundred and fifty miles towards the sea in each direction. The valley was slowly filling up from the middle to the ends in what looked like slow motion because of the sizes involved, but in reality there was tremendous violence going on.

After three minutes the show was less spectacular. The wild reaction of that soccer stadium crowd was shown. Everybody in the conference room applauded me for a spectacle that served no practical purpose. Other video replays from a dozen helicopters at the scene were beginning to appear onscreen showing the crash from different angles. Films of the event would be shown a thousand times and I didn't need to watch them now. It was time to get back to business.

"It will take four days to move Korea down seventy miles" I said to Sonwu. "That will give the North Koreans time to come to their senses."

"I don't think they will change their minds."

"Get me Prime Minister Blair."

Blair was reached. "Magnificent display, Mrs. Hartley."

"It's still a shame I couldn't sell tickets. Do you think I should go into Pyongyang in four days or wait for the leadership to collapse?"

"That is very difficult. There could be a long period of internal political fighting. The loss of life might be high. On the other hand, if you go in soon that could be tragic too."

"Yeah. It's a no win. I'm leaning to ending this thing quickly."

"That has much to argue for it. Rapid offences will destabilize the enemy. Waiting may renew their confidence."

"That's what I was thinking. I'll go in in four days unless you can talk me out of it."

"I don't want to. Good luck, my dear."

I hung up. "You heard, General?"

"I did" Sonwu answered.

"When we go in I want loudspeakers on trucks to talk to the people. I need headphones to speak to them and a translator."

I wouldn't need makeup. It's hard to look beautiful when you're staring down millions of people who were ordered to kill you.

During the four days of waiting, the controversy over whether I had asked anybody's permission to move Korea was the top news story. The South Korean government said that when I announced my intentions, the generals working with me didn't resist. The truth was they didn't say anything at all.

Prime Minister Blair made another courageous political stand. He spoke to Parliament to take the pressure off me.

"Mrs. Hartley and I spoke on the phone when she was thinking of the move. She sought my advice about moving Korea. I encouraged her. She further said she would go directly into Pyongyang unless I could talk her out of it. I must assume much responsibility for these actions. I could have talked her out of both. I did not."

The four days were up. I changed parameters on the HAL program to slow down and stop Korea. Then I had a final powwow with Sonwu.

"Did we hear anything from the leadership, General?"

"Only that the order for the people to attack stands."

"OK. How do we proceed?"

"We penetrate a hundred kilometers into the North and camp for the night. We enter Pyongyang the next morning."

"Let's get this thing going."

The South Korean expeditionary force started rolling. The first task was to clear the border of mines. This was done with special bulldozers that scraped the ground to trigger the mines. Then a line of what looked like steamrollers advanced to flatten and pack the soil while triggering the mines.

For a few miles only scattered civilian North Koreans could be spotted watching from long distances. None dared get near the column. There were no North Korean military personnel in evidence. They had been told that this was not the place to take on a fight. It was better to let the South Koreans penetrate farther in and then their long supply lines would make them vulnerable.

We stopped miles from the city and camped for the night. I got my own tent since I was the only female.

Sonwu and I watched the tent being set up. Soldiers walking by stared at me with looks of surprise.

"What's the matter with them?" I asked Sonwu.

"They didn't know you were here."

"What!"

"The commanding general never goes to the battle with his troops. If he is lost the war is lost."

"You mean our own soldiers weren't told I'm here?"

"No. One of them might be a North Korean assassin."

"What about the people back home?"

"Nobody knows you're here. Telling them tells the enemy."

"But I said I'd be here."

"Nobody believed it."

This was absolutely incredible! Nobody knew I came on the expedition, not the soldiers themselves, and not the folks back home. I'd talked with Steve about going into North Korea, but plans for what would actually be done on the peninsula were sketchy at best. In fact, I left Washington with no plan. Neither Steve or even President Stinson knew what I'd do when I got here, and surely nobody knew the North Koreans would order their poor people to attack without arms. Steve had to be going nuts wondering what I was doing!

"My God! Nobody knows. This is unbelievable."

Poor Steve. How did he put up with me without complaint? He had not bargained for this when he married. He too wanted nothing more than a quiet life, a regular job, the little house with a picket fence, an occasional night out at the movies, the American dream of secure comfort. Look what he got!

The propaganda planes flew overhead. These were South Korean cargo planes loaded with millions of leaflets bearing my picture, and explaining what I was doing. They said I was going to free the North Koreans, and that at my insistence, North Korea's food distribution and other public services would be administered by North Koreans chosen by myself. There was no mention of the South Koreans. It was all about me, me, me. These leaflets were thrown out all over Pyongyang for the people to consider through the night. Could the people fear me? I didn't think so.

Morning brought the day of decision. To proceed or not to proceed? No news had developed during the night. "We go into Pyongyang," I said.

The column now split up into two columns separated by twenty feet. This would allow the soldiers to leave the vehicles and all shoot their weapons at once while the double line of vehicles would give them some protection.

We entered the beginning of the long boulevard leading to the government building complex where helicopters watched the major part of the crowd.

The number of curious civilians increased as our army got closer to the government center. I was riding in a vehicle that looked like a large armored SUV in back of six tanks. Troop carriers were immediately behind me. I sat on the left side of the rear seat next to General Sonwu and watched the civilians standing at a safe distance. I spotted a man holding what looked like a radio.

"There's a radio."

"Yes. Without it they wouldn't know we were

coming."

That was true. The North Korean Army was gone. There was nobody to report on the South Koreans' progress except the South Koreans themselves through their radio stations.

The groups of civilian onlookers became more frequent and bolder until one mile from the government center they formed unbroken lines along both sides of the boulevard. A few hundred yards from the center the lines were two or three hundred people deep. My soldiers were surrounded by a crowd many times their number. We were in it now, up to our necks.

The boulevard was the widest street I'd ever seen, easily three times as wide as the Champs-Elysees in Paris. It could be used as an airport. In the final stretch to the government center the crowds filled this vast empty space to within a hundred and fifty feet of either side of the double column. The lines of people were so deep I couldn't see the end of them.

'How many of them are there?" I asked.

"Four million. Some came from other cities."

"This is far enough. Stop."

The column stopped. Fifty thousand South Korean soldiers jumped out of vehicles and laid on the ground to be able to shoot at the crowd over each other's heads without shooting each other. They held their guns ready to fire. Soldiers on top of tanks waited with 50 caliber machine guns. One of those bullets could pierce a dozen people. Would the crowd attack at this close range? I didn't believe it. They had to know a hundred thousand people would be shot down in the first second. It was frightening to think of it.

The slaughter would be like a nuclear attack.

Everybody stayed where they were. The soldiers looked at the crowds and the crowds stared back. It was a standoff. Nobody wanted to start a fight.

After a minute I said, "At least they're not attacking." I put on the headphones. "Am I on the air?"

"Yes," said a female voice from somewhere in South Korea.

"Everybody stay here. I'm going out."

I got out of the armored SUV-like vehicle which was between the twin columns. Soldiers with television cameras in the troop carriers behind me got out and aimed their cameras at me and the crowds. The pictures were going to be broadcast live to the world.

I walked through the left side of the column between soldiers and stopped to stand facing the crowd. People near me recognized me and talked to each other.

"I think they figured out I'm here. Hi, Steve!"

The crowd could hear my voice from the loudspeakers mounted on many trucks. My remarks were immediately translated into Korean by the female translator in the South.

Steve, President Stinson, Prime Ministers Blair and Scherzer and everybody else in the world were watching me on television. The President must have understood what I was doing. I was focusing the crowd's attention on my own personality rather than on the army to change their view of the situation and calm them down.

Another minute went by. I spoke again.

"The North Korean leaders fled to safety, but they still want the people to attack us unarmed. That's arrogance."

Actually, I didn't know where the leaders were, but a little fib seemed like the right thing to do. The leaders were almost certainly not in Pyongyang.

The quick translation over the loudspeakers made the people murmur to each other. This point must have been already considered by them. I hoped to capitalize on it.

My ad lib gave me another idea. I started walking forward to the head of the column. Some hundreds of yards further down the crowd had spanned completely across the boulevard in attempts to see better. I kept walking beyond the column until I reached a point a hundred yards beyond it and stopped.

"I could be back home living in luxury, but here I am alone with four million North Koreans. I'm risking my life to save theirs. That's humility."

Now I simply stood staring at the crowd until the translation was over.

"I could be home enjoying freedom of speech, freedom of the press, and freedom from fear. Why am I here? I guess I want everybody to have freedom of speech, freedom of the press, and freedom from fear."

That should get them thinking.

I let a half minute pass before speaking again.

"When Steve and I went to a Paris restaurant, we were ignored because we weren't sophisticated. I may not be as sophisticated as Parisians, but I don't see four million dead bodies around here."

That was calculated to re-focus them on what was at stake.

I pointed my left arm and index finger towards the direction we had come.

"My first order is to open the border and let everybody through. If there's no border there is only one country. The road to South Korea is open. You can start walking down there if you want. Nobody will stop you."

When that was translated, it met dead silence. The concept of having the option to leave the North at will was totally new to them.

I lowered my arm. "Or, you can just go home and you'll be free. We're not leaving you."

I think that scored points. The people were talking with each other.

More time went by.

"What do I have to do to make them understand we're here to help them?"

Moments after that I heard General Sonwu's voice.

"General Hartley."

"What is it?"

"China says the North Korean leadership fled to China last night."

I jerked my head back and closed my eyes. It was overwhelming. My eyes teared up. I put my hands to my face. The body language was unmistakable. The world could see how relieved and grateful I was.

"Why do they tell us that now if they knew since last night?"

"They didn't know you were in Pyongyang. They said you're recklessly endangering yourself and the world. You are needed to control HAL."

I watched the crowd. People were excitedly talking to each other.

"Don't you get it? You're free. You have a new life."

This was translated for them. They understood.

There now arose a sound unheard since the acclamation in the Forbidden City. The millions cried out as one voice in a single, unwavering sound. Half of them were wailing submissively like the ten men outside my apartment because that's all they'd been trained to do for 'our dear leader' all their lives, while the other half cheered joyously. The roar was deafening .

General Sonwu and the soldiers carrying television cameras walked over to me. I thought it was time to show confidence in my four million new friends. I walked to the side of the street. Sonwu and the cameramen followed. The people were still disciplined enough to stay where they were. I walked to the edge of the crowd and extended my right hand to them with a smile. Their own leaders had never done that! Immediately people grasped it. I walked down the street extending my right hand out to them. Up to a dozen hands at a time would touch my hand or arm in some way. Sonwu kept shouting instructions to them in Korean. I guessed he was telling them not to grab my hand too tightly and to let me go down the line unimpeded. At least, that's what the people were doing.

I went down the street a couple hundred yards holding my right hand to them when I realized I was going the wrong way. I was going towards the rear of the column but most of the people were towards the front. So I walked through the column and began on the other side. It took an hour to go around the horseshoe shaped crowd up the right, across the street, and back down to the left where I had first met them. The time passed quickly. The experience was exhilarating.

The South Korean soldiers seized the television station center in a few hours. It was announced that I would give a speech the next morning from the 'Leader's Balcony'. This was a round balcony on the corner of one of the buildings in the giant square where the grandiose military parades had been put on. Sure enough, the next morning millions of people were in the square.

What could I say to make them understand the new reality? The answer was simple. I'd quote the opening paragraphs of the Declaration of Independence. I read from a piece of paper.

"When in the Course of human events it becomes necessary for one people to dissolve the political bands which have connected them with another and to assume among the powers of the earth, the separate and equal station to which the Laws of Nature and of Nature's God entitle them, a decent respect to the opinions of mankind requires that they should declare the causes which impel them to the separation.

We hold these truths to be self-evident, that all men are created equal, that they are endowed by their Creator with certain unalienable Rights, that among these are Life, Liberty and the pursuit of Happiness. — That to secure these rights, Governments are instituted among Men, deriving

**their just powers from the consent of the governed,
— That whenever any Form of Government
becomes destructive of these ends, it is the Right of
the People to alter or to abolish it, and to institute
new Government, laying its foundation on such
principles and organizing its powers in such form,
as to them shall seem most likely to effect their
Safety and Happiness. Prudence, indeed, will
dictate that Governments long established should
not be changed for light and transient causes; and
accordingly all experience hath shewn that
mankind are more disposed to suffer, while evils
are sufferable than to right themselves by
abolishing the forms to which they are accustomed.
But when a long train of abuses and usurpations,
pursuing invariably the same Object evinces a
design to reduce them under absolute Despotism, it
is their right, it is their duty, to throw off such
Government, and to provide new Guards for their
future security."**

Nobody could translate such elegant language on the fly and maintain its beauty. I anticipated that. I'd given the translator the English text the day before and she worked all night at it. When I finished speaking she read what I'd said in Korean with all the emotions and nuances only a Korean could express. My speech, or rather the translator's rendition of it, was a spectacular success. The crowd cheered their hearts out. Witnesses said President Stinson cried when I gave the speech. This event, broadcast to the whole world, was called my greatest achievement.

Chapter 26

An old English poem says there's a Newton or da Vinci buried in every village graveyard, his genius never revealed by educational opportunities or recognized by other people and himself. Life is what we think about all day in the search of what we can and should do. I was the first to admit I had many advantages: nurturing parents, a free country, an excellent education, and a loving husband. Minus any one of these I might have turned out differently.

"Theresa is a genius," President Stinson said at a press conference. "Everybody knows that." I didn't argue the point. What made me different was going after the difficult, and with a little luck, doing it.

After two months in North Korea, acting as a head-of-state figurehead while bureaucrats took over the country, I was satisfied that the North Koreans were well on their way to democracy, and returned home promising, to come back if I was needed. I left behind thousands of South Korean bureaucrats who helped the North Koreans organize their resources so there wouldn't be a famine or other such problems. The previous central planning economy had to be transformed into a supply and demand economy which is not easy to do with an entire country. When Russian Communism fell, the people suffered for years because there was nobody to take care of them.

One of the first things I had done during those two months was to invite the German Chancellor to come to North Korea and explain how East and West

Germany had reunified after the fall of communism. I told the people, "Reunifying under the government of the South is the fastest and surest way to democracy and freedom. The South already has everything in place." People could see the wisdom of that.

General Walters, the Chairman of Joint Chiefs of Staff, was interviewed. He outlined our meeting in Col. Palin's office. The General said that as soon as I told him my plan to lead South Korean soldiers into the North, he approved it. It reminded him of Gen. Douglas MacArthur's occupation of Japan at the end of World War II. MacArthur was treated like a god by the Japanese. They clung to every word he said. Gen. Walters believed I would have a similar reception in North Korea. People are basically the same everywhere. He knew I would be another MacArthur.

I turned my attention from the very large to the very small. Before the North Korean adventure I bought a large sampling of biology textbooks. Now I had time to read them. I was interested in the human body, in how it stayed alive, why it aged, why it got sick and why it had to die. Could anything be done to keep it in good health?

From my two college biology courses I learned these matters were about cells, DNA, and biochemistry. There was a difference between macro and micro biology. A liver didn't get sick. The cells making up the liver got sick. The sick cells may die, but the liver itself might yet recover and become healthy again. This was to be my grand strategy in the world of biology.

After learning something about molecular sizes and shapes I turned to getting HAL to manipulate molecules one by one. An atom was mostly empty space. HAL should be able to get his dark matter particles into an atom and push the nucleus around. With the nuclei of atoms rearranged in three-dimensional space, the electrons would naturally fall into their proper places to make any kind of molecule.

My first experiment was with methyl blue. This was a histology stain used in microscopy. It stained collagen and made the collagen stand out from other substances in cells. Without this and many other stains biologists could not see much in cells under the microscope.

I made a three dimensional model of methyl blue and programmed HAL to find and recognize it. Then I dissolved some of the stain in a glass of water and set HAL to finding the methyl blue and pulling the molecules apart. If he did so the water should become clear.

I fixed HAL on the glass of methyl blue solution and started him on the task in the usual way, putting an X on a small strip of mat board related to a larger mat board nearby. There were umpteen gollygeedrillion molecules in the glass and it might take a long time for HAL to find and pull apart every methyl blue molecule. I left the glass on the kitchen table and went off to do something else.

Steve was surfing the internet in the living room. "Don't drink the glass of blue water on the table" I warned. "It's my methyl blue experiment."

"Right."

I sat down to do some biology textbook reading. A while later Steve went into the kitchen. He came back holding a blue thing in his hand.

"You making a new kind of Jello?" he said with an amused smile.

He was holding the methyl blue water without the glass. I took hold of it. It was floppy like Jello. My eyebrows went up.

We went back into the kitchen. I plopped the wiggling cylinder of blue water into a glass bowl and turned off HAL's task. The blue water Jello turned back to liquid.

"It's not the methyl blue," I said. "I know enough chemistry to know it's not the right kind of molecule to polymerize."

"Try it with plain water," Steve suggested.

I emptied the bowl of blue water in the sink and filled a new glass full of water. I turned on the HAL methyl blue killer program as before. Then I lifted the glass, tilted it, and let the cylinder of wiggling water fall on the table.

"It doesn't matter if there's methyl blue or not. HAL goes in looking for it and because he's there the water stays where it is. Do you remember when I was supposed to be dead for two weeks?"

He joked around. "When did this happen?"

"This is 'deep sleep' HAL used to preserve me. He just pushed himself into me and kept everything together."

"What was he looking for?"

"Probably nothing. I don't know how to make him go into something like that, but I can make him go in searching for a molecule that's not there. It makes no difference. Do you know what I can do with this? There's hospital patients who need a life-saving operation but their condition makes the operation itself kill them. They're inoperable. I can immobilize them like this while the surgeon operates and save thousands of lives."

"And get yourself thousands of lawsuits when things go wrong. Hell, the families will hope something goes wrong so they can go after your money."

"You're right. I'd spend the rest of my life in courtrooms. It's a shame. Greed keeps me from saving lives."

"Everybody has to die sometime. It's not your job to change it."

We developed a routine of spending a week in New York and a week on West Point. We did have a small circle of friends in the city. New York had plenty of up and coming young people our own age, highly talented people who had already made a name for themselves in the business world in their mid-twenties. They quickly learned that any discussion about what I did with HAL was off limits. This was accepted.

For the North Korea adventure I programmed HAL to find things. However, with my black and white vision I could find things myself and at tremendous speed. Having a general idea of where to look, I could find an archeological treasure in minutes that would take an archeologist years to find. I found some things in my spare time. They would blow people's socks off.

One day, while I was programming HAL to find weapons, Steve walked into a Yeshiva University Jewish Studies department with a large cardboard box. He put it on a table. Professors quickly filled the room. Steve had previously separated the sides of the box and taped them together. Now he slit the tape to let the sides fall and expose what made the professors hold their breath. It was a scroll, obviously very old, and crumbling. It was still in fair shape.

"What is this, gentlemen?" asked Steve.

The scholars examined the treasure for an hour while Steve wandered around the campus. He returned and they gave him their assessment.

"It's an ancient Hebrew copy of Leviticus. The script makes us believe it dates from the Babylonian Captivity period. That would make it the oldest document every found. Where did you get this?"

Steve only smiled and said, "Theresa will want it back sometime". He walked out.

The Jewish world went nuts. The big question was whether I had more scrolls. Various Jewish organizations went on television asking for more information. We didn't give any but what Steve did next was a strong hint. He bought a failed supermarket five miles north of NYC and had contractors put in climate control equipment to control the temperature and humidity. The equipment could keep the temperature at forty degrees and the humidity at near zero. Hint, hint, hint! Then, without waiting for building code approvals, as if anybody would have the nerve to stop something the World Empress wanted, Steve had construction crews build an impenetrable concrete wall around the building. The concrete wall went ten feet higher than the building's roof. It had watch towers. There was a large opening in the wall in the front of building and a twenty foot wide sideways rolling door was put in the building. Everything was ready except me. I was in North

Korea making sure democracy had a fair chance to get started there.

Once back in the U.S., I settled in for a few weeks to get something done, and then it was time for the grand opening of Steve's supermarket building. He called Prime Minister Scherzer and invited him to New York to update me on the development of the new Jewish island. We could hear Scherzer laughing. There was no way I could be interested in the island's development beyond what I saw on the local news every day and Scherzer could update me in a five minute phone call. He came to New York.

Scherzer was driven in a limousine from his hotel to the walled off supermarket building. Steve and I had arrived in our own limousine and greeted him. A large group of people, probably most of them Jewish, were in the parking lot. Steve announced that only two hundred could be let in at a time, but everybody would be accommodated by day's end. Prime Minister Scherzer walked alongside us through the gap in the concrete wall and through the wide rolling door of the supermarket building. Tension was at a peak. What did I have in store for them?

We walked up to a glass wall that protected the climate inside. The light was dim and it took a moment for the eyes to get used to it.

Inside the climate protected area were thousands and thousands of ancient scrolls mostly in large earthen jars but some scattered on the floor as I'd found them. The spectators cheered with tremendous enthusiasm. Some were crying. Their history, secrets of the early Hebrews, were now before them. People walked up to hug me.

The potential wealth of information in these scrolls was staggering to imagine. Besides scriptural books lost for millennia, there was sure to be reams of historical information. What did Moses do while a young man in Egypt? Was he in love with Pharoah Seti's daughter? Where did the story of the Flood come from? How long was a cubit? What happened to Enoch? Where was the Red Sea parted? Where did Cain find a wife? Who was the Queen of Sheba? The possibilities were endless.

"Where did you find this?" Scherzer asked Steve.

"That, sir, is a secret Theresa will take to the grave. She won't even tell me."

Scherzer smiled. He'd already guessed where the treasure came from. The Yeshiva professors said the scroll Steve showed them was from the Babylonian Captivity period. Babylon was in Iraq. That had to be where the scrolls came from, unless I found them under the Dome of the Rock or some such politically sensitive place that could start a war.

Steve followed up. "Everything is exactly as Theresa found it. There's nothing left at the site. What you see is what you get."

"That's a lot."

"Theresa presents these scrolls to the Jewish nation under your personal care, sir. Good luck trying to keep everybody happy."

"It can't be done."

"We're guessing you'll take them to the island when appropriate facilities are in place?"

"That's what we'll do."

"You'll win the lottery in the tourist business."

Steve has another surprise.

"By the way, Mr. Scherzer," said Steve. "Theresa found eight Egyptian burial sites near but not in the Valley of Kings. They're full of treasure. Looters never found them. Egypt will have to build a new museum the size of the Louvre to display everything. Here are the directions." He pulled a wad of papers out of his pocket and gave them to Scherzer.

Scherzer looked through the papers. They had diagrams of the complex burial sites with hidden entrances carefully pointed out. He swooned at these revelations. "Egypt will go mad," he said.

The Hebrew scrolls called the greatest archeological find in history, outdoing the discovery of King Tut's tomb which, while it provided interesting objects to look at, only provided a few pages of writing, all of it about Tut himself. The scrolls I found, if they contained new stories about the Hebrews, could inspire dozens of movies, hundreds of books, and thousands of paintings to look at. Even the fabulous Egyptian treasures I found couldn't match that.

Could I ever top finding the scrolls? I'd give it a try.

A week later, Steve and I boarded a billionaire's yacht to go to England. We checked into a London hotel. Word leaked out that I had asked Professor Pierre Labarre, a Middle Ages scholar from the Sorbonne, to stand by in our hotel. Labarre knew Latin, Old English, and Old French as well as all the history of the period. What he didn't know was why I asked him to come to London. It drove everybody crazy. Labarre was entering his twilight years and had never done anything worth remembering outside the little circle of his fellow professors, but in London I might have something for him to do that would win his place in history. His emotions can be imagined.

He promised to let me announce the find.

Speculation was that I was looking for William the Conqueror. He was a Frenchman, the Duke of Normandy, France, who conquered England in the Battle of Hastings. Four hundred years later, his tomb in France was disturbed, and his remains scattered and lost except for one leg bone. He had been King of England. Was it possible his bones were brought to England? Had I found William the Conqueror?

There was also the possibility I'd found King Arthur. He was mostly a legend but there was evidence that some tribal chief had organized the tribes into a primitive nation with himself as king. If Arthur had existed, somebody in the Middle Ages would have known about him, and Labarre's specialty made sense. Also, people moved across the English Channel all the time. In fact, King Arthur organized the tribes to fight off the invading Saxons. Who better to know how to fight invaders from the continent than somebody who was himself from the continent! Arthur's name was thought to be derived from Celtic words meaning 'bear man'. The Celts came from France and other parts of the continent. Arthur might have been French. People speculated I had proof. Had I found King Arthur?

Steve made some arrangements in the next several days. Then, he called Prime Minister Blair and asked him to invite the French President and five hundred Frenchmen to England. Blair was invited to join the fun.

The time arrived. We boarded twenty buses and all went to a very old church on the eastern edge of

Middle Ages London. We went inside. It was a medium sized church with seating for only five hundred. The church pastor came up and Steve gave him a check for ten million dollars. Then Steve walked to the side door and brought in a group of men with boxes of heavy duty military ear protectors. These were the ones that covered your head, neck, and most of the face to keep all noise out. They made you look like an alien from outer space. Next, he called in construction workers with jackhammer equipment. Long rubber hoses from air compressors outside the church led through the side door to the jackhammers near the altar. We all put on our ear protectors. I pointed to a spot a few feet in front of the altar and the construction crew went to work. It was a weird sight. The jackhammers tore into the floor while everybody in the church wore alien ear protectors because of the 190 decibel noise. Workers gathered the debris and hauled it away.

An eight foot wide section of the stone block on brick floor was removed. Then, workers with shovels dug up the dirt. Everybody shed their ear protectors. One of the workers hit something. Steve directed the workers to remove dirt around the object. Then, he took over. He jumped in the hole and felt around until he found the object. He lifted a cubic foot box made of bronze. He placed it on the floor for a moment, crawled out of the hole, and placed the box on a small table which a worker had set nearby as planned.

The French President, anticipating an important event, had chosen five hundred French people with tremendous enthusiasm and patriotism for France. They would cheer a French victory in an obscure soccer game. How would they react to the recovery of an important historical French hero? All eyes were on the box. Hearts stopped. Breaths were held.

Steve looked at the entrance of the church. "Gentlemen, please."

Twenty London police officers had been standing near the entrance. They moved forward down the aisle and divided into two groups standing on either side of us to let the crowd see the proceedings. This crowd might turn into a rioting mob when they saw what I hoped was in the box.

I took over. I removed the lid of the box, looked around inside, and pulled out a book with a wood binding. There were papers inside.

"Monsieur Labarre?" I called. Labarre walked up to inspect the papers. This was his claim to a place in history and he was already emotional. He examined the papers and looked up at me with astonishment. Tears were streaming down his face as he checked the papers again. Finally, he pointed out a name in the papers to me and whispered, "Oui. C'est certain. Pas de chance d'un autre ".

I wrapped my arms around Steve's neck and buried my face in his chest. Can you blame me for a moment of fragility? I'd been through so many emotional roller-coasters. A person gets tired. Courage is not about how you emote but how you overcome.

Labarre, true to his promise, left the announcement to me. After getting myself together, I reached into the box and pulled out a cloth bag, about ten inches long and eight inches wide, presumably made of wool, and tied with a string. I undid the string and pulled out a handful of perfectly preserved black hair. At this sight

Labarre broke down and cried like a little girl.

I carefully put the hair back in the bag, tied it off, and put the bag in the box to prevent somebody from stealing it.

I lifted a skull and lower jaw bone out of the box. All the teeth were present and I easily fit the skull to the jawbone. I held the head high to let the crowd see and made the announcement.

"I present to the people of France Saint Joan of Arc."

There was total bedlam in the church! I couldn't keep track of what every person in a crowd of five hundred was doing and can't describe the reactions. Use your imagination. I tried to keep a neutral, dignified expression while holding Joan, but it was difficult.

Joan was the greatest hero of France. She set up six hundred years of history as we know it. Without Joan there was no independent France, no European nations' interactions as we know them, no Christopher Columbus, no New World as we know it, and no United States of America. Something else would be on the North American continent and probably not as good. There were thousands of Saints, but did any of them change history like Joan? Forget it! Churchill said, "Joan is a being so uplifted from the ordinary run of mankind, that she finds no equal in a thousand years". Mark Twain said, "In the history of the human intellect, nothing approaches this. Joan of Arc stands alone".

The church was in danger of floating away in the sea of tears from the French people. I had done them something wonderful.

The crowd rushed forward. but Steve, Blair, the French President, and the police kept them from disturbing me while I held Joan.

When the hysteria died down, I placed Joan on the table and walked away from it. Now the people could approach me to express their profound gratitude. I was crushed in their embraces. The police surrounded the table after I moved away from it. Steve kept his eye on them!

After watching this joyful scene for a while, Blair and the French President walked up to Steve. Blair said, "This is a trick that would confound Houdini. How did Theresa do it?"

"Theresa was born on May 8, the day Joan relieved the siege of Orleans and saved France. She's always been interested in Joan. The records say the English killed Joan in Rouen, France and dumped her remains in the Seine River. Theresa didn't believe it. Wouldn't you save a souvenir of the greatest person of the age? The records say the English were sorry they killed Joan, Before the fire died out, one of them said, 'We are all lost, for we have burned a saint'. Would they dump Joan in the river? Theresa didn't believe it. She searched all the old buildings in Rouen but found nothing. She suspected that some Englishman brought Joan to England. She searched the old buildings of London and voila!"

Blair asked, "How did she know it was Joan?"

"She could see the cranial fissures were still open like a young person, and the front teeth were oval like a woman. What other young female would be buried this way six hundred years ago except Joan of Arc?"

"She risked an embarrassing situation. It might

have been a forgotten lord's daughter."

"Yeah but if she dug it out with no witnesses some people would say she faked it. She couldn't fake the Hebrew scrolls."

"Magnifique, monsieur," said the French President.

"It was brilliant," said Blair, "absolutely brilliant".

There were week-long celebrations in France. Church bells rang day and night. Crowds filled the streets. Joan was coming home.

The hair was Joan's. As a final humiliation, a prisoner's hair was cut off before he went to the stake. The French people gave me a small sample of it. I promised to build a Saint Joan of Arc Cathedral somewhere in America to preserve my small hair sample forever, and maybe a long overdue gigantic Joan of Arc University the size of a small city. That would cost one month's worth of my oil revenues. I could give it an endowment ten times that of all the Ivy League schools combined. I could do anything. Maybe I'd raise the needed land off the coast of New York, Maryland, Virginia, or some desirable location with a land bridge leading to it. The Saint responsible for the existence of the United States as we know it today, and a lot more, deserved no less.

On my insistence, the President of France promised that Pierre Labarre would study the papers found in the bronze box. Otherwise, I would keep the papers myself! Yeah, I was a badass. Labarre's published report with his name written on it would assure him immortality in the academic world.

That was the end of my archeology activity. I could never top finding Joan.

There was one other thing I planned on doing that had high visibility. The International Olympic Committee held a meeting in New York City which 'by pure coincidence' just happened to be where we spent half our time. The agenda leaked out. The IOC wanted to talk about skiing, and they hoped I would drop by.

Reducing the Earth's declination to five degrees had been a wonderful benefit for the world, but it was a disaster for the ski industry. The American ski slopes were put out of business altogether. A few European resorts could operate on their highest slopes.

"Let's go have some fun for a change," said Steve.

We showed up at the meeting. I sat in the audience while Steve helped himself to a seat on the stage with the IOC officials. Invited to speak, he said that I would raise islands along the coasts of any country that wanted them, raise land bridges to the mainland for easy access, and slide 20,000 foot high mountains I'd carve from the ocean floor up onto these islands. I would carve the mountains according to the IOC's specifications.

These ski resorts would operate all year long and would cater to millions. I envisaged four of the mountains along the East Coast, four more on the West Coast, and maybe two in the Gulf Coast. I was flexible about creating these places in Europe, Asia, Africa and South America.

Steve said that I wanted a federal ski commissioner to deal with the horrendous political problems involved in building these places. It would take years to iron out the issues. I couldn't be bothered with politicians.

Steve then read the IOC the riot act.

"Theresa is not naïve. She knows special interests will try to take over the resorts and make them monopolies. That's not going to happen. Every resort will be owned and operated by a corporation, but Theresa will own fifty-five percent of the shares. If she doesn't like what the corporation is doing she'll step in and kick butt. That's her deal. Take it or leave it."

You'd think they'd be happy with that. They weren't. An official on the stage said, "The Winter Olympics have been cancelled for lack of snow. We will reschedule them for two years from now to coincide with the Summer Games year as in the twentieth century, but none of the old venues can be used and there's no time to build facilities for indoor sports. We need a new mountain,…. near a big city,…. with indoor facilities already in place,…. and lots of fresh water to make ten feet of snow in a hurry."

"Where's that?" Steve asked.

"In Lake Michigan close to Chicago."

Me and Steve expressed our surprise. Was this guy nuts? I couldn't move that much rock around Lake Michigan without causing an earthquake. People will ask for what they know you can't give hoping you'll give them more than they deserve.

"Impossible," I said, loud enough to be heard in the silent room.

That was the wrong word to use. Steve stared back at me for two minutes while everybody patiently waited. The tension was high. I was sure he was stumped this time. I could not make a four mile high mountain so close to a major city without causing horrible damage and that was that. Then he smiled and looked up to Heaven. I could see the little wheels spinning in his head. He was getting one of his crazy ideas. What was he thinking this time?

He continued, "You need the mountain with all the slopes and level areas for a Winter Olympics?"

"Yes, sir."

The guy needed to be sent to an asylum. There was no way I could do that in Lake Michigan. I gave Steve the thumbs down sign but he didn't give up.

"When do you need this mountain?"

"In one month, sir, or there'll be no Olympics."

"Give us the shape you need and you'll have your mountain in a month."

I said, "Aren't we a little optimistic?"

"You crush rocks to raise islands. Dump crushed rock in Lake Michigan."

You could see how excited the IOC officials were at this amazing idea. They almost fell out of their chairs craning their necks at me.

"A pile of rock that high would be thirty miles wide" I said. "Is Lake Michigan big enough?"

"It's a hundred miles wide" said that IOC official who came up with the crazy Lake Michigan idea.

"The slopes will have three mile drops. How do you get a million people up the slopes?"

"We use a cable car system like San Francisco. The cable never stops moving. When a car is loaded with people a simple device grabs the cable."

"OK, but all the athletes in the world will have to move to Chicago to practice."

The IOC officials huddled together for a quick

conference. Steve could only shrug his shoulders to show me his confusion. That IOC nut said to me, "What about the Alps?"

"What about them?"

"The tops of mountains are too steep to ski. If you filled in the space between three mountains with crushed rock, we'd get gentle slopes a mile above the highest mountain peak. They would be covered with snow all year.

I thought about that while the officials figuratively bit their nails.

"OK. I'll do it."

The room was filled with cheers.

By the time we got back to the apartment scientists were on television saying the Lake Michigan mountain's snow line would never get below 16,000 feet.

"Damn!" I said. "That's no good. I'll make the mountain 25,000 feet high."

In a week I programmed HAL to build the mountain. I had HAL crush ocean floor rock to fine size, stretch it out to a long, thin stream that wouldn't cause serious damage if it fell, and bring it down to Lake Michigan. Putting in all the needed contours of the mountain was simply a matter of moving this stream around. The IOC gave me a complicated design. One necessary feature was a long, winding road a hundred yards wide to quickly shuttle huge crowds up to the 16,000 foot level where the snow would begin. These crowds would be moving between Chicago and the mountain every day to see all their favorite sports. In a month the pile was ready.

As soon as the rock started coming down doubts

about my ability to pull this off vanished. The mayor of Chicago assembled an audience to make an announcement.

"Are you ready for this? I am negotiating with the IOC to make Chicago host to a combined, simultaneous Summer and Winter Olympics."

The audience rose to their feet and set new decibel records. It was an exciting idea. It had never been possible before and a survey of the world's cities showed why it probably never would be possible anywhere else. No other city in the world and its surroundings was laid out in such a way it could handle the unimaginable visitor traffic like Chicago and its surrounding communities. Chicagoans went nuts. People would quit their jobs to watch the spectacle on television.

"I can see it now" said Steve. "Somebody trains a girl to win gold medals in both gymnastics and figure skating the same week."

"Wow! I have to see that."

The Winter Olympics had played second banana to the Summer Games because not that many people in the world stepped on the ski slopes. I would change that. The Lake Michigan mountain was gigantic. It was meant to accommodate a quarter million people at a time with hundreds of slopes instead of the usual dozen. But that was an ant hill compared to the monster offshore mountains they were sketching in the newspapers, mountains sixty miles wide that could take on over a million people. When I'd installed sixty or seventy of these giant ski resort mountains around the world, a hundred million people could be on the slopes at once all year. There was already talk of a billion people taking up skiing. The poor Summer Games athletes would look around and say, "Hey! Anybody watching us?" No, they're all skiing.

It's always hard to predict what will happen. Everybody thought it would take six months for the Lake Michigan mountain to develop a snow cap down to the 16,000 foot level. We were all wrong. The mountain was not solid rock. It was a pile of crushed rock. This meant there was no source of heat from below, that is, from the ground and below ground. Telescopic infrared cameras showed that at high elevations surface rock temperatures fell below zero *in one night*. Phew! Were we wrong! Furthermore, rain and melting snow leaked into the pile between the rocks and quickly cooled the pile down to the freezing point at lower levels. Finally, air temperatures at an altitude above one mile often dropped down below freezing at night. The net result was that the snow line reached down to the 5,000 foot level in a few weeks. Who knew? "So much for scientific experts!" I said.

It would take a long time to install lift systems up the mountain, but Steve and I didn't want to wait to try the slopes. So, we made arrangements. There are helicopters specially designed for high mountain rescues like in the Himalayas. We had one of these helicopters brought to the United States and flew up to near the top of the rock pile mountain. Since neither of us had any experience in skiing we opted for one man bobsleds. They were adapted from two man bobsleds in which the driver steered and the man in the rear controlled the brake. In our sleds, the driver controlled the brake with a foot peddle. Mechanics had attached one motorcycle ice racing tire on each sled connected to speedometers to tell us our speed.

The helicopter took us to a level 24,000 foot high area. Nobody had ever skied or sledded at this height. The view was breathtaking. We could see Chicago miles below us, and all the land in the next two hundred miles.

"We should build a house up here" I joked.

Steve said, "It'll be hell on the mailman".

Every square inch of our skin was covered with impermeable material to protect against the severe wind chill effect of these conditions. We took off at the same time, each in our own sled. The helicopter flew ahead to guide us along the carefully chosen route. Where the hill was steep we used the brakes to keep our speed down to something reasonable like sixty miles an hour. Any faster than that would be suicidal. Most of the time we just let the sleds go free. It was a thrilling experience. The total distance down was something like twelve miles. Wow! What a ride! The skiers had something to look forward to.

There was a food market a block from our New York apartment. I went there every other day or two stopping along the way to look at this or that store. I was always surrounded by government agents who had every secret security device you never heard of. When I had to stand still waiting for a traffic light to change they made a tight circle around me to frustrate any sharpshooters who might be five hundred yards away. The Secret Service had kept every President alive since Kennedy. I was even more important. You can always get another President. There was only one me.

I set out one morning and it happened so fast I

didn't see it coming. A fast moving car hit me from the side. I flew over the car and landed on the street. The government security men were all over me. They were smart enough to let me lie there.

An ambulance came quickly. I was gently put on a stretcher and placed inside the ambulance. Two EMS people were poking me all over.

We arrived at some hospital. I was wheeled into an x-ray room for some pictures. Somebody did a blood draw. Then I was rushed to an operating room and placed on a table. There was already a team of ten people waiting for me. Something was injected into my arm and I went to sleep.

I woke up one day later with a body cast immobilizing my torso. Steve and my parents were in the room. I could tell from their faces they didn't have good news.

"Hi, hon," said Steve, trying to sound cheerful.

To avoid the bad news I asked, "What was his beef?"

"He's a Middle East terrorist. He had somebody helping him to get the timing just right. He phoned your movements to the car driver and the driver got in position. They must have tried it a dozen times to get the timing perfect."

"When do I get out of here?"

"It will be a while. Your back is broken." He stopped for a moment, delaying the worse as long as he could. "The doctors say you won't walk again."

I broke down and cried. This time I had a good reason and didn't have to hide it. I had a long cry to get it all out.

The world's reaction was touching enough to preserve my faith in humanity. People organized in hundreds of kinds of demonstrations. Large groups of children were assembled to sing pretty little songs to give me hope. Military bands and symphony orchestras gave special concerts in my honor. Air Force planes flew over my hospital daily. Thousands upon thousands of people marched in silence in every city. There were pro-Theresa demonstrations even in the Middle East countries where people were beginning to understand the importance of the mountains I was starting to raise there.

I cried every day. The loss I'd suffered at age nineteen had no consolation. I don't have to mention the effect on my married life. But there were all the other things—the simple pleasures of walking through the park, of driving a car, of being independent—all were lost. It was like being a corpse. I cried every day.

There were weeks of physical therapy in the hospital. I had some feelings in my legs in some areas of the skin called dermatomes. But I'd lost the use of my leg muscles. I couldn't walk.

Steve was with me most of the time except during therapy. Gradually I adjusted to my situation. I had the use of my arms, and that made me far better off than some people in this place. Steve was as loyal as a husband could be. He told me a thousand times he loved me and wouldn't let me down.

Finally, the boring routine of the hospital ended and I was brought back to the West Point house. A wheelchair ramp had been installed.

After a couple of days President Stinson came to

the house. We traded small talk for an hour. She told me how much the world owed me, how proud I should be of my accomplishments, and all those clichés. Then she asked me about my plans. I had been thinking about that for weeks.

"I'm getting into biology. HAL can work on matter one molecule at a time. If you think about that for a while you can see that if you can work on matter one molecule at a time you can do some really amazing things. Imagine what a surgeon could do if he could operate on one cell at a time. You could repair severed nerves. The spinal cord has a couple of dozen nerve tracts. I might be able to copy some other girl's spinal cord and rebuild my nerves."

President Stinson must have thought I was losing my mind, but all she said was, "That's an ambitious project."

"Yeah, and I don't want to get it done when I'm ninety years old. I'm working on another project. I'm working on ways to stop my aging. There are many ways to do it if you have HAL. For example, one reason cells grow old and die is they accumulate unneeded proteins. When the proteins clog the cell, it dies. I'll get HAL to squeeze out five percent of the fluid from my cells once in a while. The way the mathematics works, the unwanted proteins that are accumulating have a greater chance of being kicked out. Over time the cell is stabilized. There are lots of other techniques I'll look into."

The President must have thought this was all pure fantasy, but she didn't have HAL.

Chapter 27

Two hundred and four white spheres hovered miles over Eastern Massachusetts. A little less than a yard wide each and swirling around several yards from each other, they weren't visible from the ground.

They slowly drifted down to a height of two miles. A commercial jet flying towards Boston from the west flew almost directly over them. The pilot reported the strange phenomenon to Logan Airport.

Another commercial jet sighted the spheres. This second sighting was passed along to the Air Force along with the first. Jet fighters were sent out.

The spheres drifted down to half a mile as they headed towards the Boston downtown area. Army helicopters took over the job of following the spheres.

A dozen Army helicopters moving together towards downtown Boston was an unusual event that could hardly go unnoticed. The television stations scanned military channels and picked up the conversation. They learned about the spheres.

Television programming was interrupted for live coverage of the strange event.

President Stinson called me. "Theresa. Are you watching what's happening in Boston?"

"No. What is it?"

"Hundreds of white spheres are moving toward the city."

"Oh crap!"

I hung up on the President. "Steve! Come here."

Steve came in the living room as I got the

television going. A news helicopter was shown following the two hundred white spheres approaching downtown Boston.

I said, "If those are HALs we're in big trouble."

The spheres came straight at the 907 foot Prudential Building and appeared to be about to crash into it, but at the last minute they diverted to one or the other side of it in two packs that rejoined once past the building.

There was a change in the spheres' behavior. They stopped and hovered over the open spaces in front of the skyscraper. Crowds of people were running out of nearby buildings to watch this phenomenon.

"God!" I said. "Do you think they'll merge with people?"

Steve said nothing. We both understood the horrible implications if that happened.

The spheres simply swirled around hundreds of feet in the air like a school of fish. The crowd gathered. There were soon thousands of people looking up at the spheres. Then, what we feared most happened. A sphere suddenly sped down to a spectator and appeared to disappear in him just as my HAL had jumped from the fox to myself. This man was surrounded by people asking how he felt.

Other spheres similarly sped down to spectators. They moved so fast there was no way to evade them. When the crowd realized what was happening they started running, but this only increased the rate at which the spheres zoomed down to individuals. It seemed that the spheres were attracted to people in motion. In three minutes all two hundred and four spheres had merged with people on the ground.

I began to cry. No worse disaster could be

imagined than having hundreds of people infested with HALs. The world would expect me to do something about it. I could see nothing I could do.

The phone rang again.

"That must be Stinson," said Steve who walked over to answer it.

"Mr. Hartley? Prime Minister Blair. What is happening?"

"Your worst nightmare, sir. It looks like a lot of HALs have infested a lot of people."

"Where did they come from?"

"It was probably from Theresa's HAL. When she was nuked it must have been a trigger for HAL to divide himself. One of them stayed with Theresa and the others wandered off to find somebody else to infect."

"But that was nearly two years ago."

"What's two years to something that's been around billions? It's not a coincidence these HALs showed up in Boston. It's where HAL first merged with Theresa and maybe HAL has been here a million years. They've been wandering around the world looking for Boston. They probably recognized the Massachusetts coastline and came down. The original HAL learned that Theresa spent time in buildings. These HALs came to the biggest buildings they could find looking for Theresa. Unfortunately there were a lot of people there."

"If you don't mind I will fly to New York."

"You're welcome, sir. You saved her life."

There were no more phone calls. It was easy to guess Blair told President Stinson of his conversation with Steve, and that there was nothing more to say for the moment.

We settled in to the ordeal of watching developments on the television news.

One of the new HAL hosts had already discovered his strength. He proudly demonstrated it by lifting the front of a Cadillac with his bare hands. The reporters eagerly discussed this feat, as if it were worth the attention! Did they have no inkling of what the day's events meant?

Videotapes of the HAL invasion were analyzed. It was determined that two hundred and four HALs had invaded people. The problem was identifying the hosts. Only ninety of them had announced themselves by six p.m. A few more were reporting themselves each hour, but it was thought the total number of identified hosts wouldn't approach two hundred. A lot of them were hiding.

The evening talk shows got into the more important issues. Commentators wondered if the new hosts would get control of their HALs as I had done, if they could interfere with each other, and if they could be talked into cooperating. If a few started doing destructive things, could the rest stop them?

"They're so stupid," I said, at the end of my patience. "Of course they can learn to control their HALs, and they can't stop each other. You can't stop a cloud with another cloud. This will be chaos."

The next day the Secret Service appeared at our house to announce the President and Prime Minister were coming. Shortly after, the two politicians arrived in a limousine. We met them in the driveway. All was as friendly and cheerful as possible under the circumstances. My distraction at the new challenges couldn't be covered up completely. We went inside.

President Stinson started it off.

"How likely is it the new hosts will get control of their HALs?"

"It's a sure thing," I said. "I did it all by myself. They'll have plenty of people who will be glad to help them."

"Can we keep them from doing something wrong?"

"No. HAL is not a weapon you can aim at somebody. I don't see how the HALs can do anything to each other. They each live in their own world."

Blair asked, "Are we in trouble?"

Steve answered, "We're in big trouble. It's only months before these people get control of their HALs. You and I know what ordinary people will do when they get unlimited power. They'll go nuts with it. They'll try to grab this and that and anybody who stops them will be eliminated."

"That is pessimistic," said the President.

"But realistic. You know what people are like."

"Is there anything we can do?"

"Yeah." Theresa wants to try putting one of these people into the deep sleep and see what happens. If it puts his HAL out of business she'll put them all into deep sleep until she figures out something more permanent. We don't have much time."

"Only a hundred and twenty-two have been identified. Many are in hiding."

"Maybe Theresa can find a way to locate the rest if deep sleep works."

The President promised to look into it. In a couple of days her people found a new HAL host who was willing to cooperate in this experiment. He was a twenty year Marine veteran loyal to his country to the end. He knew what two hundred HAL controlling people would do to the world and wanted to stop it. George Catlin was a retired sergeant and jumped at the chance to defend his country once again. "Thank God for men like him," said President Stinson.

George Catlin was brought down to West Point and introduced to Steve, Peter Blair, President Stinson and me. Steve explained the procedure.

"Theresa was put in the deep sleep when she fell from the plane. We think the bomb triggered HAL to divide. What we don't know is if these two actions are related. What we want to do is put you in a deep sleep and see what happens. There won't be a bomb. If your HAL doesn't divide, our problem is solved. Theresa can put everybody to sleep until she finds a permanent solution."

"How long will that take?" the sergeant asked discretely.

"It may take years. There's no predicting. She has to find out what she can do with HAL, but we don't have much time before the hosts get control of their HALs."

"I understand. Let's do it."

"Bravely spoken, sir."

I said, "We have to duplicate conditions. Let's go outside."

We went out to the front lawn.

"Now, sir," Steve continued. "When you go into deep sleep your body will fall down, so lie down."

George Catlin laid down. I wheeled myself closer. I fixed HAL onto him and put an X on a slip of mat board. Nothing happened. George Catlin just lay there looking around at us but not going unconscious.

"So much for that idea," said Steve.

I was nearly in tears again. I removed the X and wheeled myself back into the house alone.

"What happened?" George Catlin asked Steve rising to his feet.

"It looks like Theresa's HAL couldn't get into you. Your own HAL keeps him out. It makes sense. They can't occupy the same space."

President Stinson shook the man's hand. "Thank you for your assistance, Sergeant."

They went back into the house. I had disappeared into my room. Steve started the talking.

"Theresa's HAL couldn't be the only one in the universe. There must be trillions of them everywhere or there wouldn't have been a snowball's chance in hell of one finding Earth. They have to reproduce themselves somehow. How would they do that, do you think?"

Blair said, "I assumed the death of the host would signal the time to reproduce."

"We thought that too for a while, but it doesn't work. The mathematics is impossible. If the HALs multiplied every time the host died, before long there would be more HALs than there were creatures on the planet. The HALs would be locked up and immobilized. Something else made them divide and go back into space. In the early universe there were a lot of giant stars going supernova. The HALs were ripped apart. The pieces clung to rocks drifting out into space and became new HALs. This became part of their reflex collection. Most of the new HALs never found another creature to host them, but a few did. These learned more reflex tricks including putting the creature into deep sleep when it was under stress and reviving it later. When the atom bomb went off, it was like a supernova. HAL started to divide. But this time his host was still around. Theresa was in the water. One HAL reattached himself to her and put her in deep sleep. The other HALs just drifted off looking for Massachusetts."

President Stinson asked, "Is there anything Theresa can do to control all the HALs?"

"Maybe she could find a way in fifty years. We don't have that much time. We might think of something to do sooner. Leave us alone for a week. Nothing's going to happen in a week."

The two heads of state left and Steve went looking for me. I had pulled myself up on the bed and was thinking of the situation. We had already decided on a desperate last resort plan if the HALs couldn't be controlled.

"Are you going to do it?" Steve asked.

"Yup. There's no choice."

"That's throwing all the chips in the pot!"

"I'm open to alternative suggestions."

"All right. I'm with you. We're getting out of here."

When you have the money you can buy properties in remote places under fake names. We'd already done so for the day when we just wanted to get away from it all without having the curious watching us. Now we'd use these places.

We disappeared. Nobody knew where we were.

A tanker from Theresa's Island was crossing the Indian Ocean some nine hundred miles east of South Africa. Its radio went silent. All attempts to hail the tanker resulted in silence. It is an alarming situation when nothing is known about what a giant oil tanker is doing.

A plane was sent to investigate. As it approached the area in question, it too went silent. The ground continued calling for eight hours and gave it up. The plane had vanished.

President Stinson ordered the American Ambassador to South Africa to rush to the coast and report whatever he found. He positioned himself in Durban, a busy city with many people riding or walking around. Hours passed. Something reached the coast. He looked towards the shoreline and saw people falling to the ground. Vehicles stopped.

"Everybody is going unconscious!" he exclaimed. "It's like a giant nerve gas attack. It's coming close to me. I'll keep talking as long as I can. It's close. I can see people falling down. They don't seem to know it's coming...." After that his cell phone went silent.

President Stinson and twelve members of her staff were quiet for a moment. The Secretary of State was first to speak the obvious.

"Theresa is putting the world into deep sleep."

Chapter 28

Once again I dominated the news twenty-four hours a day, and this time no one knew where I was.

There was understandable alarm when people realized what was happening in Africa and Australia, soon to be followed by India. President Stinson made an address to the nation.

"My fellow Americans. The last time Prime Minister Blair and I met with Theresa and Steve, Steve said something which I considered a statement of pessimism and hopelessness. He said it might take Theresa many years to find a way to control the other HALs, and we didn't have that much time. What Steve was really doing was giving us a hint of what Theresa was about to do. She is putting the world into deep sleep to arrest any activity of the other HALs and their hosts until she can find a way to control them. This is a reasonable course to take and the only one that will rescue us from a political and social nightmare we can't even describe.

"I know it's frightening to think about being put to sleep for years, but consider that it is Theresa doing this. She has saved us more than once. She will do so again.

"My advisors tell me when the deep sleep comes near you are advised to sit or lie down. That's what Jack and I will do.

"What Theresa is doing is not without risk. Many things could go wrong. But she hasn't failed yet. I can't believe a God who has brought her this far without mistakes will let her make one now. From her ingenious self-preservation in the fall from the plane to her suicide mission in Pyongyang, she has shown a remarkable ability to survive and triumph.

"Have courage. It will seem to pass in a moment and Theresa will have everything under control. Good night and God bless America."

Simple and quick was always best in an address to the nation.

Inevitably a staff member asked her a question about what she had not said.

"Why didn't you invite Theresa to come in and talk about her plans?"

"If you have a better idea for how Theresa can control all the HALs tell it to me and I'll go back on television and explain it to her."

President Stinson had set the tone. Most people agreed there was no other way to get the other HALs under control and prevent disaster, although exactly how I would get the HALs under control was not known. They would have to trust me.

Prime Minister Peter Blair went on television and summed up the situation.

"Even if we found Theresa we couldn't stop her. I don't believe we should want to. Do you want to see a hundred unstoppable Adolf Hitlers in the world?"

However, the media were saying that I should at least talk to President Stinson and her advisors out of courtesy. Maybe an alternative idea could be found. Steve jumped on his computer and emailed a reply to several networks.

"You can't move a cloud with a cloud. Theresa's HAL cannot stop or influence the actions of other HALs. If just one of these 204 people decided to be evil he could destroy nations and Theresa couldn't stop him. For the last time: there is no alternative.

"Theresa needed three months to get control of HAL. One of these other people might do it in a week with the help of a bunch of people in another country. We don't have time to fool around. Theresa had to act."

No more could be said than that. There was no alternative to what I was doing. Everyone had enough knowledge of human nature to know what would happen if a large number of people acquired limitless power. The rest of humanity would be crushed. Death might be preferable to living in that world.

People waited for the deep sleep to come. It covered Africa, the bottom half of Asia, and Australia. There was only silence from these regions. Initially, some people had tried to flee to America on airplanes. President Stinson ordered all international flights canceled. There was no point in trying to flee. The deep sleep zone would cover the Earth within eighteen days of its first discovery.

Europe went silent.

The deep sleep zone spread over the oceans. It was nearing the East Coast of the United States.

President Stinson held a last meeting of her cabinet.

"The deep sleep will be here in four hours. Electric power generating systems are programmed to shut off at that time. Hospitals will run on generators.

"I want to commend everybody for remaining calm in this troubled time. I believe this comes from Theresa's sterling character. We know she will take care of us.

"Ladies and gentlemen, I wish you luck."

Veronica Stinson and the cabinet rose. She walked around the room shaking everybody's hand and giving some hugs. The cabinet somberly walked out, and Veronica went upstairs to be with her husband.

They went to sleep.

Veronica Stinson woke. Jack was still asleep next to her. She felt for his pulse and found none.

"Jack! Jack! Oh my God!"

She raced to the door and opened it. Two Secret Service men were outside.

"Jack is dead."

"No, ma'am. People are waking up randomly. You were first. He'll come around one of these days."

She calmed down. "What's happening?"

"Some of the staff are downstairs. They'll brief you."

She walked towards the staircase leaving the two Secret Service men behind to guard Jack.

As she walked downstairs to the lobby, White House personnel saw her and cheered. They were all second string staff members. One of them suggested, "Would you like a briefing in the cabinet room, Madam President?"

"Of course," she said, feeling much more confident.

More personnel along the hallway cheered as she passed by. She entered the cabinet room. General Holmes, her new Chairman of Joint Chiefs of Staff was there, but none of the department Secretaries. The rest were office managers. She sat down. The General was senior man here and did the briefing.

"People have been waking up one by one in

random order for three weeks. It's being done in a manner that makes sense. First were the people in critical infrastructure areas such as power plants, water supply, and other services needed to be in operating order before everybody else came to. Then the police stations were targeted. Then the fire stations. Now adults of every kind are being randomly aroused. The children are still asleep; they're helpless without the adults. We think the last to be aroused will be the people in hospitals. It takes the entire community to keep the hospital going."

"How many people are awake?" she asked.

"Approximately forty percent, but many still asleep are the young.

"The astronomers say six hundred years have passed."

President Stinson was astonished. The staffers were amused to see her reaction.

"Did you say six hundred years?"

"Yes, ma'am. It's a long time. The astronomers say today is June 18."

"Can they prove it's six hundred years?"

"Yes, ma'am, from the positions of the planets. Theresa might have fooled around with them, but there are two new supernovae hundreds of light-years from here. She couldn't have done that."

"Did Theresa get the other HALs under control?"

"We talked to known hosts of HALs. They all say their HALs have disappeared. They don't have super strength or throwing accuracy. It seems Theresa did find a way to put them to sleep a year later but couldn't destroy their HALs. "

"So they're all gone?"

"We can't be sure. Some hosts were never identified. If one of them has a HAL, we still have a problem."

"What else has been going on?"

"There are countless new medical devices to do things we never dreamed of. We have thousands of new drugs to treat every disease, and specifications for how to manufacture them.

"The South Pole has been eliminated except for a few small islands. Greenland has been cut up in many pieces and moved South. The ice is gone and nothing can ever change ocean levels. The salt content of seawater has been reduced by half. It multiplies marine life and keeps bacteria under control.

"There's a new building near the beltway. It's a library filled with millions of scientific books and articles on every subject: the complete genomes of every creature on Earth, every kind of chemical compound and their syntheses, physics of the complete set of subatomic particles, the resolution of the unified field theory, designs for workable commercial hydrogen fusion power generating plants. The list goes on and on."

"Who wrote them?"

"A large number of fantastically intelligent beings. The authors have numbers instead of names."

"Why numbers?"

"We figure it makes it easier to look up who did what. Names can be confusing when they're similar. Numbers are unique. It simplifies the paper trail. We have found four hundred and twelve numbers."

"Not our people?"

"Couldn't be. They would all have to be

Einsteins."

Veronica Stinson's face saddened. Her mood spread to all. They knew what she was thinking.

"Theresa died hundreds of years ago."

"Yes, ma'am."

President Stinson nearly cried. Theresa was everybody's darling. It was hard to imagine a world without her.

The waking of people continued randomly but at an accelerated pace. In another ten days all adults except those in hospitals were awake. Then the children woke up. Finally, people in hospitals not connected to life support systems were woken up, soon followed by the most dependent patients. It was all over.

President Stinson had been scheduled to attend a July 12th dinner hundreds of years ago and she went. She gave the last word on me.

"Peter Blair told me something about Theresa. Theresa was never that popular with many people. She wasn't cool, hip or totally awesome. Do I date myself? What people don't understand is the cool, hip, totally awesome don't save millions of lives and change the world. Theresa did.

"Theresa meant many things: order, kindness, intelligence, humility, faith, hope, and common sense. She was the exemplar of all virtues.

"Theresa could not bring us back and do all the other changes, but before she died she found somebody who could. Her reputation will stand for all time as the greatest contributor to the human species.

"I think the most important thing she did was what

she didn't do. With all her power she left us alone. She didn't try to bring in a new order. She was wise enough to know the world is improved by the individual people living in it, not by governments or dictators.

"Steve once said Theresa never got in trouble because she was perfect in every way. That's what got her in trouble. A lesser person would not have risked herself to go after the terrorists which is what lead to the OPEC and Israel situations, and she certainly wouldn't have gone to North Korea. She triumphed over everything because her real power was her character.

"I'm at a loss to say all that can be said about her. Let me give her a toast."

She picked up a glass of wine and so did everybody else.

"Here's to you, Theresa. You did a wonderful job. May you rest in peace."

She and all the others drank. They put their glasses down and gave a final round of applause for Empress Theresa.

Powerful military radar detected something flying up from the South Pole. It was traveling four hundred miles an hour at a height of twelve thousand feet. It appeared to be coming up the Eastern side of South America.

Planes were sent out to investigate. Telescopes showed it was a silvery metallic object in the shape of a modern coffin. It was not designed to calm the nerves.

President Stinson was briefed.

"This thing is four hundred feet long and a hundred feet wide and tall. There could be a lot of beings in there."

"Martin worried this would happen, and it happens to me. The landlords are coming for the rent. I'm supposed to have the check. Prime Minister Blair said it. 'Better to be a fisherman than a governor of men'."

She put her elbows on the desk to rest her face in her hands for a moment.

"All right. If they land in the United States let's do everything we can to make them feel welcome. If they don't like us, we run for it."

The chances of them landing in the U.S. were very good. The scientific library was in Washington. No similar structure had been found anywhere else. Why these beings were interested in the U.S., how I found them, or how they noticed my problems, were questions to put on hold for now. They were powerful beings and had to be dealt with immediately.

It was late in the evening. Veronica Stinson went to bed leaving instructions to wake her if there were any developments.

When the President woke up, she learned the "flying coffin" was over Cuba approaching the latitude of the Florida Keys. It had swerved toward the West to cross over South America. Its current flight path put it on a direct course to Washington.

"Could pass right over us," General Holmes suggested.

"What other big city is on its current flightpath?"

"None, really."

"Set up a speaker's platform on the Capitol steps in case they land here. There'll be a big crowd. Have the

Air Force send out more planes to watch it," she ordered.

"Why?"

"It might separate into parts going in different directions. Who knows what it will do."

"We'll be ready."

The coffin flew on some two hundred miles off the coast of Georgia. It entered airspace over land at North Carolina. The Air Force had thirty-six planes 'escorting' it. Every AF General wanted one of his planes in the party. They noted its altitude was decreasing.

General Holmes said, "I think we can be sure it's coming in for a landing in the Washington area, or it might do a low altitude pass over."

The object's speed gradually slowed down to three hundred m.p.h., two hundred, one hundred, and finally sixty m.p.h. The Air Force planes had to veer off. It was forty miles from D.C. General Holmes listened to his cell phone.

"It appears to be headed for the Mall."

"My God!" exclaimed President Stinson at her staff. "Get all the police out there. Keep people off the Mall. Let's get over there."

The National Mall was a 1.9 mile long open space running west to east from the Lincoln Memorial to the Capitol Building.

The object lowered down to a thousand feet. A few miles from the Mall it turned around ninety degrees to become parallel to the Mall.

Police had cordoned off the Mall with yellow tape. Half a million people had already gathered.

The object slowed down to 15 m.p.h. One mile

from the Capitol building it began a final descent. In total silence, and with a kind of beauty in its movement, the object gently came to ground some three hundred feet from the Capitol steps. It landed with a dull thump. Nothing more happened.

Numerous small, dark, round windows lined the object on all sides some fifty feet above ground. They had darkened glass. Helicopter crews could not see inside.

A foot deep recess was noted in the object's end facing the Capitol. Some police officers walked over to investigate this recess. There appeared to be double doors. The separations were so tight they couldn't slip a piece of paper through them.

Veronica Stinson stepped up to a microphone on the steps of the Capitol to welcome the landlords. One and a half million people had gathered. There was a sea of television cameras.

Two minutes went by after the President's arrival. All waited patiently.

The double doors slowly spread, or rolled, apart from each other. The interior was dark. Nobody had been allowed to get close enough to the ship to get a look inside. Some movement was seen.

Steve and I walked out with a crowd of what looked like ten year old children.

The crowd roared in delight. The line of "ten year olds" coming out the doors behind us was endless. There were a hundred of them in sight and still they were coming out.

I smiled proudly. Steve maintained his cool as did the children who looked out casually at the crowd. They didn't act like ten year olds. But neither were they adults. I'd kept them in a pre-puberty state so they wouldn't fool around with each other. They didn't mind. All of life experiences in the ordinary world were still ahead of them.

Two hundred children were visible. They wore multi-colored armbands on their left arms. Red, green, blue, yellow, purple, and black stripes of various widths and arrangements signaled in which areas the children were most expert. The boys looked like Steve and the girls like me. They all had my nearly black very dark brown hair.

Three hundred children were outside. Millions of mothers throughout the world squealed in excitement or cried happily at my experience.

The imperial couple was getting close to the Capitol steps. The last of the children left the door. There were four hundred and twenty of them, most of them twins and triplets.

We walked up the steps to the hastily assembled temporary wooden platform. President Stinson stood at one microphone and we walked to another ten feet away. Steve went up to the microphone first and stood with his hands on his hips, standing proudly erect like he'd done it all. It was very funny. Men cheered him on. When the noise downed down Steve loosened up and said words he'd been waiting hundreds of years to speak.

"You should see our bathroom!"

The crowd roared again. Steve finally smiled and waited for them to quiet down.

"We figured out the physics of the HALs. Theresa's HAL has absorbed all the other HALs and will absorb any other HAL that comes in from space.

When Theresa dies HAL will merge with the Earth and never do anything again."

He stepped to the side and I advanced to the microphone.

"Don't be fooled by our children's appearance. They're older than Methuselah and they all have the equivalent of a hundred college degrees. They know what works. We enter new eras but the old laws still rule.

"Now that we're back we will age like everybody else. Steve and I don't want to outlive our children. We will age too.

"We've been saying good by to them for years. With all the things they'll be doing, they'll be too busy for us, and our time is short. We give our children to the world. Take good care of them. Farewell, and be kind to each other."

The people moved in to meet the children.

Steve and I were smiling. Our work was done.

The End

ACKNOWLEDGEMENT: My heartfelt thanks to Pierre Groussac who proofread the text.

Pierre is the editor and publisher of "Don Quijote 1 & 2 Español – English", a bilingual edition of Cervantes' great classic. The corresponding Spanish and English paragraphs appear together on the same page but in different fonts, making for an easy comparison of the two texts by students of Spanish or English as the case may be.

DISCLAIMER: It is doubtful that any American President would try what President Martin attempted, or that men could be found to support him. The event in chapter four was included to set up interesting "what if" situations which would otherwise not be possible to consider in a story.

FINAL NOTES: In chapter 1, Theresa names the alien entity HAL after viewing the movie *2001: A Space Odyssey*, but there is no similarity between the two HALs.

One of Prime Minister Blair's comments in chapter 8, "In dealing with truth we are immortal, and need fear no change nor accident", is from *Walden Pond* by Henry David Thoreau. See the chapter titled 'Reading'.

In chapter 7, Theresa makes a one sentence reference to *The Hunger Games*. This was a recent change. *Empress Theresa* was written years before *The Hunger Games* came out. There are no similarities in content in the two stories, but if readers find any similarities in style or atmosphere let me assure them it's a coincidence.

September 2020

Printed in Great Britain
by Amazon